Elizabeth Lor_____lon
but at the age of_____has
lived ever sinc_____and
when she was_____s a
legal secretary until she remarried in 1968. She has a
son and two daughters, all married; her second husband died in 1984. Elizabeth is an ardent traveller and
likes to spend her spare time visiting ever more exotic
locations.

The Turning Tides

Elizabeth Lord

PIATKUS

For more information on
other books published by
Piatkus, visit our website
at www.piatkus.co.uk

First published in Great Britain in 1997 by
Judy Piatkus (Publishers) Ltd of
5 Windmill Street, London W1T 2JA
email: info@piatkus.co.uk

This edition published 1998
Reprinted 2000

*A catalogue record for this book is available
from the British Library*

ISBN 0 7499 3058 6

Set in Times by
Intype, London Ltd

Printed and bound in Great Britain by
Cox & Wyman Ltd, Reading, Berkshire

To Rosemary and David
with gratitude to David
for all his help and advice

There is a tide in the affairs of men,
Which, taken at the flood, leads on to fortune;
Omitted, all the voyage of their life
Is bound in shallows and in miseries.
On such a full sea are we now afloat,
And we must take the current when it serves,
Or lose our ventures.

Shakespeare, *Julius Caesar*

Chapter One

'Marry me, Amy darling.'

The girl sitting beside the earnest young man in the driving seat of the stationary Riley Tourer turned her pretty, oval face towards him and burst into a spasm of tinkling laughter that entirely upset him.

Dicky Pritchard, who preferred Dicky to Richard which made a rather silly alliteration of his full name, frowned and shrugged his narrow shoulders in a dramatic gesture of offended pride. 'If that's how you feel about it, then forget it!'

The huffy remark sobered her. 'I thought you were joking.'

'Well, I wasn't.'

'You sounded as though you were joking.'

'I said I wasn't,' he persisted, still nursing umbrage.

Piqued by his stupid attitude, Amelia Harrington, Amy to all her friends, turned to gaze through the late November drizzle at the small exclusive nightclub from which they had not long emerged, and for something better to do deciphered the wording on the rain-spattered placard beside the well-lit door: NEW YEAR'S EVE, it read, SPECIAL LATE EVENING – SEE 1926 IN – WITH STYLE.

More people were emerging. It stayed open to the small hours, but some preferred to go home earlier or go on elsewhere. Out they came in couples and groups, chattering, laughing, brollies unfurled as the rain was discovered; men in evening dress and shiny pumps, most of them slightly tipsy from two too many champagne cocktails, while their

1

ladies, with shingled hair and knee-length silk and chiffon dresses, handkerchief-pointed or fringed hems of uneven lengths fluttering and dancing below brocade or silver lamé wraps, hung giggling on their escort's arm to huddle closer beneath the wavering umbrellas as they scuttled along the shining pavement on Cuban heels to waiting cars and taxis.

'I wasn't joking,' Dicky said again. 'After what happened last night.'

The reminder brought Amy's hazel eyes back to glare at him, her thin pencilled eyebrows arching to disappear beneath the brim of the cloche hat that hid her brown hair. She didn't wish to remember last night. 'All right, you weren't joking. But I don't see why I need marry you just because we got carried away.'

His slim elegant form slumped in his seat. 'You didn't say that last night.'

'That was different. I wasn't thinking properly.' She should have been thinking properly, now she was regretting every second of it.

Dicky had sat up straight again. 'I love you, Amy. If I didn't love you, I would never have done what I did. I assumed you'd *want* to marry me.'

'Oh, don't be silly.' At eighteen why ever would she want to get married? She was having too much fun to settle into stuffy old marriage. 'Come on, Dicky, start up your motor and take me home, there's an angel.'

'But we made love last night.'

'And you forgot to be careful,' she shot at him. 'How do you think I feel? I wish it had never happened in the first place. Now take me home.'

'Don't you love me, then?'

'No.'

'But last night . . .'

'Oh, for God's sake! Take me home!' Her exasperated cry made heads turn in her direction and she hastily lowered her voice. 'If you don't want to take me, I can get a taxi.'

'There's no need. I'll take you.' His face was a study in the glow of The Golden Turkey's electric sign as he leaned forward and viciously punched the starter button, throwing forward the handbrake as the engine came to life with a deep rich roar. 'You've made a fool of me, you know,' he hissed.

'You've made a fool of yourself,' she hissed back and fell silent, remaining so for the rest of the journey through the shiny-wet streets with the West End traffic becoming slowly more sparse as they approached Bayswater and Queensway Terrace, one of the nicer parts of London where she lived with her parents, her younger sister Kay and twelve-year-old brother Henry, who was away at public school.

Still annoyed by Dicky's silly attitude, she didn't even say good night as she got out of the car and hurried on through the wrought-iron gate, heels clicking angrily on the tiled path and up the steps to the porticoed front door. She knew he was still sitting there watching her as she pushed the bell for one of the servants to let her in, but she didn't turn round.

She'd see him again, of course. He'd soon get over this evening, all that maddening attentiveness as they danced, hardly giving her a chance to dance with anyone else, mooning over her even to the point of ignoring the couple of friends they had gone there with.

He could be good fun if he would only stop being so possessive. It would do him good to stew a little over what happened last night. It had been at Marjory Broome's coming-out party. She and Dicky, borne off on the warm wings of a very potent punch, had found themselves in some maid's attic bedroom in the quietening hours of early morning, the girl being occupied downstairs with the guests. Under the influence of punch and a variety of cocktails, lovemaking had been a new and wonderful experience, and terribly wicked for someone who had never done such a thing before. But he'd insisted she could trust him. And then he had got carried away and she, even with her inexperience, instinctively felt that something had gone horribly wrong.

Embarrassed, he had apologised profusely, hastily adjusting his dress while she lay on the maid's bed aware of the damp place beneath her and becoming more angry and frightened by the minute, hardly able to think straight. Since then she had been thinking very straight. It was said that a mistake on one's first-ever affair seldom came to anything,

3

and although there was a chance that it might, she had grown more and more sure that it wouldn't, had made up her mind that it wouldn't. Then had come Dicky's silly proposal, bringing it all back.

He should have known by her angry reaction at the time it happened that she would want nothing more to do with him, *that way*. Obviously he hadn't – to the extent of his ridiculous offer of marriage. He *was* fun to be with. But marriage? To narrow-shouldered, slightly-built, fatuous if marvellously wealthy Dicky? Not in a million years. If something had happened to her, God forbid, she wouldn't marry him, not even to save her good name. How she could have let him do what he'd done last night, him of all people . . . But she had been pretty squiffy at the time.

She heard the car pull away as Alice, the parlour-cum-housemaid, opened the door to her, but she didn't turn to watch it go.

He was making himself scarce. Sulking no doubt. Whether he was really keeping out of her way or was genuinely unable to see her, she did hear that he'd gone up to Scotland for Christmas and would be staying until well after the New Year and might not be back in London for weeks.

'He's avoiding me,' she told Polly Brooke who was on the point of becoming engaged to the tall, handsome and rich Meredith Quinn-Martin.

'Why should he be avoiding you?' Polly's cornflower-blue eyes regarded her from the huge gilt-framed mirror as they retouched their make-up in the powder room of the Grosvenor where everyone was attending the Christmas Ball.

'Because he proposed to me,' Amy supplied.

'Lucky old you.' Polly's eyes were concentrating on the rouging of her lips. 'His family are stinking rich. Titled too. You heard his father was knighted last year. By King George himself. Something to do with industry – munitions or something during the last war. But, darling, what makes you think sweet, fascinating Richard Pritchard is avoiding you?'

'Because I refused him.'

Polly stopped rouging her lips to stare at her from the

mirror as though Amy had lost all her senses. 'My dear – you didn't! You must be stark staring mad!'

'I'm not in love with him – not in the least.'

'Who cares? It isn't as if he's not good-looking. In fact he's extremely good-looking. Those lovely shaped lips of his, and those gorgeous brown eyes, like almonds. And his eyebrows – they make a person tingle all over. He's divine.'

Amy's own rouged lips pouted. 'I suppose he is, in a limp sort of way.'

Polly busied herself fishing in her gold lamé envelope bag for face powder. 'I admit. But he's only twenty. He'll fill out after he's twenty-one. They do, you know. All that little boy look gone. Pity. Though I imagine sweet Richard will always be slim and boyish and have every girl falling at his feet. You can't allow it, Amy. You simply can't. To miss a chance like that, refusing such a marvellous offer.'

Amy didn't reply. She was visualising the man of her dreams – tall, broad-shouldered, slender-hipped, strong handsome features: a man who'd pick her up in a pair of muscular arms and sweep her away with him. Someone like Rudolph Valentino, or better, Ramon Novarro, whom she considered far better-looking. But even her giddy young brain under its shingled light brown hair told her that such men existed only on the silver screen. Dicky *was* good-looking even if no one could call those ever-so-well-bred features strong, but she didn't love him. Not really. And wealth could never compensate for the lack of love. For all his father, now *Sir* John Pritchard, was wealthy and Dicky as his eldest son was heir to everything, she just couldn't see herself accepting him as a husband. Not that he was here, of course, to renew his offer, sulking up there in the Highlands of Scotland.

By the time he did return to London, however, circumstances that had nothing to do with his being heir to pots of money had her reconsidering his offer of marriage.

Over Christmas she developed a nasty cold, most annoying when one needed to look one's prettiest. She managed to weather it with paint and powder and a cheery smile, but four days into the New Year it developed into 'flu, putting her to bed. She lay there with every limb aching, praying Dicky wouldn't come back to London and take it into his head to pay her a call. As much as she still had no intention of accepting his absurd marriage proposal, the last thing she wanted was to have him see her with a face all mottled and ugly beyond belief and a thermometer sticking out of her mouth, which Dr Lombard seemed to be coming daily to do as though it were his sole delight in this world.

'He says you must stay there for at least another three weeks,' her mother said after he and his beastly thermometer had departed for the umpteenth time.

Dr Lombard was their elderly and fussy Harley Street physician who charged the earth for each visit. With him it was two pounds a sneeze.

Not that his sizeable fees bothered them much – Daddy a City stockbroker with his Clubs, Mummy with her Good Causes rubbing shoulders with people such as Lady Harper and quite a few other titled ladies; a country retreat in Berkshire (a four-bedroomed 'cottage'); summer holidays in France, in Provence mostly; here in Bayswater employing almost as large a staff as anyone in the area. It was just that, her thoughts inclined to ramble in her feverish state, she found herself dwelling on the fact that just one of Dr Lombard's fees would be a fortune to someone like their parlourmaid Alice – would probably keep her type of family in food for months.

The girl had been with them for about four years and she often noticed the girl's peaky looks spoiling her otherwise extremely pretty face, but it had hardly concerned her until now. She knew little about her. Employers didn't concern themselves with the lives of their employees outside work. It was fatal, as Amy had found out after having once had a chat with the girl. For a while she had become beset by thoughts of the poverty her family apparently endured in the East End of London, though in a totally different way to the Good Causes her mother indulged in with meetings and fêtes and charity dinners. She'd even slipped Alice a shilling on odd occasions, but after a while it had died a natural death, and just as well. Her mother would have had a fit had she known. Tipping servants in secret – Mummy

6

would have made something out of nothing, just as she was doing now.

'Dr Lombard says it could be quite serious, similar to the epidemic in nineteen-nineteen. It carried off thousands, especially the poorer classes.'

Amy grimaced. 'Don't be silly, Mummy. It's just ordinary 'flu. I shall be fine in a week's time.'

'Nevertheless,' her mother said firmly, 'Dr Lombard says you have to stay in bed for three weeks. By the way, that young Richard Pritchard called. I told him you had 'flu. He asked me to convey his sympathy and loving regards.' She gave Amy an enquiring smile. 'Is there something between you two, my dear?'

'He's just a friend.' Friends had been calling all the time during her illness. The telephone had hardly stopped ringing.

'He sounded more than *just* a friend, dear. So dreadfully concerned for you.' Her tone was eager – the names of her daughter and the young Pritchard heir coupled together would be something to boast about to her own friends. It didn't do to tell Mummy too much. She always made so many mountains out of molehills.

She frowned as a 'flu spasm made itself felt, her feverish head throbbing. 'Just friends,' she said. 'I'd like to sleep a little now, if you don't mind.'

'Yes, of course, dear.' Quietly her mother tiptoed from the room, leaving her alone to nurse her thoughts about Dicky's call and its implications.

She was becoming worried. Her monthly period which should have arrived, most inconveniently, around Christmas, hadn't. In a way she'd been relieved at the delay, then without too much concern, had put its total absence down to her horrid cold. Her next usual should have begun two days ago, but again nothing. Probably 'flu was at fault this time she told herself, more occupied with the illness, and dismissed it to concentrate on overturning Dr Lombard's predictions of three weeks in bed.

She was in fact out of bed in two weeks – one in the eye for Lombard, she gloated. But with more time to think, the two missing periods had now begun to concern her a little. It had to be just being ill for so long. She pushed the more unutterable thought, pregnant, from her mind and prudently fell short of disclosing their non-appearance to her mother, but there was no hiding such things from her.

'Is there anything wrong, dear? You are all right, aren't you?' she asked as Amy sat at her dressing table applying a little colour to her still-wan cheeks. Her mother, wearing a rather out-of-fashion afternoon dress of slate blue stood tall and dignified above Amy. Her brown hair, with only slight traces of grey, drawn loosely back into the same sort of chignon she'd probably worn as a girl of Amy's age before the War, made her face seem far more narrow and gaunt than it really was. Amy lowered her eyes from her mother's anxious regard in the mirror.

'Of course I'm all right, Mummy.'

'You would tell me if you were not?'

'I'm quite recovered.'

The hollows in Constance Harrington's high-cheekboned face became even more hollow. 'I am not referring to your recent illness, my dear. I mean in . . .' She hesitated and then continued more firmly, a hint of distaste and disapproval in her tone. 'In *other ways*.'

She waited, but when Amy did not respond, drew her elegant figure to its full five foot eight inches, and keeping her tone mild with an effort continued: 'To my mind, something is not quite as it should be concerning . . . *certain things*.'

Again a pause while Amy occupied herself looking for hand cream, avoiding having to look directly at her in the mirror. She knew what was coming. 'There has been nothing in the bowl left in your room, Amelia. In fact not for two months.'

Amy doggedly kept her hazel eyes averted from her mother's enquiring gaze. She had been expecting this. The missing of one's menstrual cycle couldn't be kept secret when the small square towels used every month for that purpose had to be left in the covered porcelain pail of cold salt water to help dislodge the worst of the blood before a maid took them away for boiling clean again in the copper down in the scullery. These were things the men of the household never saw or apparently even knew about, kept discreetly out of sight and swiftly secreted away below stairs to be dealt with ready for re-use. But mothers were great inspectors of things personal to their daughters – especially *her* mother, already including her younger sister Kay in her realms of investigation. She never kept such a close eye on Henry. Then Henry, at twelve, was at Rugby and came home only seldom.

But for Katherine, Kay for short, coming up to fourteen and learning the facts of life by devious means, Mummy's responsibilities tended to fall short of explaining *that* sort of thing, apart from the significant placing of a covered porcelain pail in her bedroom and saying she would *know* what it was for when the time came. Kay would more likely learn them from someone bolder, a servant perhaps. Someone like Alice perhaps, who coming from the poorer classes had, Amy imagined, a more casual approach to life. She had heard somewhere that in lots of poorer families with houses so small and cramped there was little room to spare, parents actually had to make love in the same bedroom they shared with some of their children; and brothers and sisters had to sleep together to quite a grown age. It probably meant girls learned about women's problems at first hand, their mothers never having to resort to embarrassing instruction as did mothers of higher social classes.

Mummy was gazing down at her, her sharp grey eyes clouded by an unwillingness to acknowledge the suspicion forming in her mind. 'How do you account for it, my dear?'

'I've had a cold, Mummy, then this 'flu.' It was the best reason she could think of, eager to believe it herself. 'Doesn't that sometimes delay things?'

'It is rather unusual.'

'But it could, couldn't it?'

Her mother's lips tightened. 'Once perhaps. Twice . . . It is probably your health then,' she concluded tersely, and her expression as she turned away to leave the room conveyed the fact that she wasn't convinced, while at the same time something like fear that she wasn't.

Lawson Harrington glanced up from his *Sunday Telegraph*

9

as Amy replaced the telephone receiver on its hook. 'Not going out, Amelia?'

'I'm not much in the mood,' she said, giving him the same reply as she had just given Dicky asking if she cared to go for a spin this afternoon, it being an exceptionally nice day for early February. Poor Dicky, he'd sounded so woebegone at her refusal. It was obvious he was still madly in love with her, but the way she was feeling, she couldn't face him yet; hadn't the courage yet to face him with what was pounding away in her mind.

Her father grunted and went back to his *Telegraph*. 'Bit of fresh air would do you good. All this mooning about the house, not going out. Bad for you.'

It was true. Since her 'discovery', for that's how it seemed as she anxiously awaited the middle of this month to disprove it, she had kept away from everyone as if at the first sight of her they would *know* what was wrong with her – she would betray herself, her fears. No, better to keep away until she was really certain.

Poor Dicky, constantly ringing her up, was confused, she could tell by the sound of his voice. Kay thought she was crazy not going out when she had such wonderful opportunities. Friends too were ringing, asking where she was.

'We haven't seen you for simply weeks, Amy. Where *are* you? Everyone's asking after you. Have you been so terribly ill?'

'It has been a long bout,' she excused herself to Sylvia Fox-Carter telephoning for the umpteenth time. 'It took longer than expected.'

'I should say it has. But surely you're ready now to be up and about again?'

'I'm getting stronger. I will be about very soon, I expect.'

'Oh, you must, darling! You simply must be better by Saturday. It's that gorgeous party Fram Lassington's people are throwing for her twenty-first. You couldn't have forgotten, Amy. We are all relying on you, and Dicky Pritchard, to be there. I have heard that you and he are very much together these days, that he even proposed to you before Christmas.'

Amy remembered now her idle remark to Polly Brooke

at the Grosvenor Christmas Ball – the entirely wrong person to mention anything like that to, the news spread around in no time.

'I heard you turned him down.' The voice on the phone sounded animated with interest. 'But you've been seen together since. Absolutely *everywhere*. Do tell, Amy darling, is it *serious*? Terribly exciting if it is. Now you will be well enough to come on Saturday, won't you?'

But she hadn't gone. Dicky, disappointed when she'd refused his offer to escort her, had rung to say what a wonderful evening it had been and how sorry he was that she'd missed it, and did she feel up to going for a spin this afternoon.

'Thought you'd have jumped at the chance,' her father was saying into his *Telegraph*. 'A fine crisp afternoon like this. That young Pritchard's a fine young fella – not one to be sniffed at if he's an admirer.'

'Lawson,' Constance looked up from the book she was reading. 'Must you be so crude, dear? Sniffed at – it sounds so . . . animal.'

'She knows what I mean,' he chuckled. A tall, stiff-faced man, greying at the temples, he had the welfare of his three children sternly at heart; especially for Amy, his first-born, in that she should be thinking along the lines of a good marriage.

'That one's a young man you should be considering very seriously indeed, my girl.'

Amy didn't reply. Avoiding her mother's gaze that followed her everywhere these days, she retrieved the fashion magazine she had been reading before the telephone rang. But her mind was not on fashion. February and still no sign. She shivered, despite the blazing fire Alice had built up after lunch, and secretly planned to consult the girl at the first chance. There was no one else she could speak to. Alice would put her right, she was convinced of that – someone who had no axe to grind, who could be trusted to keep a secret; sworn to secrecy. More than any fear of possible pregnancy loomed the fear of having to face her parents if she was.

As for Dicky, he hadn't referred again to his proposal

that evening before Christmas. Perhaps he was waiting for some sign from her. But should she begin trying to encourage him? If her condition was as she, now terrified, suspected, were he to repeat his proposal she would jump at it. Yet what if there was nothing wrong with her at all? For all Dicky's fine prospects, she couldn't see herself as his wife. But waiting another two weeks to the middle of this month to be sure which way she should jump might be too late and Dicky, tiring of asking her out with no success, might give up trying. She could hardly ask him herself to marry her.

The following morning, all uncertainty was swept away. An early morning rush to the bathroom immediately confirmed her condition as she vomited into the toilet, hoping that no one in the house had heard her. There was nothing for it but to ask someone entirely neutral, Alice, what to do. It was a horrible Monday.

In bed that night, she listened for the house to fall silent, with only the scullery maid left up to set everything out for the morning. It was always a long day for the lower domestic staff. Not that they weren't treated kindly. So independent had they become since the War that they had to be. The Government had even set up training schemes, denying women the dole to entice them back into domestic service. Trouble was, once they were trained they were off looking for higher wages and better conditions with other families. Amy had overheard one of her mother's friends saying: 'You just can't get them. My maid left last week and I haven't been able to replace her. I feel so humiliated answering the door myself that I have to put on a hat to appear to be going out when the doorbell rings.'

Even her own family was short of a housekeeper and still advertising. Alice, thank heaven, had proved a loyal girl. Amy prayed she would stay so and not be lured away by another employer offering better wages. She needed a friend.

Once the house was finally asleep apart from that wretched scullery maid still wearily setting things up for the morning, Amy was unable to contain herself any longer. Creeping out, she went up the narrow uncarpeted stairs to the attic rooms, fearful of every creaking step, for some reason imagining it could wake her father and bring him to investigate – foolish, she knew, but her nerves were so on edge.

At the door to the tiny room on the right which Alice shared with the scullery maid, she tapped lightly.

'Who is it?' came a muffled sleepy voice.

'Amelia,' she whispered.

The voice brightened. 'Come in, Miss.'

She found the girl already perched on the edge of her bed ready to receive her. In the meagre glow of a tiny table lamp Amy had once given her, no longer having a use for it, Alice's pretty, heart-shaped face looked resigned, her small round chin lifted stoically, her lively brown eyes now clouded with sleep, her short fair hair tousled.

'I hope you don't mind my disturbing you at this time of night,' Amy said, realising how presumptuous that must sound. It was past midnight. Of course the girl minded. But she wouldn't say so.

'No, Miss, not at all.'

'I've something I need to ask you,' Amy continued. She must get this done before the scullery maid came up. She closed the door but didn't come any further. Space didn't allow it with two narrow beds, wardrobe and washstand.

'I need your advice,' she hurried on. 'I can't ask my family. I thought you'd be the best person to advise me.'

'I don't know, Miss.'

Ignoring the dubious note in the reply, she hurried on. She needed to hurry. 'You might be in a better position to tell me what I should do. The thing is, I've discovered I have got myself pregnant.'

In the faint yellow glow of the tiny lamp, she saw the girl's lips twitch. 'You can't get *yourself* pregnant, Miss. It takes a man to do that.'

'Don't be facetious!' She didn't mean to sound over-bearing, but the remark annoyed her.

The lips straightened instantly. 'I'm sorry, Miss Amelia. I don't know what you want me to do.'

'I hoped you might give me some advice. You would know

13

more about these things than I, you being...' She broke off, already regretting what she'd been about to say, but Alice had already interpreted it, her face taking on a look of simple dignity far more forceful than if she had put her feelings into words.

'Beg pardon, Miss, but what makes you think *I* know about such things more than you? When it comes down to it, it don't make no difference where a girl comes from, she can still get herself into trouble if she plays them sort of games.'

Amy found herself apologising, but stuck to her guns. 'There's no one else I can turn to. I daren't tell my family. It's so awful. People will think straight away that I am *that* sort of girl. And I'm not. That's what makes it so dreadful.'

Sympathy had replaced the hurt pride. 'I know you're not, Miss.'

But Amy didn't want sympathy. She wanted help. 'I don't know where to turn. I don't know what to do.'

'Can't you marry the person?' Alice offered.

'I could, but I'd rather not. It could still be a false alarm. I don't know. I know so little about these things. And you see, I don't really love him.'

The shoulders under the flannelette nightdress gave a small shrug. 'I don't think you've got much choice, Miss, if you are expecting. More a case of getting him to marry you. And quick, before he realises. That's if he *wants* to marry you.'

'Oh, he does,' Amy said hurriedly. 'He loves me.'

'Then there's no problem as I can see.' As Amy continued to look forlorn, the girl gnawed speculatively on her lip. 'It wouldn't be right, trying to get rid of it – if that's what you're thinking. I mean, getting rid of it professionally. It's against the law. It'd be sort of murder really. And dangerous to you as well. Your best bet is to marry 'im and have done with it. That's all I can say on it, Miss.'

Amy nodded dismally. The girl was right, she had no choice. 'I hope you didn't mind my asking you,' she said lamely.

Alice shook her head vigorously, her short fair hair jiggling. Amy had never seen her without her maid's cap, the

14

frilled band of which came right down to her very eyebrows, covering brow, ears and hair. Now she marvelled how shiny that hair was in the little lamp's poor glow, and extremely fair for a brown-eyed girl.

'I hope I've bin of some help, Miss.' She had a pleasing voice for all it still held faint traces of the Cockney accent one heard from barrow-boys. Working with a good family had improved her speech over the years. There was the odd dropped 't' or an 'h' occasionally left off, but its natural timbre was not at all coarse.

'I'm glad I spoke to you,' Amy said. She heard the stairs creak beneath the heavy tread of the scullery maid coming up to bed at last. 'I am grateful to you for sparing me your time. You must be tired.'

It sounded outrageously patronising. Without waiting for a reply, she let herself out, ignoring the enquiring look from the plump scullery maid, who gave a small ungainly bob as she passed her.

Chapter Two

Pauline Carpenter, fiancée of one of Dicky's friends, was apparently throwing an impromptu party on the Friday. Dicky, naturally invited, had asked Amy to go with him. Resigned now to the fact that mid-February had come and gone without event, there was really nothing left to her but to accept, much to the innocent Dicky's obvious delight.

So they arrived together at the extensively modernised house in Chalfont finding it already filled with young people, its modern rooms with their masses of art deco furnishing echoing their babble and high bursts of laughter. With one side of the main reception room given over to a massive buffet, and the adjoining room to a jazz trio – piano, saxophone and percussion – in the corner, there was hardly room to stand, much less dance, though some were managing it, carving out a small space for themselves there to kick up their heels in a Charleston or a one-step.

'Pauline does give awfully good parties,' Polly Brooke was saying as Amy and Dicky stood with her and a few friends in the room where the buffet was. 'Does anyone know what it's for? My invitation merely said to come along. It only arrived yesterday. There was no time to ring and find out, I was so busy elsewhere.'

'It's not really *her* party anyway,' Sylvia Fox-Carter said, her slightly horsey features conspiratorial as she sipped her champagne cocktail in its wide shallow glass, at the same time gazing around at the room.

'Then whose is it?' Amy asked.

'Haven't the faintest. A birthday party I've been told.

Twenty-first. But whose, I haven't the foggiest. I'm glad *you* people were invited though. I hardly know a soul – at least not *everyone*. How about you, Dicky?'

'I do know a few,' Dicky said nonchalantly, knowing most anyone who was anyone.

'Of course, darling, we all know a *few*,' Sylvia said, still gazing about as she continued to sip daintily.

'It's an awfully good party though,' Max Shaughan put in. 'I don't know about you lot, but I'm about ready for another dance. Sylvia?'

'Oh yes please, Max. Divine.'

Led away into the other room, followed closely by Polly and the extremely tall Meredith Quinn-Martin, Amy and Dicky were for the moment left on their own.

'Care to dance?'

Amy shook her head. She had been feeling queasy all day. This morning she'd had to rush to the bathroom again. She had expected to emerge feeling clear-headed and fine again, but she wasn't feeling as bright as she ought. For all she smiled and laughed and chatted with the rest, every now and again fear of the future reared up to take a front row in her brain, clamouring to be heard until she almost believed everyone else could hear it, especially Dicky whom she mustn't allow to notice a glimmer of her condition, not until he again asked her to marry him.

He hadn't mentioned it since that time in November, and that was worrying. It looked as though he'd shrugged his shoulders at the whole idea for all his longing gazes with those moony brown eyes of his. But how on earth to open the subject of that previous proposal, she couldn't imagine.

'I think I will dance,' she burst out, changing her mind. Better that than think, and there was a wild idea that abandoning herself wholly to the crazy number now being played might dislodge something inside her and mercifully leave her as she had been before that stupid escapade in that maid's vacated bedroom. Alice had said that doing something utterly energetic, like jumping off something high, could do it. But that sounded terribly drastic. She had suggested hot baths with mustard, but they had done nothing for her. She had also mentioned drinking gin until it came out of her ears, but that was how it had begun, she getting herself squiffy. For some inexplicable reason, Amy felt she couldn't do that again, and besides, where could she go to get as drunk as Alice had intimated she should?

'Come *on*, Dicky,' she urged, already making her way towards the crowded other room where the music blared across the babble of conversation.

She danced like a mad thing. Slim, bare, slave-bangled arms flailing above her head, long shapely legs in their rolled knee-length silk stockings below the short skirt of her beige sequinned dress kicking out at all sorts of clever angles, the fringe around her skirt adding to her amazing gyrations as it swung and fluttered; admiring eyes were turned on her. She was a good dancer and so full of energy that poor Dicky, trying to keep up with her, was becoming completely out of breath.

Finally he all but collapsed. 'I've had enough, Amy,' he managed between gasps as he ceased struggling to match her steps. 'I'm pooped, utterly. I have to sit down.'

'No, darling!' she called breathlessly. 'We've hardly started.'

'I'm sorry, Amy. I have to sit down. I've really had enough.'

There was nothing for it but to follow him as he made for the edge of the tiny dance area that had been created, amid a round of appreciative clapping before the onlookers turned back to what they had been doing before turning to watch her. She trailed after him to a couple of empty chairs he'd spotted near the musicians. They gave Amy a little bow as they continued their playing, a gesture of appreciation for her entertainment, but she barely looked their way, her hazel eyes centred angrily on her erstwhile partner.

'Dicky, you are a stinkpot – you really are. You made me feel a complete idiot,' she said as she sat down next to him. 'Walking off like that. I shall never forgive you.'

'It was just a bit too much for me,' he sighed by way of apology.

Suddenly she too felt tired. Exhausted. The fine filigree gold watch on her slim wrist showed quarter to two. She found herself needing to take note of her physical condition.

Her body felt limp and she was developing a slight weary headache. And her stomach? Was that a pain? One tiny twinge that might indicate a disturbance of the minuscule life that lay there? No, just imagination. No pain. Nothing. Her hopes faded, then rose. Perhaps later. Perhaps it took a while to happen. Yet something else had stirred, in her thoughts: the words minuscule life, the first time she'd ever considered it a life, provoked the oddest sensation, quite suddenly. Life. Inside her she held life, and something within her wanted to keep it there. Dicky only had to propose and all would be well. Plans were now beginning to form in her head, full of hope.

'I'm tired, Dicky,' she said suddenly.

'I don't wonder,' he said, not looking at her.

'I want to go home. I've a headache coming on.' She expected him to say again that he didn't wonder, but he looked at her in concern.

'You do look a bit pale around the gills, old thing. You must have some air.'

'I need to go home.' She needed desperately to talk to him, in the quiet of the countryside on the way back to London, in the dark before they hit any of the lights of town: dark, where he couldn't see her face, nor she his. 'Please, Dicky darling, take me home, there's an angel.'

He relented. 'I've had enough myself.'

Quickly she gathered up her coat and hat, collected for her by a waiting maid who executed a little bob as Dicky dropped a threepenny bit discreetly into her hand before the all-seeing eye of the family butler could turn in their direction, but he suspected the tip would be confiscated for sharing out later, according to status.

'Good night, sir, madam,' the man offered, his tone low and expectant, and Dicky dropped a ten shilling note into the waiting hand, a tip befitting the top rank of household staff. It would probably not be included in the portioning out after the house fell silent. Butlers were butlers, the highest of the high in the domestic world, above sharing out their own gratuities with lowlier staff.

Returning the good night casually, for he was only a

butler, they made their way to where Dicky's Riley stood alongside others on the gravel drive.

'Damn!' Dicky swore, the car's exit blocked by a badly parked Rolls-Royce.

A few minutes later, the butler persuaded by another tip, the Rolls-Royce's owner came to unblock their way, cheerfully tipsy and not at all put out by the inconvenience of being summoned to do so, and soon they were rumbling through the dark lanes.

After motoring a few miles, Amy took note of a cluster of trees coming up ahead, looming out of the clouded night to make an even darker cloud of their own, a perfect stygian place to pull the car up and talk.

'Stop,' she commanded, pointing ahead. 'There. Stop there.'

'What for?' They were almost up to the place.

'For heaven's sake, Dicky, stop!'

'Are you ill?' But he slowed, noting a small clearing enough to park in, and pulled off the road to come to a halt. Switching off the engine he turned to her, his face almost invisible in the even deeper darkness beneath the great oaks, for all their branches were bare of leaves. 'Anything I can do? Do you feel sick?'

'No, I'm fine. I just thought it would be nice to sit and talk for a while.' It was an invitation if ever there was one. He put an arm lightly around her, then after a while it grew firmer, slowly bringing her nearer to him. It was obvious he was imagining some unspoken message.

'We haven't done this for ages.'

'We haven't been alone together for ages,' she said.

'That's true.' He was silent awhile. Then he bent and kissed her, his lips coming lightly on hers at first, but quickly becoming urgent. 'Oh, Amy, darling, darling,' he breathed against her lips, and she felt the tension mounting within him, knew instantly what was happening to him, what he wanted. It would help her plan if she did allow it. She let herself melt into his arms and let him lay her back, awkwardly easing himself across her in the cramped Riley. Her coat had fallen open, she could feel his solidness through her flimsy dress, even in this cramped space. Her need now as keen as his, all earlier thoughts of plans swept from her mind, she felt herself being half-eased, half-carried from the car onto the damp leaf mould of the copse floor. There they made love with a pent up desperation from him as though this would be his last act, his gasps and sighs close to her ear, mingling with her own final cries of culmination, unstifled, for here in this dark place there was no one for miles to hear her. 'Oh, Dicky! Dicky! Darling, darling, darling . . .'

She recalled little of getting back into the car. Her head spinning, somehow that was where she arrived, her coat damp, her shimmering dress dishevelled, her hat having somehow got onto the back seat with her handbag, her bra – those flat things designed to give a girl a boyish line – undone so that her breasts had leapt up to their normal roundness, and which she recalled now, he had fondled and kissed and sucked before taking her.

He was sitting next to her, slumped in his seat as though ashamed of himself. He sat like that for a long time, not speaking, and she waited quietly beside him with no idea herself what to say. When he finally spoke, his voice was low and trembling.

'Have you done any considering, Amy?'

'About what?' It sounded quite silly.

'My asking you to marry me. Last November, or was it December? I can't think.'

'The end of last November,' she supplied.

'And you laughed at me.'

'I'm sorry about that.'

'That's why I never asked you again.' He paused, but when she didn't reply, went on, 'If I were to ask you again, now, would you still laugh at me?'

Amy took a deep breath. This was what she had wanted. 'No, I wouldn't.'

She was aware his face had turned to her, heard the hope ringing in his voice. 'You mean that, Amy? You really mean . . . You mean you'll marry me?'

'Yes.'

Without seeing his expression, she knew his face was one huge beam. His voice held a strangled sound. 'My darling . . . I can hardly believe it. You really mean you'd have me? Oh,

21

my good Lord, I can hardly . . . Oh, dear Amy – you've made me the happiest man.'

'Yes,' she said again, wondering at her lack of emotion now all her emotion had been spent there on the damp forest floor. She felt herself smiling at his rush of plans.

'I'll have to speak to your father, of course. And to my parents. They'll have to see you, approve, that sort of thing. But I know they will. They will have to. If they don't I shall whip you off to Gretna Green, my darling, and we'll get married there. But they will approve, I know they will. Oh my darling, darling Amy . . . there's so much to be done.'

'Yes,' she said again, lamely.

'We must set the date immediately,' he continued, not hearing her. 'We'll get engaged straight away. Monday. As soon as the stores are open we shall buy the ring. Harrods. God, how wonderful. We won't delay. Then we must set the date for the wedding.'

This was what she wanted to hear. She sat wrapped in her own ecstatic thoughts as he switched on the car's engine and revved up, swinging the motor back onto the road to speed off, the car's very speed conveying his excitement.

Amy sat back without talking, feeling the wild wind in her hair. Within half an hour he was dropping her at her home, finding his voice again, whispering his love, and she hers, a lingering kiss and an arrangement to see her this afternoon. Then he was off, speeding away in his joy at this evening's achievement, while she made her way up the short flight of stone steps to her door and rang the bell. Late though it was, Alice would awaken and come down to let her in. Amy passed her with hardly a thank-you, her mind in the clouds. Dicky wasn't so bad a catch. She could have done worse.

At the top of the house, Alice lay listening to the voices below, raised in argument.

After letting Amelia in she had crept back up to her room and wriggled shivering back into bed, grateful for the warmth it had retained. She had been as quiet about it as her creaking bed had allowed and Lily was still sleeping soundly, snoring loudly. She hated the scullery maid's snoring – a deep and sonorous man's snore, snorting at the back of her throat with a regularity that could drive anyone mad unable to sleep for it. And so close, they might have been sharing the same bed.

There was hardly room between the two for the tiny table lamp to sit, on the floor, let alone enough to ease sideways to get into them. The thirty inches between the foot of the beds and the shared single boxwood wardrobe and tiny table with its washbasin, jug and pockmarked oval mirror afforded the only space in which to dress and undress, that having to be done one at a time. At least the plump Lily was required to be first up and downstairs before anyone else, which left her in peace to wash, comb her hair and get into her uniform and cap uninterrupted.

Intrigued by the voices and despite the cold, Alice now eased her bare feet back into her slippers, also given to her by her young mistress at some time or another – but then Amelia had so many clothes and shoes and things, one pair of slippers meant nothing to her. Careful not to wake Lily, if that was possible, she eased herself along to the greater space at the foot of the bed and opened the door just a crack.

The voices became instantly more distinct. On the floor below, Amelia's bedroom door stood open, her parents apparently both in there, the light from it filtering up the narrow stairway to the attic landing. Watchful that neither door to the two larger rooms on the opposite side to hers, those of Mrs Penruth the cook-general, and the chauffeur/handyman Mr Gardner, didn't open suddenly to find her lurking there, Alice listened to what she could catch of the argument below, half hoping her young mistress was in hot water, for she had felt a little peeved at the way she had ignored her when she came in, taking her for granted and not at all apologetic for having awoken her at four in the morning. But that of course was what she was paid for – not much but better than nothing at all, and it was a genteel job working for some well-britched family rather than in some factory or other. She was conscious of feeling very much a cut above those sort of girls. Her family might live in London's poor, often poverty-stricken East End; her father and brother Tom might merely be stevedores loading and unloading ships on the Thames, their pay better than some but still mostly intermittent as they waited at dock gates between jobs for something else to come along, but she had escaped the rut and bettered herself. Being in service only across London allowed her to pop home whenever she had a night or a Sunday off, so life wasn't all that hard for her. Poor Lily who came from Wales, never able to get home, was more or less stuck. Alice thanked her own lucky stars as she held her head to the crack of her bedroom door to listen to the voices below.

Her employer was asking his daughter what time she called this, his voice, though low, carrying perfectly well, and obviously angry.

'You informed us that you would be at an all-night party and therefore well taken care of. Now you come home at four in the morning. What d'you think you are playing at?'

'I was tired, Daddy. And I had a headache,' came the protest.

'Then you should have asked someone where you could have slept, Amelia,' came Mrs Harrington's high sharp voice. 'You might have put yourself in all sorts of danger coming home at this unearthly hour when all types of unsavoury people are about. I don't know what you must have been thinking of. And who brought you home? I take it someone did.'

'That's what I want to tell you,' Amelia said angrily. Listening, Alice failed to catch the name. 'I was so excited when I came in. That's why I woke you both up. But all you've done is to go on at me about the time. You haven't given me a chance to say what I want to say. I have to tell you my wonderful news or I shall burst. He has proposed to me and I have accepted. He wishes to come here tomorrow ... no, this afternoon now, and ask you for my hand in marriage, Daddy. And all you can talk about is the time I've come home.'

In the few seconds of silence that followed, Alice strained her ear to catch what would be said next. So her young mistress was out of hot water. She would marry quickly and no one any the wiser. The baby could be passed off as slightly premature.

Mrs Harrington's voice interrupted Alice's thoughts. 'You have a proposal of marriage from young...' A slight creaking of Alice's half open door made her miss the name again. She strained her ears but Mrs Harrington had already gone on.

'Amelia, how simply marvellous. But why haven't you given us any intimation of this before now? Surely you must have known he was going to propose.'

'I wasn't sure, Mummy. I knew he was sweet on me.'

'Sweet on you! How you young people talk these days.' But all the anger had gone out of her tone. 'Far too modern, all you young things. But my dear, I am so very pleased.'

'He's coming this afternoon, you say,' boomed Amelia's father. 'In that case, we must be ready for him. And you, young woman, need to get to bed or you'll be fit for nothing when he comes. But well done, Amelia, well done. You couldn't have chosen better.'

Alice hastily withdrew her head from the doorway as she detected the sound of her young mistress's parents moving from the room, and closed the door softly. Very soon Miss Amelia would be marrying. Her earlier chagrin at being expected to get up in the early hours to open the street door for her had melted away. She would miss her, especially since the way she had come up here seeking advice from her. Her! It had made her feel important. But now she would be a mere housemaid-cum-parlourmaid again.

'How did it go, Dicky?' There was no need really to ask, Daddy following him from his study into the parlour, Mummy trailing behind them, all three beaming, Dicky looking very pleased with himself.

'It's OK, Amy. Your father said it's fine as long as my people agree. But I've already prepared them,' he went on, laughing happily as she threw herself joyously at him, her slim arms clasping him around his neck. 'It wasn't any surprise to them when I told them what was on my mind. I've been babbling on to them about you for months. So we'll pop off to see them now, shall we?'

'Oh, yes please!' she gasped, her hug tightening still more until he could hardly breathe. Over his shoulder she could see her mother and father smiling their satisfaction at such a suitable match, and at this moment she knew that nothing in this world would ever again be as wonderful, as marvellous as this very moment.

It was the better part of an hour's drive to Lyttehill, Surrey, Dicky's home and he seemed set to talk the whole way, beginning the instant he started the car up.

'I have it all planned,' he said, his eyes trained on the road. 'I did it while I was driving here. I hope you'll agree, Amy darling. In fact I just know you'll agree. We'll buy the ring tomorrow, then have it announced next weekend – my parents will undoubtedly throw a party to celebrate it. Everyone, but everyone'll be there. No expense spared. The oldest son and heir, they'll splash out, you can bet. After that, we'll make marvellous plans for the biggest society wedding of the year – if no one beats us to it, that is.'

'Can it be as soon as possible, darling?' she said, finally managing to get a word in.

He glanced sideways at her with an understanding smile before returning his eyes to the road ready for a left turn to take them to the Great West Road. 'I know how impatient you're feeling, darling. I feel impatient too. But we can't hurry this if we want a grand society wedding.'

'I don't want a society wedding. I want something quiet – and soon.'

Dicky's eyes didn't leave the road. ''Fraid not, my love. My parents would expect it. Their first son getting married. I owe it to them.'

'How long would that take to plan?'

'Oh . . .' he smiled at the road ahead, slowing the car as their turning loomed. 'I'd say possibly about a year. We can have a spring wedding.'

'A year! I can't wait a whole year.'

Straightening the car up, Dicky threw back his head and laughed. 'I know how you feel, darling, but we'll have to be patient. Things like this have to be carefully arranged, you know. The revered Mater and Pater would hope the bride's parents would think of St Pauls, with the reception at

Mansion House perhaps.' He grew suddenly serious. 'Listen, my darling ...' he glanced in the rear mirror for any traffic following close behind, and with his right hand signalled his intention to pull over to the kerb and stop. He came to a halt. Switching off the engine, he turned to her.

'Listen, Amy my love. My family have always wanted this for me when I got married. My mother, bless her heart, has always had wonderful dreams about it. And who can blame her? All parents want the best for their children, I expect. And my parents can afford the very best. Now my father has a title, how can they not want the best? My sister Effie is only fifteen – it'll be years before she marries. And next year I shall be twenty-one – a good respectably marriageable age, and you'll be nineteen – a lovely age to be married. Of course they'll want to do the best by us.'

Amy sat gazing down at her gloved hands, glad that much of her expression was hidden by her cloche hat. Her heart seemed to be sinking as low as the threatening clouds above them, the car's hood up against possible rain as well as to keep them both warm. In the dimness of its interior she prayed he wouldn't see the fear that had pulled down the corners of her lips, though the huge fox-fur collar of her coat must be hiding much of that too.

She had to say it now: that it wasn't possible to wait six months, much less a whole year. She had to say it.

'Dicky ... I ... I'm pregnant.'

Looking at her as he had been, he just sat silent. Dumbfounded, she suspected. Shocked.

'I'm sorry,' she mumbled as if it were her fault. Then felt angry with herself for apologising. It was as much his fault as hers. But he would blame her. And something oddly womanly in her compelled her to do the apologising. Yet he didn't answer, and it was fear of his reaction that made her anger rise up against him too. 'Well, say something!'

'I ...' He seemed unable to form any words for a moment or two. Then: 'I don't know what to say.'

'It's yours,' she reminded him.

'Yes ... I suppose so.'

'It isn't anyone else's.'

'No, I suppose not.'

She wanted suddenly to shout at him, lift her head and bawl at him to say something more constructive. Where was his spirit? Dicky had no gumption at all. She almost wondered why she was marrying him, except that she knew why only too well. And now he too knew why. If only he'd say something. But he was just sitting there, useless.

'Say something, Dicky.'

'What do you want me to say?'

'You said yesterday that you'd whip me off to Gretna Green if it had to come to it.'

'I was joking.'

'I suppose you were.'

'I don't know what to say. Amy, darling, how long before you . . . have it, the baby?'

She found herself smiling, but it was a bitter smile, her lips curling downward. 'It happened in November. Just count nine months from then. It'll be born in August.'

She saw him wince. 'How can you say that so calmly?' he burst out. 'You're having a baby, for God's sake.'

'*We're* having a baby,' she corrected. 'It's yours as well as mine.'

'But a baby . . .' He said it as one might mention something nasty seen in the gutter. Suddenly he came to life, twisting towards her to take her by the shoulders, glaring at her. 'You can't have it! You just can't. Oh, my God, what will people say? Can't you get rid of it?'

'What?' she felt strangely stricken.

'You know. *Get rid of it.* Whatever they do, to do that. *You know.*'

'No, I don't know!' she cried. 'I couldn't do that – have an abortion, that's what you mean.' Again she saw him wince, at the very word, but she ploughed on. 'You are a worm, Dicky. It's all very fine having a bit in some attic bed or in some wood, but when you have to account for yourself, that's different. It's, can't you get rid of it? Well, darling, I can't. And I won't. I won't subject myself *to that*. Why should I? We're going to get married, so what's wrong with that? It just means we'll have to think again about all the trimmings your parents will be dreaming up and get married quietly and quickly.'

'I can't do that.'

'Why not?'

'Well . . . because.'

'Because?' she echoed as he let go of her and slumped back in his seat.

Seconds later he turned to look at her with determination shining through the appeal on his smooth features. 'Amy, can't you see. We can't get married as you ask and then produce a baby six months later for everyone to put two and two together. Not in our walk of life. It might do if we were ordinary common people, but we're not. I'm not. My family is not. We have a certain reputation to keep up, and this . . . well, it's not on. I really don't know what to say.'

'So you keep saying,' she muttered, her mind becoming set on overcoming all these problems he was presenting her with. 'You say you love me. Nothing anyone can say or do can alter that. So now prove it, darling. I'm having your child. Say you are pleased. Say that it doesn't matter what people think – you are proud and you want to marry me. You love me. Say you love me.'

Plans were already forming: she would find some way to redeem him from this predicament. He only had to be strong. But all he said was, 'I'm turning the car round, taking you back to your house.'

'Why? I thought you were taking me to meet your parents.'

'I shan't be now.' Letting off the brake, he started the engine up, and hardly glancing over his shoulder, viciously swung the car round the way they had come, ignoring the angry tooting as surprised drivers pumped their motor horns.

For a moment they drove in silence and now it was she who didn't know what to say. She already sensed what was on his mind, and yet was stunned when he said, his eyes trained doggedly on the road ahead in the gathering gloom of winter's early afternoon: 'I'm sorry, Amy. I can't possibly marry you. You do see, don't you? My family's reputation. I'd never be forgiven. I can't be underhanded with them and yet I can't tell them. It's better we call the whole thing off.'

'But . . . the baby?' she said stupidly, so close to tears that she could put up no other argument without breaking down completely and pride wouldn't allow her to break down.

'We'll come to some arrangement about that.' Like a common servant he'd seduced. Fury bit deep into her, smothering any thought of pleading. Sitting next to him in the car, she drew herself up.

'You needn't concern yourself about *arrangements*, Dicky,' she said haughtily. 'I don't need you, Dicky. I don't need anyone.'

But inside, her heart fluttered in fear and her limbs felt like jelly for not knowing what she would do now.

Chapter Three

From the dining room came the sound of women's voices, bright, urgent, brittle in discussion. Constance Harrington was holding her monthly lunch meeting for the hospital charity group of five ladies over which she, being in the chair, presided. It was always held on a Monday, the only day all could spare at the same time in their busy lives.

Two were titled ladies, but having been voted in the chair for this year, on these Mondays she considered herself of somewhat more importance than even they, ruling like a queen over the proceedings for some ninety minutes or so. In her new role she intended to carry out her year to her utmost ability: an acceptably modest but well-chosen lunch; her best china and silver cutlery, the everyday silver consigned to the sideboard out of sight; Alice, as always briefed beforehand lest she make some mistake, and Gardner, having swapped chauffeur's uniform or handyman's clothing for a butler's suit, attended the commands of their employer's wife as smoothly as they'd been instructed.

From the half-open door of the morning room, Amy could see Alice hurrying to and fro across the black and white chequered linoleumed hall in her neat parlourmaid's uniform, donned in place of her housemaid's dress and apron, the lace-edged band of her cap suitably low and tidy over her forehead.

The meeting migrated to the drawing room on the same side of the hall for a final brief social cup of coffee before leaving. Alice hurried past the morning room on the opposite side, arms laden with coats edged with fox and fashionable monkey fur for handing to Mummy's guests as they emerged. There was not long to wait. Within ten minutes the drawing room door opened, the parting conversation becoming instantly loud as it surged into the hall.

'Goodbye, dear Mrs Harrington, Delightful lunch, as ever.'

Constance beamed at the heavy-breasted woman. 'Thank you, Lady Edge.'

'Till next month then, my dear?'

Constance's beam switched towards Mrs Forsythe. 'I look forward to it.'

'A most productive meeting, dear Mrs Harrington. We managed to cram a lot in, in a short while, don't you think?' Lady Parsley's thin lips touched each of her hostess's cheeks in turn, her bosomless frame held well away, pearls swinging free as she bent forward.

'Most productive,' echoed Mrs Forsythe while Daphne Moss, the youngest of the committee, passed by with a smile and a quiet good bye and thank you.

Lady Parsley hardly glanced at the departing young woman. 'I do so enjoy coming here – such a charming house – so cosy. One does tire of huge rambling places.'

Whether it was meant to be a compliment, through the half-open door of the morning room Amy noted her mother's acid smile, slightly hostile, as the woman swept on to retrieve her coat from the parlourmaid.

Maud Aimsley, one of Mummy's guests, and friend of many years' standing, glimpsed Amy sitting quietly and beamed at her, fluttering her hand. 'I hardly saw you, my dear, sitting there half-hidden like a little waif and stray. You should have joined us.'

'I did ask her to,' rejoined her mother, 'but she didn't seem inclined. And we were talking shop, my dear Maud, were we not? Too boring for a young girl, I should imagine.'

But her eyes were censoriously questioning and Amy once again felt the foreboding she'd had ever since yesterday rise up in her.

She had evaded her parents' surprised interrogation after coming home alone shortly after she left with Dicky Pritchard by telling them that on the way she had begun to develop a sick headache. So much so that he had promptly turned the car round and brought her back home, and that all she wanted was to go to bed.

'Migraine,' her mother had said, noting her white strained face. 'Nerves, dear. But I would have thought Richard might have come in with you if only to be sure you were all right.'

'I didn't want him to,' she had said in excuse, to which her mother with a resounding tut had replied: 'Young people of today!' and left it at that as Amy took herself up to her bedroom.

Away from everyone, she had let the tears flow, giving herself up to the misery, the desperation, the lonely confusion eating into her. This morning, her eyes heavy from weeping, it was all she could do to stop her mother calling in Dr Lombard.

Anger towards the feckless Dicky almost consumed her. He hadn't even telephoned to see how she was, but she had been thankful that her mother's concern that he hadn't yet telephoned had been allayed by her even greater concern that her house and table were in proper order to receive her monthly committee. Soon, however, she'd begin to notice Richard's absence and start asking questions.

Having waved the last of her committee off the premises, her mother turned towards her daughter. Amy watched her come into the morning room where she sat with every nerve in her body cringing. She'd been trying to rehearse what she must eventually tell her, but it would still come down to the fact that she was pregnant, that Dicky had discontinued their relationship because of it, and that there was no solution to the disgrace she must bring upon the family.

'My dear.' Advancing on her daughter, Constance Harrington was struck by how ill the girl looked. She should have paid more attention but had been so busy. 'I am so sorry to have ignored you this morning, Amelia dear, but my mind had been so taken up with this wretched committee of mine. It is so very important – the less privileged classes do so need our help wherever we can give it. But that's over for another month and I can devote my time to you, dear. You do look so dreadfully off colour. I wish you'd let me call Dr Lombard. If this goes on, I shall.'

Taking one of her daughter's hands, at the same time feeling her brow, she was surprised not to find the feverish temperature she had expected. 'I expect that will show itself later, but one ought not to take chances. I think you should go back to bed, my dear, for a little while. I shall telephone Richard and tell him how you are.'

'No!' The sharp cry took her by surprise.

'My dear, why ever not? He should be calling soon to take you out to buy your engagement ring. I really should telephone and warn him that you aren't well enough.'

'There's no need,' came the strained reply. 'We ... We decided to postpone it until next week. I was feeling so unwell yesterday ...'

'Of course,' Constance cut in, smiling understandingly down at her. 'How very thoughtful of that young man to realise you wouldn't be up to such excitement after such a sick headache. Do you still have it, dear? Yes, I know. I'll send Alice up with some aspirin. I shall tell young Richard how highly I esteem him for his understanding when he comes to see how you are. Now back up to bed, dear.'

'You do look peaky, Miss.' Alice came on tiptoe into the room, carrying a glass of water and two aspirin, together with a square of toast and a small pot of tea, all on a tray.

Propped up on pillows, her eyes even more swollen from another bout of tears, Amy signalled to her to leave the tray on the dressing table.

'You're the only person I can talk to,' she said, beckoning her over to her bed. 'I'm in such trouble.'

'How's that, Miss?' Alice stood before her, hands folded neatly in front of her plain apron. She was such a pretty girl, and well composed; Amy noticed with envy that she had nothing to be discomposed about, unlike herself. Smallish, slender, she carried herself well. Through her misery Amy found herself thinking how well presented she would have been had she been of good background, even that with a little training no one would guess her true upbringing.

'You're due to be married, Miss,' Alice continued. 'What've you got to be worried about, if you don't mind me saying so?'

Was there a ring of jealousy in the statement? Amy's lips curved downward in a bitter smile. 'I shan't be getting married,' she said tersely.

'You won't?' The brown eyes looked shocked.

'He turned me down,'

'Oh, he didn't, Miss!'

'Yes he did. I made the mistake of telling him.'

Alice's expression was one of genuine horror. 'Why ever did you do that?'

The horror turned to avid interest, as of someone listening to a story, as Amy briefly explained the expected niceties of such things as society weddings, the length of time required, by which time her condition would have been apparent to everyone and her shame uncovered.

'I see what you mean,' Alice said slowly, nodding her head. 'What're you going to do now?'

'I don't know. I am going to have to tell my parents eventually.'

'Then what?'

'I don't know,' Amy repeated dismally, then pulled herself together as the bedroom threatened to blur before her eyes. The last thing would be to allow a servant to see her in tears. 'That's all for now, Alice,' she said, and added as an afterthought, 'Thanks for listening to me.'

'That's all right,' Alice said and made her way to the door. But there she paused and looked back, the door half open. 'If there's anything I can do, Miss Amelia – any 'elp I can give, don't 'esitate to ask me. I'll do whatever I can.'

Without waiting for a reply she was out of the room, leaving Amy to stare at the now-closed door. Her lips tightened. What could a mere servant do? Yet she sensed an ally in this world grown suddenly hostile. It was of little comfort though; in fact finding herself with just a servant for an ally made it all the more isolating. Very soon, she guessed, her friends would be friends no longer. Fingers would be pointed, whispers behind her back overtly sibilant. Giggles coming from some far corner of a crowded room would be interpreted as aimed at her. Boys would cease asking her to dance. The gaze of older people, parents of her friends, would be averted as she neared, to follow after her as she passed. And in all this her only friend would be a parlourmaid.

And what about her parents? How would they react when she told them, as she must eventually? There was only one way they could react. Knowing they could never again hold up their heads in society, she'd be sent off far away to some expensive nursing home to have her baby alone. The child adopted, she'd be returned home with some hopefully satisfactory excuse for being away so long. But who'd believe a prolonged holiday abroad, when nothing had been previously mentioned to all the right circles that she had indeed intended to go abroad on holiday? And alone. Such things must always be suspect. And facing those friends when she returned home – how could she ever bear it? The prospect was all so horrible. Turning her face into her pillow Amy's body convulsed with a welter of devastation.

Closing the door, Alice could already hear the muffled weeping, but it wasn't her place to go back into the room to cuddle the girl in an effort to comfort her.

Making her way along the passage the weeping followed her, begging her return. She compressed her lips and carried on down the stairs towards the kitchen where she'd be required to help Mrs Penruth with dinner as usual. Mr Harrington always liked his dinner on time when he came home from his office – a hurried brandy and then dinner.

Miss Amelia's weeping seemed to follow her all the way down to the hall, even down the stairs to the basement, not so much a sound as in her own head. She did feel sorry for the girl. What would she do in her plight? But then, she wouldn't have allowed herself to get into that plight in the first place. Miss Amelia had brought it all on herself. No girl of her station should behave so free and easy with a boy as she had. Something had gone wrong and now she only had herself to blame.

Despite her sorrow for the girl, Alice couldn't help feeling a twinge of wry scorn. Perhaps she had thought her fine upbringing would vindicate her in some way. But playing with fire, fingers can get burned whether rich or poor. All the money in the world couldn't take away the shame of

36

what she'd done. Perhaps it helped a bit. Or perhaps it was worse for someone in society than for someone like herself from a family that had hardly a penny to bless itself with. Mind, if she'd had to face her parents as Miss Amelia must face hers, the result might be the same. Cast out. What a dreadful thought . . .

'What're you standing there dreaming for, girl?' Mrs Penruth's soft West Country accent, now sharpened by exasperation, startled Alice, who found herself at the kitchen door without much recollection of how she'd reached it, her mind had been so far away. 'I've been waiting ages for you. What took you so long taking that tray up?'

Quickly, Alice came into the room, instantly enveloped by the lovely smell of roasted beef mince and the sound of clashing pans, Lily up to her chubby elbows in soapy water scrubbing them free of baked-on residue with wire wool and soda. The family always had a freshly cooked dinner on Mondays, but the remains from Sunday were reserved for the staff, shepherd's pie with the leftover lamb, with rice pudding to follow.

'Miss Amelia detained me,' Alice said. 'She's not well and she was crying.'

'That's none of your business, girl. Here, take these.' She thrust a duster and a tin of lavender furniture polish into her hands. 'Those banisters need another going over. Why I should worry myself on them when I've all the cooking to do and all, I don't know. It'll be nice when we get a proper housekeeper. All this chopping and changing staff we get these days. Not like in my time when servants stayed with their people for years and years. What's wrong with her?'

'I don't know,' Alice said as she took the duster and polish. Keeping Miss Amelia's secret was becoming a burden, but she daren't break her promise.

'Well go on, girl. Get them banisters done, before the master comes home.' In her old-fashioned way, all her long years in service, she still referred to her employer as the master rather than Mr Harrington.

Polishing industriously at the top of the stairs from the hall, Alice strained her ears for any sound of weeping from Miss Amelia's room, but there was nothing. Perhaps she

37

had fallen asleep, snuggled under the thick eiderdown of her beautiful bed with its creamy cotton sheets and soft puffy pillows.

Her own bed at home had only blankets and hard flock pillows, a bed she shared with two younger sisters – three in a bed. Her home in Stepney, part of London's sprawling, squalid, poverty-ridden East End, was two-up two-down, one of hundreds just like it, homes pressed together in faceless rows like endless packs of cards, door opening onto the street, and a back yard just big enough to hold an outside lav and a bit of rubbish. Her parents had the other bedroom while her twenty-one-year-old brother Tom shared a pull-out sofa in the downstairs front room with his nine-year-old brother Willie. The sofa-bed would be packed up each morning by Mum in case they had visitors worthy of being shown in there. It was a squash, but they were luckier than some with even bigger families with only two rooms in what were called dwellings. But it was just as well for Mum that she seldom slept at home.

Here in her tiny attic room she at least had a bed to herself, still blankets and a hard pillow, good enough for a domestic, and there were some nice things, like the little table lamp handed on to her by Miss Amelia for her to use. But what was it like to sleep between Irish linen sheets; to be Amelia Harrington with all those nice clothes, going with friends to posh houses and tennis parties, attending speedway races and things, drinking champagne and eating caviar and smoked salmon sandwiches; and lovely evenings dancing at balls and going to nightclubs and theatres in the expensive boxes? If she went to a theatre it was up in the gods with a few mates, queuing to get in, and often standing room only. She did go to the pictures, queuing for the cheap front seats. Did Amelia Harrington go to the pictures? Too common, Alice supposed.

It wasn't jealousy. Just a wish to know what it was like. She would often ape the way Amelia Harrington spoke, the way she walked, would remodel some old dress to look the way hers did. Fortunately she was good at needlework and with a yard and a half of material at eleven pence three-farthings a yard – the skimpy fashion not calling for a lot of material – she could copy Miss Amelia's dresses pretty well. But it wasn't the same. So many times she had yearned to be like Amelia Harrington. But not now. Certainly not now. Some things had their compensations. Alice smiled grimly as she polished hard, her slim elbow going like a piston.

It was the worst week she had ever had. With an effort she managed to put on a brave face, stop crying, make an effort to unravel the mass of tangles inside her head. Mummy was not convinced that she was recovered from whatever had ailed her. On the Thursday she breezed into the morning room where Amy was sitting gazing out of the window.

'You haven't set foot outside this house in days, my dear. Haven't you anything to do, or anywhere to go? Surely you must have.'

'I don't feel like going anywhere.'

Her mother came over and, putting a finger beneath her daughter's chin, raised her face to hers, frowning, perplexed.

'You still look a little pale, dear. It must be nerves. I can think of no other cause. You haven't any misgivings, have you, over Richard's proposal?'

'I . . .' she got no further as her mother hurried on, taking her hand away from her chin.

'Of course you would be a little overawed by it all – such a sudden proposal. Aren't you and he buying the engagement ring this Saturday? So marvellous. Even my breath has been taken away by it all.' Again she frowned. 'But I would have thought Richard might have telephoned or come to see how you are. He knew you weren't well on Sunday. It is strange. I do hope he isn't going to turn out to be one of those uncaring young men. It's all very well, and fine, to marry into good prospects but a husband should be caring towards his wife.'

'There's a long way to go,' Amy managed to get in, returning her gaze to the window, 'before we become husband and wife.'

'Of course, my dear,' came the reply. 'Such a lot of planning to do. If your father has any say in it, yours will be the wedding of the year, or I shall be asking why not. We cannot start too soon. To start with we will have to find someone to design the wedding dress. Something quite outstanding, fashionable, something breathtaking. Something by Vionnet, or Chanel, or Lanvin. And then . . .'

'Mummy!' Stopping her in full spate, she had nothing to say.

'What, dear?'

'Nothing. It just seems a bit too early to talk about it all.'

'It's never *too* early. We want the best for you, Amelia, on your special day. And when Richard calls, we can discuss it all more fully. After all, with your feeling so under the weather this week, you haven't even been formally introduced to his people, even though they seemed to have approved, sudden though it was.'

'They might have second thoughts.' She pounced on the prospect, knowing it to be the only way to keep her mother's enthusiasm at bay.

What she really wanted was for Richard to call to say that he himself had had second thoughts and would marry her, come hell or high water and in the face of all gossip. But deep inside she knew it would not happen. It would have by now had he changed his mind. But he had been only too glad to escape in time from a sticky problem. She felt nothing but contempt for him – wouldn't marry him now after all the heartache he'd caused her, even if he came begging. And yet, to save her shame, if only he would come begging, she'd fall into his arms. But he wouldn't. He had brushed her off to do the best she could for herself. Again the tangles in her head began to weave themselves in and out in confusion. Now was the time to put an end to it all, at least to know where she stood.

'Mummy . . .'

'Of course they have not had second thoughts. Whatever put such an idea into your head?'

'Mummy, listen to me.'

'I can understand how it all seems too good to be true.'

'Please, Mummy, listen to me!' She almost had to shout to overcome the ongoing flood of enthusiasm. Now her mother fell silent, shocked by her cry. Now she must explain.

'If they haven't had second thoughts, then Richard has.

That's why he hasn't called to see how I am. You see . . .'
God, how could she go on?

Her mother took immediate advantage of the pause.
'What do you mean, he has had second thoughts? I really
don't understand. Amelia, are you trying to tell me that you
and Richard . . .'

'Yes, we are not going to get married.' Now was the
opportunity to tell a few white lies, that they had both
thought better of it and had parted amicably. But that
wouldn't do anything for the noticeable bulging of her
midriff soon now. There was no way to explain that away
with a few white lies. Yet she hesitated. 'Richard and I have
decided to call it off.'

'But you have only just . . . Surely, the whole thing can't
have been called off when he's only just proposed. Jilted?
No. I shall telephone him at once.'

'No! Please!' she cried jumping up, her hand outstretched
in an appeal as her mother made for the door and the
telephone in the hall. 'It was my idea.'

Already at the door, her mother turned, stared back at
her, her own eyes narrowed discerningly. 'No, Amelia,' she
said after a moment. 'I don't believe that. You and he had
an argument on the way to see his parents. That is what
made you so ill. That is why he hasn't come to see you.
Well, we shall see about this.'

There was no way to stop her march into the hall. Amy
hurried after her, protests falling on deaf ears. Lifting the
earpiece, dialling the exchange operator and asking for
the number seemed to be executed in one smooth motion. In
a few seconds her mother was speaking into the mouthpiece,
asking if Richard was available. Unable to stand by and
listen, Amy fled. In her room, her head seemingly about to
explode, she paced back and forth, wishing her head really
would explode and she could die.

It seemed so long before the door opened. It opened very
slowly, as she knew it would. Her mother stood framed in
the doorway, her face like stone, as she knew it would be.

'Amelia – I am appalled by what I have just been hearing.
What . . .'

Amy came to life, moving halfway across the room in a

41

gesture of appeal before stopping short of her mother, her hands clasped to her breast as if for protection. 'Mummy! I'm sorry. I should have told you. But I couldn't.' Her words came hurriedly and disjointedly and with no relief in what she was saying. 'It was only that one time. At a party. It got out of hand. I never dreamt one could get pregnant as easily as that. I'm so sorry, Mummy. What am I to do?'

As her babbling died away, she saw her mother's face had grown more granite-like. Her words when she spoke were low and measured, not like her at all. 'I was about to say, Amelia, what could he mean, that you and he would not be married after all? He would give no explanation. He refused to say more. But you have said it for him, haven't you?'

Amy stood in the centre of the room unable to reply. A great trembling had begun somewhere inside her. She could feel her face growing white as the blood drained; felt cold perspiration on her skin, numbness spreading through her limbs, the muscles of her legs fluttering, hardly able to support her weight. She felt herself sinking down, knowing she must try to remain upright yet unable to control herself from crumpling, ever so slowly. She was vaguely aware of her mother's cry for assistance, felt herself lifted onto her bed, yet she couldn't bring herself to come round, not until her cheeks began to be slapped, gently and rapidly.

When the room came back into focus through a gradually clearing blur, she was crying helplessly. Above her hung the faces of Mrs Penruth and Mr Gardner staring down anxiously at her, but her mother's voice held an unsympathetic ring now that she was back among them.

'Stop this wailing. It will do you no good.'

Her very tone implied that it was not for the sake of her condition she was being told to cease weeping but that she was hoping to melt her mother's stony attitude.

Controlling herself with an effort, she sat up carefully, oddly ashamed at being looked upon by servants who normally never saw her lying here on her bed and in so distraught a state too, and who must now be aware of her condition. Though how they could be, she couldn't say.

Her mother must have sensed her feelings, for seeing her daughter's eyes flicker from one to the other, she turned to them, her voice sharp, imperious and without any tone of gratitude. 'That will be all. She is fully recovered. You may return to your duties.'

Swiftly they let themselves out. As the door closed she turned back to Amy, her tone brisk, lacking all sympathy, her lips still tight. 'How far along the road are you?'

'It must have been about the middle of November,' Amy replied woodenly. 'At Marjory Broome's coming-out party.'

'I care not a jot whose party it was. It is now nearing the end of February, so we can estimate you are some three months . . .' She paused before going on, as though the next word was unutterably distasteful, finally allowing it to come out as a whisper: 'pregnant.'

Amy didn't answer. She saw her mother straighten up, reminding her of a long thin stick protruding from the ground, dry enough to snap at any moment.

'Your father will have to be told.'

Amy stayed silent, watched her mother turn and leave the room. Now was the time to throw herself down on the bed and cry her heart out. But there was nothing there. Just an arid ache that wouldn't go away, and an emptiness in her head that precluded all effort to think. It was like being sealed inside a vacuum.

Chapter Four

In the drawing room, dinner was being delayed. Lawson Harrington fixed his glare on his eldest daughter. His younger daughter, Kay, was banished to her room for the moment, such unsavoury business deemed unsuitable for her young ears.

Amy stood with her hands tightly clasped together, the only outward sign of the apprehension churning within her. The clasped hands should have conveyed repentance but her refusal to meet her father's gaze, hers travelling about the room rather than staring down at her feet, obviously made her appear to him even more the slut than he already considered her. But she didn't want to bend her head like a supplicant. She was feeling bad enough as it was.

Her roaming eyes took in the well-furnished room, its faintly Edwardian style contrasting ludicrously with the modern cabinet of the recently bought gramophone and the one or two fashionable art deco originals in their pale frames.

'Look at me, Amelia, when I am addressing you.' The deep voice, hollow with anger and disappointment, but mostly with anger, made her jump slightly and brought her gaze back to meet his.

'I am asking you what you have to say for yourself.'

What could she say? Had Dicky not been such a cad, had he kept his promise, impetuous though it had been, to marry her no matter what, there would now be none of this outrage from her parents. They had been so excited and thrilled by the prospect of their daughter becoming engaged to the son of a now-knighted father; going up in the world, all they had once probably wished for themselves when they were young and struggling towards the top of the tree, hers for the taking. And now this.

She blamed Dicky Pritchard entirely. It was he who had led her astray. She had believed everything he had said. Then he had let her down with a click of his fingers and a shrug of his shoulders. Let her down to face this. She hated him, his very name. Even if she *had* loved him in the first place, she would have hated him now, with all the intense hatred she could master.

'I'm asking you a question, Amelia. May I have the pleasure of a reply? What have you to say for yourself?'

'I don't know, Daddy.'

His brows drew together. 'You dare call me that. You, a cheap little slut!'

Even her mother, standing behind her, leaving this distasteful business to her husband, gasped. 'Oh, Lawson, dear . . .'

'Don't oh dear me, Constance. You're as appalled as I am, and you know it. Don't start defending her now.'

'I wasn't about to, dear. But such strong words to your own daughter.'

'She is no longer a daughter of mine. There are no other words for what she is. All the apologies in the world aren't going to detract from that. She did what she did in full knowledge of what the outcome could be. And now assumes a simple apology is all that's needed to put everything right.'

It was no good telling him that she hadn't yet apologised, that she knew any apology would make not the slightest bit of difference to things. Yet an inbuilt social code prompted her all the same, fatuous as it was. Her father pounced on it immediately.

'No use trying to get round us that way, my girl. We want none of your apologies. But I tell you this, you will leave this house immediately. I wish never to set eyes on you or hear from you or of that thing you're carrying ever again.'

'No, Lawson . . .'

He waved away his wife's protest. 'She thinks she can bring disgrace on this family with impunity? Well, I tell her

45

this, she must think again. I shall settle a small allowance on her – a cheque. I would not see any woman turned out to starve.' It was as though he had washed his hands of her already, talking about her rather than to her. 'With it she will be able to find herself a place to stay for a while. She may put some of it in a bank for herself. I shall replenish it occasionally – enough for her not to starve, if she uses it wisely. But I do not wish to hear any further from her. What she does and how she looks after herself is up to her. She has washed her hands of this family in what she has done, as I now wash my hands of her.'

'But if we were to send her to a private nursing home ...' This was what Amy had hoped her mother would say, and her heart rose a little at her mother's words. 'She could have the child and it could be adopted quietly, no one knowing a thing about it. And when she comes home ...'

'Constance, I am not throwing money in that direction,' he blared at her, compelling her to silence. 'I am not prepared to live a lie. I have always dealt honestly with every man, and will not start changing my code now, nor the honour of this family.'

'But when people ask, her friends wanting to know where she is?'

'They will be told she has gone away. Gone to Canada, or New Zealand, a long way off, to live with relatives.'

Amy stared from one parent to the other. It was as though she was not there, had already left this place. When she tried to put in a word she was totally ignored as though she were invisible. There could have been no greater punishment. Even her mother, pleading for her, sounded as though she were pleading on behalf of some stranger, one of those poor unfortunate girls her good works sometimes involved. Her sole instinct now was indeed to leave, go as far away as she possibly could, to inflict her condition on her family no longer. In her heart she knew it was an attempt to punish them, or perhaps even to punish herself with a sort of martyr's need to prove some obscure point. To hurt herself and thereby hurt them. What was it – cut off one's nose to spite one's face? The most foolish thing, but all she wanted to do was go.

'You don't have to worry about me,' she got in. 'I shall leave right now.'

'She can't,' her mother gasped, still referring to her in the third person. 'It's dark outside. You can't let her go at this time of night to find herself somewhere to live. It's too dangerous.'

'She's exposed herself to danger already, she can come to no worse harm.'

For the first time since the argument began Constance Harrington stood up to her husband, drawing herself up to her elegant and majestic full height, the way she did when presiding over her charity committee meetings. 'She will sleep here tonight and leave in the morning.'

For a moment he looked as though he would override her, but her eyes met his with such steadiness that he gave an exaggerated deep-throated cough to combat the moment. 'Very well, Constance. But she goes up to her room now, and her meal will be served to her there. I shall go to my office tomorrow, at my normal hour, and ask that she wait until I am gone before leaving this house, and not venture downstairs for anything until she is ready to leave. Her breakfast will be served in her room also. Is that understood?'

His wife remained silent and his grey eyes at last settled their gaze upon Amy, their message understood immediately. Obeying it, Amy moved past him wordlessly. She wouldn't have spoken to him even if he had expected or asked her to. Not now, not after the way she had been treated. She in turn wanted no more to do with him. Her breast seethed with fury at him, yet also with a suffocating love borne from loving her parents with all her heart from the instant of her birth.

She left the silent room feeling unendurable pain and ran up the central staircase to her room. In her haste her foot caught the last step, flinging her headlong onto the landing above with an audible clatter and thump.

Involuntarily she cried out, but no one came from the drawing room to her assistance or even to see if she had hurt herself. She could imagine her mother starting forward but her father staying her with a firm hand.

47

Amy didn't move from where she had fallen. It was the proper culmination to this terrible day. A welter of sobbing began to consume her. Lying on the floor, head cradled now in her crooked arm, Amy let her sobs fill the house. But still no one came.

Gentle hands were helping her to rise. 'Oh, Miss Amelia. Are you hurt?'

'How they must hate me,' Amy heard herself saying as Alice helped her towards her room. But there was no more opportunity to continue what she wanted to say to unburden herself. From below came her father's voice.

'Alice! Dinner has been delayed long enough. Gardner is waiting for you in the dining room. Kindly be about your proper business. We are waiting to eat.'

'Yes, Mister Harrington, straight away, sir,' Alice called down, then turned hastily to Amy. 'I'm sorry, Miss, I must go. You all right?'

'Yes, I'm all right. You go now. I'm having dinner in my room, Alice.'

'Is that right, Miss?' But she hurried away, leaving Amy to go to her room on her own.

No more tears now. Moving and feeling like an automaton, with only a deadness inside her, hardly power enough to think any more, she pulled down a small suitcase from her wardrobe, not too large for she would have to carry it on her own. Her mother would get her a taxi. She'd have enough consideration to do that for her, surely. Slowly she selected the items to take with her, folded each garment with deliberate care as though folding up her life here to take with her. And all the time was the one thought, where to go. Pride forbade the seeking out of a friend; the same with any relative. There was a brief, rather wild idea of appealing for help from Mrs Daphne Moss, one of her mother's more outward-looking circle of charitable friends who'd always impressed her as having a real wish to help people in distress rather than just basking in the euphoria gained from doing good works as she suspected her mother and most of her friends did. Mrs Daphne Moss was a woman who didn't mind getting her hands dirty; who would sink them in mucky washing-up water and handle the filthy clothes of poverty-stricken men and women while the others enjoyed the more wholesome tasks of dispensing soup and little packets of plain cake.

There was also Mummy's old friend, Maud Aimsley, who had always been so cordial towards her. Would her cordiality reach as far as taking in her friend's daughter who had fallen from grace so spectacularly? Would either of them stretch to that, so near to home? After a moment's debate, Amy knew they wouldn't. Compared with dispensing sympathy and assistance to strangers, for either of them this would be too near home, asking too much of even their magnanimity. But where else was there to turn?

The thought of being alone in London left to find herself a small cheap hotel suddenly terrified her. She wasn't alarmed by hotels by any means, but had always gone to events held in the grander ones in the company of others, there to kick up her heels and take part in outrageous exhibitions which those of her class always got up to, sure in the knowledge that when the madcap escapades were done, her home and parents would be waiting for her.

She was still wondering what would happen to her now when Alice came into her room with her evening meal set out nicely on a silver tray – obviously Alice felt sorry for her, was aware of what had transpired for gossip travels fast below stairs, and had taken special care to make her dinner attractive.

'Are you all right now, Miss?' she asked as she set the tray on the place Amy cleared for it on the dressing table. 'You're not hurt?'

'No, thank you, Alice. This is kind of you.' She surveyed the lovingly prepared dinner tray. She had never made a point of over-thanking any of the staff, but Alice's sympathy in a desert of inclemency touched her. The next second she had broken down, overcome by the maid's open commiseration.

'I don't know where to go, Alice. What am I to do?'

Alice stood awkwardly by. 'Perhaps by the morning your father might've got over it,' she mumbled ineffectually. 'By then he might think better of it and let you stay.'

'No, he never will,' Amy gulped. 'Not after this.'

'I only wondered, Miss.'

'Yes, thank you, Alice.' She was doing far too much thanking.

'Have you got anywhere to stay, Miss?'

'I shall find an hotel somewhere, for the time being.'

Alice's brown eyes opened wide with shock. 'You can't do that! A well brought up girl like you.' For once she had forgotten to add the obligatory 'Miss'. 'You can't go to a hotel alone, a nice girl like you.'

Amy's laugh was bitter. 'A nice girl!' she scoffed.

Alice looked confused. 'You know what I mean. It's not thinkable. You'll have to stay with people you know.'

'No one will have me,' Amy said glumly. 'I know that before I start. And I refuse to reveal my condition to any of my friends – have them laughing at me, gossiping behind my back, ignoring me openly. I have my pride.'

'You told me,' Alice said, as though considering herself among her friends by virtue of having been confided in above anyone else. There was even a ring of pride in her voice.

'You were the only one I could turn to. There was no one else.'

'That's what I mean, Miss. You turned to me. And I'm appreciative of that.' As though in sudden embarrassment, realising her station in life, Alice busied herself lifting the cover from the dinner plate and setting knife and fork and the small glass of wine beside it. 'Here, you eat this, Miss. It'll make you feel better.'

Amy felt she couldn't stomach one morsel. 'I'll eat it later.'

'You sit down now, and eat it, Miss,' Alice said forcefully. 'You need to keep up your strength. You're not really intending to go to a hotel, are you?' As Amy nodded, picking up the fork to play with the food, pushing it around the plate, she added, 'I don't think that's wise. What I was thinking, if you don't mind me saying so, is that if you don't want to go to someone you know, you could go and stay for a few days with my family – until the air clears. I still think your father will come round. After all, blood's thicker than water, and he loves you, in spite of everything. I'm sure my mum and dad would forgive me, after a while. It was a shock. And I don't blame your parents for having a go at you and wanting to send you away. But they'll come round. So as I say, our house is only little – tiny compared to yours, but I know my mum'll put you up at the drop of a hat, for a few days. She's that sort of person, my mum. At least you'd be safe there and no one will think you were a ... well, you know ... one of them night ladies that frequent hotels on their own. That's if you don't mind being in a place like mine. It's nothing compared with this, but it's clean. My mum's a very clean person. She's always cleaning the house. She makes sure it's clean even if we've not got much.'

It seemed, while offering shelter, Alice was at the same time apologising for its humbleness. Suddenly Amy felt ashamed, though of what she didn't know. But it was this very feeling of being ashamed of herself and her surroundings while others like Alice lived in poverty that prompted her to look up at the girl and nod her acceptance.

'I am very grateful – if I can take up your offer, Alice.'

'Oh, that's lovely, Miss.'

'But only if you warn your mother of my coming.' After all, she wouldn't know what to expect. 'Can you telephone her that I shall be coming?' Amy saw her frown.

'We don't have a telephone, Miss.'

'Why ever not?'

'We can't afford that sort of thing. No one around our way can. There's one in the corner shop I think, but that won't help. They can't go running up the street eight-thirty at night to tell someone they hardly know about a telephone call. And a telegram would startle the life out of my mother.'

It was the first hint Amy had of exactly where she was going. She assumed everyone had a telephone. She had never before thought that many people couldn't afford this apparent necessity. Poverty. She knew about it, saw it in the newspapers, saw it on street corners where beggars stood, but she had never stopped to wonder what it was really like to be poor.

She hastened to correct her mistake. 'I didn't realise your family were as poorly off as that.'

Alice drew herself up, insulted. 'We're not poor, thank you.' Again there came no respectful title. 'We have enough to live on. We don't owe anything to anyone, and my mum has never had to pop anything.'

Amy had no idea what 'pop' meant, but Alice had more to say. 'My brother Tom and my dad both work – not all the time but most of the time, when there is work, and they get good money when there is. We can't go in for things like steak and pheasant or afford a telephone, but we don't ever starve.'

Again, Amy found herself apologising, with deep humility now and a great deal more thoughtfulness. What Alice's home was like, she had never given any deep thought to, except on one or two occasions, then merely to assume it a very much smaller version of her own, the woman of the house doing her own chores with the aid of a labour-saving vacuum cleaner, eradicating the cost of keeping a housemaid. Perhaps they couldn't afford even a vacuum cleaner, and Alice's mother got down on hands and knees scrubbing her own floors and doorsteps like a hired daily woman. Drudgery. She couldn't begin to imagine it of Alice's mother, even though she had seen women doing that sort of thing. It was what Lily, their scullery maid, did every Monday and Friday early in the morning so that visitors coming wouldn't see her.

'I'd still like to take up your offer, Alice,' she said, trying not to sound condescending yet sure that was exactly how she sounded. To lessen its effect, she added, 'please,' as humbly as her upbringing allowed.

Her offended expression faded and Alice smiled. It seemed to light up her face. So seldom allowed to smile in her work, her expression dutifully composed to ensure her employers and their visitors were not made to feel ill at ease by any hint of a lapse of servility, now, quite suddenly, she was her own person, with feelings and thoughts and impulses like anyone else.

'I know you're supposed to leave in the morning. But if you're really certain your father won't change his mind tomorrow, you could leave later tonight. It'd be a lot easier really, getting it over and done with instead of going to bed on it and fretting all night. I can take you there myself, you see. It's my evening off anyway. I sometimes go to the pictures with my friend Elsie. She's a between-maid just down the road. You might know the family – the Whitcombes?'

Amy shook her head, intrigued by the girl's almost unstoppable flow as she continued with hardly a pause.

'Now and again she gets the same evening off as me. But if she don't, I sometimes catch a bus home for an hour or two, just to see them all at home. I could do that tonight, if you want, after I've cleared away dinner. I could take you there myself so you won't have to find the address on your own and have to explain what it's all about. Would leaving tonight upset your parents?'

Did it matter if it did? Nothing she did now could distress them any more than they already were.

'I doubt it,' she said. 'Tonight would suit me ideally.'

Alice gave her a look, detecting the note of bitterness underlying the statement, then broke into another of her flashing smiles. 'Right then. As soon as I've cleared dinner away, tidied up and got my dress on.' She indicated her maid's uniform, then glanced towards Amy's untouched meal. Her smile faded a little. 'You ought to try and eat at least some of that, Miss. You are eating for two now. And you've got a journey to make – on an empty stomach if you don't try to eat something.'

Amy was too wound up to eat. 'I can't,' she said, and saw the girl nod understandingly, going and taking up the tray to bear it away. 'But I'll have this,' she added, sweeping up the glass of red wine as Alice passed. 'I need to keep my courage up.'

Alice paused in the doorway, smiling again. 'You don't need courage, Miss, what you're doing. You've got all the courage in the world. I couldn't do what you're doing. And you don't have to be scared of my family, you know. They're the best family a girl could ever 'ave.'

Deftly balancing her tray on her other hand, she closed the door gently behind her, leaving Amy to stand gazing at it, her wine glass in her hand, those last words reverberating in her head: 'the best family a girl could ever *'ave.'* The 'h' so rarely dropped, a sort of insight into how Alice, when away from here, conversed with her family who most likely spoke far worse; with the prospect of going home for just an hour or two, she was already a girl at ease with herself as she never was here, pushed by circumstances into what was for her an artificial world. Would the world to which she, Amy Harrington, of a good upper-class family, was soon to be introduced, seem to her just as artificial? Perhaps not, but definitely foreign to all that was familiar to her.

For all she knew, it might have been better going to an hotel no matter how lonely and forlorn. Amy shivered apprehensively and drank her red wine in one go.

For a while she stood looking at the empty glass, noting the pink stain at the bottom. The import of what she was doing came like a blow inside her head. To combat it she quickly put the glass back on the dressing table and resumed the rest of her packing, choosing items with a more deliberate care now.

She felt quite sick at the thought of the place she was going to but she'd burned her bridges and anyway it wouldn't be for ever. In time, someone kindly and sympathetic, someone such as Mrs Daphne Moss, someone of her own class, might take her in and perhaps mediate between her and her parents. In time things would come right. Parents couldn't stay cross and bitter for ever.

It did briefly occur to her to make a detour to Dicky's home to confront him before his parents with her condition, but it was a very brief and foolish idea. He'd deny everything, leaving her looking stupid and ashamed, casting himself as the wronged one.

She had just put the idea aside when there was a light tap at her door. Alice – already? But it was Kay.

Her sister's eyes, a hazel-flecked grey so like her mother's, were as round as marbles with her eagerness to know what was going on.

'What's happening, Amelia?' No one at home called her Amy. 'Daddy made me leave the room this evening. He looked so utterly cross and it worried me. He said he had to talk to you and that it wasn't for a child's ears. But I'm not a child, Amelia. What have you done that's so wrong?'

Reluctantly allowing her into her room, although Kay was already halfway in, Amy wished her sister were away at school like Henry, instead of being tutored in an exclusive London girls' college where her parents had preferred she study before being sent on to finishing school as Amy herself had.

'What is going on?' Kay demanded, looking at the empty wine glass. Amelia didn't usually drink wine in her room, and as best she could Amy explained briefly and in a round-about way, something of her troubles without actually managing to say what it was in so many words.

Kay's eyes had grown even rounder. 'You mean you're going to have a baby? But how can you be having a baby?'

The blunt question shocked Amy, though she knew it had been innocently said. Fourteen-year-old girls were not supposed to know too much about what men and women got up to. 'It doesn't matter how,' she said. 'It's just that I am, and I shouldn't be.'

Kay became suddenly wise, frowning knowledgeably. 'That's true. You can't have a baby if you're not married. I know people have to be married to have them. So you must have made some mistake, Amelia.'

Amy almost smiled at the fourteen-year-old's naïvety, not knowing how near to the truth she had come with her innocent presumption of it being impossible for unmarried women to conceive, not even knowing *how* conception came about. She most probably assumed it to be some special gift bestowed on a woman as a reward for being married. She'd believed much the same thing herself until finishing school had taught her more than the school had intended she be taught.

'Something like that,' she hedged, adding that she would be going away for a while to find out if a mistake had occurred, pushing Kay out of the room before Alice came dressed in hat and coat ready to take her off to Stepney.

Chapter Five

Constance Harrington eyed her husband, occupied by the *Financial Times* he'd brought home with him. As though nothing untoward had happened. Yet she knew how he must be seething inside, how deeply hurt by what he'd learned tonight.

He had always cherished Amelia, more, she suspected, than Katherine, perhaps even more than young Henry. Because he was away at school, affection between father and son tended to be less, though Lawson was hugely proud of him. But it was always Amelia he held up as a shining example of how a daughter should be; how bright she was, how clever and pretty, how one day she would make a most excellent marriage and prove herself an excellent wife to someone; meantime what a good daughter she was – a little giddy maybe, too much the modern young woman with modern ideas – but she would grow out of that in time and settle down.

There was no especial reason for such loving favouritism as he had for her, except that it was there, in the way he watched her and watched over her, though he had never cuddled her, nor any of his children – he wasn't that way inclined – but his love for her glowed, always had. And now this. How he must be hurting inside. For that alone, Constance felt she could never forgive Amy. Perhaps he had brought it on himself – it was wrong to favour one child above another, and could lead to disaster – but to hurt and disappoint her father so, who thought so much of her. For herself, she might come to terms with it in time, but Lawson never would.

Already she regretted blurting out her horrifying news to him. She should have kept it to herself, giving it a while to sink in. Had she done so, there might have been a more prudent moment to broach it so that the impact of it might not have been so drastic. Instead, it had hit him exactly the same way as it had hit her, and just as she had recoiled, so had he.

But to order his daughter from the house, that was too much. Hurt as she was herself, it was too much. But how to persuade him out of his resolve? Her book lay open on her lap, the same paragraph read over and over with none of it making sense. Constance searched for a way to approach the delicate subject without making things even worse. Yet approach it she must. Her narrow chest filled with a deep resolute breath.

'Dear?' She heard him grunt behind the newspaper, the paper rustling slightly, and tried again. 'I was thinking, dear . . .' She allowed a pause.

'What?' The newspaper, muffling his voice, rustled again. Otherwise there was no sound in the room, the gramophone on which he listened to his favourite records, mostly Sibelius or sometimes Bach, forgone this evening, as was the hourly news the round-topped radio conveyed, another of his regular pleasures.

'I was merely thinking . . .' Again she tailed off.

Now the newspaper tipped forward slightly, revealing his eyes, his stern gaunt features even gaunter this evening, betraying what churned in him. 'What were you thinking, Constance?'

She took another deep breath, filling her lungs to capacity. 'I was thinking, ought we not allow Amelia to stay a few more days. To get her affairs in order. There's quite a lot . . .'

'It's done,' he interrupted. 'Finished. No more need be said on the matter.'

His tone swept away hope of persuasion at this moment. In a few days, a few weeks perhaps, she might change his mind, to forgive enough to recall Amelia and have her packed off to a nursing home. It wasn't a question of money, and there were ways to account for Amelia's absence. All this she had planned to say now after he had calmed down sufficiently to listen, but his harsh interruption told her this wasn't the time. He was already back to his newspaper, using it like a shield.

It was then that the door opened, causing him to lower his paper again ready to query the maid he expected to walk in. He even began irritably to ask, 'Yes?' but was stopped by the sight of Amelia standing there, wearing a brown felt cloche hat, a fawn fur-trimmed outdoor coat clutched about her by one kid-gloved hand, the other holding a suitcase.

'What's this?' His voice shattered the earlier quiet of the room, the very paintings on the wall seeming to shudder. She didn't even flinch.

'I've come to say good bye.'

Constance came to life, started up from her armchair. 'No, you can't! Not tonight, dear.'

'I merely need to order a taxi.' She met her mother's eyes coolly. 'I know where I'm going.'

'Where, dear? Where will you be?'

'What do we care where she'll be?' came Harrington's voice. 'So long as she's out of this house. And now's as good a time as any.'

'No she can't – not this time of night. You must wait until morning, Amelia. In the daylight. Where will you be staying? With whom?'

'Someone has offered me accommodation for a day or two.'

'Who, dear? Is it someone we know? Is it someone reliable?'

'It doesn't matter who, and yes, she is reliable. More reliable than many I could name not too far from me.'

'Get out!' Her father was on his feet, waving his now-crumpled paper.

Amelia met his eyes with a cold steady stare, saw his face redden at the hatred he had detected in it. She heard him say again, 'Get out,' but this time his voice was small as she averted her gaze to pick up the telephone and ask the operator on the other end to put her through to the taxi service she often used in happier times.

Her father had gone to the bureau that stood beside his precious radiogram. He extracted his cheque book and, taking a pen, dipped it into the silver inkpot on its stand and began to fill in one of the cheques. All of it was done with a slow methodical intent that radiated every last measure of the bitterness he felt. Watching him, Amy felt a shudder inside her. There would be no forgiveness there. Not for a long time, if ever. It seemed she was looking at a totally different man to her father. How could he be so unforgiving? It came to her that she had never known him, even though she had always thought she had.

When the taxi was ordered, she wordlessly took the cheque her father had given her mother to hand to her – not even demeaning himself to hand it to her personally – and went out of the silent room, closing the door on them; on her life it felt as she heard the barely audible click of the door catch. For a while she stood with her fingers curled round its brass handle, breathing deeply to compose herself. Then she went on across the hall and quietly let herself out.

Alice, dressed in her one winter coat and hat, was already waiting for her outside as Amy had requested. 'It's not far to the bus stop in Bayswater Road. A number twenty-three takes us all the way there – if we get one. Otherwise we'll have to change . . .'

'No need,' Amy broke in through the hearty gabble. She was already a little wary of this incessant chatter, so different to the incessant chatter of her own circle of friends, Alice's voice flat where theirs lilted up and down, full of refined modern idioms and lively invigorating excesses. 'No need. I've ordered a taxi. It should be here any moment now.'

Alice looked horrified. 'That's too expensive, Miss. It's no journey by bus.'

Amy grimaced at the thought. 'I'm not dragging a damned great suitcase half across London by bus.'

'It's not that big, Miss. I can carry it for you.'

'We'll use the taxi,' Amy said firmly. She saw the girl's face in the light from the street lamp – its awed expression a study.

'I've never ever been in a taxi,' came the daunted whisper. 'All that way, by taxi. Can you afford it, Miss?'

She was going to afford it, with what cash she carried in her purse, whether it broke her or not. Her last gesture of defiance.

She wished now that she had been a person to save at least a little from the allowance her father gave her at the end of each month, but she had never felt the need. Cash was always available, a little borrowed on account, though her father usually indulged her and forgot to ask for it. Now all she had to her name was a few pounds in her purse and a cheque.

She still gripped the cheque her mother had handed her, at arm's length, crumpled now in her gloved palm. She let her fingers uncurl. The crisp paper opened readily, still slightly creased. In the figures section she saw the sum of £250 written there. A decent sum, enough to keep her modestly for a few weeks if she lived like Alice's family apparently did, certainly not near enough to keep her in luxury for much longer than ten days. It occurred to her that this figure was the extent of her father's so-called love for her – two hundred and fifty pounds. He couldn't even stoop to rounding off the sum. Well, so be it. She made a small vow, as the taxi rumbled up and she ushered a frightened Alice through the wide door the cab driver opened for them, that she would not be indebted to her father for long for two hundred and fifty pounds; that as soon as possible she would return it, and without any accompanying note. He would understand implicitly.

Alice was silent during the whole journey, seemingly unable to know what to say to her mistress, and Amy had no wish to force conversation as she stared dully from the cab window, her mind going over and over what had happened, the cruel suddenness of events now beyond being changed, and what lay ahead.

Moving through the London streets, now busy, now quiet, now busy again, and again quiet, the brightly lit West End giving way to the now dark and deserted commercial Square Mile, that too dwindling to huddled rows of dingy single-fronted shops on Commercial Road with tatty-curtained flats above. Narrow side turnings appeared with regularity, dim caverns lined with rows of narrow tenements. Alice had grown suddenly lively. 'We're nearly there! The next street but one!'

The taxi turned into a cavern on the left, turning twice more, deeper into the maze. Enthusiastically Alice pointed, her finger moving to the slowing speed of the cab. Her voice, shrill, had changed, had become faintly more coarse.

'There! That one there! Stop! Just 'ere, Mr Taximan. This one! This one's my home.'

While Amy paid the cabby, Alice bundled herself and the suitcase out, almost bumping her head on the door rim.

She laughed gaily, happy to be home. 'Oh, Lord! Silly me!'

As the taxi rumbled off, Amy stood looking at the place Alice called home. A front door and one window, and above that one more. On either side and across the road, barely lit by a street lamp, every house was identical. Nothing to tell one from another except for an occasional drainpipe that left a shiny greenish stain across the narrow uneven pavement to the gutter. Each of the front doors had a single stone step lifting it from the pavement, otherwise no railing or even a strip of grass separated dwelling from pavement. A caller could tap as easily on a window as on a front door. Amy had never seen such a place.

A couple of street lamps were out, leaving puddles of deep shadow. A nearby one was alight, though two of its four downward-slanting glass panes were missing. There was a ragged rope dangling from its iron arm, swinging idly in the damp late February breeze, used, she imagined, by children as a swing during the day.

Alice knocked on the door. 'Mum will be surprised, seeing you here.'

Her cultured tone had been restored but Amy hardly noticed, eyeing the closed door. 'This is all rather an imposition on your mother.'

Already she was regretting this move – and not merely because Alice's mother might object to being sprung upon at this hour. She had begun to notice a disagreeable smell about the area: a sweetish stale reek, unidentifiable except that it was very unpleasant and seemed to waft in waves. It brought a sudden fear that if she remained here too long it would attach itself to her like fungus and wherever she went, this air of poverty would cling to her. If Alice's mother invited her in, *if* she did, she'd excuse herself immediately to the bathroom and counteract the cloying odour with a quick dab of the *Adieu Sagesse* perfume she'd brought along.

The door opened. A square-bodied woman in a flowery printed wrapover apron stood there, her hair an indiscriminate faded colour cut square about her ears to give her face a pudding-like shape. Seeing Alice, a huge smile transformed the features completely, small teeth revealed in two even rows and cheeks puffed out.

'Caw, luv! I didn't expect ter see you. You wasn't coming 'ome this week. Wasn't you going to the pictures with your friend Elsie?'

The smile still on her unrouged lips, her gaze moved towards Amy whom Alice hurriedly introduced.

'This is Miss Amelia Harrington, the daughter of my employer.'

Consternation replaced the woman's smile. 'Oh my!' she whispered, but Alice gave her no time to quail at such an illustrious visitor.

'I've brought Miss Harrington with me, Mum. I wonder could she stay here for tonight. It's important. Would you mind, Mum? I'll explain when we're inside.'

The woman seemed to come to from her trance. 'Oh ... yes. Of course. Come in.' Put into a sudden fluster, she stepped back for the two girls to enter, apologies already tumbling out for the apparent state of her home as she closed the door and followed them up the dim narrow passage unlit but for the light coming from an open doorway to the left at the far end.

'We didn't expect anyone tonight. I'm afraid we're in a bit of a pickle. We was on the verge of going ter bed, really. The place ain't much ter talk about. Fancy bringin' your employer's daughter all the way 'ere ter see us. You should've warned us. Look, wait 'ere a moment, would you both? I'll just see if my Tom and Arthur, my 'usband, are in a fit state to receive visitors. Won't be a tick.'

Bustling ahead of them, she hurried into the room from which the light came, half-closing the door behind her to

62

plunge them into even deeper dimness. 'Dad's probably in his braces,' Alice whispered. 'Mum's very particular, you know.'

From the room came the muffled sound of voices, urgent and sibilant, and the swishing of some hasty activity. Moments later, Alice's mother came bustling out. 'You can come in now. Sorry about that.'

The room into which Amy was ushered completely stunned her by its humble proportions. A sagging brown armchair, a two-seater sofa, and a wooden chair with arms and a cushion, all but swamped the tiny area between the four green flowery wallpapered walls. Yet also crammed in was a drop-leaf dining table with a cotton crocheted runner, two wooden chairs, two stools, and in the shallow recesses on either side of the tiled fireplace low cupboards displayed photographs, vases, and bric-a-brac, with shelves above them holding a variety of faded china, several stacks of magazines, a few books and more bric-a-brac.

The strange odour outside hadn't penetrated into the house, thank goodness. Instead there was the lingering trace of some recently cooked meal together with a slightly sooty smell from the low fire in the grate. A little more pleasant was a faint perfume rising from the polished linoleum that covered the floor apart from a home-made rug in front of the fire. Amy could well imagine Alice's mother down on hands and knees polishing industriously, working hard to keep her home clean, which came as a relief. All the way here Amy had had visions of some grimy hovel, of having to sleep between unwashed sheets. There was no question that these people were poor, and that where they lived left a lot to be desired, but they were clean enough. Alice had always proved herself spotless, and, it seemed, so was her mother. Even so, her first impression of this place made Amy shudder, resolved to be away the moment she'd got her wits together, for she had no intention of staying longer than she could help.

Alice's father, who had no doubt been lounging in the single armchair prior to her entry, was now standing stiffly to attention ready to receive her as she approached, his jacket on although he was collarless. At one end of the sofa

63

sat Alice's brother, Tom, whom her mother had mentioned, also collarless, and Amy had the impression that he had hitherto been stretched out full length. Now he too stood up as she came forward and she marvelled how tall and strong-looking he was; strikingly handsome too, with strong even features. But her observations were interrupted by his mother embarking on a rather gauche effort at introductions.

'This is my 'usband,' she began awkwardly. 'Mr Jordan.' Amy was suddenly struck by the knowledge that in all the years Alice had been in service with her family, she had never bothered to know her surname. Obviously her father knew it, paying the girl's wages, but it had never occurred to her to know any more about her than that her name was Alice. Alice Jordan – it sounded quite nice.

'And this is me oldest boy, Tom.' She paused for Amy to acknowledge him, then went on: 'Me other girls, Vi and Rosy is already in bed. Workin the mornin', they don't go out much weekdays. Willie's in bed too. That's me ovver boy. 'E's nine, be ten in May. 'E's still at school, but 'e's a paperboy at weekends. A real quick runner – beats nearly all the ovver boys, runnin' wiv 'is papers,' she added proudly and Amy smiled.

She'd always seen armies of paperboys streaking through West End throngs, each with a bundle of a latest edition under his arm, one being frantically waved as each yelled at the top of his lungs, '*Star-News-Standard-* extra edition!' to have it snatched up, replaced by a coin to be dropped in a hip satchel and another paper plucked from the bundle, but she had never thought to pause to consider who they were and where they lived. Apparently one of them lived here. It was intriguing.

Mrs Jordan had quite forgotten to introduce Amy herself, and Alice, having studied etiquette well, hastily stepped in to introduce her properly.

Mrs Jordan looked directly at Amy, her first awkwardness conquered. This was her home, and her smile, though still friendly, demanded explanation. 'Alice said you needed to stay 'ere tonight, Miss 'Arrin'ton? I don't want ter be rude nor nothing, but it seems a bit – well, unexpected, if yer know what I mean.'

'I'll explain in the kitchen, Mum,' Alice broke in as Amy looked towards her for help. 'Make yourself at home, Miss Amelia. Mum and I won't be a tick.'

Left with two men looking awkwardly at her, the older sitting down again and clearing his throat in embarrassment at being faced in his own home by a well-dressed young lady from a world he only ever saw alighting from cabs in the West End, Amy sat on the sofa edge, returning their smiles, and waited.

It seemed an age before the women returned. Mrs Jordan's face, plump, lined, but still faintly echoing a once-pretty young woman, was wreathed in a sympathetic smile as she regarded Amy. Whatever Alice had related had obviously pulled at her heartstrings.

'Me and Alice 'ave decided, if you don't mind, we can put you up in the girls' room. With Alice 'ardly ever here, they 'ave the bed ter theirselves. It's a big double bed an' there's plenty of room. They can both shove over an' make room fer you an' Alice.'

Her gaze took in Amy's expensive coat and hat she was still wearing, the fine shoes and leather handbag she held on her lap, fingers nervously curled about its handle, and her expression grew apologetic.

'I'm sorry we don't 'ave a lot of room, dear. You're used to a lot bigger place by what Alice described where she's 'ousemaid.'

'No, Mrs Jordan,' Amy hastened to reply. 'It's fine. I feel I am being such a trouble to you.'

'Of course you ain't, luv.' On top of her embarrassment, Mrs Jordan grew motherly, now in charge of the situation. 'No decent girl should be out there at night on 'er own lookin' for somewhere to stay. There's some not very nice places in London, and some not very nice people, doubtful women ... Your only other choice would've bin to go to one of them there 'ostels what take in girls what are ... well, you know.'

She paused, loath to complete that doubtful description, then went on hurriedly: 'They ain't for decent girls. They look after you, of course, but they make you work 'orribly 'ard for your bed and board while you're waitin' for . . . well, you know.'

Again she hesitated, giving her two menfolk a wary glance. Amy could read her thoughts clear enough: her visitor's problem was none of their affair and not to be spoken of in front of them to show her up. But the very significance of the sharp way she had pulled herself up made instead painfully obvious what the problem was as Mrs Jordan went on, supportive, well-meaning, and in the process, glaringly informative.

'It really ain't for gently brought up young ladies like yerself, luv. My Alice was right ter bring you ter me. I know we ain't got much, but I can see you all right for a day or two, until you can sort yerself out.'

'I'll be able to pay for any inconvenience I'm causing,' Amy said quickly, feeling a hint was being given.

Mrs Jordan looked instantly mortified. 'Good Lord, child, I wouldn't dream of takin' yer money.' She threw a sharp glance at her husband who had given a significant cough at that remark, but took note. 'Of course, if you did 'ave to stay longer, I wouldn't think of charging rent, but I'd 'ave to ask for a bit towards food, if you know what I mean. I don't want to look grabbing but my men don't bring in a lot. Money's good when they're in work, of course. Stevedores' money ain't bad, but it's gettin' work, you see. When an unloading job's finished, it's a case of 'aving to stand around outside the dock gates fer whatever other job comes along, and sometimes there ain't no jobs for a while. They usually get something though. Good workers, my two. Strong and tough, both of 'em, and willing too. And Alice's sister, Vi, she left school last year and got 'erself a job as a packer down at Billin'sgate – the fish market, yer know – she brings in a bit as well. And . . .'

'You must be tired, Miss Amelia,' Alice cut through her mother's chatter that threatened to go on well into the night. 'Mum, perhaps Miss Amelia would like something to eat – a sandwich or something.'

'Oh, my – there's me goin' on like there's no tomorrer. I

was forgetting. I can cut you a cheese sandwich. The cold meat from Sunday is all gone.'

'I'm not hungry.' Events had taken away any appetite. That and the realisation that these people had next to nothing to give. 'I just feel weary, that's all.'

Mrs Jordan made for the door. 'Right then, I'll get them girls ter shove over. I changed the bedsheet this morning when I got the other one off to wash, so it's clean. I 'ope you don't mind sharing with Alice as well, do yer? This weather it do 'elp everyone ter keep warm.'

From the door Mrs Jordan smiled at her little joke, but the idea of sharing a bed with her own housemaid as well as two other people struck Amy as thoroughly unsavoury. She felt her flesh squirm but there was little she could do except smile back as graciously as she could. Alice and her mother were trying to be kind. Very few people would have been so kind, certainly not the people she knew. Despite the prospect of sleeping four in a bed, she could have wept tears of gratitude for these people.

Within minutes, Mrs Jordan was down again. 'All ready,' she declared. 'Yer can go up soon as you like. A skinny pair, my kids – don't take up 'ardly any room.'

Much as she didn't savour the thought of getting into a bed warmed by other bodies, Amy felt exhausted, worn out by the worry of her condition and the hurt of her parents' reaction; though half-expected, she hadn't imagined it would go to the extremes of their throwing her out of her home without any consideration as to the alternatives. All she wanted was to fall asleep, anywhere, the desperate unhappiness consuming her muffled by oblivion.

Nor did she relish making conversation with these people, good-hearted as they were. Mr Jordan looked most uncomfortable, his home invaded by a stranger. His son's opinion of her and her condition was as transparent as if his handsome head were glass. Unexpectedly she found it concerning her far more than it should what this big, well-made man thought of her. Why it should, she didn't know. He was nothing to her. He'd not spoken to her once since being introduced, except to give her that first awkward smile while Alice and her mother had been in the kitchen. Now as she looked towards him any friendliness he might have shown to her had disappeared, the brow knitted, the dark eyebrows drawn together, the blue eyes she had noted before anything else about him lowered away from her, shadowed beneath their thick dark lashes.

'All right, luv?' Mrs Jordan was saying. 'I'll take you upstairs then. Alice can follow you up in a little while – give you time to sort yourself out and get undressed. That all right, dear?'

Amy nodded, and throwing a last look at Alice's brother, uttered an oddly humbled good night.

Following Mrs Jordan up the shallow flight of creaky stairs, bare of any carpet and narrower even than those to the staff quarters in her own home, she found herself shown into a bedroom perhaps just a little bigger than the one Alice and the scullery maid shared. She had expected this, taking in the smallness of the room downstairs, but she was still taken by surprise, as, without too much consideration for the two girls now kindly moved over to one side of the double bed to make room for her guest, Mrs Jordan flicked down the brass light switch.

'I know you two are awake so it don't matter,' she laughingly defended the intrusion of a bilious glare from beneath a cheap yellow shade on the ceiling set close to the flimsy beige window curtains to avoid throwing silhouettes of the room's occupants for every passer-by to see.

The room was stuffed with cheap furniture. Between the bed and the wall stood a Victorian commode, probably second-hand, serving as a bedside table, its cupboard door half-open to reveal a jumble of underwear instead of the chamber pot it had once held, its flat top littered with a few well-thumbed girls' picture magazines, various jars, some Woolworth's knick-knacks and a battered old alarm clock.

There were no framed pictures on any of the walls, though several garish prints of film stars, Ramon Novarro, Douglas Fairbanks, John Gilbert, all carefully cut from magazines and smoothed out, had been tacked up. There was no dressing table, Amy noted – no space for one – but a chair under the window had a square mirror propped up on it. Against the wall where the door was, an ancient wardrobe dominated the room, the flimsy veneered oak raised in places, another secondhand article she imagined, and she shivered at this enforced scraping of a living compared to her own hitherto accepted standards of living, splendid home, fine furniture, well-planned furnishings and decorations. She felt strangely ashamed at having taken those high standards of living for granted all her life when there were such poor people about as these.

There was no washstand either – again no space, and she wondered vaguely where these girls did wash. There had been one other door upstairs, slightly ajar to reveal another bedroom, probably belonging to the parents, but no sign of bathroom or toilet. That they could be downstairs seemed odd, but the life of these people was certainly odd by comparison with what she was used to.

From above the coverlet of the occupied part of the bed the faces of Alice's younger sisters peeped at her, eyes squinting against the sudden light, dim as it was. Mrs Jordan gestured towards them with a mild smile.

'You two go to sleep, now. Miss 'Arrin'ton don't want you garping at her while she's trying ter get 'erself ready fer bed. Go on now, turn over an' go back ter sleep.'

Instead, the covers were pulled down even further and Amy found herself regarding two pretty faces below heads of fair, slightly wavy hair.

'Go on, I said,' continued Mrs Jordan, her command not to be flouted by their curiosity. 'Vi – turn over and mind your own business. You too, Rosy. Miss 'Arrin'ton wants a bit of privacy.'

'Privacy! What's that?' came a pert retort from Rosy, the eldest by two years, Amy judged. Violet looked about fifteen.

'Now we don't want none of your cheek. Just shut up, both of yer, and leave Miss 'Arrin'ton in peace.'

'I ain't said nothing!' came Violet's affronted voice, but her mother smiled even as she admonished.

'I don't care. Yer can talk all yer want in the mornin', so let's 'ave a little bit of 'ush now. Alice'll be up soon, and Miss 'Arrin'ton wants ter be in bed before she does.' She turned to Amy. 'All right, luv, I'll leave yer to it. Goo'night.'

'Good night,' Amy returned. 'And . . . thank you for all you're doing. It's very kind.'

'Gaah,' came the reply by way of dismissing her gratitude. 'Ain't nuffink. Turn orf the light whenever yer want to.' With that she left Amy to it, closing the door gently with a scraping sound across the bare linoleum.

Left to herself, Amy smiled at the inquisitive faces turned in her direction despite their mother's warnings, and then moved away to put her small case on the chair and open it, hoping her back might persuade the watchers to indeed turn over and go to sleep. But she knew she was being watched with more than avid interest – a strange visitor being offered a bed for the night; a woman who spoke, as she now realised, with what Alice had once called a plum in her mouth; one whose attire was worlds beyond their wildest dreams to possess. They were awed, speechless now that they'd been left alone with her, yet full of wonder and curiosity, almost as though royalty had entered their bedroom.

She was glad neither of them found enough courage to start asking her questions. Left to herself she hurriedly unpacked her nightdress and dressing gown, and went quickly over to switch off the light so they wouldn't see her undress.

Plunged into darkness, she clambered into her nightwear, fumbling, glad to slip into the unsavoury, noisily creaking bed before the dim glow from the street lamp outside could begin to penetrate the flimsy curtains to show her up.

She lay very still. The girls gave a hesitant, whispered, 'Goo'night,' and she responded, her pronunciation of the word so different to theirs. She felt the soft tug of the bedclothes as they turned over. There was a moment or two of whispering, a muffled giggle, then silence. She felt grateful for the silence; offered up a small prayer for her future, and continued to lie very still, not daring to move lest it provoke the other two into conversation. But, as is always the case, deciding to lie very still started up an itch somewhere on the body, in her case her upper arm, provoking the need to scratch. With an effort, she endured it, willing it away.

In the gloom she gazed up at the ceiling. She was still in her make-up – had not washed, brushed her hair or cleaned her teeth. No one had invited her to, and she hadn't thought to ask, so weary was she from this evening's turn of events.

Was it just this evening, when she'd been told to leave tomorrow but had been persuaded by Alice to go this very night? It seemed ages ago. It felt as though she'd travelled half across the universe, so far away did this world seem from hers. Yet it was only three hours before that she had left the one she'd known all her life; that comfortable, safe world taken for granted, with no thought that there could be any other way of life. Now she felt unclean, desperately in need of a long hot soak. But hardly the thing now to go back downstairs asking for a bath ... if indeed they had such a place. It hadn't seemed like it. Where did they bathe?

The bed too felt unclean; still warm as she'd clambered in, unfresh, sagging at the middle, used by another; horrible. It possessed an intrusive taint of cheap perfume. Rosy's perfume? Probably worn all day. Did she ever bathe before going to bed? Oh, God, it was all too horrible to contemplate! *Everything* was too horrible. All she wanted was oblivion, to forget this nightmare of an evening and imagine herself not here at all. She prayed for sleep.

Amy awoke with a start, the bed rocking to the weight of someone climbing in beside her, its springs creaking. There was a moment of panic, the end of a confused, unrecalled dream, except this final part, caused no doubt by the tangible disturbance itself, giving her to imagine the bed's movement was from Alice's well-built brother climbing in with her, to maul her, have his way with her. She started up with a little cry of terror.

'Oh, I am sorry, Miss. I didn't mean to disturb you.'

Amy sank back in relief. 'You startled me.'

'I am so sorry, Miss Amelia ...'

Irrational irritation swept over her. 'Please, Alice. Don't call me Miss, or Miss Amelia. My name is Amy. Everyone uses it. Apart from my family.'

Alice sat looking down at her. 'I couldn't, Miss ... I'm only your maid.'

'You're not my maid any longer, Alice, remember? Just call me Amy. All my friends call me that.'

In the darkness she felt Alice's body relax, thought she was smiling, heard her say, softly, 'Oh, that *is* nice. Thank you,' and at that moment knew that she had, quite inadvertently, invited Alice to be included as a friend. There was no way to remedy the error, but as Alice lay down very carefully beside her so as not to cause too much disturbance, Amy now finding herself completely restricted by the recumbent forms on both sides, she wondered if it wasn't perhaps a bad thing to have Alice as a friend – a far truer friend by her actions this night than many she could mention.

Chapter Six

Morning came with a rude shock of noise and bustle, a scramble to get out of bed leaving Amy quite alone in it, the light switched on, raw after the soft darkness; outside it was still dark with hours to go before any glimmer of daylight. Girlish voices, high and quarrelsome, battered at Amy's ears as the bed creaked and bounced. The room suddenly became a hostile place. Amy closed her eyes tightly, unsure whether she too should be getting up or staying where she was.

She stayed where she was, half wanting to break into tears at the stark recollection of her situation, the desolation of that knowledge now she was fully awake. At home it would be hours before she arose, leisurely, Alice bringing in morning tea, her tone gentle, respectful of her mistress's drowsy senses as she quietly drew back the curtains.

Here, there was nothing gentle about Alice's voice. It might have belonged to a different girl, raised in conflict with her younger sisters to be first to the wardrobe to dress for the day ahead; it seemed the first dressed probably had a better chance to be first getting to the bathroom, wherever that was, to wash and tidy herself up. Amy never dressed before her morning bath. A dressing gown was all that was needed, a few moments spent sipping at her morning tea before slipping into a ready bath, then on with a little make-up, then dress and go down for breakfast.

Alice was still half dressed, but ahead of the other two, pausing only to whisper in Amy's ear, 'I've got to be off, Miss Amelia. Mustn't be late back. I'll be up again before I go. You stay here for a while, then Mum'll have a bit of breakfast ready for you.'

She was out of the door before Amy could reply. Peeping over the blankets, her eyes now adjusted to the harsh light bulb, she saw her and Violet surge out of the room together followed closely by Rosy, still hastily dressing herself. The door left open in the rush, allowed in the concerted sound of their scurrying down the uncarpeted stairs like a horde of heavy-footed mice.

From below came the deep mumble of men's voices, both of them long since up, then the crash of the street door as they went off to work. Amy glanced at her watch, having gone to bed still wearing it, she had been so tired. It showed the unearthly hour of six thirty-five. It had never occurred to her before that men did go off to work at such unsocial hours. The girls would follow in their own allotted time – Alice a little before the others, obliged to travel half across London to be in Bayswater ready to begin her duties in the Harrington household for the next week or so. It dawned on Amy with a shock that she wouldn't see her again until her next day or evening off. That could be ages. What was she expected to do in the meantime? No one had said.

Hardly had the thought gone through her head than Alice was in the room again, creeping in on tiptoe, her voice gentle now, just as if she still waited upon her employer's daughter.

'Miss Amelia. Are you awake?'

Amy stirred, as she would have in her own bedroom. She sat up. Alice was holding a cup of tea which she put on the converted commode, pushing aside the pile of magazines to do so.

'Mum said I could bring this up to you, being as you are a guest.' From the raucous tones of a few minutes before, she was once again the maid, well-mannered, her diction studied, conducting herself as would be expected of a ladies' maid. 'She says you may stay in bed for as long as you wish. She isn't sure how long well-brought-up ladies, as she puts it, stay in bed. But it's up to you, Miss Amelia.'

'No, I shall get up,' Amy said, glad the menfolk had gone and she would only have Mrs Jordan and her daughters to face. 'I'm not sure, though, what will happen now. I take it

74

you're off back to my parents, and of course, you'll not be back here for a while. I don't want to make you late, Alice, but what do I do?'

Alice smiled as though she had achieved the most wonderful solution. 'I've had a little talk with Mum and she says it's quite all right if you want to stay a few days with us until you know what you want to do. Or even until I have my next day off.' She gave a small giggle. 'I think she feels quite honoured having someone of quality staying here. She can boast about you to all her neighbours. She does enough of that about my being in service. In her eyes it makes me almost as high-class as the people I work for, when all the girls around here work in factories and workrooms. Some work in shops and a few in offices and they think they're very up in the world.'

She spoke with pride of her own achievement and Amy smiled. She had always liked Alice, as a maid, but now she found herself liking her as a person in her own right. She would miss her company. A pang of fear gripped her as she envisaged the days ahead, staying with this family, alone without Alice's support. She made an effort to overcome the fear.

'Thank you for everything you've done for me, Alice. And thank your mother for being so kind. Tell her I'll be down shortly. I don't want to be a disruption. And I won't overstay my welcome. I'll try not to get in her way, but I shall give her something towards my keep, of course. It can't be easy for her, having someone like me staying here.'

It was as if she were talking about someone other than herself. She'd never been in such a position before; rather as though she were some sort of beggar. But she *was* a beggar. Yes, she had money, could probably get more if she went cap in hand to her parents, yet here she was, like any beggar pleading for a roof over her head; a few days of security. It was the most awful feeling.

'You'd better go, Alice,' she said, taking firm grip of her emotions. 'You'll make yourself late. I don't want you to be in hot water with my parents because of me. Do take care, Alice, and thank you again.'

After the girl had gone, Amy draped her dressing gown

about her, her need to refresh herself greater than ever. She'd spend a while in the bathroom – she'd have to ask where that was – making her face up, combing her hair, dressing, all done slowly so that she wouldn't be in Mrs Jordan's way as she got her remaining daughters off to work.

Creeping downstairs, she found all three in the tiny kitchen at the end of the downstairs passage. There was a small table against the wall, littered with used heavyweight cups, saucers and blue cereal bowls from the men's breakfast. That was as far as crockery went. Instead of sugar bowl and milk jug, the sugar seemed to have been used straight from its blue and white cardboard packet, and milk from a half-empty bottle without a top. Jam too, from a jar on the green baize-covered table, the lid lying beside it, the rim caked with old jam. A paper bag of cornflakes stood with the top open, and a quarter loaf of bread lay on a stained breadboard, a half-used, half-squashed packet of some deep yellow, indescribable margarine next to it dusted with little black bits of toast residue from a careless knife. The kitchen itself smelled of washing, just as the scullery in her own home did, but here it permeated the whole house. She had smelt it even as she came down the stairs.

Mrs Jordan looked up from clearing away what there was of crockery as Amy entered. Her motherly face beamed.

'Ah, there you are, luv. Come and 'ave a bit of something to eat. We've got cornflakes or bread'n'jam if you want, or I could make some toast. Whatever yer want.'

'Thank you, Mrs Jordan.' She eyed the dubious jam pot and the congealing milk on the inside of the bottle, the spotted margarine. 'I'll just have a small slice of plain bread. I eat very little at breakfast. Can you tell me where the bathroom is?'

She saw a significant look pass between the two girls, their lips curling, suppressing a giggle. Mrs Jordan's face was a study of blank bewilderment.

'Bathroom?' She seemed suddenly flustered. 'We don't 'ave no bathroom. Did you want a bath then? We've got ours outside on the wall, but we only 'ave it on a Friday – at least us women do, when the men are down the pub or at the union. They always go to the union on Fridays when it's on. Or else they go down the pub. They 'ave theirs on Saturday when the girls're at the pictures and things. But if yer like . . .' She'd begun to look positively worried. 'I can get it down for yer I suppose, and 'ot up some water. Though it do take ages to fill up with the kettle and saucepans. I 'ave ter start well in advance and bank up the fire till it's nice and warm to have it in front of, and a good fire going in the range out 'ere so's I can put lots of saucepans on it.'

Looking at the black-leaded range with its low glow, it came to Amy that bathing wasn't the accepted thing here. Bath night was a ritual, a once-a-week exercise. It was her turn to feel confusion, embarrassment. There was no bathroom. No room for any such. The idea of standing wet and naked before a living room fire, the possibility of someone coming in on one by accident, maybe the men for all Mrs Jordan said they were expected to be sent out of the way during the womenfolk's Friday ritual, made Amy shudder, remembering the seclusion of her own home. This was what she must endure if she stayed here too long. Oh, no, it was all quite unthinkable. A day or two at the most, then she must think seriously of some other arrangements.

By that time her parents might have got over their shock and, worrying about her wellbeing, still loving her deep down, would welcome her home again, her father hopefully moved to considering a private home where she could have the baby, have it decently adopted and no one the wiser. Her father must have been in bad shock to dismiss such a sensible solution out of hand. In a few days, she'd be back home, so if she could just endure this next day or two as best she could, this would all be behind her and never again would she set foot in such an unwholesome part of the world as this, in which these people lived with quite an astounding complacency about it all.

'You mustn't go to such trouble, Mrs Jordan,' she managed. 'I need only to have a quick freshen up, if you'll show me where I can do that?'

This time there was open giggling from Violet and Rosy, now busy spreading jam on a piece of bread each. Their mother gave them a sharp look.

'Mind it, you two! And get yerselves off ter work, quick

77

as yer can. Yer goin' ter be late, both of yer. I still got ter get Willie up fer school yet an' I can't 'ave all of yer millin' about me feet.'

She turned back to Amy, her expression mellowing. 'You can use the sink 'ere. There's 'ot water in the kettle. Soap's on the side and the flannel's 'anging on its 'ook there. I expect yer'd like ter make yer face up in the girls' room afterwards. I'll pour you out another cuppa tea while you're doin' that.'

Breaking off, she moved to the open kitchen door, leaning forward to raise her voice enough to reach the half-closed door of the front room where Willie was slumbering on, enjoying full use of the sofa bed with his brother up hours ago.

'Willie!' From the room came a muffled protest, but she ignored it. 'Willie, get up now, luv. Yer've got ter get ter school.'

Turning back to Amy, she smiled. 'Kids! It's like shiftin' lumps of lead. But I can be a navvy in that direction if I want to.'

She looked warningly towards her two daughters, who took the hint, swallowed the last of their breakfast and kissed her on the cheek, then made for the passage for their coats and hats and handbags. The door slamming, Mrs Jordan gave a deep sigh of relief. 'Two down, one ter go.'

Now she became business-like. 'I've got ter go out shoppin' this mornin'. I don't know what you'd want ter do. Yer can come with me if yer like. But it's a cold mornin' and it ain't much fun, shoppin'. Or yer could go ... well, I don't know, whatever yer fancy, I suppose. Or yer could stay 'ere in the warm.'

Amy leapt into the breach. 'I'll be fine here, Mrs Jordan, if that's all right with you. Look ...' she fished in the handbag she had brought downstairs with her, and took out her wallet, hastily extracting a pound note. 'Will this help towards my keep for today?'

Mrs Jordan pulled back as though threatened by a knife. Her face was a study of horror. 'Oh, no, luv, I can't take that!'

Amy held the note further out. 'I really must pay my way.'

'That's far too much. A couple of bob'd do. Not a *whole pound*.' Pride had for a moment improved her speech, but for a moment only. 'I could do a week's shoppin' fer the 'ole family and 'alf the street too on a quid. I ain't takin' all that.'

She bounced away towards the door, her voice agitated. 'Willie! Did you 'ear what I said? Get up! Yer'll be late fer school again.'

Amy had to give something. Replacing the note in her wallet she drew two half-crowns from the purse, a quarter of the first offer so that it wouldn't appear so patronising, which is what Mrs Jordan's face had told her she was being. It seemed hardly enough to feed a baby. 'Mrs Jordan, please, take this. I want you to.'

The woman began to relent, stared down at the coins, her mouth working with the force of need, her eyes eager. 'I'll take just 'alf a crown.'

Willie had come dawdling into the kitchen, half-dressed, his legs in his short trousers seeming too long for the rest of him, his arms protruding from his vest like a couple of piston rods. It was a runner's body well enough; Amy smiled.

Seeing her, he stopped as though he'd walked into a wall. His eyes bulged, taking in the cream silken dressing gown only ever seen between the pages of a fashion magazine or on a cinema screen. 'What's that?'

''Oo's that,' his mother corrected. 'That's Miss 'Arrin'ton – come ter stay wiv us fer a little while.'

'Wha' for?' His mother gave his head a mild cuff.

'Don't be rude. Just mind yer p's and q's and 'ave a bit of bread'n'jam ter see yer off ter school. An' *wash* yerself before yer go.'

Leaving the boy to himself, she turned back to Amy and held up the half-crown. 'I'll do yer proud on this, luv, you see.'

Returning an hour later, her expression was at once penitent at having spent the whole amount and triumphant at the wonderful food she had bought.

'I got a lovely bit of stewin' steak. I 'ope you don't mind, luv – fer us all. And a tin of cream ter go with some bananas fer afters. Sure you didn't mind, luv?'

'Not in the least.' It brought an odd feeling saying that – her heart suddenly light to see the pleasure of spending on Mrs Jordan's face. She hadn't intended to behave like Lady Bountiful, and didn't want to feel she was, yet it was such a pleasant sensation, her heart lifting without any prior warning, that it took her by surprise. In the past she'd given Alice the occasional sixpence or a cast-off trinket, the pleasure of giving quite anticipated. This was different. There was no feeling of superiority; in fact she felt humbled, but in a pleasant way and she felt easy in her heart for the first time since arriving here.

'What do you usually do during the day?' she asked.

Mrs Jordan looked round. 'Why, there's ironing ter do of yesterday's wash, and I'll 'ave ter 'ang some more bits and bobs around the range ter dry. There's beds, an' dusting, and dinner ter get, an ... Gawd, there's umpteen things.'

'I'd like to help if I may.'

'Well ...' Mrs Jordan looked speculatively, even hopefully at her. 'I don't see why not. If yer want to, that is.'

'I'd be happy to.' It would help use up her day and take her mind off her present situation as well as her condition. The less she dwelt on that and her future, the better.

The day went by before she realised it, helping to dust, make beds, peel potatoes, for the most part clumsily, experiencing something she had never experienced before, and though her hands felt oddly sensitive by the afternoon and her back ached a little, before she knew it Rosy and Violet were home, the house coming alive to their voices shrilly exchanging snippets of their day, arguing over whose make-up belonged to whom, who had used whose dress unasked, and who should set the table for dinner, each insisting the other had 'got away with it yesterday', both appealing to their mother to play arbitrator.

Entertained, Amy stood back enjoying it all. But with father and son coming in from work as the meal was being dished up, the atmosphere changed, at least for her, none of the women noticing a thing out of place. To them it was a time of relaxation, the girls relating their day to their father, Mrs Jordan bustling happily in and out, Willie pummelling his older brother whose deep laugh filled the room.

Tom hadn't taken the slightest notice of Amy, although his father gave her a cautious nod as though not yet quite sure how to conduct himself before her or whether he was really easy with her being here at all. But there was no tangible animosity in it. Tom's off-handed dismissal of her was far more intentional, and for some unaccountable reason it hurt, plaguing her all through the tea, as they called this evening meal, the stewing steak having been made into a meat pudding and served up midday – dinner-time as Mrs Jordan had called it – for the girls coming in from work and Willie from school, their mother and herself, Willie going back to school afterwards and the girls back to work. At home, Amy had reflected as she'd forced her way through the huge meal for the sake of good manners, far too large for that time of day, they would have eaten lunch – a light repast, with dinner served in the evening about eight o'clock.

The men's dinners, put aside after dishing up at midday, had been steamed hot again between plates for them. The rest of the family had bread and jam and fish paste, and home-made seed cake, left from Sunday, Amy gathered.

Sitting round the pulled-out old gate-legged table she found her eyes turn again and again towards Tom Jordan. He was so startlingly handsome, and so terribly rude, totally ignoring her as he readily conversed with everyone else. She might not have been there.

'This is lovely, Mum,' he praised, his mouth full of meat and potatoes, his voice with a deep, pleasant timbre. It sent little ripples up and down her spine, partly pleasurable, as she felt hopeful of his glancing her way at least in passing, and partly frustrating at his persistent refusal to do so.

'We don't usually get meat pudd'n on Tuesdays, Mum,' he was saying. 'In fact I can't remember when we last did 'ave meat pudd'n – someone's birthday?'

'No.' Mrs Jordan's face bore a proud smirk, her cheeks, shiny from years of application of soap and flannel and little else, puffing rosily. 'Miss 'Arrin'ton gave me some 'ousekeeping an' that's what I got with it. And we've bananas and cream fer afters. Don't yer think that's generous of 'er? And she's only bin 'ere a day.'

81

'Didn't expect to look after a lodger on nothink, did yer?' he rejoined, his gaze on his plate. 'But yer didn't need to blow it all in one go, nice as it is, thanks ter your cookin', Mum. No need ter go bloody barmy. A bit of scrag would've done.'

'I wish you wouldn't keep on usin' bloody,' his mother said amiably. 'Well, it's bought now, so you do me a favour, and eat it up.'

His father was already noisily scraping up the last of his gravy with the somewhat battered dessert spoon she'd laid out for his bananas and cream. 'Any more bread?' he asked, and reached across for a thick slice to wipe around his plate.

'I made two bob last weekend,' Willie announced, cramming the last of his piece of seed cake into his mouth, his narrow jaws going up and down.

'And gave me one an' six out of it,' his mother added. ''E's a good boy.'

'We all need to 'elp while it's there,' Tom said, to which his mother nodded innocently, but Amy took it as a dig at her for some reason and squirmed.

She ate sparingly. She'd never had a large appetite and all her life it had been dinned into her that only common people ate like pigs, that it was good manners to eat slowly, leave a little on the plate when finished. For all she'd contributed she began to feel herself a parasite. Her gaze riveted to the yellow cotton tablecloth, she became aware of eyes staring at her.

Instinctively she looked up in time to catch him studying her eating, not her face so much as her hands delicately holding their knife and fork, the fork bearing the tiniest morsel of butter bean on it. She thought she detected a smirk on his lips, not the amiable happy smirk his mother had displayed, but a derisive smirk, ridiculing her manner of eating as against his own accepted one. In it she read all the antipathy of the poor towards the rich, condemning them for having striven to gain their place in the world where the less fortunate apparently saw themselves as dogged by ill chance. In it she read too his opinion of a girl of good breeding getting herself pregnant during some madly expensive escapade. That she was having to pay for her escapade hadn't struck him. All he could do was smirk. All this she read into it the second before he noticed her watching him and looked quickly away.

'And I've no care for you either,' she said silently as she returned to eating, what small appetite she'd had now having to be forced. But there was no combating the leaden weight which that look of his had hung on her heart.

In neat cap and apron, Alice bent her back and rotated her elbow as she polished the master bedroom. It was a bright airy room, like the rest of the Harringtons' fine home. It lifted the heart to be here after her dismal journey by bus and tube and the long walk through the barely light streets with the cold rain coming down in stair rods, her umbrella buffeted all over the place by the accompanying wind.

It had been good to get inside, going round the back to have the door opened to her by Mrs Penruth who cast an eye at the clock over the big kitchen range to check that she wasn't one minute late. In fact she'd been ten minutes early, transport on time for once and the inclement weather making her hurry even more than usual, breaking into a run now and again, eager to be in the dry.

Mrs Penruth had humphed her disappointment in that she had no reason to tell her off and immediately set her to helping prepare breakfast for their employer. Mr Harrington, stern-faced and silent, had eaten his alone in the breakfast room, Mrs Harrington appearing as he was setting off for his office. There had been a quick peck on the cheek for her, but neither of them had spoken. Mrs Harrington had eaten little, and Alice had to empty the best part of it into the bin after she had cleared the table while Mrs Harrington took herself upstairs to the little study adjoining her bedroom and Mrs Penruth, Mrs Gardner and Alice drank a welcome cup of tea. Lily would have hers after she'd washed up the breakfast things.

Refreshed and ready to face her day, Alice's next task as parlour/housemaid had been the master bedroom, now filled with sunlight, the rain ceased and the sun up. Such a contrast to the dingy home she'd left just two hours ago. Yet it never really entered her head to consider that contrast. This was her place of employment, as different to her home as any office or shop might be, and she felt no envy of it because it was a futile exercise for people like her with never a hope of achieving such opulence, try as they might. Acceptance of the distinction between the two worlds was inbred. True, it would be nice to have a little more money, a nicer house, to spend without worrying about the next penny, or shilling, or even pound. But to want to ape the way her employers lived? She didn't think she'd fancy it much with all its social observations and petty rules, especially now after the way Miss Amelia had been treated.

Her own parents would never have been so cruel. Shout and hoot they might have; slap her face they might have – or her mother would have; remind her of the fool she was, even have a full-scale row with the offending boy's family, demanding he marry their daughter. But throw her out, like the Harringtons had their daughter? Not on your nelly they wouldn't. And her mother would have been the first to defend her against the opinion of the outside world, would probably have thumped any neighbour who tried to cast aspersions on her girl. Families might fight like cat and dog, but woe to the outsider who tried to air a single unsavoury view about any one of them.

Alice was quite aware that in the past she had known a pang or two for the things Miss Amelia had – the lovely bed she slept in, the lovely rooms she moved through, the lovely clothes she bought, but it hadn't ever been the sort of jealousy that would turn her against Miss Amelia in person in the way some jealousy can. It had been more a mild envy. Now, as she worked, Alice wondered how she could ever have felt even envy of the girl. In her own humble way she was far better off than Miss Amelia was now. Far better never to have than to have and then to lose it all. How on earth must the girl be feeling at this moment?

It was not very nice of her, but Alice was actually conscious of a small surge of self-satisfaction as she polished Mrs Harrington's beautiful walnut kidney-shaped dressing table, and she felt quite happy and content with her lot. Funny how it took the fate of the person one had wished to be to make the other thankful for her own lot, no matter how humble. Yet she couldn't help feeling suddenly buoyed up by her own sense of wellbeing at this moment. She even began to hum as she worked, a snatch of a current hit song: 'No gal made who's got the shade of sweet Georgia Brown . . .'

It had been a terrible day. A drawn-out day. Constance wondered how she was ever going to reach the end of it.

Her usual Monday committee meeting for her good works for the hospitalised poor had not helped divert her thoughts of last night and that aching worry as to where her daughter had gone and with whom, and how she was faring.

Her members had looked at her from time to time, wondering at her strange preoccupation, she who, with her swift decisions and exciting ideas, was normally the pivot around which they all revolved Even Lady Parsley, shallow-minded to the nth degree, looked bewildered, while perceptive Maud Aimsley asked her if she might not be feeling well. There was no question, of course, of divulging the truth to any of them and Constance had decided to admit to a slight headache, so breaking up the meeting a little earlier than usual, which wasn't the best of ideas, leaving her with no respite at all from her anxiety for Amelia.

Nor had her younger daughter helped, still moping and scolding and short with her replies whenever she was spoken to, and she just a child with no right to be short with her parent. Distracted by concern for Amelia's wellbeing, she had ignored Katherine's rudeness for a while but in the end had been sharp with her. As a result, Katherine's young voice had screamed through the house in a most unseemly and quite unacceptable fit of temper at being treated so. Now banished to her room, she was crying.

Yesterday evening, her father had been forced to admonish her severely for her wilful determination to follow after her sister when she realised Amelia hadn't so much left home as been ordered to leave. She had been at the top of the stairs, eavesdropping as her sister left the house; had come rushing down demanding to be told the rights of it all. How could one explain to a fourteen-year-old the rights of such things unfit for such young ears? But even a fourteen-year-old had the wit to glean that there was a great deal wrong. She had turned on her father for his callousness and had finally to be ordered to bed for her rudeness to him. It was all too unsavoury to bear. And now Constance could only fret her day away.

It was a relief when Lawson arrived home in the evening, even though she knew there would be a silence between them, he again brooding after having put it aside for the day at his office, and she wanting yet fearing to open the subject which would only awaken yesterday's upset and send him stomping off to hide in his study until time for bed, leaving her to brood on alone. In a day or two perhaps they might speak of it more rationally.

Dinner was quiet with just the two of them. Katherine was so swollen-faced from crying and still recalcitrant, hardly touching her food, that they excused her shortly after she came to the table.

Alice alone served them; it needed no more than one person. Constance noticed how set her face was. Even the staff were feeling the strain. It was too unforgivable, and Constance blamed her daughter. She was entirely respons-ible for this tension in the household. But her father could have been just a little more sympathetic to a girl who had made a mistake. Mistake! Constance toyed with her food. They were the ones to have made a mistake, the parents, all parents; it was the times they lived in, allowing girls such rein; the girls of today imagined themselves so modern, outside conventional rules of conduct their mothers had observed – they were just as vulnerable when it came to being taken advantage of by young men as they had been in her time. They weren't modern, they were fools! And they didn't realise what despair they brought upon their parents. But it was the parents' fault for being far too lax with these headstrong young people of today. Even as she worried for Amelia out of the home God knows where, she felt acute anger towards the times that had ruined her daughter, towards herself for bowing to them, and towards Amelia for taking such advantage of them that she had landed herself in that state. With a need to express her anger, she directed it at the housemaid.

'For heaven's sake, Alice! I can't stand your long face at table. What's the matter with you, girl?'

Alice gave a tiny curtsey. 'I'm sorry, madam.' But her expression did not change, in fact grew more tight-lipped.

'What is wrong with you, girl?'

She saw a determined expression creep over the girl's face. 'Begging your pardon, madam, I feel sorry for Miss Amelia.'

'It isn't your place, Alice, to feel sorry for your employers. Go about your duties.'

At her sharp tone, Lawson looked up, first at her and then at the maid, then back to her. 'What's the trouble?'

'I will not have my servants airing their opinions of us as though they have the right,' she stormed, throwing her napkin down on the tablecloth. 'My meal has been ruined by that girl telling us how she is sorry for us. How dare she! I am upset enough as it is. Am I to sit here and listen to my staff making free with their opinions?'

Lawson raised his grey eyes to Alice, making the girl quail a little. 'I don't pay you, girl, to concern yourself with your employers' problems. Tell Gardner to wait on us for the rest of dinner. You may go.'

Alice felt herself trembling, not from fear but from anger. 'But I do feel sorry for Miss Amelia. I can't help that.'

'That's enough!'

She saw his back straighten, become very stiff. It meant a dressing down if ever there was one, but something drove her on, her words tumbling out in her need to defend her young mistress.

'How can you turn her out like that? She had nowhere to go. Anything could have happened to her. She could have been set upon in the street or something. Don't you care that she could be lying dead, or robbed, or wandering about in that rain last night with nowhere to go?'

'That's enough, I say!' As his wife gave a small cry of distress Mr Harrington sprang to his feet, his chair almost toppling back but for the hand he put out to save it. 'Any more of this, and you'll find yourself out on the street. Fired!'

'I'll tell you where she is,' Alice ploughed on, standing

her ground, she was so angry with these two inhuman people. 'She's with my family. She had nowhere to go and I took her home with me last night. To save her walking the streets or ending up in some seamy hotel. I know she had enough money for a good one, but at that time of night all hotels are seamy for a young woman on her own. She could have been taken for a streetwalker and . . .'

'No more!' His thunderous shout made her jump. 'You can leave this house immediately. And you'll get no reference out of me either, young woman.'

His wife too was on her feet. 'No, Lawson dear. We need a maid. We have such trouble getting staff. You can't . . .'

'I can. Damn the staff problem, I'm not sitting here being insulted by one of my own servants.'

'Is that all you care about?' Alice shot at him, beside herself now with fury. Damn her job. 'Miss Amelia, your own daughter, needs you at a time like this, and all you can care about is staff problems. I wouldn't want to stay in this house anyway. You can both stick your job right where it disappears!'

Already she was tearing off her apron and cap, all but throwing them at her erstwhile employers. She'd done it now, so it didn't matter. 'I'll tell you this much, for what it's worth to people like you, you can rest assured your daughter will be in good hands with my family. They've more soul and heart than a dozen of you rich lot! And I wouldn't work for people like you again for a pension.'

Her parting shot as she made for the door, leaving them both standing outraged and thunderstruck, was: 'You've got my address to send my cards to, so you know where Miss Amelia is. I'm making sure she stays there so you'll know where to find her if you ever want to get in touch with her again.'

Outside the door, she stood a moment, panting. Then, gathering herself together, she went to collect her belongings and tell Mrs Penruth why she was leaving. Mrs Penruth would be mildly sorry to see her go as a good, normally passive, obedient girl, but her main concern would be the fact that she'd be left to cope with hardly any staff. Well, serve them all right!

Saying her quick goodbyes, Alice let herself out, her small, tatty suitcase held determinedly, and set her face towards the bus stop and home, eager to tell Amelia – no, from now on it would be Amy – tell her all about how she had stuck up for her.

Chapter Seven

'It would be simpler for me to leave.'

There was nothing else she could say. Since Alice's totally unexpected return home with news of her dismissal, there had been ineffectual suggestions as to where their pregnant guest should be put, ideas batted back and forth and getting nowhere, juggling who could be moved to make room to accommodate her, ending up at square one again with no conclusion come to, because there was no conclusion other than what she now suggested. It was up to her, the intruder into this already overcrowded home, to make the decision to leave it.

But she didn't want to leave. In the back room of the Jordan household, Amy sat looking dejectedly from one to another, starkly aware how quickly one's view can change.

All day she had thought of little else but how soon she could be away from this miserable little house to whose occupants, knowing nothing else, it was a home they were proud of, as comfortable as any they knew. Yet once the opportunity to leave raised its head, the hostile world outside began to loom and Amy's heart trembled as suddenly this home, poor though it was, began presenting itself as safe. But she had made her suggestion. She'd have to stick by it.

'I can't take up what little room you have now Alice is back here.'

But she ached to hear their protest, to have them say to her, no, love, you can stay here for as long as you wish. What would she do out there? Where would she go, if they agreed it was best she leave? There were decent hotels and she had enough money. And surely, if asked, her father would send her more, even if he refused to let her back into his home. It still seemed incredible that he could have thrown her out as he had, with no compunction, or that he might not relent sooner or later. Until then, she'd be alone in the world.

'I'll get my things together now.' The decision had been made. 'I can most likely get myself a taxi somewhere.'

Outside some nearby public house perhaps. Mr Jordan would probably see her that far. She still knew very little about him but he seemed decent enough to do that for her. All through the evening meal she'd shared with his family, he had hardly said a thing. She imagined that had she not been here, conversation and laughter would have flown back and forth as freely as birds in a tree. It was Mrs Jordan, proving herself a natural chatterbox, who had kept going what conversation there had been. The two girls had been chatty between themselves, and the boy had been like any nine-year-old boy, oblivious to all but his own wants, noticing no strain. His older brother on the other hand had been taciturn to the point of rudeness, but his father's silence had been purely one of awkward self-consciousness and Amy was sure he meant no ill will as his son seemed to. She felt he'd not balk against seeing her safely to a taxi.

Mrs Jordan was staring at her in almost offended astonishment. 'What yer talkin' about, luv, gettin' yer things? Don't be silly. No one's ask yer ter leave, 'ave they? I wouldn't be so in'uman as ter turn you out at this time of night. Not now, nor anytime. And certainly not in your condition. So no more silly talk like that.'

In control of matters at last, the question settled, she turned to the rest of them. 'Now look, you lot, Miss 'Arrin'ton 'as ter sleep somewhere.'

'Please, I don't want to impose,' Amy protested, but had the woman turn on her, the pudding face set firm.

'You just keep quiet, Miss 'Arrin'ton. Let me do the talking now.'

'Please, Mrs Jordan, would you call me Amy?'

Mrs Jordan hardly flickered an eyelid, so set was she in her determination to solve the problem before her. 'Orlright . . . Amy. Now Amy 'ere can't sleep in with the gels. There ain't much room as it is all in one bed, and she's gonna get bigger round the middle as time goes on. I know she don't show yet.' It was no longer any secret as to their guest's condition. 'An' we'll 'ave ter allow fer that. She'll need a bed to 'erself. Now my suggestion is, we push the gels' bed up in the corner and put down a mattress on the floor in the other corner fer the time bein'. We can get an 'alf decent second 'and mattress from up Whitechapel. One of you men can carry it 'ome.'

Amy might have smiled at the vision of two men struggling with an awkwardly bouncing mattress through the streets of East London if she hadn't felt so horrified at the thought of sleeping on something countless unknown bodies had used. Who might know what sort of disgusting germs lingered there? She had a nightmare vision of ancient, suspicious stains on its surface, babies were known to wet beds, adults could wet beds, people could be sick . . . it didn't bear thinking about.

'I can pay for a new bed,' she blurted out, and knew instantly that she had committed herself to accepting their hospitality and that from now on there could be no backing out to find her own life, at least until the birth. Now they all turned to her expectantly as she went on more calmly, though her heart pumped heavily with the knowledge of her commitment. 'I hope you don't mind if I do? And when I do finally leave, it's yours. I shan't want it. And thank you for all you've done – for all you're doing. I can't thank you all enough. I'm very grateful.'

She lapsed into silence, and silence wrapped itself slowly around her as they stood looking at her. She stood looking back at them, not knowing what else to say and how to breach this all-enveloping absence of sound. The people looking at her began to mist before her eyes. She was aware that her eyelids were feeling wet and that her cheeks were too – twin rivulets were sliding slowly down her cheeks with a tickling sensation. She didn't for a moment realise she was crying, without any noise.

She must have moved forward just a fraction towards

92

the watchers in an unspoken need for help. The movement prompted Mrs Jordan to hold out her arms.

'Oh, luv, don't!'

Simple words, negative to some ears, but to Amy, brimming with promise of comfort. She found herself falling forward into the outheld arms, felt them wrap about her shoulders, drawing her in, and suddenly she was crying her eyes out, great gulps of weeping she thought would consume her whole body as the woman rocked her gently backwards and forwards as though she were a baby. This is what had been lacking – lonely, holding her emotions within herself for so long, unable to let go, it felt as if her soul was tumbling out of her and she let the woman, the stranger, cuddle her in her own mother's stead. It was cruel, the truth of it, and Amy gave herself up to all its cruelty and to its tenderness and to her suffocating need for comfort.

'So what're yer gonna do, Alice? Yer'll 'ave ter find a job.'

Alice's eyes stared pleadingly at her mother. 'I can't go into a factory. I'm not used to it.'

Her accent had remained cultured, even after a month at home. She intended to keep it that way for as long as she could. But to go into a factory, talking the way she did, was to ask for a life in hell being ridiculed at best or at worst ignored.

'You'll 'ave ter get used to it, luv. There ain't nothink else. You just ain't qualified fer nothink else. Ain't as if you were bright at school and got yerself a certificate fer 'igh school. Yer didn't. Yer went straight inter service what didn't call fer anythink clever except scrubbin' floors and dustin' furniture, at the beck and call of the posh lot what never dusted nor scrubbed fer themselves in their life – might spoil their nice soft 'ands. An' look where that's got yer. An' now you ain't even got a reference ter go anywhere else. The way you talked to your employer, I doubt 'e'd give you a reference now if yer pleaded on yer knees to 'im, after the way you acted.'

'I'm not going into any factory.'

'Yer could try shop work. But again you ain't got no qualifications fer shop work.'

'I shall keep on trying for something in service.'

'Yer've bin trying, an' a fat lotta good that's done yer.'

It had been going round for weeks, this argument. Bringing no money into the home, Alice felt herself fast becoming a parasite on her mother and a sponger off Amy who would slip her hand into her purse every now and again when she noticed Alice in need of anything. Not that Alice had ever asked for money, but it was too much of a temptation to refuse the odd shilling when offered so openly, almost gratefully, as though Amy felt indebted to Alice for her shelter.

They had become good friends this past month. Who would ever have thought that she, a maid to her mistress, would end up as her friend? Amy hadn't even attempted to contact her family. There was a certain bitterness there Alice had never dreamed her capable of, and the slightest mention of them would send her pretty face into a tight expression and she'd change the subject abruptly.

She still had a good deal of money. Two hundred and fifty pounds she'd said her father had given her. She'd said that at one time she'd have gone through such a sum in half a month, on dresses and entertainment, without even thinking about it. Now she guarded it with all the thrift of a Scotswoman, had put it in the bank and drew out a little each week to pay for her board and lodging with Alice's mother, and a little for her own use at weekends. Alice seemed to love nothing better than to take her up West to see the lights and to window-shop. They'd have a cup of coffee and a bun somewhere, then go to the pictures, Amy lining up for the front stalls as though she'd been used to it all her life instead of sharing a box at some grand theatre.

She said that when her money ran out, her father wouldn't see her starve; that he was probably quite taken aback that she hadn't sent for more before now, had no need of his help. This she said with some pride in her voice, as though her abstention from spending was something to hit him in the eye with, in some odd way a means of getting her own back on him for throwing her out as he'd done. Alice knew that rankled above all else, and as he hadn't forgiven her, so she would never forgive him. But she could only guess how deeply it went. Very deep she imagined, and shuddered, thankful to be a daughter of her own parents.

But the crux of it for Alice wasn't the handouts, but the opportunity to be around Amy so that her speech didn't suffer. One day, speaking as she did, who knows, she might meet someone of worth and settle down like the lady her hidden dreams imagined her to be.

'I'll get a job in time,' she pouted at her mother's persistent nagging, but received a sceptical snort.

'Even yer bruvver Willie gets 'imself a few bob doin' what 'e's doing, and 'im still only a schoolboy. I'm proud of Willie. 'E'll make 'is way in the world, 'e will. But you, Alice, you can't go on moonin' around all yer life dreamin' of bein' better than you ought ter be. You ain't, fer all yer bein' in service, Miss 'Igh'n' Mighty. Git yer feet back on the ground, and go an' look fer some proper work. 'Oo knows, termorrer yer dad or Tom could be out of work. They've both bin doin' well since Christmas, thank Gawd, so I ain't 'ad no worries. But all that can change, and you know 'ow easy it can change. A few weeks without work is all it takes. Then we're down to the pop shop wiv me best tablecloth and things, tryin' ter make ends meet like we did last year. Remember? So don't you go on thinkin' yerself so grand, Miss. If yer dad or Tom falls out of work . . .'

She didn't finish, but shook her head slowly, allowing the significance of having again to live on the breadline sink in.

At six-thirty in the morning, the bar of The Blue Posts pub in West India Dock Road, the call-on point for stevedores and dockers seeking work in the West India and Millwall Docks, was packed with men awaiting call-on, their voices an unbroken droning hubbub.

At one end of the bar, its surface awash with the overspill of countless brimming pints and cups of tea and Camp coffee, Tom and his father hovered, waiting, with a slowly growing gang of men, men they trusted and with whom they'd worked many times before on a regular scratch basis and would again, maybe within the next quarter of an hour if all went well.

Work had become somewhat irregular of late. Times were

lean, but Arthur Jordan could be reckoned to know what was about even as he drank and chatted. A man to be trusted, he'd put himself about where he'd be noticed and discreetly approached by someone who had some good work going. Many knew him well, putting worthwhile jobs his way while others less in the know had to 'go on the stones' shaping up for a chance of being called on if there was any work at all for them. He was a tough man, tall and wiry, one to be reckoned with when it came to stamina. He'd work fourteen hours without a break, methodically, doggedly, shaming the younger men who threw themselves into their job with too much zest at the beginning only to flag as the gruelling hours dragged by.

A man like Arthur Jordan was usually a ganger, in charge of eleven or sixteen men, depending on how big a gang was required. He would gee them along to his own rhythm, clocking up the hours of overtime which every one of them needed, whether they could stay the course or not. Enthused by him, they often did, going home better off than they might have been under their own steam or some less worthy ganger. Known for being honest and hard-working, he was often one of the first to get the best job – not always but nearly always, and by that token sought after by the men.

He was also known as one to hold his beer, drinking most men under the table and this morning was no exception. While they waited for the call-on time to arrive, a couple of hopefuls, known as floaters, had each stood him a pint as a primer to being favourably looked on for his gang should it happen to be short of a man. It was always possible a regular member would be late or sick, and then a replacement was crucial to make up the number. A man could only hope.

Arthur Jordan had already downed two pints of brown since the pub had opened half an hour ago and now had another in front of him. Tom nudged his father's shoulder.

'A bit early in the mornin', Dad,' he warned, low, so no one else heard.

Three pints wasn't too much for the man, but Tom's own pocket was a bit light this morning. As the son of Arthur Jordan, ganger, he too would come in for a treat by anyone hoping to look good in front of his father, and he'd already been asked what he was drinking. He'd said coffee, ignoring the wry grin. It was more prudent to refuse anything stronger than have to buy the offerer one back another time. Nor was he one to hold his drink all that well, as Dad could. Took after Mum who'd get tipsy on half a glass of sherry at Christmas and preferred not to indulge at all because, as she said, it showed a person up. And if they were called on, as undoubtedly they would be any minute now, knowing Dad, he'd need a clear head to get through the gruelling hours ahead, hopefully with overtime thrown in. Mum needed the money in these lean times.

His father grinned, his leathery, hatchet face creasing in every direction like glass suddenly crazed by a flung stone. 'This'll be the last. Call-on in five minutes. That'll put a stop ter this lot yacking on about their troubles.'

The morning's talk had been all of ruinous pay; the fluctuating job market; strikes that had failed and the few that had worked, but mostly how unfair everything was, especially bosses.

'Bloody lot of blood-suckers, all of 'em,' one was still going on. Charlie Gifford, a brawny twenty-six-year-old, a good worker but with a tendency to be a troublemaker. 'Work yer arse off fer three 'n 'alf quid fer a flat week – that's sod-all if there ain't no overtime. Then kill yerself wiv piecework. They don't care.'

'Yer know,' came a reminder, 'I remember it was over four quid around nineteen twenty. Three years later they shoved it down ter fifty-five shillings, and union dues ter pay too.'

'Fat lot o' good the bloody union ever done me,' Charlie moaned.

'If it weren't fer the union,' Arthur Jordan began as he swung round on him. Compared to Arthur who'd seen forty years as a stevedore, Charlie was still wet behind the ears, married or not, with two kids or not. 'Yer'd be in a worse state. Yer get a damn sight more'n them in engineering an' that's all down ter Bevin what fought fer us when we went on strike all them years ago when that bleedin' Lord Davenport said he'd starve us inter goin' back. You're too young ter remember them times. Things've changed.'

'An' I say, they ain't.'

A union man to the last drop of his blood, Arthur flared back: 'Whyn't yer stop belly-achin', yer miserable young sod.'

'Oo you callin' a miserable sod?' Charlie, known to be a mixer, began to flex his biceps under his work jacket. His chin jutting as he locked eyeballs with his adversary from beneath his flat cap, he began to make ready to shape up to the older man. 'Come on, yer daft ole geezer, 'oo yer callin' a miserable sod? Whyn't yer move over and make room fer younger blokes what can do the job, ole man!'

In the docks few men moved over for others. They worked until they caved in, some into their seventies, for who could ever live on what the government doled out? At fifty-one, Arthur Jordan still considered himself in his prime and no one bossed or knocked him about. A fist short-jabbed as the younger, beefier Charlie reached out to tip him under the chin, and caught his a somewhat harder blow, not intended to knock him down but to unsteady his balance.

There came a roar. Charlie put his head down with the idea of wading in, but Tom stepped beside his father, his graceful bulk bolstered by two other well-muscled supporters, and gave the would-be attacker a little food for thought.

Glaring at the four tense faces, he gave a light cough of defeat, and swung away, dragging his half-empty pint glass with him.

'What do I care anyway? Yer can stick yer gang up yer arse,' the mumbled sentiment rumbled in his throat. 'I've had enough wiv you lot. I'll sort meself out.'

A floater was straight in, eager to step into his place as soon as Charlie moved off to the other end of the bar. Floaters were always on the lookout. Arthur accepted him readily, seeing that he appeared strong and able.

Seconds later, a small, neatly-dressed man sidled up as the pub, almost as though on a given signal, began to empty for the call-on. No one ever moved out a minute before the due time – an unwritten law which every man obeyed. Now they began their surge to the designated call-on point. On the stones it was every man for himself – it was often said that some men waving their brass tally could slice off another's ear in their need to be noticed – but none ever stepped out before the rest. An eager crowd, they followed after the several foremen and ranged themselves opposite the foremen as they halted. Hands started to signal to attract attention for a day or week's work, tallies held aloft as the sign of registered perms and not mere unskilled casuals; all jostled for the best position, unless like Arthur Jordan's gang they'd been discreetly approached by some local contractor such as the neatly-dressed man had been and all that was required was to wait for him to come along and take them up. Obviously the practice was against the rules, but beneficial to both gang and contractor who could be sure his already picked workmen would not be snapped up by some other foreman before he could get to them.

Half an hour later, Jordan's men were at work. Holds numbers One and Three held general cargo. Number Two had sugar, stacked to the hatch in two-hundredweight bags. They'd work for as long as it took, since once the basic rate had been earned there'd be an increase on piecework assured, and if more work came in rather than the spasmodic way it had of late, they'd be contracted again by a regular company as they had been in the past. If luck held this time, their families would again see a decent table, the rent paid and whatever china or linen had been popped into Uncle's that week to tide the family over to next payday, redeemed – all thanks to Arthur Jordan for being well-known as a good worker. They might have blessed him, but no one said anything.

Tom bent to the job. It was always hard, the work, the long hours. Time had little meaning. For a while the March morning sunshine penetrated the hatchway, though never reaching to the wings of the hold, which would have remained in darkness but for the lights that swung slowly in response to any gentle rocking of the ship. As sunshine always does, it lightened the spirits briefly, but as the sun moved round, the golden shaft disappeared, and from time to time Tom, glancing up for the rope to come down for its next load, studied the blue square of sky beyond the open hatchway criss-crossed by the black shapes of cranes and derricks and ropes, and wondered what it must be like to be a bird, flying free without thought of tomorrow.

He hated working sugar; sweet stuff enjoyed by most but detested by those who had to handle it. Sacks rubbing continuously against the backs of the hands scraped the skin raw, it rated alongside lamp black that got into the pores and stayed there; copra – coconut husk shot loose and shovelled amid choking dust into baskets to be taken out; hides dry or wet which stunk to high heaven, dry hides, a man could get deadly anthrax from them. This started as a small pimple with a mauve ring around it, accompanied by a throbbing headache. It meant a hospital job as soon as recognised which some people didn't, and an operation to have it cut out, and then just pray.

This morning it would soon be time to break for lunch, he assessed by the changing colour of the blue square above him. Tom was working alongside his father, the work continuous – each pair of men operating at three corners of the hold, one pair making up a set, one pair sending theirs up and one pair guiding the looped rope ready to making up their set, with no break in the rhythm. Three hundredweight bags, nine bags made up a set – the first three laid across a rope, three on top, then another three; the rope looped around them and up and out of the hold it went, then the rope came down to start all over again. As a well slowly deepened in the tons of stacked bags, the best way then to make a set on the laid-out rope was to dip three, roll three, kick three in with your heels, shove one looped end through the other, secure to the dangling hook, and up she went.

Scant time to think. But Tom thought as he worked, longed to be up in the sunshine. He had never shirked hard work, but neither had he ever felt content in the bowels of a ship. He'd have preferred to be up there, a crane operator perhaps, with a clear view across the clean sweep of the Thames, the water flowing faster than it seemed to while looking so smooth. Or out on the river itself, a lighterman or managing a tug, to see the estuary, its banks slipping to a far horizon. Freedom. He longed to be free of the stink of hides; the dust of grain and the scream of it as pipes

100

sucked it from the hold; the squeal of cranes and derricks captured and held within the cavernous confines of the ship. Even dockers had the open dockside to work on and could also work in the holds. Stevedores never worked on the dockside.

Alongside the ship, lighters would be taking on the sugar for the Tate and Lyle wharf. He had been on them, drawn by tugs, taken to another dock, his only experience of the river and one he longed over and over again to repeat. Oh, to be a lighterman. But lightermen were the sons of lightermen. He was the son of a stevedore. He could change jobs, just as they could, but few did. What your father was, so were you. It was simpler all round not to seek change when jobs were as scarce as they'd ever been.

The sun had set with hardly anyone but Tom noticing. Though it was getting higher in the sky with approaching spring, by the time they'd come up to eat their midday sandwiches it had already gone behind the tall ragged line of Canary Wharf although the buildings of North Quay had still been bathed in golden light, free of Canary Wharf's uneven shadow. Sandwiches eaten, tea in his flask drunk, he had descended into the hold with the rest, even more dingy after the brightness up top. The afternoon had worn on, the cargo considerably lowered, the square of sky above the hatchway had turned pink, dimmed, had grown dark, and now all that lit the fast emptying hold were the bilious lights strung up.

'What's the time?' His voice rang across the now echoing hold. He had never possessed a watch. Few did. But the hatchwayman could see the clock on the docks illuminated by the dock lights.

'Eight fifteen,' came the call. They'd been working over twelve hours with still a bit of a way to go. That meant overtime, extra in his pocket, an extra couple of bob to give Mum. That's if she'd take it with Madam Moneybags still living in with them. She was giving Mum six bob a week. Mum thought herself living in the lap of luxury these days and that the sun shone out of Madam Moneybags's arsehole.

But the place wasn't their own. *She* was there all the time, taking up room, another chair crammed up to the table, turning up her nose every time he looked her way, never so much as a smile, let alone a word to him. No one seemed to be concerned by her lengthening stay, no one grumbled, not even Dad who said very little about her even when he, Tom, mentioned her. They all treated her like visiting royalty, awed by the way she spoke, the way she behaved, doling out her money for her keep like the lady of the manor handing out largesse to the starving peasants – he'd heard that somewhere – no one saw that she was making a convenience of them all, and the moment things were all right with her again, she'd be off without a word of thanks. The wealthy, the rich snobs, were like that – sod you, I'm all right.

God knows what she had to look down on his family for. Tom's lips curled into a sneer as he helped make the last few sugar bags into sets to be hauled up through the hatchway. Her in her condition, no shame, acting as if people of her class had every right to behave as loose as dogs in the street. He'd seen them up the West End showing off, making a bloody nuisance of themselves, having parties in the trains on the Circle Line tube, going round and round till the early hours, kicking up their legs, spilling champagne everywhere, annoying ordinary decent people with noisy shrieking laughter and their bloody silly behaviour. *She* had been one of them, Miss Moneybags, until she'd got herself up the spout. The Bright Young Things the press called them. The name had stuck. But there was nothing bright about their brains, he was sure, if they got themselves in the state *Miss* Amy Harrington had got herself into, still thinking herself a cut above ordinary decent working-class people. He would love to tell her what he thought about her, with her nose in the air and her pretty face – it was a pretty face – refusing to look his way, or looking quickly down should their eyes meet accidentally. But why *did* she disturb him so whenever he looked at her?

Chapter Eight

Perhaps for the first time in her life Amy was beginning to recognise the value of money.

She had been with the Jordan family for three weeks – like a lifetime – like another life, and it amazed her how little they could live on. The cheque her father had so disdainfully handed to her mother to pass to her, her contemptuous receipt of it, noting later with a twinge of bitterness that all he thought her worth was two hundred and fifty pounds, hardly a couple of months' allowance, now presented a fortune. Even the expectation that when this was gone she might write for more, if she could smother her pride, had taken on a different aspect and it came to her how quickly one's conception of money could change. Already she was thinking like a poor person. It was horrible.

To the people here, ever praying that what little came in would be enough to last them to the next payday, the money she had was beyond their wildest dreams and she was growing almost ashamed to have been so affluent, swearing Alice to secrecy about the amount deposited in the bank.

It was a lot compared to what people here had, but how long would it last? Other questions too. How long could she stay with this family? Until they were sick of her and asked her to leave? Until she had the baby? And afterwards, how would she fend for herself, alone, with a baby, perhaps by then needing to work? She had never worked in her whole life. How did one go about it? In the light of last week, all those questions bombarded her with even more dread.

Last Saturday, in a moment of panic, she had written to

103

her parents saying how she was and where she was, hoping to jog their consciences into forgiving her. Posted that morning, it would have reached them that evening. Even if they hadn't replied until Monday, taking time to consider, she'd have received it by now. But they hadn't replied. They might still, but she didn't think so.

She was left bitterly regretting her action. It would have been better not to have written at all, for in refraining from it, there had been some hope of their reconsidering their earlier action and at any time writing to ask her to come back home. But her letter, while temporarily relieving anxiety, had brought a whole week of uncertainty only to realise their true sentiments. Their lack of a reply could only mean that they had no intention of forgiving her.

She had written to Dicky too, again in a moment of impetuosity. And now her entire soul squirmed with humiliation recognising how much she'd demeaned herself. Of course there had been no reply from him either. Pride and resentment welled up in her and she vowed that even if she were dying she'd not put another pen to paper and give any of them the satisfaction of ignoring her again.

Their treatment of her, Dicky Pritchard's spurning of her, gnawed away at her each night as she tossed and turned on the little bed she had bought to go in the Jordan girls' room under the window. Each night was fraught with bitterness and hatred and hurt; hatred for Dicky in particular, but for her family pure, stringent hurt, a far sharper pain, blood being thicker than water. She fruitlessly planned revenge – on Dicky in particular.

These last two days, planning had taken on more solid form, so much so that she had become quite possessed by it, to such an extent that she almost forgave her parents in her need to get back at him, the root cause of it all.

'Don't you ever fancy spending an evening in the West End?' she asked Alice, once her plan had taken shape. She chose to ignore that it was the silliest plan ever – could only come about on the silver screen, certainly not in real life. But even the silliest plan of revenge was better than this continuous feeling of humiliation. 'We could go together, Alice.'

Alice hadn't yet found herself a permanent job. A few days on two occasions but she had been sacked from both jobs. Her mother had said she'd got too above herself. 'You ain't a ladies' maid no longer so you can come down out of the clouds,' she'd told her. 'Knuckle down ter bringin' in some money. I can't go on keepin' yer. It don't grow on trees, yer know.' Which Amy took to include herself and couldn't wait to hand over her six shillings a week, which was all Mrs Jordan would take, loath to be thought of as a greedy woman.

Alice looked at her erstwhile mistress, now on virtually the same footing as herself, no longer one to bow and scrape to. 'Where am I going to get money to go gallivanting up the West End?'

It was Saturday night. She and Amy were alone, the two of them sitting at the table in the back room, Alice reading a tatty issue of *Peg's Paper*, Amy a slim novel she had recently bought, a little guilty at having forked out on such a thing. From the horn of the cheap wireless set which Alice had twiddled into life a few moments ago, tinny music crackled faintly. Her sisters were at the local picture palace. Her parents had gone down the local pub with some friends, Willie had gone to bed in the front room to read an old comic he'd picked up during his paper round, not wanting to be stuck with two women. Tom was out somewhere, probably with a girl.

Amy, with her eyes on her book but not seeing the words, thought about him and the unknown girl, and tried to ignore a twinge of jealousy, visualising him kissing and cuddling. Towards herself he was unremittingly distant. His whole attitude was one of putting up with her presence only because his mother had taken her in and was practically mothering her, being a motherly soul anyway.

He seldom if ever spoke to her, as if it were too much trouble to do so. She in turn never knew what to say to him. And it was irritating, the way her heart would flutter when he appeared. It irritated too, this jealousy that sprang up at the thought of him taking himself off somewhere. Even more irritating, this wasn't the first time she had felt it.

She closed her book and concentrated her gaze on Alice.

'My treat. I'm sick of staying in night after night. Soon I'll start to show around the middle, and then I won't be able to go out at all.'

Alice's lips tightened with hurt pride. 'I don't expect you to pay for me.'

'Of course you don't,' Amy placated hurriedly, 'but I want to. If I stay here a moment longer, I shall scream. I don't want to go on my own. I'd be so grateful if you'd come. So it's my treat. Just this once.'

'I don't know about that.'

'We can put on our best dresses. We could go dancing.'

'Not in any of the things I've got. I couldn't go dancing anywhere posh up the West End in any of them. I'd feel a fool, you in one of those marvellous dresses you've got and me in my home-made things. Anyway, it's far too expensive.'

'You could wear one of mine. We're the same size. I'm not that much taller than you.'

She could hardly wait to see what Alice would look like in a Bond Street creation, several of which she'd brought with her when she'd left home. Lately she had wondered why she had bothered to bring them, going nowhere and doing nothing. But now she knew. It was a golden opportunity. She knew what haunts Dicky Pritchard frequented. With luck – he might be in one of them. It would only be by sheer luck, but even that was worth trying.

'I bet you'd look stunning in my gold lamé one,' she urged brightly. 'It's just hanging in the cupboard upstairs doing absolutely nothing.'

'I couldn't wear one of *yours*.' But Alice's pretty brown eyes were already beginning to sparkle.

An hour later, looking positively ravishing in Amy's gold lamé, a matching band around her head, a long string of real pearls around her slim neck and dangling pearl earrings swinging with each movement, two gold slave bangles on one upper arm, her lips painted red and eyebrows freshly plucked, she shyly entered the bright noisy dance hall where the clarinet of an energetic four-piece band echoed above the general hubbub. Her eyes opened wide with awe at the well-dressed young people jigging like crazy or standing

106

about looking elegant. She looked a dream. Beside her, Amy appeared positively dowdy.

That was the intention. She had deliberately dressed down this evening, for Alice must shine like a beacon – if, as she hoped, Dicky was here.

But there was no sign of him. Several males seeing the lovely new blonde standing so wide-eyed and shy came fluttering up, moths detecting the scent of the female, unable to control their desire to close in on her. One after another they whisked her off to the dance floor. She would arrive back breathless, glowing, to be swept off immediately by another.

'I never dreamed . . .' she whispered time and time again, her hand no longer uncertainly seeking Amy's, her accent automatically mimicking the cultured ones about her. Well, Amy thought with a satisfied smile, she'd already had plenty of training, hadn't she.

Amy was hardly noticed at first. Then after a while she gave up her plan, for what was the point of keeping in the background when there was nothing to keep in the background for? Dicky wouldn't be coming here tonight. Perhaps after a while they could go on to another haunt she knew. He might be there. In the meantime, why not enjoy herself, kick up her heels?

A notion still lingered that abandoning herself to the strenuous dances might still dislodge what was inside her. If that were to happen, how wonderful. She'd grieve a little perhaps at the knowledge of her loss – the hint of that had been there the first time the thought had crossed her mind, when she'd danced Dicky into the floor – but only for a while. It would soon disappear and she would be Amy Harrington again, slim, beautiful, eligible daughter of Lawson Harrington, successful, wealthy City broker. And if Dicky Pritchard came begging for her hand, what a shock he'd be in for.

There was no sign of him in the dance hall, nor in the two busy nightclubs, two of his favourite haunts, to which she dragged Alice. No one she knew at all there. She returned home disappointed, Alice none the wiser about her scheming. There was always next Saturday, but time was running out. Should she fail to find him next week, the idea would have to be abandoned altogether, or wait until the baby was born. It could be too late by then. But how she would have loved to see Dicky's face if her scheme had come off.

Alice's mother was waiting up for them as they came in, her podgy benign face not so benign as she opened the door, her gaze going straight to her daughter, though Amy knew her annoyance was directed at herself as well.

'And what time do yer call this? Yer dad's in bed. Needs 'is sleep. Got ter be up crack of dawn tomorrer. But 'e's real angry an' 'e'll get yer tomorrer, he will. Where the 'ell 'ave you been?'

Alice looked quickly at Amy, who took her cue. After all, it had been her suggestion they go out, and West End entertainment seldom finished early. Although a taxi had brought them straight home, it was nearly one o'clock in the morning.

'I'm afraid it was my fault, Mrs Jordan.'

'*You're* afraid!' There was no awed respect for her at this moment. She might have been one of her own daughters needing to be scolded. ''Ow d'yer think I feel? Me an' Alice's dad 'ave been pacin' the room lookin' at the clock. He nearly went out ter look for yer at one time, and 'im tired out after a day an' 'alf's work wivout a break. We couldn't think where yer'd gone.'

It was stupid. She ought to have left a note. She said so now. 'I just thought it would be nice to take Alice out for a while. We went dancing in the West End.'

'The *West End*? You got money ter throw away up the *West End*? Well, if yer've got money ter throw away, a little more from you each week'd be welcome. Be put in the right place.'

It was as if she were indeed part of this family, accepted and able to be spoken to as such. Miss Amelia Harrington no longer existed. Amy didn't know whether to be pleased or sorry. What she did know was that suddenly she wanted to stay here, accept the telling-off, and any more that might ensue in the coming months. Oh, please, the coming months must not witness her being asked to leave. She must learn to toe the line, just as she was learning to accept the way of life she saw all around her: the mean housing; the poor, barely adequate food; the everlasting penny-pinching; the smells; the grubby, pasty-faced, very often ragged children wearing hand-me-downs from brothers and sisters; the quiet acceptance of women with not enough housekeeping to feed their families going off to the pawnbrokers' with bits of crockery or linen to tide them over; and the look of defeat she saw so often in the men's eyes as they searched and waited for work that seldom came along. And yet they always found an excuse to be cheerful, a sort of raucous, defiant cheerfulness that at times wrung her heart.

Mrs Jordan had switched her attention to her daughter. 'And just look at the way you're dolled up! That dress, and that face ... Yer look like a painted tart! Go an' wash it all orf. An' get ter bed, both of yer. Vi an' Ros 'ave bin in bed fer ages. An' I'm whacked, waiting up ter this hour. On Monday mornin', Alice, yer go an' look fer a job. Any job. That'll keep yer mind orf fancy living. Dancing up the West End indeed!'

After the dim passage light had been extinguished, they felt their way up the narrow stairs, Mrs Jordan close behind, having shot the bolt of the front door as a final act to her anger.

So was this the end, Amy debated as they went into the bedroom that smelled of stale perfume and recently-worn clothing, to all her plans? It mustn't be. She must try one more time. Wait until towards the end of the week and with Mrs Jordan in a better frame of mind she would ask permission to take Alice out one more time, using her need to get out before her thickening figure made it too late. Already she could feel her stomach beginning to distend just a fraction.

The thought lay heavy as she slipped into her small single bed and tried hard to sleep. A few weeks from now she would be unpresentable. It had never felt quite real before. Now it felt only too real. She wanted to rip this thing inside her out bodily, throw it away, pretend it had never happened, but it was part of her and would not leave until the time was ripe. God, how she hated it, hated Dicky Pritchard, hated herself – mostly herself.

Alice was full of it all on Sunday. If she went over her evening once, she went over it half a dozen times: first to Rosy then to Vi the moment they awoke; to Willie, who hurried back to the front room out of the way, a boy quickly bored by silly sisters; over breakfast to her dad and Tom while her mother moved back and forth between kitchen and back room frying eggs, a bit of streaky and lots of fried bread. Breakfast on Sundays was a special occasion as was Sunday dinner. High tea with shrimps, winkles and cake rounded off the day – Amy hated winkles, which as far as she was concerned tasted chewy and slimy.

The house filled with the smell of frying bacon and Alice's tinkling voice could be heard in the kitchen excitedly regaling her mother with every last detail of her evening as she trailed around after her helping to set the fried breakfast on plates for the waiting mouths in the back room. Her mother suffered it without comment except for the odd, 'Well, I never,' opinions on her daughter staying out until all hours done and finished with.

Finally coming to sit down to eat, Alice was still full of her evening out. Last night in the taxi home, she hadn't stopped talking about it. Amy took pleasure in the girl's reaction to an evening she could hitherto only ever have imagined.

'I never knew what it could be like,' she had burst out again and again. 'Oh, Amy, I want to do it again. Can we go next week? I'll try to pay my way if I can. All those wonderful dances, and being asked to dance by all those men. All those rich people. I thought I'd feel out of place, but I didn't. I loved it! I wish I could be one of them. I wish I was rich. If only I was rich.'

There was avarice in her voice. What Amy had opened for her was a floodgate. While contained in her small East End pool, even in her more elegant world in service to a good class of family, she could only wonder briefly, vaguely, what their lives were like. But now, having experienced a little of it, Alice was unstoppable, she was like a Midas, wanting more and more. The once would never be enough.

'We must go again, Amy. We must. Who knows, I might even find a simply wonderful young man for myself from all those who asked me to dance. Wouldn't that be simply divine?' Her diction had become studied, fashionable idioms already creeping in, as though in training for that simply wonderful young man when he came along to make her rich. Alice would never be the same again, leaving Amy to question herself for what she had done.

Even here at the Sunday breakfast table, ignoring the sidelong looks of her parents, she had become a different girl overnight, no amount of looks and titters from Willie and his sisters dampening her enthusiasm for those words she had picked up in that one evening, interspersing every other sentence with 'divine' and 'utterly' and 'terribly'.

Arthur Jordan had obviously had enough. Fixing his eyes on his gabbling daughter, he growled through a mouthful of streaky: 'What's all this bloody silly talk yer've picked up? 'Ow about shuttin' it fer a bit and usin' yer mouth to eat with. Yer breakfast's gettin' cold, and yer givin' us all the ear-ache. Yer mum still ain't pleased wiv yer comin' in all hours, and neither am I. Yer made 'er lose 'er beauty sleep waitin' up for yer, and mine too. So give it a rest.'

He resumed his chewing, leaving Alice to gaze at him, her mouth open, her face growing pink. It was seldom her father spoke so much in one go, and seldom that he told her off like this. 'I was only trying to tell everyone what a wonderful evening we had. And it's all thanks to Amy.'

'All right. Yer've told us. Now shut up abart it an' give our ears a rest.'

Amy too felt herself squirm, his chagrin obviously directed at her as much as his daughter, though he was too polite to her still to include her.

Alice said no more, but her face was tight and her lips set. Looking across at her, Amy knew that whatever might be said, she had already made up her mind that next Saturday would see her visiting the West End yet again. Like a strong drug, it had only needed that one dose to make her want more. Amy felt something like compunction at what she was doing. She hadn't meant to use Alice to such an extent. She ought to feel overjoyed at the girl playing right into her scheme, yet shame gripped her as she hastily bent her head to the greasy breakfast set before her.

In all this, Tom had said not one word, eating his meal as though he were the only one at the table who existed. Now he spoke, his deep voice low.

'Be careful what you're doing, Alice.' It was as though he spoke from a distance; a voice disembodied. 'Be careful yer don't get out of yer depth.' And from beneath his lowered brows, his eyes, shadowed and deeply blue, glanced towards Amy, their message clear. 'I don't know what you're up to, but I don't like it.'

He might as well have spoken the words aloud, and Amy felt a shiver run through her, unable to escape the keen awareness of how deeply his dislike of her went. Instinctively she felt her back go up. He had issued a warning, but far from alarming her, it made her all the more determined to get Alice out of the house the following Saturday if she could. How dare he, a common labourer, tell *her* what she should do and not do? How dare he issue warnings as though he had rights over *her*? Then she remembered she was a guest in this house, at their mercy to have her to go or stay. It was insufferable having to be so humble. Even so, she must get Alice out next Saturday. It might all be a wild goose chase but she did so want to attempt her wonderful plan once more. It *was* a good one. And, who knows, it could work. Anything was possible. It sent thrills down her spine just to think about it. She ignored Tom's cynical eyes slewed in her direction, and thought of next Saturday.

'May I, Mum?'

This time Alice thought to ask permission first. The effect was immediate. Her mother, with one look at those pleading eyes, smiled her consent. 'So long as yer come 'ome at a decent time.'

But Alice wasn't satisfied with that. 'It could be a bit late. But we will behave ourselves.'

'No one said yer wouldn't, luv. I know yer a good gel. I know Amy'll look after yer well enough. She ain't in no condition ter do otherwise. Once bit twice shy yer might say. No offence meant,' she added swiftly, but Amy understood and smiled back at her. But the woman was already babbling on. 'Yer'd better 'ave a key – save disturbin' me. But don't tell yer dad. He ain't so easy-goin' as me. Me, I'm a bit of a fool, but there you are.'

'Thanks, Mum.' Alice's pretty face adopted an earnest expression. 'We won't make a habit of it, I promise.'

Mrs Jordan's smile broadened her already broad features. 'I don't suppose you will.' Her eyes flickered towards Amy's middle. 'You won't be goin' out Up West fer much longer, luv. Not lookin' like yer will in a few weeks' time – if yer don't mind me saying.'

There still lingered a little awe of her that made Mrs Jordan careful of her words. Even though she had dispensed with the 'Miss 'Arrin'ton', she used her name as little as possible. Amy strove to put her at ease. She had come to like Mrs Jordan immensely for all her slovenly speech and rough-and-ready ways.

'I expect so,' she agreed, and Mrs Jordan's smile seemed to surround her. She felt suddenly protected. This was a woman who wouldn't throw her out the moment it suited her; who would see her through her pregnancy and afterwards, even be there at the delivery, taking the place of the mother who should have been present. It occurred to Amy that soon she must make arrangements for her stay in hospital. She could quite easily afford to, but a hospital's clinical face would remind her of her own isolated state. She had learned that these people, if they were wise, were in the Hospital Savings Association at so much per week, and perhaps the Jordans were. Many who weren't still had their babies at home but whether in Mrs Jordan's home or in the cold dispassionate atmosphere of hospital, she knew Mrs Jordan would be the first to visit and applaud her. She knew that implicitly with an ache for the mother who would not be there.

In the glittery little nightclub with Alice close beside her, Amy surveyed the scene. Despite the squally weather outside, the place was crowded. Most having arrived by taxi or in their own vehicles, not one girl had a hair out of place or her make-up damaged, not one escort had his bow tie spotted with rain or his trouser bottoms splashed by mud. She too had chosen to come by taxi – expensive but worth it; Alice looked perfect, again in her gold lamé.

But Amy's hopes were once more dying. How could she imagine finding Dicky here in this one nightclub out of the hundreds in London? It *was* a wild goose chase, a fool's errand. She was utterly mad, this whole idea too outlandish for words. But somewhere there must be faces she knew.

Her eyes roved desperately, then stopped, glimpsing a small group of young people in one corner. Just for a second as the crush of people around her parted briefly before closing up again, she recognised Sylvia Fox-Carter, Max Shaughan, and two or three other familiar ones, and . . .

It took her a moment or two to believe what she was seeing, to believe such incredible luck. The next second she had grabbed Alice by one arm and, half-dragging the girl with her, pushed through the noisy chattering throng, skirted the tiny dance floor to end up standing breathlessly before the group she sought, her face animated, her eyes sparkling as they fixed on the one she'd picked out, her voice high and bright with assumed surprise.

'Dicky! Dicky, darling! Fancy your being here.'

Recognising her voice, the small group swung round as one person. 'Amy!'

But her gaze was for Richard Pritchard only. 'Dicky, it's been simply ages.'

'Darling,' burst out Pauline Carpenter. 'Where on earth have you *been* these last weeks? Not a word. We thought you had *died*!'

'I went abroad for a little holiday.'

'*Alone*? My dear, how could you?'

'My mother and I were supposed to have gone together, but she had to cry off at the last minute.' Dicky was looking like a man condemned to death. 'We were to go to Ceylon to see a friend out there. But I went alone.'

'My dear, all that way, alone. How brave.'

Amy dramatically shrugged off Pauline's sentiments, savoured Dicky's still-horrified face, watching his gaze travel to her midriff. He was behaving like one about to be exposed, accused of some horrible crime. Don't worry, her mind said the words, I'm not going to expose you, but I am going to give you a lesson you'll never forget. Revenge, she mused as she smiled blithely at him, was the sort of dish one did better to serve up cold.

'Everyone – this is Alice,' she announced brightly. 'I brought her back from Ceylon with me for a short vacation here. We travelled back together.'

She heard Alice's intake of breath at the bold lie, hoped desperately that she would play along with the joke and not show her up by being suddenly open and honest. This Amy had not rehearsed, taken by surprise by her own ad lib. But already they were all around Alice, giving her no chance to deny what had been said, all asking at once how was her passage to England, when had she last been here or had she been born 'out there', and when was she going back, and how was she liking it here?

In all this, Alice, confused and flattered by the attention heaped upon her by people she had never dreamed she would ever associate with, had said nothing except to gulp and smile and nod. But soon she'd find her tongue. And then what?

'Her father's a diplomat,' Amy chipped in, glad for once of Alice's awkward shyness in such, to her, elevated company. 'She's never travelled before, or gone to many places.'

Alice bore out perfectly the picture of a girl fresh from a sheltered life in the Far East, her first time in England, London, awed and speechless by all these brash and noisy socialites. It was all working out splendidly, far better than she'd hoped.

Dicky had forgotten Amy's threat to his peace of mind. He was all over this stunning newcomer already, his eyes devouring every inch of her. 'Did you find it pleasant out there, the climate, the people? Were you born out there? I hope you aren't going back too soon.' He was babbling, bubbling over with eagerness.

Alice found her tongue at last. Her eyes opened wide with appraisal as she looked at the slim handsome young man dancing attendance upon her. 'I ... we ... we lead a very quiet life.' She was doing her best to support the fib Amy had concocted, but it was obvious it was going against the grain, that she felt unsure how to handle it. 'I'm ... I'm not used to ... parties, or ... or nightclubs and things.'

'What, no parties out there?' he interrupted. 'No nightclubs?'

'No ...' This was part truth as far as she was concerned. 'Not like this.'

'But you must have met lots of people, your father a diplomat?'

'Not really.'

'Good Lord! But there must have been ...'

'For goodness sake!' Amy slipped in quickly. Any minute the girl was going to let her down. She could see it coming. 'All these questions. For God's sake, you'll upset her utterly.'

'Yes, you're right.' Dicky hadn't taken his eyes off the girl. He had even reached out and taken her hand. He was still holding it. 'Didn't mean to be rude.'

Now he swivelled his eyes towards Amy and there was a look in them that said, don't you dare spoil this for me. Amy returned his gaze, silently saying, of course I'm not going to, and the look of relief lighting up his narrow handsome features made her smile. How delectable it was savouring the thought that he had no idea just how hollow that relief would prove to be. She could hardly wait to drop her bombshell.

We've been lying to you, Dicky. Alice doesn't come from anywhere so far east as Ceylon; she comes from the east all right – the East End of London – her father works in the docks unloading cargo and hasn't a bean to bless himself with. She's a Cockney, Dicky darling. Not your sort at all. Now you know how it feels to be let down with a crash.

But not yet. If all went well, and by the way he was drooling all over her, it all looked perfect, he must first fall madly in love with this devastatingly pretty girl whose father was alleged to be a foreign diplomat of some standing. He must take her home and introduce her to his family. He must propose to her and set the date for the fine society wedding he had once planned for herself before she'd told him she

116

was pregnant with his child. He must do all those things. Then she would reveal Alice's true birth, her upbringing, her family. She hoped Alice wouldn't fall too much in love with Dicky. If she did, her heart would be broken, just as her own had been.

Amy cringed momentarily and turned her thoughts hastily away from the prospect that she would be instrumental in this unsuspecting girl's desperate unhappiness if it should be so, and set her thoughts to exacting her revenge upon the spoiled, spineless, irresponsible, falsehearted Richard Pritchard.

Dicky was looking at the girl. The band had struck up with a lively one-step. 'I say, do you care to dance? Do you dance?'

'Yes,' came the shy reply. It was all he needed.

'Oh, wonderful! Splendid! May I then?' His offered arm hesitantly taken, he guided her away from the group that surrounded her, and out on to the tiny dance floor, already filling with couples.

Amy watched them, trying to ignore the prick of guilt that kept making a nuisance of itself. Dicky looked thoroughly besotted, and Alice demure but soaking up his every word. By the end of the evening, having fought off every competitor, he was asking if he could see her again.

Alice's eyes turned towards Amy. 'I . . . I don't think I can.'

'Of course you can,' Alice almost shouted. 'I'm sure your parents would approve. Dicky's family are . . .'

'I've explained all that to her,' he broke in. So that was why Alice had been soaking up every word he'd said – she was overwhelmed. Amy smiled as he turned back to his conquest. 'May I see you tomorrow, Alice? We could go for a spin. I could ask Sylvia and Max to come along, so it would all be above board, if you see what I mean.'

Alice's eyes were like saucers, her eyelashes fluttering, her head nodding vigorously. 'Oh, I would like that very much. It'd be all right, wouldn't it, Amy?'

Dicky gave a little giggle. 'Are you sure you've not lived in Australia at some time? You really do have that sort of accent that reminds me of that Australian I told you I once knew.'

'I am sorry.'

'No, don't be. I told you, I find it exquisite, the way you speak. So it's a date then? Say after lunch – about two? Where do I pick you up? Are you staying with Amy?'

'Yes. Well, you see, I . . .' Alice broke off, her face colouring. She looked desperately at Amy for help, unsure how far this white lie was supposed to go.

'I think it best,' Amy put in, thinking quickly, 'if I bring her, shall we say to Marble Arch? And I could pick her up from there, say around four o'clock?' He was looking at her questioningly. 'She doesn't know her way around London at all, you know.' This was becoming more complicated than she had anticipated. But it was Pauline who broke the tension with a light laugh.

'Amy wants to play chaperon. Well, it's not on, darling. Let the lovebirds be. Can't you see they've eyes only for each other. My God, it *is* love at first sight. I never believed in that, not until now. How perfectly adorable.'

Alice blushed. But Dicky was in command of himself, his eyes admiringly on his choice. 'I find her the most charming person I have ever met. All I want to do now is to get to know her better. If you'll let me, Alice.'

Pauline threw up her hand in a dramatic gesture of defeat. 'Oh, come away, everyone! This is becoming too sick-making for words! But the night is young. We could all go on to a darling little club I know of. You've been there, Dicky . . .'

'Not for us,' Amy interrupted. 'I've promised that Alice must be home at a reasonable time. And it is getting late.'

'Oh, how miserable!'

Dicky was looking forlorn but hopeful, ready to concede to any arrangement so long as he could see this delightful girl again. 'Two o'clock, then. Marble Arch.'

Hardly giving her time to nod her consent, Alice had whisked her away before there were any more complications to deal with. The last she saw of Dicky was his face, looking quite lovesick, gazing after them.

That night, Amy could hardly sleep for thinking about how splendidly it had all gone. Soon she would turn the

118

tides on Dicky Pritchard – or was it the tables? Whichever, it couldn't have gone better. To see his face when she told him the truth was something she could hardly wait for.

Chapter Nine

Grace Jordan was in the middle of her Monday wash, the kitchen filled with steam, the walls running with condensation from the boiling copper in the corner, when Tom and his father walked in.

In the act of manipulating a well-smoothed copper stick to hook a twill bedsheet from the bubbling suds for easing through the rollers of the portable mangle, she paused to stare at the two men, half in surprise, half in the trepidation most women would feel at seeing their menfolk troop in unannounced in the middle of their working day.

'What you two doin' 'ome? You ain't bin laid off, 'ave yer?'

Arthur Jordan threw his cap onto the damp baize of the kitchen table and yanked off his choker. 'We're on strike.'

There had been plenty of strikes at the docks in the past and many an unsympathetic soul not familiar with dock conditions had seen it to be a docker's regular pastime, like some sort of hobby. That there could likely be another dispute Grace Jordan wasn't that much surprised, but she was concerned, visualising more days of eking out what money they had, perhaps finally forced to hock something until they went back to work, sometimes with their claim, whatever it was, unsettled.

'What's it about this time?' she demanded, letting the sheet drop back into the soapy water and drying her hands on the already wet sackcloth apron she wore for doing the washing. 'For more pay I suppose. Well, I don't reckon you'll get no better than you did last time you was all on strike.

All I want is a reg'lar bit of money comin' in each week. I can manage with whatever bit I get 's long as it comes in. All this strikin' . . .'

'It's more'n just a dock strike,' Tom butted in. 'This one's goin' ter be the 'ole country by the sounds of it. You've read the paper, Mum, about bosses wantin' ter cut miners' wages. The miners ain't 'avin' it, but that Baldwin's supporting the bosses fer a wage cut.'

'That's what it said in the papers,' Arthur added.

'Now the Trades Union Congress 'as called all transport and 'eavy industry out in support,' Tom went on as his father offered no more explanation. 'That's us as well. So we're out too. An' there ain't nothing we can do about it. It's a matter fer the unions. But I agree wiv' 'em, and so does all of us.'

'That's all very well,' Grace turned on him. 'It don't do the likes of me any good though, do it? Havin' ter scrimp and scrape again.' But he wasn't listening.

'Damned employers – they think they can do what they like because they think we come two a penny, the ordinary workin' man. And Baldwin's backin' them all the way. His bloody government ain't interested in people like us so long as the bosses can get away with cuttin' wages and still 'ave us silly buggers working fer 'em. But the miners ain't 'avin' any of it, and nor are we.'

'Yes, Tom, I 'eard yer the first time. I don't want no politics in this 'ouse. Go outside and talk politics. All I want ter know is 'ow long d'yer think yer'll be out?'

''Ow d'we know?' Arthur groaned. 'Blame us fer it all, go on, why don'tcha? We're just doin' what we're told. Me an' Tom only come back ter tell yer an' get ourselves some tea and a sandwich – God knows 'ow long we'll be 'angin' around them dock gates waiting ter see what's goin' ter go on. They've closed the gates at West India Docks. But if they open 'em again in the next few hours, me an' Tom want ter be there ter be first on the stones.'

'Well, I'll get yer something to eat, and then yer can get out of my way. I've got work ter do, if you ain't. Bloody men! Bloody country! Bloody governments and unions.' It was seldom Grace Jordan swore, but she could see hunger stretching ahead of her. What the union paid from its strike fund wasn't enough to keep a canary alive.

Upstairs in the bedroom, the door open, Amy heard it all. As she often did these days, she had been helping Mrs Jordan a little, but at six months pregnant the strain was beginning to be felt and Mrs Jordan had packed her off upstairs to rest for a while.

She listened to Tom's deep voice, trying not to acknowledge the pleasure it gave her to hear it without having to meet his eyes, which after more than two months of living in this house were still unfriendly. Yet sometimes she was conscious of his looking at her more than was necessary. He would switch his eyes hastily away should she turn to meet his gaze, and lately it had become a game with her, to catch him out. With the rest of the family, she was unassuming, respectful, careful not to let her good breeding diminish them in any way. She was after all still their guest, at their mercy to be allowed to stay, and she *was* grateful. But with him, she allowed all she was to show, paying him back for his persistent condemnation of her – as if he had never done any wrong in his life. A handsome, well-built young man, he must have had his fair share of girls. Amy felt the jealousy rise at the thought. How dare he condemn her who had only allowed a man free rein on one ... no, two occasions, but the same man, who had proposed marriage to her and to whom she had given herself trustingly.

Tom's voice had risen a little, angered by the way Stanley Baldwin's government was treating the working masses. But Amy was no longer listening, her thoughts flying to the man who had wronged her; to the plan she had thought so clever, gone utterly awry. Nothing was so sour-tasting as a well-laid plan thwarted.

Alice, honest Alice, unable to sustain the lie, had blabbed to Dicky about where she came from. Not so stupid Alice ... scheming Alice ... by the time she'd bared her lily-white soul like a prostrate little nun, Dicky had been so head-over-heels in love with her that he was vowing to marry her, no matter if he had to defy the whole world to make her his. Why was he doing that for her when he hadn't done it for

122

herself, Amy? That was what really galled, more than any defeated plan. Alice went around putting on airs and graces, visualising herself lady of the manor in time, and no doubt thinking herself above the girl to whom she had once been a mere maid, even though she hadn't said as much.

But it still might not last. There were Dicky's parents to consider; their views on their son wanting to marry a common East End Cockney maid. That would take Alice down several pegs or so. And her own family didn't seem so keen on the idea either, her father giving forth sneers, and her mother looking thoroughly worried, her sisters' looks pure vitriolic stabs of jealousy and her younger brother chanting whenever he accosted her: 'Al's in luv wiv Dicky, and Dicky is a pansy!' which to him all wealthy blokes were. Nevertheless, it was obvious that Alice was in love with Richard, as she called him, and spent every moment she could talking of him, almost as though she were taunting her one-time mistress.

Angrily Amy thrust aside thoughts of the new high and mighty Alice, and concentrated on what Tom was saying. His voice had become indistinct, but she was intrigued to hear more. A strike would mean he'd be home more often. She saw very little of him under normal circumstances. Perhaps he and she would be more thrown together and thereby get on closer speaking terms.

She got up from her bed, and taking the now-empty teacup she had brought upstairs to drink while she rested, she made her way awkwardly down the narrow stairs, the lump over her stomach as prominent as an outsize football, emphasised by her otherwise slim build.

What made the cup rattle in its saucer, she didn't know. Perhaps her hand had trembled involuntarily in the knowledge that her presence downstairs might intrude on Tom and his father's conversation. She took her hand off the banister to steady the cup, but the fingers caught the rim instead, sending it flying off the saucer.

Automatically she tried to catch it, a silly thought rushing through her head that the thing belonged to Mrs Jordan, but with her mind taken off her descent for a second, her heel slid over the edge of the stair immediately below, throwing her backwards. She made the rest of her journey on her back, landing in a heap at the bottom, still desperately clutching the empty saucer.

The noise of the fall brought the Jordans hurrying from the kitchen. Tom was there first, picking her up, asking if she'd hurt herself. Of course she'd hurt herself. Her back hurt and so did her bottom, and one arm where she had tried in vain to save herself, giving it a nasty wrench. The shock of her tumble had started her crying. Tom was holding her to him, patting her back, saying it was all right – it was all right. It wasn't all right. Amy clung to him, letting the tears flow.

'I . . . I'm sorry about the cup,' she heard herself sobbing foolishly. As if the cup mattered now.

'It's not broken, luv.' Mrs Jordan bent and retrieved the undamaged cup. 'I'd've sooner it 'ad bin and you 'adn't slipped like that. That was a nasty tumble. Bring 'er into the back room, Tom. We'll sit 'er down till she feels better. Where are you 'urt, luv?'

'My back, and my arm.'

'You're goin' to 'ave a few bruises,' Tom soothed as he gently sat her down on one of the upright chairs. 'But there ain't nothing broken.'

'Not even the cup,' she said as she looked up at him, her face white and tearstained.

For a moment he gazed down at her, then he gave a chuckle. Soon they had all joined in, relieved that she could crack a joke even in her shocked state, even though she hadn't intended any.

Mrs Jordan was the first to sober. 'Look, luv, I think you ought to go back up ter bed. Yer don't know what damage a fall like that could do – the baby an' all. Yer certainly went down a thump, and that's the truth. I'll take yer upstairs.'

Amy got up from her chair, trying not to wince from her strained arm. 'No, it's all right, Mrs Jordan. I don't need any help. I shall be fine.'

'Are yer sure, luv?'

'An' we'd best be gettin' back,' Arthur Jordan observed. 'Come on, Tom, let's go and see what's doin'.'

Tom led her to the foot of the stairs while the other two

returned to the kitchen, Mr Jordan to get his cloth cap and choker.

'Will yer be all right?' Tom's voice sounded more concerned and gentle than she could ever imagine it to be.

'Honestly,' she breathed. 'I shall be fine.'

But she was feeling just a little giddy. With a need to steady herself she held onto his arm for support. In response, he bent to help her regain her equilibrium. Their faces came close together as for a moment their glances met. He paused, his breath brushing warm across her cheek. A fraction nearer and his lips would have touched hers. It almost seemed that he wanted to, the moment giving a distorted impression of an eternity before he drew his head suddenly away. The look on his face was odd, too swift to be interpreted but enough to provoke an unsettled feeling inside her. Then it was gone.

'Take it careful up them stairs,' he said gruffly. 'Don't want another fall.'

'No,' she said limply and began her ascent, feeling his eyes following her the whole way. She didn't turn round.

It was Willie's birthday. The seventh of May, the strike in its fourth day, it wasn't an auspicious one for any boy's tenth birthday with no prospect of any wages coming into the house this week and no likelihood of a birthday present of any sort, not even that pair of roller skates he'd set his heart on. They cost half-a-crown in Dimmonds in Commercial Road which sold bikes and skates and toys.

He should have gone to school, but he'd cried off. It was his birthday, he'd protested. Bad enough as it was without being stuck at school for it, and that didn't help bring money in. Mum had conceded, too concerned by the times to argue with him. She knew what was in his mind and a few pennies coming in weren't to be sneezed at.

He'd got up early and gone off instead to where his usual gang of paperlads collected outside Stepney East station on the corner of Commercial Road and East India Dock Road to await the first delivery of the day. Most of the boys were older than him, had left school immediately they turned fourteen for a more lucrative activity, but he knew he looked older than he was, was as tall as many of them and could hold his own against any of them, loudmouthed and aggressive as they when the need arose. He let them believe he was thirteen coming up to fourteen.

It was quite pleasant standing around in the warm early morning sunshine waiting for the drop with the older boys who swapped dirty jokes, talked about parts of girls' bodies, some bragging about what parts they'd seen and breasts they'd touched. Willie did his best to brag, but at ten he'd only ever seen his sisters when he peeped through the crack of their half-open door while they were undressing until angrily chased away. Mum was called to give him a swift clip round the earhole and a lecture that boys, and men didn't behave dirty towards women. Which he didn't believe, because if they behaved as she said they did, how did women get babies? The older boys had told him how men stuck their things between women's legs and that was how babies came. And if that wasn't behaving dirty, Willie didn't know what was. He'd once seen the private underpart of a girl in his class behind the outside lavs when he was nine. He'd given her a farthing Golly Bar to show hers and he'd shown his. They'd giggled and then parted company. It hadn't occurred to him to stick his thing between her legs, which the boys here said felt ever so smashing. Hearing them he wished now that he had, except that he doubted he'd have felt anything, his little diddly pressing back into itself wouldn't have gone anywhere between her podgy legs. He was still in the same class as her at school, but she wasn't podgy any more. She had grown tall and slim and her hair was long and blonde, tied back in a bow, and her nose tilted upwards and her eyes were cornflower blue, and he was in love with her. Her name was Edith Bates. But these days she ignored him. Perhaps she was still ashamed about that day behind the outside lavs.

The papers came up around seven, tied in ragged bundles with string to be slit free with a penknife and a pile grabbed, as many as would tuck under the arm, without being dropped all over the pavement, and made off with as fast as a lad's legs could go.

The streets were quiet, as they had been all week. Few

people were going to work. Those that did were on bikes or walking. A sort of silence hung over London, not the silence of Sunday when one expected everything to be quiet, but a hovering silence of uncertainty as if nearly everyone had gone off to live in darkest Africa or on the moon, leaving everywhere deserted.

But there was noise. Willie heard it growing louder as he ran, racing his competitors the half-mile towards the docks area where he knew men would be who would snatch up a Friday paper for one precious penny to see what was going on about this general strike, as it was called.

Surrounded by the low murmur of men waiting around, he sold his papers, not quite as many as he would have on a normal day. Few men had pennies to splash around. They gleaned the news from others.

Every now and again the murmur would rise to a roar as the dock gates, guarded by soldiers with rifles, which made Willie's awed eyes stick out like corks, opened to let a loaded lorry pass; that too was guarded by steel-helmeted soldiers. The crowd would sway and hoot, fists raised, but no more than that. Surely the army wouldn't shoot at its own countrymen, though no one was willing to tempt it even though it went against the grain to see them there as though dock workers were their own sworn enemy. Now and again an armed and helmeted soldier would nod and exchange a chummy remark with a nearby docker. He had nothing personal against these men so long as they didn't try to attack. He was only following orders and probably hoped they wouldn't become aggressive, for obvious reasons.

The dock gates opened again. Another lorry emerged to hoots and boos, a huge notice on it, like all the others, stating that it was acting under the authority of the TUC.

'TUC!' spat a man whom Willie was squeezing past to get nearer the gates hoping to get rid of a few more papers and earn his meagre percentage for that morning. He still had too big a bundle under his arm for his liking. 'The bleedin' TUC. They're all workin' against us.'

This time there had been an angry surge forward, taking Willie with it. He was almost at the front now and he could see the guarding soldiers begin to level their weapons, but looking worried in case they had need to use them.

It seemed they might have to as one man raised his arm, a large stone in his hand to aim through the lorry driver's window. Others would follow suit. A riot would break out. Men injured or killed. Willie felt his innards cringe. He was right at the front now, in the line of fire. And there was no way to squeeze back into this slowly surging, increasingly infuriated crowd already intent on surrounding the lorry despite the army's presence all around it.

The gates had remained open. Another vehicle was emerging. A silence descended over the crowd, then suddenly cheering broke out and hoots of laughter at the small donkey cart bearing a pile of vegetables and driven by a very elderly man in a battered bowler hat. He too had put a large notice on his cart. It said boldly: 'Acting under the authority of my own bloody self!'

Tension broken, the tight-packed throng parted for it, and the little donkey cart was cheered all the way down the road until it turned left into the main road and disappeared from sight.

Willie had taken the advantage and moved back into the less dense crowd, the joke rippling through it. Men, still chuckling and better spirited for the moment, readily found a penny to buy a paper. It was a better morning than he'd expected and returning with not one paper left, Willie received the handsome sum of eightpence, thinking perhaps he might go to school this afternoon, saying he had not felt too well this morning.

His mother received him cheerily. 'I made yer a cake,' she said in a confidential tone as he came in famished.

'Thanks, Mum. I could eat the lot meself.'

'Yer probably will. It's only a small one. But it's got a little bit of fruit in it, what I 'ad left in the cupboard, and I've put candles on it from last year. I know there's only nine, but you can pretend. And I've got yer a present. A bag of Golly Bars what you like. Yer like that there toffee. When things get a bit better I'll get yer a proper present – them half-crown skates in Dimmonds. But yer'll 'ave ter wait.'

Yeah, Willie thought as he flopped onto a kitchen chair and dropped two threepenny bits on the kitchen table. It's goin' ter be a long wait. He had kept back tuppence for himself, a penny to spend and a penny to save. He was saving for a bike. With a bike he could really get into the newspaper selling business, and run errands too – all that sort of thing. So far he had one shilling and eightpence in his Post Office Penny Saving Book. Once in it, the amount written down between the brown, printed covers with its Post Office emblem, nothing would entice him to draw it out again and see the precious sum diminish. A second-hand bike could be got for ten shillings and sixpence from Dimmonds. They had them chained to the outside doorpost. Ten and six, it was a fortune when you could only afford to put away a penny or tuppence at a time.

He looked longingly at the two threepenny bits on the table. He didn't have to give his mother anything, but a head made wise by having to go without at times told him that he must do his bit to help.

His mother gave him a guilt-ridden look. 'Oh, Willie luv, I can't take that.'

'Yes you can,' he said and saw her snatch it up as though any slower movement might make the money sear her fingers.

'Yer a good boy, luv. I could do with every bit we can get, them all out on strike. An' I *will* get yer them skates, luv, soon as things get back on an even keel.'

'Yer could buy 'em now, if Miss 'Arrin'ton gave yer a bit more.'

Grace Jordan shot him a warning look. 'Keep yer voice down. She's upstairs in bed. She ain't feelin' so well. Got pains in 'er tummy. She gives me quite enough money as it is She's upped it ter eight bob now, and I can't take no more off 'er. She 'ardly costs anythink to keep, the way she eats, and she did buy 'er own bed and linen. And she buys us little odds and ends as well. I think she gives me enough.'

'She could afford a pair of half-crown skates.'

'Willie!'

'Or yer could borrow off 'er.'

'That's enough, Willie! I wouldn't dream of askin'.

Besides, she needs any money she's got fer the baby. Now you'd better go off ter school. I'l give yer a jam sandwich before yer go.'

To which Willie agreed, his stomach already sticking to his backbone.

Upstairs Amy tried to sleep. She'd taken a couple of aspirin to help ease the nagging pain which at times seemed to be more in her back than her stomach. When she looked at herself in the wardrobe mirror, twisting herself as far as she could to see, there was a large blue bruise developing where her back had bumped down each stair in her fall, but her arm had stopped hurting. She just felt stiff all over.

She heard Willie come in, his exuberant voice filling the house, but his mother seemed mostly to be whispering. She lay only half-listening, heard her name mentioned at one time and wondered idly what they were saying about her. As she always did, she wondered Mrs Jordan was still willing to allow her to stay on, although if she wasn't, she'd hardly discuss it with a ten-year-old boy. Willie's birthday, she remembered. It was the reason why she had upped her keep by another two shillings. She had tried to make it ten shillings, but Mrs Jordan had looked almost insulted, as though she was being thought unable to manage on her men's wages. Prudently, Amy hadn't tried again.

Perhaps in a few weeks, she mused, changing position in the bed, as she grew larger and needed more help, she might try again to offer something more. Meantime it was Willie's birthday and she must buy him something. Listening intently, the word 'skates' drifted up to her, and Mrs Jordan saying she would try to make it up to him as soon as better times came. It was an idea. She could go out tomorrow, if she felt better, and buy him the best pair of roller skates she could find. He'd be so pleased and . . .

The musing was broken abruptly by a sharp pain shooting from her back to her front, making her gasp. In an instant it had gone, leaving just the dull ache as before. She must have moved too quickly and pulled at the already stiff muscles.

Lying quietly, she closed her eyes. Perhaps if she tried to

have a little doze. Against the lids she saw Alice – Alice still with Dicky, and putting on airs and graces, her parents as awed by her conquest as they were concerned, convinced that people like them couldn't ever associate with people like that. But Alice was convinced that they could, and no one was going to dissuade her. Alice was in love.

She had told Amy that Richard, as she now called him, deeming Dicky to be a silly name for such a wonderful person, was even prepared to confront his family with his intention to marry her. 'He's so very gallant,' she'd gushed, dewy-eyed. 'He's prepared to brave any protest they put up or any threat to disinherit him. He's quite adamant about it.'

Yesterday, coming home from where she now worked behind the counter at Lipton's Dairies, she told her that his father had relented and agreed to his taking her to meet them. She was going this very weekend. Amy had never even met them and she felt the chagrin that thought brought rise up inside her, but she had kept her expression tranquil as she listened to Alice going on.

She must have slept for a little while for she awoke to Mrs Jordan calling up to say it was twelve o'clock and did she want to have her midday sandwich upstairs or did she feel like coming down?

'I've made yer a nice boiled bacon sandwich if yer want it,' she called loudly at the foot of the stairs.

Amy grimaced. If only it had been ham. But Mrs Jordan, careful with the money Amy gave her, would search for the cheapest cuts of cold meats like boiled bacon or ox tongue or brawn. It never occurred to her in times like these to indulge in some decent ham. That was for family visitors on a Sunday, her sisters and their families and Mr Jordan's brothers and sisters and their families, when times were good. Ham was special, not for Friday middays.

Amy's grimace wasn't aimed purely at the stringy salt-laden sandwich filling, but at the fact that Mrs Jordan still deemed her to be above the rest of her family and given the best she had when they must put up with bread and dripping or jam. It irked, made her feel different when all she wanted was to be one of them. It also provoked thoughts of her former life with even ham sneered at in preference to chicken and game and caviar; thoughts of her own people, wondering how they were and what they were doing, and the hurt re-awakened that they had never bothered at all to contact her to see how she fared, She wanted no longer to belong to them, but to these warm, great-hearted people who had taken her in, yet how could she do that when Mrs Jordan persisted in holding her up above her own family?

'I think I'll come down, Mrs Jordan,' she called back. Bad enough without being served in bed, the woman waiting on her like a skivvy.

'Righto, luv. It's in the kitchen then, with a nice cup of tea.' Mrs Jordan would probably have the inevitable bit of bread and jam. 'Sorry there ain't no cake. I want ter save Willie's birthday cake fer when we all sit down this ev'ning. We're 'aving a bit of scrag end tonight. I'm makin' it nice and thick with split peas and a bit of cow-heel the butcher let me 'ave. Sticks ter yer gills that do.'

Amy smiled. Even shouting up the stairs, Mrs Jordan couldn't keep her talk to a minimum but must tell the whole story inside out and outside in – what Tom had once described as the ins and outs of the cat's arse, that expression never again repeated after his mother had admonished him for being so coarse in front of their guest. He had given 'their guest' a sharply annoyed look that had made Amy blush.

'I'll be down,' she called down and sat up, swinging her feet to the floor. A shriek escaped her lips as another pain, this time excruciating, shot through her, bringing the woman hurrying up the stairs, already aware of what it could be.

Chapter Ten

She was dying. She had to be dying. Who could go through such pain and not be dying?

Amy lay in the labour ward of the London Hospital, her desperate gaze roaming about the white painted walls, the clinical instruments, the nurses who looked down at her in sympathy and the doctor who hadn't once looked at her as far as she in her agony could tell.

When Mrs Jordan had seen the pain she was in, the blood coming away from her, she had made her lie down on the sofa, hurrying to put a sheet and a piece of baize under her so as not to stain the old cushions further. With gabbled instructions not to move a muscle she had then run for the doctor, no thought as to how she would pay him; in her panic to get him, that hadn't entered her mind at all. It had been an emergency and that was that.

One glance at Amy had told him that the situation was beyond his skills.

'This isn't right,' he'd said, almost angrily, his moustache bristling while Amy looked up at him with imploring eyes to do something. 'I'll get an ambulance to her. She needs to be in hospital as soon as we can get her there.'

And now she lay here in this place, her cries filling the whole ward and people leaning over her telling her to be brave, that it would soon be over, that they were doing all they could. What did they mean by that? Did they mean her situation was hopeless; that they expected her to lose the baby; that they expected her to die?

Through bouts of excruciating pain that seemed to

consume her, she prayed for release, for the baby to come away, alive or dead, anything, so that the pain would stop. Between the bouts she cursed Richard Pritchard who had put the baby there inside her to cause her all this agony, only to walk off with Alice, the girl she'd befriended – she cursed Alice too – as though she, Amy, mattered no more than a stone under his shoe. She wished him here now to witness his damned handiwork. If only it was last November and she able to live those moments in that maid's bedroom over again and she could push him away from her. But there was no going back, and here she lay suffering the results of that stupid, drink-promoted lark.

'Push now!' ordered the nameless doctor, faceless too behind his white mask and cap, only his grey eyes visible. She felt she would remember those grey orbs to her dying day . . . if she didn't die this very minute as she obeyed.

The push was the most terrible thing of all: the pain of bearing down, the feeling of being strangled, of bursting.

'And again!'

Did she have any strength? From some hidden reserve she found enough to satisfy the heartless man for the moment, the veins standing out from her forehead as though they would break open and pour blood all over her.

There was blood. She caught sight of it on his hands as he lifted them for a second. And it was on his apron, and on the bed. So much and so bright. She was bleeding to death. She panicked and gave out a shriek, only to be told, 'Enough of that!' by one of the senior nurses standing above her.

'Rest a moment,' commanded the faceless doctor, his eyes flicking to her and then back to her lower parts, her legs strapped up high above her head. Things, awful things, were being done to her down there. There was nothing she could do about it; she had never experienced anything like it, as though some mighty instrument was being thrust inside her, prising her body apart, seeking some vital part of her to rip out and kill her. Terror. She had never felt such terror. And it hurt oh, so much. How could she avoid screaming out? Crying out in fear and pain.

'Now push . . . gently! *Gently* . . .'

If only to get it over with, she stopped screaming; did as she was told, pushing firmly but slowly. Something wet and slippery came away from her and there was instant relief from all that pain, except for the discomfiting feeling still of her underneath having been torn apart and left to fall together, the feel of those cold steel instruments that had been used on it. She wanted to cry, but now she wanted more to see her baby. All that pain. Now it was born, a living scrap that would develop and grow into a person with its own character, its own feelings and experiences. Suddenly she wanted very much to hold it, cuddle it, feel it in her arms instead of just something that had lain inside her. Love for the child she hadn't yet seen began to flow out of her.

Where was the baby? Perhaps they would bring it to her soon. Lying back, allowing the nurses to unleash her ankles and place pads between her legs and settle her a little more comfortably on a pillow, she searched for the tiny scrap she had given birth to.

'Where is it? What have I got? A girl or a boy?'

They didn't reply. Looks passed between the nurses. Amy repeated the question. 'Can I see my baby?' Then the truth began to dawn. She was unmarried, not a fit mother, the child was to be taken away and adopted. But surely, were there not rules, could a mother first be allowed to agree, to choose? She wanted her baby. Amy felt panic begin to rise.

'Where is he ... she?' Already the scrap of life was taking on a persona, must very shortly have a name. In time she would have opinions about her future, her past – she automatically knew her baby was a girl – who her mother was ...

'I don't want her taken away from me,' she gasped. 'I have to keep her. Please. I want to hold her.'

Still the silence, the looks. Then the nurse who seemed to be in charge, the sister, came forward, her stiff face unstiffening a little, her harsh voice moderating.

'Miss Harrington,' she said slowly, her voice low. 'I have some sad news to tell you, my dear. You lost your baby.'

'Lost?'

'The child was stillborn, my dear.' She might have been trying to be sympathetic, but her profession made her incapable of speaking other than in cold, clinical terms and

135

any semblance of sympathy was lost, even though she smiled gently down at her as Amy continued to stare, unable to take in what was being said to her. 'I believe you had a fall last week. Mrs Jordan, who says she is looking after you, explained that you fell most of the way down her stairs. It was noticed that you have an extensive contusion on your lower back. I think the baby had been injured in the fall.'

'Lost?' Amy repeated as though drugged. 'How could I lose her?'

'It was a boy, Miss Harrington. Perhaps it was just as well. It isn't easy for a young unmarried woman or for the child. The stigma. The child would have been better adopted. You could not have brought it up by yourself with fingers pointed at you.'

'But I couldn't lose her. I wanted her. She was mine.'

A cold hand was laid on her arm. 'Try to rest, my dear.'

'But I want her.' Amy's voice was rising. 'I want her. I want to see her. Let me see her!'

'We can't do that, my dear. It's impossible.' The forceps had done their job on the stillborn, easing the dead child from the mother's womb with little need for delicacy about what had already died save that the mother must not be too injured in the process. The results of those gripping forceps were not for displaying before a grieving mother. 'You must try to rest now.'

The room was suddenly deserted. She lay alone in the centre of it, the white emptiness creeping all around her – a horde of shrouded ghosts coming to mock, or was it to grieve? Their whiteness hovered, the pale walls scintillating before her arid sight, seeming to dance. All the ghosts were dancing, going away, bearing her child with them. She saw herself reach out a hand to stop them. They mustn't take her child. Her dead child. Those unspoken words wafted towards her, embedded themselves in her head, and as all the ghosts fled, she began to cry, great buffeting racking sobs that shook her entire soul.

On the lighter alongside the cargo ship's towering hull, Tom watched from the top of tons of stacked sugar as his father and two other stevedores climbed down the twelve-foot mound built up from the lighter's combing with as much again in its hold. Like mountaineers, hooks dug into sacks instead of rocks to support their weight, they descended, glad of a job finished, already thinking of the money earned.

The general strike had been over more than a month. Little had been gained from it. With the miners still fighting on alone, people with no axe of their own to grind had contemplated their own jobs, had made their point, their own jobs in jeopardy. Nine days' support for the miners had to be enough and like Tom and his father they were grateful to be earning again. It had been a struggle, nine days without pay.

But Tom wasn't thinking about that. He was thinking of Amy, the way she moved about the house as though half-dead, eyes vacant, movements slow as if she was exhausted in body and spirit. She'd sit idle, saying nothing unless asked a direct question, and then her reply came only after a pause as though she hadn't quite understood the question.

Of course he was sorry for her – they were all sorry for her. It was a bloody awful thing to have happened to her, no matter that she might have had to give up the baby anyway – it would always be pointed out as a bastard, fingers pointed at her too. But why she should concern him so, he couldn't understand. Time and time again he shrugged off his thoughts of her, but they kept coming back.

Before losing her baby, all that standoffishness, thinking herself too good for the likes of him and his family yet glad to accept their help, had at once annoyed and put him in awe of her. Now she merely seemed pathetic. He wouldn't want to trade his life for her way of life, not for all the tea in China if she was the product her sort turned out, even with all the money her parents had. Perhaps now that she wasn't pregnant any more, she'd go back to them and it would be the last he'd ever have to see of her. His family could settle back and be themselves again. They hadn't been since her arrival, in dire straits or no dire straits. She'd never shown any humility for her condition, and had hardly given any thanks except to provide a bit for her keep, her with money in the bank, she could have afforded even more, where they had to grub about for everything they needed. Well, she could go . . .

Tom paused in the act of climbing down. Never having to see her around the house any more. Suddenly he knew it wasn't what he wanted. It shook him unexpectedly. For a moment came a wild thought – if only he could find a way of getting money, he'd show her that he was as good as her any day of the week. But how in hell's name would he ever get the kind of money she was used to?

Shrugging off the damned silly nonsense, Tom put one leg over the side of the high stack of sugar and began following the other three down to the combing. But the thought had sparked off a chain of others: his work, doing what his father and his father's father had done; stevedores and dockers knowing no other life. Whatever other life he'd have had, he'd still be tied to the river, couldn't imagine it being any other way. His people were Thames people, connected to it by birth like an umbilical cord. He could no more visualise a life not connected with the river than contemplate migrating to the other end of the earth.

But how much was he really connected to the Thames, unloading or stowing cargo deep in some ship's hold, his world no wider than its dingy wings? What he'd have liked would be a job where he could breathe the clean air of the tideway instead of his lungs remaining forever full of dust of hides and cement and grain, his hands rubbed raw by sugar, his flesh full of splinters from timber. If only he could have been a lighterman driving his craft from reach to reach, visiting the ships and wharves and docks. Or a sailorman as they called those who took their brown-sailed Thames barges out beyond the estuary. Or a pilot taking a big ship up river. Or on a tug manoeuvring those ships through narrow dock gates. But those sort of jobs required skills he'd never have. Loading and unloading was all he was good for. No wonder the Amy Harringtons of this world looked down on the likes of him.

There was no chance of ever bettering himself enough to be on the same footing as people like her. He felt anger ooze out at the thought that before she came he'd never had these wild thoughts. To work on the open water, perhaps, but to feel such an urge to better himself, never. Angrily, he put them from him because they would only destroy him, and climbed on down the stack of sugar, the hook he wielded to support himself digging viciously into each sack as he passed.

'You lot! I've got a job for you if yer want it.'

It was the last day of June, the weather warm but cloudy. Arthur Jordan's gang had just finished two days of the skilful loading for which stevedores were known and were now making their way for a well-earned cuppa with their sandwiches.

The voice came from the dock foreman. 'That's if you lot wants ter make yerselves a bit extra.'

Arthur Jordan paused, the rest with him. 'What's the job?'

'Bin a bit of a collision between an American cargo vessel and one of the Woolwich ferries. Just a moment ago. People on the ferry can't git orf by the sounds of it. The bloody landin' stage is damaged. Two of them barges yer've bin unloadin' 'ave decided to make for it and see what's doin'. I'm thinkin', gettin' some of those passengers orf, we could make a bit out of it – sort of salvage if yer like, if we get there before the big boys. What yer say?'

'You're on!' Arthur Jordan yelled, and with his men eagerly following, he clambered back across the ship they'd been coming off from and down its side to settle themselves on the roomy forward end of one of the two lighters below.

In minutes they were pushing off, the lighterman standing aft wielding a twenty-nine-foot sweep, as he called the oars, like a man gone mad, shooting his craft into the tideway.

Sitting gazing down at the tumbling moustache of the bow-wave, below him, listening to its hollow sloshing echoing under the lighter's flat bow, Tom's thoughts were already weaving dreams as he breathed in great gulps of fresh moisture-laden air, carrying with it all the smells wafted from every wharf, of timber, of spices, of coal, the stink from the gasworks, and from the very mud on the river's bed. At high tide, the river was alive: the big ships moving off from wharves and moorings; barges, skiffs, lighters crossing back and forth from one bank to the other or being towed six at a time in a double row by a tug.

That was what he should be doing. Driving a tug. Tugs did well out of salvage. Money in it, between manoeuvring ships in and out of docks. For a moment or two Tom's mind flew off on its own course. If he had a tug, a couple of tugs – no need to know how to drive one, just employ others to do that while he sat in an office taking command of things and watching the money roll in. Seconds later he was laughing silently at himself. And where was the money coming from to buy a tug with? Stupid sod. Having pipe dreams.

It was Amy making him think like this. End of June and she was still with them. Hadn't even attempted to contact her family. Something about pride, making her own way in the world. She had to be stupid too. All that money her family had. If money like that awaited him, to hell with pride, yet she was willing to throw it all away. He had no idea why.

She had come out of her stupor at last, and these days she seemed a totally different person, more thoughtful, somewhat more approachable, sort of less stuck-up – the complete opposite of his own sister, Alice, once so level-headed, now happy to muck around with that rich bloke she'd found, talking like a silly little flapper, getting more self-willed and stuck-up by the minute.

But Amy . . . one could say that losing that baby had done her a power of good, made her more human. Sometimes he found himself almost liking her, so long as he could control that strange turmoil inside whenever she came near him. The way she looked at him at times, so damned odd. He still had the feeling that she continued to think herself above him, yet there were times when she did relax enough for him to wonder that if only they could continue to talk more easily to each other for longer periods, maybe the turmoil he felt when with her would cease.

The last day of June – how could she have been here all this time? She was slowly coming to terms with losing the baby. Everyone had said perhaps it was just as well and she had to agree with them, but sometimes a tiny stab of emptiness would creep there inside her, where the baby had lain, and she had to fight hard to control the tears; wanted only to get away from everyone so she could indulge in the luxury of a good cry.

It should have meant, if one thought about it sensibly, that without the burden of a small baby growing up she could go back to the life she had known. It wasn't at all like that. She was still here and looked like staying here. But to say she had become used to her life here was far from true. She would never become used to it. She dreamed of home, constantly: the comfort, the *joie de vivre*, the spending, going off with a horde of friends to parties, to afternoon tea dances, to dances, to tennis parties or hilarious afternoons spent boating, or being driven down to Brookfield motor racing circuit, going to theatres and nightclubs, dancing till all hours to noisy jazz bands.

Compared to all that, what was there here? Here was how she imagined hell to be – not fire and brimstone but a grey, dragging existence.

Several times since the loss of the baby she had gone off to Bayswater to stand and gaze at her home from the end of the road. But she had stopped going. It was too painful.

Alice, full of the joys of life with Dicky these days, couldn't understand. 'I really don't know why you continue to stay in this miserable hole,' she said, 'when you could toddle off home any time you wish.'

'That's the last thing I shall ever do,' Amy told her and saw her arch her finely pencilled eyebrows.

'Not your silly pride still? You only have to ask your parents nicely to have you back.' To Alice pride had become an idiotic word lately.

She still worked at Lipton's, though under protest these days of high living, her lovely summer dresses hidden beneath the white coat the girls had to wear. These days Alice's wardrobe was well and truly guarded from her sisters' envious hands: the several pairs of high-heeled shoes with comfortable straps instead of those cheap things that pinched at the toes and whose straps cut into the instep; the well-cut suits reaching just the right height above the knees showing fine silk stockings which she often rolled down to display rouged knees to her mother's prim and proper disapproving looks. But she didn't care. She was growing away from her place of upbringing as fast as she possibly could go, continually boasting about the fun she had, the clothes she had.

'Richard . . .' she persisted in calling him by his full name. 'Richard bought me this handbag for my birthday.' Which had been two weeks ago. 'We got it in Bond Street, you know.' Or, 'Do you like this adorable little hat?' She had several hats now, summer ones, cloche hats of fine straw in pastel shades to match whatever outfit she was wearing, and sparkly bands for evening wear. 'Dicky said he'd pay for it. He's so gallant, such a terribly terribly thoughtful old darling.'

Even her speech had taken on the outrageous colloquialisms of those she now mixed with, except that as always with the newly converted it was even more stressed. Not only that, but she was becoming a snob, looking down on her own family as though they were a nasty smell under her nose. She hadn't once brought Dicky here, as though she were too ashamed of the home and area in which she'd been born, even though she had been dreadfully honest, as she put it, and had told him all about her upbringing.

Amy still felt the devastation caused by Alice's honest confession not long after he had asked her out; in those days she'd still been guileless. Even so, Amy could see her scheme of sweet revenge working. All very well Dicky seeing his new love through rose-tinted glasses, but once he took her to meet his parents, which for obvious reasons, Amy smirked, he hadn't done yet, she would be out on her ear, Dicky threatened with choosing between her and his inheritance. And Amy could guess which it would be. She'd had personal experience of Dicky's train of thought. And then she would see her desire for revenge satisfied. Shame for poor Alice, but it would serve her right, carried away as she was, the unbearable snob as she was becoming.

Amy looked at her as Alice took off her hat after coming in from work to sit on the edge of the bed she still had to share with her sisters, much to her chagrin.

'I don't ever want to go back home. Things that seem to glitter to others aren't always gold, you know.'

She heard Alice's brittle laugh at the cumbersome paraphrasing. Alice's laugh had become very brittle of late, aping those she went around with. 'How quaint. Before long I shall be having some of those glittery things when Richard and I are married.'

'He *has* asked you then?'

'Well, he hasn't quite gone down on bended knee yet, but he talks about it an awful lot.'

As he once did to me, Amy thought bitterly, and couldn't help furthering it. 'And when is he going to take you to see his parents?'

Alice pursed her lips, toyed with her hat. 'I'm to meet them soon. He just wants a little time with them beforehand.'

'How long have you two been going out together – three months? I should think he's had ample time in three months.'

'One doesn't rush these things,' Alice said haughtily, suddenly annoyed, and shot to her feet to put away her hat in one of the several hatboxes she kept in the small space between the window and the wardrobe away from her sisters' envious filching fingers.

She swept out of the room leaving Amy alone with her thoughts. Nothing on God's earth would induce her to go back to her parents. Not after the unselfish way these people had taken her in – how could she go off with a thank you and forget all they'd done? Mrs Jordan was like a mother to her, more so than her own mother. Not a word from either of them. They had no idea she had lost her baby. As far as they were concerned she was still going to have it, and she wasn't prepared to enlighten them.

Yes, it was pride that kept her from going home. Pride and ... Amy paused mid-thought – pride, and Tom, she had to admit it. Every time he came near her, it seemed he was ravaging her heart. She often could hardly breathe for its pounding. It was so silly, they were classes apart, and yet ... If only I had been otherwise, how wonderful everything would have been, for she was sure he felt the same way about her. But he was just a working man, common sense spoke softly in her ear: how could she ever come down to his level, her memories full of the life she had once had, no matter that she chose not to have them again? Before long she would resent him, and where would the love go then, the pounding heart, the adoration? If only there was a chance for him to become rich. But that was just wishful thinking, a pipe dream, a silly pipe dream.

Chapter Eleven

Alice was becoming worried. August, five months since she had first met Richard, and for all he professed to love her he still hadn't proposed marriage properly, as though reluctant to for some reason. Besides, she'd never got over that look Amy had given her back in June when Richard's name had come up, as though she knew something she, Alice, didn't. And asking so pointedly: had Richard taken her to meet his parents yet, almost hinting at something wrong.

It had put questions in her own mind. Perhaps Richard *was* worried about how his parents would receive her. It made her tremble – what if in the end they refused to meet her? Perhaps he hadn't even said anything to them about her yet. Perhaps he was trying to hide her from them. Somehow it all combined to make her conscious of her own roots where mostly she almost forgot them when with him and his many friends. Another thing – he'd never let on to them about her, as though secretly ashamed to let it be known, perhaps laying himself open to ridicule. He might be head over heels in love with her, but when class got in the way, that was a different kettle of fish. It had begun to plague her, just as it was plaguing her now.

Despite a simply wonderful evening, seeing the new Ivor Novello play *Downhill* at the Queen's, then to a party above the Strand Theatre given by the great man himself, having got in with one of Richard's theatrical friends, and now Richard driving her home via the Embankment with all the lights romantically twinkling in the Thames, her uncertainty about Richard rose up afresh.

'Richard, darling, you do love me, don't you?' she burst out suddenly. He'd leave her at the top of her road, dull and empty after the West End's bright lights. She still insisted he come no further, still a little ashamed of her neighbourhood, which was silly when he could see enough of it from Commercial Road. He never argued. Why? Was he ashamed too? She found herself dreading taking that vital step when he would truly see her for what she was, a girl from the poor East End and not the one of his dreams, all the romance and adventure in courting her bursting like a bubble. Was it for that same reason he hadn't told his parents about her, for she was becoming more and more convinced that he hadn't. What if after all this she was merely one of his flings, a diversion from his usual pursuits?

'*Do* you love me, Richard?' she persisted.

'You know I do.'

But she wasn't satisfied. 'I'm not sure if I *know* that you do.'

Richard's foot came down sharply on the brake, taking her by surprise and throwing her forward a little. Ignoring the angry hooting of car horns he lifted his foot and let the car glide into the kerb and stop. There he turned to her.

'Alice, my love, what do you want me to say? I love you. I really do.'

His arm came around her shoulders, pulling her towards him, and he kissed her with . . . was it contrived passion?

She pulled away. 'That doesn't prove a thing.'

His handsome features peevish under the Embankment's bright lights, he sat back in his seat, 'Then tell me what I *have* to do to prove it. Tell me and I'll do it.'

Determinedly, Alice ignored his peevishness. She had to know one way or another if he was playing her about. She gazed across the dark water of the Thames where the lights from the opposite bank made dancing reflections on its stygian surface. 'Have you ever spoken to your parents about me?'

'What kind of question is that?'

'A question that will tell me if you really love me or not.'

'I don't follow.' He was sulking.

'Are you ashamed of me?'

She felt him turn towards her. 'Of course I'm not ashamed of you. Why should I be? I love you . . . Oh, no, that doesn't prove anything, does it?'

She ignored the sarcasm. 'Have you mentioned me at all to your parents – who I am, where I come from, my upbringing, my common upbringing? And don't tell me you don't follow,' she added sourly. 'You know full well what I am. You still say you love me, but how do I know you're not just dangling me on a piece of string, a little diversion from your usual capers?'

'Five months! Good God, Alice, you call that a little diversion? If it had been a little diversion it wouldn't have lasted a week. And if you want to know, I *have* spoken to my parents. Well, I've hinted that I am going out with someone. And they've said they would like to meet her . . . you. You see, Alice, darling . . .'

He paused before going on, and she turned away from the river to look straight at him. 'Yes, Richard?'

Bitterness was already growing in her tone. Had she been some highly bred young thing he was so in love with, he wouldn't have hesitated a second to tell his parents, and they would have insisted they meet her straight away.

He had read her thoughts. 'Listen, my darling. I love you with all my heart and with all my soul . . .' How bloody melodramatic, she thought sourly as she let him continue without interrupting. 'And I don't care a jot about where you were born and who your parents are. To me you're the most beautiful thing that has ever happened to me. And I swear that on my own . . .'

'Don't say things like that,' she burst out. 'Not things God might ask you to prove.'

'But it *is* true, my darling. I can't begin to tell you how much I love you. And I'm prepared to move heaven and earth and defy God Himself for you. But you see, my love, others might not see it the way I do.'

So there was that barrier, but Richard was ploughing on.

'I have to approach my people very carefully. Prepare them, rather. I want them to love you the moment they see you. But I can't lead them up the garden path any more than I would lead you. The moment I make our alliance official, they will want to know what your circumstances are, who your people are, how far do they go back, where they live and what they do and how much they are worth. Marriage union in the circles I live in isn't a bit like the way your people go about it. You fall in love and marry and it's all straightforward . . .'

Not all that straightforward at times, she thought, listening. She knew of arguments in families because a lighterman's son wanted to marry, say, a docker's daughter, the river men deeming themselves above lowly loud-mouthed dockers. And what father working as even a humble office clerk would heap blessings on his daughter's wish to marry a costermonger with only his barrow to his name? No, it was the same the world over, she reckoned, and trying to overcome the bitter feeling inside her, she listened to Richard going on trying so earnestly to put things right.

'With my people, they look for the high society wedding, the *good match* as they call it. I know my father hopes . . . no, expects me to find myself a well-bred wife whose family go back generations, whose father can give her a really smashing dowry. He wants the name of my future wife emblazoned all over *The Times* and the *Manchester Guardian* for everyone to see. He wants the best. He *is* a sir, you know. But more or less newly knighted. Well, last year, anyway. And like everyone newly lifted up, he is very aware of it. And for me to come outright with the fact that I want to marry an ordinary girl . . . I mean to me you're not ordinary, not at all. You're just the most wonderful person . . . No, Alice, don't interrupt! I'm putting all this badly, I know. But what I'm trying to say is that he and Mother would see you as ordinary even if your father was only a small businessman, or even a middle-class businessman with pots of money. He is besotted with his new title and there is nothing worse than the newly elevated. You see, Alice, he'd kill me for saying this, but my father came from small beginnings. He started with a small engineering firm well before the War, before I was born, on a few pounds inherited in an old uncle's will and by the time the War came he'd already turned to making munitions. In just four years it expanded out of all expectations. And he was shrewd too – he invested in other like industries. Now he has a thriving empire and a title, he likes to forget his small beginnings. Naturally he's looking for me to make a good marriage. But I love you, my darling. I shall fight for you and nothing he says will part us. You're better than anyone I know, and I shall remind him of where he himself originated.'

'But he was never as poor and ordinary as us,' Alice said as he finished. 'He came from a better background than I, humble beginnings or not.'

'I don't care!' Richard snorted defiantly. 'My darling, I don't want to lose you. I shall fight tooth and nail for you. Even if it means he cuts me off without a penny. Anyway I have my own money, in trust. No one can take that away. So you are assured of a decent life with me.'

'Do you mean you're proposing to me, Richard?' Alice had concentrated her gaze fully on him. 'Officially? Properly?'

'Officially and properly.' He smiled, relaxing, drawing her close once more.

She let herself melt into his arms, let him kiss her with all the passion in both their beings. But they were in the middle of the Embankment and passion could not be allowed to go too far. Richard broke away and before she could think what he was doing, he had started up the car and drove off erratically.

'Where are we going?' she queried.

'You'll see.' His voice had a grating sound to it.

Almost immediately the car took a left turn into a side street, turning again into a small dingy alley. There they stopped. 'We can be out of sight here,' was all he said as he quickly cut the engine and turned to gather her up in his arms.

Alice gave a little struggle, already sensing fear of something not quite right about this. 'What are you doing, Richard?'

'What we've both wanted to do for a long time, my darling. To make love, properly – cement our love, my sweetest.'

Alice pushed against him, really frightened now, heard herself crying out, 'No! No!' But he wasn't listening.

'I love you, Alice, and it's killing me.' His voice came with an effort. Already his hand was pushing beneath her skirt exposing her legs to the warm August air now feeling suddenly cold on the bare flesh above the rolled tops of her stockings. His fingers were at the two buttons of her camiknicks, fighting to release them. 'I love you so much, so much darling!' His breath against her face was hot. He was panting.

She was fighting him now, her words, 'No, Richard! Don't!' smothered by his kisses as he panted against her lips how they loved each other, how they needed each other, how they must have this relief from their pent-up love of each other.

The buttons had come undone, the band around her waist suddenly loose. He was now fiddling with the fly buttons of his immaculate evening suit trousers. Panic consumed her.

'Get off me!' she shrieked, managing to avert her lips a little from the crushing kiss. At the same time her struggles released her left hand. Instinctively she brought it back, then forward, the resounding smack of her palm on the side of his cheek echoing from the stone buildings lining the dark alleyway.

Startled, Richard pulled away, his frantic movements ceasing. 'What was that for?'

'Don't you dare touch me!' she screamed at him, sobbing through her scream. 'Don't you ever dare touch me again like that.'

Alice was pulling her short skirt back over her legs, trying to rebutton her camiknicks, hoping she had succeeded with at least one as the band tightened. She felt dreadful now the fright was gone – angry at him, angry at herself, feeling a new stab of fear lest he throw her over unable to get what he'd wanted, and bitter disappointment that it had all turned out like this. She was just someone he'd been going out with for all he could get even if it had taken him some while. All her hopes felt dashed. And she was so in love with him. How could she have been so let down? She felt cheap, degraded. And she'd had such high hopes, silly little fool, a girl from the East End, dreaming about being the wife of a wealthy son and heir of a sir. She sat silent.

Richard had sat back in his seat. 'Are you all right?' His voice came hollow.

'I suppose so,' she just about answered.

He seemed to be crying. Surely he wasn't crying? His voice when he spoke again proved that he was. 'I'm sorry, Alice, I'm so sorry. I don't know what came over me.'

But she had no time for his tears of remorse. She was angry, disillusioned and terribly terribly degraded, all her hopes, her silly hopes, tumbled at her feet.

'And so you should be.' She tried to control the sob in her throat. 'You tried it on with me . . .'

'I love you.' There was a sob in his voice too, but she didn't care.

'I'm not one of your free and easy tarts, even if you thought I was. I've been brought up decently even if I'm only working-class.'

She thought of Amy, product of an upper-class upbringing. Look where her money had got her. 'I shall never let any man touch me until I am married to him.' Her voice was growing stronger, more resolute, her mind making itself up to end this affair, hurtful though that was. 'I'm sorry too, Richard. But I'm not that sort of girl. It's all over, isn't it?'

She felt him sit upright in his seat. 'What d'you mean, it's all over? Do you mean you're throwing me over because of this? Alice, you can't! I said I was sorry.'

She stared at him. 'I thought you'd want to throw me over. Not able to get what you wanted, I thought you . . . I thought . . .'

Even in the dark, as her voice trailed away uselessly, she could see his eyes gleaming. 'How can you say that? All I want is you. There's no one else in the world for me but you. I want to marry you, Alice. Please forgive me for what happened just now. I promise I shall never do that again if you don't want me to. Not until we're married.'

In the dark alley Alice's world lit up like day. 'Do you mean that, Richard? You still want to marry me?'

'Of course I do. I've never wanted anything else.' She was in his arms again, this time the embrace holding no threat, only abiding love. 'And as soon as I can I'm going to ask your father for your hand in marriage.'

Happiness restored, Alice giggled, picturing him standing before her father.

'I can't believe yer want to marry my gel.'

'But, sir, I do. I do indeed want to marry her.' Richard stood facing the man who, at the first hint of who had entered, had struggled into a collar he'd found after frantically rummaging in the sideboard drawer, and put on a jacket over his braces.

He looked very aware that he still bore the signs of a man not long come in from doing a dirty job of unloading a ship's hold, that he hadn't washed properly as yet and needed a shave, that his moustache still had a remnant of gravy on it, which he quickly wiped away as Richard entered the back room with Alice on his arm.

Alice, having introduced her fiancé as she could safely call him, now sat on the edge of the sofa while Richard, having shaken hands with her father and hefty-looking brother, remained standing almost to attention in the centre of the room, so nervous did he feel after having informed the family of his intentions towards their daughter.

By rights he should have requested to speak to her father in private, in another room and there presented his intentions, his credentials, his ability to care for Alice in the way to which she was accustomed. But there was no other room. The door to the one he had passed on entering the house, the room at the front, had been open revealing a double bed. It had shaken him that someone in this family was obliged to sleep downstairs without a proper bedroom. He could hardly have asked Mr Jordan to step into that room.

So here he was standing in the centre of this one, the remains of their meal still on the table, the house redolent with the smell of that meal, his own self-confidence thoroughly shaken by it all. Nor could he speak of his ability to care for Alice in the way to which she was accustomed, for nothing could be further removed from the existence she obviously led here.

'Well I never!' exclaimed Mr Jordan, taken aback at being

called sir. He recovered himself quickly and became formal, frowning severely. 'I 'ope yer ... you intend ter ... to treat 'er right.'

'I certainly do, sir. Alice is all I want in my life. I shall be loving and loyal and I shall see she wants for nothing. I can give her a good marriage, sir.'

Mrs Jordan, in apron and old shoes that served for slippers, opened her mouth to speak, her diction as good as she could get it. 'You've really honoured us, Mr Pritchard ...'

'Richard,' he corrected gently. 'Please call me Richard.'

'Oh ... yes. And I know my Alice'll make you a good and lovin' wife, I'm sure.'

'Oh, I know she will,' he echoed fervently, his fond gaze coming to rest on the blushing, glowing-eyed Alice.

Upstairs, Amy heard the entry of the loving couple. Alice's raised and excited voice revealed the moment the door was opened that Richard Pritchard had just proposed to her and that she had brought him home to ask her father for her hand in marriage.

Amy had been sitting on her bed by the window, her thoughts as always when alone going miserably back to the baby she had lost. At such times she yearned for the child she might have had. That her future life must prove easier without the encumbrance of an illegitimate baby held no consolation but only that emptiness of something precious having been taken from her. Never in her worst dreams had she imagined how empty she could feel. That she was in love with Tom was no comfort for she was not at all certain that he loved her; still holding her at bay, still seeing her as untouchable, on a plane far above his – that wasn't love.

Up here by herself she had been sitting considering this life in limbo, neither one place nor the other. She couldn't stay here for ever and she couldn't, wouldn't, go home. So what was there? Visions of the empty years stretched ahead, growing older, growing old, friendless, childless, unloved, belonging nowhere ... And when there was no more money? Amy had seen old women carrying their worldly goods in old canvas bags, huddled into corners as the day faded – had they as young girls once been comfortably off, loved and cared for, but cast off for various reasons of their own, no longer wanted or loved? Was that to be her life?

She had let the desolate tears trickle down her cheeks unchecked, half luxuriating in their progress, allowing herself a sort of satisfaction that she could be so laid low by her thoughts. But the sounds at the front door below brought her upright, her misery swept away for the moment as Alice's excitement drifted up the stairs.

Sweeping the tears from her cheeks with an angry, almost frightened hand, she prepared herself for the girl to come bursting into the bedroom. She must not see her like this. No one must see her like this. She stood up and made ready with an easy smile, trying to ignore the fact that it trembled.

Then she heard Dicky's rather high voice saying good evening to Alice's mother as he entered, and Alice's voice again, introducing him, and more:

'Mum! Oh, Mum – Richard has proposed to me. We're going to be married.'

And Mrs Jordan's shocked response. 'Oh, Lord! Oh, what a surprise! Oh, I don't know what ter say. You'd best come through and tell yer Dad. Oh, well I never. Just a tick, luv, while I see if 'e's decently dressed. Do wait 'ere a minute, Alice, Mr Pritchard.'

Amy's heart was already pounding against her chest wall like a hammer pounding on rock. He'd done it. He'd actually proposed. He was here to make it official. Had he also made it official with his own family? He must have done, or at least was sure of their response, or he wouldn't be here. Anger and frustration gripped Amy.

Mrs Jordan had come out into the passage again, bidding the two of them to follow her. The door closed. Silence. Amy strained to listen to what was going on below her, the ceilings of this house transmitting every sound, the walls as thin as cardboard. But the words were indistinct, the voices too muffled to make sense of, though she knew exactly what they said. She gave up, and lowering herself back on to her bed, lay with her face in her pillow to silence the rending sobs of hatred and defeat that now came of their own volition.

* * *

154

In the breakfast room, the orange-flowered cream curtains half-drawn against the morning sunshine pouring full into the room, Sir John Pritchard sat regarding his son from one end of the table, this one smaller and more intimate than the long table in the dining room. Sir John's old-fashioned greying moustache seemed to bristle.

'You've been keeping company with a girl from ... where?'

Richard's mother reached for his hand and held it tightly. Extremely pretty at twenty from her photograph when she had married his father, at forty-three she was still very attractive, still slender, slightly built, her hair still golden with not a strand of grey in it, now in a fashionable shingle that made her look even younger, and following the fashion in dress as closely as a middle-aged woman dare. She was very much like him, or he very much like her: small straight nose, light brown eyes, small chin. But there the resemblance ceased. She was animated, happy bossing everyone about, and quite as self-assertive as any young person, to the point of being positively brash, whereas he knew he was far from strong-minded.

At this moment, however, he needed to be as much as possible, for Alice's sake, for both their sakes. Nothing was going to stop him. He matched his father's annoyed stare across the breakfast table.

'From Stepney,' he confirmed gamely. 'And we aren't keeping company. We're very serious about each other.'

Unfortunately an effort at self-assertiveness in those not naturally so can often come out sounding rude and impertinent. The older man's moustache seemed to bristle still more.

'I don't object to your having a bit of a laugh with girls like that from the lower orders of society – but be careful, son, some of them can be full of diseases. I know, I have to employ some of them, I've seen the sores breaking out around their mouths. Be careful what you're doing, Richard. I'm not objecting to your finding yourself a girl for a night or two's fun. I'm objecting to the *five* months of it and your saying nothing about it to us. And serious? No, young man, I'm not having that.'

155

Richard stood his ground, or rather sat it, his hands clenched on top of the breakfast table, his untouched fried eggs and grilled kidneys growing cold. 'I don't care what you say, Father. Alice and I are in love. And she is as clean living as you and I.'

'*Love!* Good God, boy, what d'you know of love?' His tone moderated a little, became advisory. 'Forget it, lad, find yourself a decent girl from a fine family. There are enough of *them* among your café society friends, surely.'

'Alice *is* a decent girl. She was a lady's maid. She's well-mannered, well-spoken and as honest as . . .'

'Don't argue with me, Richard.'

The benignity had been dispensed with, but Richard continued to entreat as far as his seething anger allowed. 'If you'd let me bring her to meet you . . .'

'Meet me? Damn it, Richard! Why should I wish to meet her?'

'To see how well brought-up she is. Not everyone in the East End lives in poverty, and her family are quite comfortable compared to many. She's a charming person and . . . and . . .' He wanted to say, 'I love her,' but saying it twice would just be tempting fate. It was his mother who rescued him.

'No harm in us meeting her, John. We mustn't cling to Victorian prejudices. Class barriers aren't what they were and she might be a very nice sort of girl.'

'But not our class,' John thundered at her over his son's head. 'It still does matter, Margaret, for all you try to be so modern. It's nonsense, and your ideas of what is modern are nonsense. That girl does not set one foot in this house.'

'John, you're an outrageous snob! We have servants here from the lower classes.'

'But we don't greet them and offer them tea.'

'I do. When I interview them for a position here, I bring them into the morning room and have them sit down and offer them a cup of tea while we chat.'

'That's different. They are being interviewed. They're not out to marry my son and imagining they'll be coming into money.' He turned his eyes sharply on Richard. 'That's what

156

she's after, young man. And you're idiot enough to fall for it.'

Richard shot up from the table unable to control himself any longer. 'OK, so you don't approve, either of you. Well, I'm going to marry her. She's all I want and all I ever shall want. I'm still going to marry her. As soon as I can. And you can cut me off without a penny – I don't care!'

'Done! Every penny can go to your sister, Effie. A nice surprise for her when she comes back home from that Swiss finishing school of hers. Not one farthing to you, Richard, and that's a promise if you don't get your silly ideas out of your head. We'll see how you like living in poverty. And we'll see if this . . . this gold-digger will have you then.'

'I shan't be in poverty, Father. I've got a damned good bit in trust for when I turn twenty-one. And that's only two months off. We can live until then.'

'And how long d'you think that will last you?'

'Properly invested, a long time. And I can work.'

There came a harsh laugh. 'Where? How? You've never done a day's work in your life. I pay you a good salary for doing nothing. You've a seat on the Board, but you're hardly ever there. I hoped you would take an interest in the business, visit the factories, but you've never set one foot in them. You're a gallivanting, ne'er-do-well parasite, and I'm disappointed in you – have been for a long time. And I tell you, this is the last straw unless you give up this ridiculous idea and settle down in the company and do what I pay you to do and find yourself a decent girl from a good family to marry. But why am I lowering myself to argue with you? I've had my say. If you leave this house to marry this creature, then you're out of my will as quick as lightning, and will be asked to tender your resignation from the Board of Directors. And see if she has you then.'

'Oh, blast you, John!' Margaret had also stood up, she and her son staring down at the seated man, his head below them. 'All this melodrama! You're so high up, aren't you? Just think, my dear, where we both started . . .'

'Not in the gutter, that's for sure.'

'Just let me finish, John. You're so behind the times. We're not Victorians, John. We've left the stuffy eighteen hundreds

157

behind. We are, should be, modern-thinking people. At least I hope I am. Class distinctions are breaking down everywhere. Richard says she is a good respectable girl and that her family are not poverty-stricken and seem upstanding enough. At least let us see her before we judge her. If we don't like her, then I agree, Richard must come to heel about it.'

'We've only his word on how respectable she is,' he shot at her, still seated, deciding not to make it too obvious by getting to his feet that he resented their standing above him. 'We don't know the first thing about the family she comes from.' Richard had not told them that Alice's father was a mere dock worker. The longer he held that back the better, he thought. 'They may have a criminal record, be out-and-out spongers for all we know. She seems to be one.'

'That's what I am asking, John, that we see her. Or I see her. I'm a good judge of character. I do all the hiring of servants. You leave that to me. Yes, I know it's my job to. But I know I shall judge this girl for what she is – good or bad, honest or scheming. I think we should see her before passing judgement on her.'

'And what if – I say *if* – he were to marry her, how do you think we'd hold up our heads before our own friends and acquaintances when they find out that the fine wedding we'd be giving will be for our son to marry a person from Stepney without any background whatsoever? We'll both look fools. Have you thought of that, Margaret?'

'If they are so desperately in love, it could be a quiet unobtrusive wedding.'

'Over my dead body!'

'But who says they are going to marry? Richard might well find someone else if we decide he should wait a year to be certain. John, my dear, indulge him a little. It's probably a phase he's going through. It's youth talking. Forbid him and he'll take the bit between his teeth and defy us. I know what I'm talking about.'

Richard could almost hear her saying it was just a flash in the pan affair. He opened his mouth to speak but realised it would be the worst thing to do. His mother was doing very well on her own, and at least once they saw Alice, part

158

of the battle would be won. She was so charming and pretty, well-mannered, demure, well-spoken, how could they not be charmed by her? It was best to leave things to develop by themselves. Something told him he would win if only he waited a little longer, bided his time. Alice would understand.

He had his fingers tightly crossed, however, as he sat back down at the table, pulling his now cold eggs and grilled kidneys towards him, while his mother also returned to her seat to nibble on her toast thinly spread with butter. She observed her figure very strictly, conscious of the current vogue that decreed all women of fashion to be stick-thin and breastless.

Chapter Twelve

Amy sat on the sofa with Mrs Jordan gazing up at an animated Alice who'd hardly stopped babbling since the first post brought Dicky's letter half an hour ago. The girl's eyes shone almost as brightly as any July afternoon, bright enough to make the entire room appear to glow on this dreary November morning. Had she stepped outside the house, Amy could imagine them lighting up the whole world like twin suns, so delirious with joy was Alice.

'To think, I'll be meeting his parents tomorrow. At last! At last! After all this wait. I can hardly believe this is all happening to me.' If she had said all this once she must have said it a dozen times already in different ways. 'I wish I knew what to wear. I must look my very best. Oh, I do so hope I create the right impression.'

'Of course yer will, luv,' her mother beamed up at her, proud as punch of her eldest daughter.

'What if they don't like me?'

'They won't be able to 'elp but like yer, luv. You, pretty as a picture. An' yer got lovely manners an' bearin'. An' look 'ow well yer talk an' all. 'Course they'll like yer.'

Alice's nervous fingers played with the single sheet of expensive blue note paper, unfolding and refolding it again and again. 'Oh, I hope so. I do hope so. I'll simply die if they don't. My first meeting ever with them. I mustn't make a mess of it. I simply mustn't. Everything ... my whole life depends on their liking me.'

Amy said nothing. It was Saturday. Alice would have been at work by now, but the arrival of the letter just before she was due to leave had put paid to any thought of working behind a counter now that there was a chance that she might never need to work again.

She should be hating Alice's happiness, but somehow she couldn't bring herself to do even that. Over the past few months something seemed to have happened to her: resignation, a form of self-preservation maybe, following an instinct to make the best of a bad job. Odd how one begins to adapt to an environment it has become impossible to escape from – as though the old life she had known belonged to another while she had slowly fallen into the one she now led, the world she had once known passing her by, going on its own way and leaving her standing.

She hardly ever went buying new dresses now, much less following any change in fashion; she had no inclination whatsoever to go out and enjoy herself. Where was there to go? And with whom? Alice had her own pursuits now, her evenings after work spent with Richard as she called him; the two girls, Vi and Rosy, were too immature to make friends with. Those she had known were long since gone, nor had she made any new ones, finding them too rough, ill-spoken, not of her class, her mind clinging still to that distinction drummed into her from birth, for all she tried to change.

Somehow the lack of friends, of the world she'd known going on without her, seemed not to matter all that much. It might have been that the miscarriage had changed her perspective on things. She had heard it could do that to a person, and other odd things too, strange frightening impulses coming out of the blue – just as she thought she was over the worst, it would flood back over her in the most unsettling way. One such morning only two weeks ago, Saturday, payday, out shopping with Mrs Jordan in a little local market, she'd stood outside a small shop seeing a woman with a thinly dressed, pinch-faced toddler hanging, snivelling, onto her coat follow Mrs Jordan into the shop, leaving a battered pram outside, because it was too huge and unwieldy to get into the crowded place.

Waiting, Amy had peeped distastefully into the horrid pram. There lay a two-month old baby dressed in a grubby knitted coatee and bonnet and covered by a single, very thin, obviously well-used baby blanket despite the cold November weather. She'd seen this a hundred times, ill-clad children, equally ill-clad mothers with husbands out of work, welfare handouts not enough to feed the cockroaches much less those they preyed upon. She had become virtually accustomed to it by now, but could never get over the strange smell that always issued from those babies in their battered, second-hand prams. This one had been no exception and her face had puckered from the faint odour that wafted upward.

Then quite suddenly came a sudden impulse to snatch the thing up and hurry away with it. She felt no conscious wish to make it her own, yet all the loss she had felt, all the emptiness she still felt from time to time, inexplicable because common sense told her she was far better off unfettered by an illegitimate baby, convulsed her in that moment enough to take her breath away. The compulsion had been such that the certainty had flashed through her mind that the mother might even be thankful to be relieved of that extra, unwanted mouth.

It was the wildest impulse she had ever experienced, so strong that it made her feel sick for a moment, her head beginning to spin, the world receding, and all that had been in her mind was that act, as needful as breathing itself. Mrs Jordan coming out of the shop was what burst the thought, almost like a physical stab of pain.

Amy had smiled at her as she'd enquired, 'Orright, luv?' confused by her apparent blank stare but turning away with, 'Right then, one more shop and we can go 'ome. 'Old that fer me, luv, will yer?' handling her the old canvas shopping bag heavy and bulging with spuds and a loaf of bread.

That, two weeks ago, and it still haunted her. She had felt withdrawn and pensive ever since.

But more, she merely felt apathetic, resigned to fitting in with this world she had been thrust into, had come to know even if not quite like. That was it: apathy, resignation, perhaps even fear, that fear becoming deep-seated, of returning to that which was fading enough to cause her to hesitate to venture back into it.

In August she'd plucked up courage enough to write again to her parents, that time to tell them that she had lost the baby and was her old self again. She had really expected them to reply, call her back home, if not with open arms then at least with some quickly conquered reservation. She even began preparing herself for re-entering that life she had left behind; spent a little of her carefully hoarded money on a modest new outfit. But as the weeks moved on and no reply came, she had put away her new outfit, her mind sinking back into apathy – like a prisoner seeing his release cancelled and no further new date set.

A painful reminder of fallen hopes, the outfit now hung, unworn, on the wall beside all her other clothes, hidden behind a small curtained rail fitted between the wardrobe and the window where her bed was. Her entire wardrobe hung from clothes hangers supported by hooks screwed and hammered into that wall by Mr Jordan, there being no room in the old wardrobe itself for all four girls. Apart from that new outfit, she hadn't bought herself anything new since losing the baby. Once she wouldn't have allowed a month to pass before spending on more lovely things, trying to be almost ahead of fashion, at least on a par with all her society friends.

She wasn't broke as yet. Of the money her father had thrown at her, there was still three-quarters left in her bank. It was beginning to bring in interest, but conditioned to this life she now led she felt the pain of every penny that had to be taken out for her keep. One day she might need it desperately. There had to be enough there for that eventuality. The thought would make her shiver, and she had come to understand the overriding fear that gripped nigh every soul in these poorer parts of London – destitution. She was even contemplating, at last, the once unthinkable prospect of finding herself a job to enable her savings to be kept to a respectable amount.

Amy brought herself back to the present with a jolt, aware that Alice was addressing her.

'Aren't you pleased for me, Amy? You look so glum. One would think you were begrudging me my wonderful good fortune. You're not jealous, are you?'

163

'No.' Amy smiled at her. 'Why should I be jealous?'

Alice still had no notion that the man whose parents she had been invited to meet was the same one who had got her one-time employer pregnant and who had promptly jilted her; entirely innocent too of the plot Amy had hatched for her. When she had confided in the girl – was it only ten months ago? It seemed like years – she had never mentioned the name of the man who had wronged her. Just as well perhaps. Better to leave it that way.

Still a sweet-natured person who didn't deserve to have her heart torn out of her, Alice had fallen into the trap of developing ideas well beyond her station. Even so, Amy found herself hoping that Dicky wouldn't let her down as he had let her, Amy, down; that his family would accept her and her life be a bed of roses. She deserved a little happiness. There was precious little of it here.

No, she didn't begrudge Alice her joy of Dicky Pritchard. She didn't feel any fury that her scheme, the silly plot she'd hatched so long ago, had backfired on her. She no longer harboured a desire to avenge herself on him. It was over and done with. She had lost her baby and must live with that. Small compensation, she had found Tom, although even that hadn't worked out as she had begun to hope. He still treated her as a lodger in this house, spoke to her, included her in his conversations, but that was as far as it went.

There had been a time when she had fancied he was growing closer, and her heart had beat a little faster, the loss of her baby put behind her. But hardly had she noticed this than he had retreated again leaving her thwarted, confused, wondering if she really would want him to be that close after all, whether she could handle the situation when it came to it.

Even so, there was no denying the thrill that clutched her to see him come home from work, grimy as he was, to see him washed and at ease, amazingly clean from just the kitchen sink, the joy of being opposite him at the table where she could study his strong face as she ate her meal. And there was no denying that her heart would thump away with its own little longings, divorcing itself entirely from the

164

common-sense reasoning her head kept insisting upon, that they were both from far too different worlds ever to become a pair, and that this was what he too knew and why he kept himself from her.

For most of her young working life as a house/parlourmaid, Alice had become used to the spaciousness of at least one of the homes of London's upper classes. How many, gazing at their drab frontages, each a copy of its neighbour, could imagine the size and opulence lying behind those deceptively narrow façades?

With this in mind, Alice approached the huge corner edifice in one of the finer roads in Chelsea that was the London home of Richard's parents with much less trepidation than had she known what lay beyond. Her only misgiving was that instead of coming to serve these people, she was coming to be greeted by them as an equal, she hoped. Oh, please God, she hoped. In itself that prospect was enough to frighten.

She had expected Richard's house to be imposing, frowning, similar to the one she'd worked in, Victorian, Georgian perhaps. There was nothing Victorian or Georgian about this. Set at the corner of two roads, it was huge and square and terribly modern, built mostly of concrete. The unexpected picture, shielded now by large bare November trees, helped to calm her nerves to some extent as Richard conducted her from the taxi and holding her arm hurried through an ornate gate with brass lion heads and on towards the faceless edifice by the short slightly curving path between two immaculate grass lawns with black and empty flower beds.

Up the half-dozen pink concrete steps they went, the bottom and topmost ones set with Grecian urns, each holding some sort of neat little tree. Richard pressed the doorbell that buzzed raucously in response on the far side of the door.

'You'll like this place,' he said, almost breathlessly as they waited. 'Mother loves everything art deco, and so do I. We've got another place in Surrey – country mansion – stuffy old place – all stairs and holes and corners. There's a

165

round tower – pseudo of course, a bit like an old oasthouse.' He spoke in short nervous tones, very fast. 'Huge fireplaces, tall, draughty windows, high ceilings, dark antique furniture, Mother hates it ... By the way, she also hates being called Mother. Prefers Margaret. My sister and I both call her that. Makes her feel youthful. She's an extremely outgoing, modern person. You'll like her ...'

The rest of the gabbled information was cut short as the door was opened by a maid. 'Oh, Mr Richard! You've arrived. They're expecting you in the lounge.'

'Lounge, eh?' Richard laughed, some of his nervousness dissipating as he and Alice stepped inside a spacious strongly-lit cream-coloured vestibule with walls displaying several geometric paintings and two angular tables each bearing a very expensive looking piece of sculpture with a white telephone on one. Beyond that, there were no other decorations. It looked stark, unlived-in, a showpiece. Alice felt her insides shrivel like a prune that had been dried too quickly. Richard might be at ease now, but she wasn't.

'They must have high hopes of you, darling,' he was saying as he took off his coat and Derby. 'They've avoided the formalities of the drawing room. I should think so too, after all the effort I went to, to get them to meet you.'

Said innocently enough, Alice felt herself quake all over again at all the cajoling he must have had to put in before they'd even consent to see her, a common working-class girl, for that was what she was, when all was said and done, despite her having held an excellent position in service. All of a sudden her prospects as Richard's wife didn't seem so certain.

It had taken him several months of careful persuasion, she knew that now, to get her this far. She mustn't spoil it. Her stomach gave an even larger churn than it had already been doing. She had a ghastly fear that it could rumble. If it did she knew she would just die, there on the spot. She had a fleeting vision of his parents' expressions becoming as sour as unripe grapes as the liquid gurgling echoed through the silent lounge where she was to be conducted

The vestibule had become a blur before her eyes; she let him help her off with her fur-collared coat, bought for this occasion. He handed everything to the maid who gave a small bob, her arms full, while Alice took off her deep cloche hat and handed that over as well.

Concentrating solely on what she was doing, she hadn't noticed that a door to one side of the wide vestibule had opened until a strong almost strident voice made her start and look up to see a tall woman with shingled blonde hair standing there. She had obviously been observing her, like a tiger, while Alice had been preoccupied with taking off her hat, and there was surprise in her tone at what had been revealed.

'Oh! You're a *fair* girl! Come on, Richard darling, do. You're late and your father's getting fed up. Now come along. Let's meet your lovely Alice. You're right, darling, she is lovely, isn't she?'

The woman, who Alice deduced to be his mother, disappeared through the doorway without waiting, her appearance, and flood of words having taken Alice's breath away.

There followed several weeks of debate between Sir John and Lady Pritchard, both at their home in London and the one at Lyttehill in Surrey where John Pritchard loved to go on occasion, before a decision could be made about Richard's intended. Richard thought she was his intended. His father didn't. His mother merely wondered, her highly active mind churning over all sorts of ideas to settle it all, and not a few thoughts on the diversion to her normal life that might be got out of it.

Not that she didn't have her son's future in mind, but she could see the possible dire results of forbidding him this girl, and she didn't want her enjoyably smooth life disrupted by a family dispute.

At Lyttehill Manor, as Christmas approached, she confronted her husband's continuing adamant opposition to his son's ridiculous whim, her manner as ever light.

'We're going to lose him, John darling, if we forbid him to see this girl. Besides, I like her. She's sweet.'

'So are puppies, even mongrels.'

Margaret gave a little squeak of laughter. 'Oh, John! What an analogy. A mongrel!'

'She's hardly thoroughbred, is she, this . . . Alice? How can you even think of welcoming such a person, a common working girl, sweet as she is, into our family? It's utterly unthinkable and the sooner he gets over this episode the better.'

Margaret's smile had faded. She became serious. 'I mean it, John, when I predict the possibility of us losing Richard. He is desperately in love. Anyone can see that.'

'Then he can fall out of love.'

'How can you expect him to do that? It's not a tap to turn on and off at will.'

'You don't think so?' he challenged in his deep voice. He wasn't a big man in height, but his girth made him appear bigger than he was, his face full to podgy with good living, his attitude authoritative from the continuing success of his industrial empire.

'You don't think so, Margaret?' he repeated, embarking now on a favourite theory of his. He had many theories which he loved to air. 'When someone loses a partner in life, what does it profit them to go on mourning for ever? In time one has to pick up the pieces and get on with life, even find another partner. It's a natural process. If this Alice were to fall down dead, would Richard go on yearning for her? No – he'd have to get on with his life. If a man can do that, he can also apply it to giving up a girl.'

Margaret shook her blonde head, her face, strikingly young for one her age, tight with irritation at this outpouring of cracked philosophy. 'Oh, stop rambling, John. You sound so ridiculous. The difference is that the girl is alive and on this earth and Richard is deeply in love, and I will not have him sneaking off to marry her in the dead of night and you cutting him off without a penny and all that rubbish. I'll not see my only precious son prostrate with misery. Besides . . .'

A cunning smirk spread over her face. A narrow delicate hand came up to touch her cheek with one finger, provocatively. 'She needn't be a disaster. I do like her, John. I really do. I could nurture her. She's halfway there already, with her nice manners, and her speech is impeccable – well, almost.'

'That's no recipe for a decent society marriage,' John grumbled, a little deflated as he always was by his vivacious, overpowering wife, his high-flown logic put down as ramblings. 'If this is another one of your crack-brained schemes, Margaret, remember this time you're playing with Richard's future. We want no *Pygmalion* situations here. Leave that for the stage. It's not real life. Can't be.'

'Would you rather he went off, married against our wishes?' She displayed no frivolity now. 'Because I can guarantee that he will. He can be as stubborn as I, as you, in some things. And this is one of them. For this girl he'll fly in the face of all your threats to disinherit him. We'd lose him, his love, and we'd gain a daughter whether we acknowledged her or not. We are faced with a situation, John, that we have to confront, something we can't dismiss with a flick of a finger. If we can't alter things, then I do have a scheme, John, that will work perfectly. I know it will.'

'I think you're mad. Margaret. Don't you know that we're going to have to face society with her if we let him have his way? Have you thought about that? Knowing they're all gossiping behind our back, poking fun at me for letting my son get married to some scheming little gold-digger.'

'Oh, I don't think she is entirely, dear.'

'Of course she is, and I forbid it.'

'Oh, don't be stuffy. Of course she's overwhelmed by Richard's place in the world. Any girl would be. That's what girls – all those of our standing – get married for, isn't it? Wealth, position, an assured future. What else? It's quite acceptable to people like us. Often love comes a poor fourth. But this girl, this Alice, I could see at first sight that she is head-over-heels in love with him.'

'Love! Marriage is more an alliance between families, to cement things.'

'Old hat, darling! Things are changing. Disinheritance! Richard will call your bluff. That's what love does, dear. Nothing moves it. No, my dear, let me play it my way. I shall make something of this little Alice, and no one will be any the wiser. I know exactly what I am doing.'

'I rather doubt that you do.'

Her laugh was tinkling yet self-assured. 'Just trust me, my dear.' When her mind was set, she always got her way, and this idea in her head was not as hare-brained as he imagined.

Alice didn't spend Christmas with her family. She spent it with Richard's.

'Ain't good enough fer 'er now, I s'ppose,' commented her father.

To which her mother replied: 'It's all new to 'er, luv. Give 'er a little bit of rope. She's spent every Christmas of 'er life with us. Now this one's 'ers, ter be spent with her fiancy – or 'e will be, come the new year, ring an' all. It's only natural she'd want ter spend it with 'im.'

'They could've come 'ere ter spend it.'

At which Mrs Jordan let out a vast rolling laugh. 'What? An' spoil our 'ole Christmas? With 'im 'ere, we'd all be creeping about 'avin' ter mind all our p's an' q's an' frightened to be our nat'ral selves. Better all round fer 'er ter spend 'er Christmas with 'er prospective in-laws. She's goin' ter be something, our Alice. Ain't you pleased at that, Arthur? Ain't you proud of 'er? Don't 'appen ter us all, yer know.'

Arthur rubbed balefully at his pale bristly moustache. 'Yer didn't mind yer p's an' q's with that Amy 'Arrin'ton when she first came 'ere.' He still used their lodger's full name.

Again his wife laughed. 'It was different with 'er, she'd got 'erself down on the same level as us, worse, 'er carryin' another man's baby and not married. No better than she ought ter be then, and all 'er 'oity-toity ways didn't mean a thing. But she's different now, Amy, just as Alice is different, and me fer one – I'm proud of her – of 'em both. I wish Alice well. I wish both of 'em well. So fer Gawd's sake let's stop blessed worrying about Alice an 'ave our usual good time.'

Arthur Jordan sucked at his pipe as he stared into the back room fire above which a garish string of home-made paper chains moved in the rising warm wave of air. 'Thinks she's too good fer us,' he grunted, not having wanted to take in one word she had said, and, leaning forward a little, spat

170

dark tobacco-stained spittle into the burning coals where it sizzled briefly before being consumed by heat.

Now that Amy's first Christmas with the Jordans was two days away, she couldn't prevent her thoughts turning to her own parents, what they would be doing in two days' time. Most likely spending it at home with a good circle of friends, the drawing room the backdrop to a quiet sedate mutter about work and politics, the dissection of other friends, the latest fashion, the latest play, as they stood around holding brandy and cocktail glasses or fastidiously helping themselves to dainty finger food on the side tables.

The children would be taken care of upstairs by nannies and nurses who would have their own Christmas dinner below stairs. A line of private cars would stand in the small gravel drive or outside at the kerb. The house staff and a couple of outside help would move silently among the gathering, hardly noticed. Cigar and perfumed cigarette smoke from ivory holders would drift up to the chandeliers and the latest, not too jazzy, tune would be playing on the radio-gramophone.

Her brother Henry would be home for the Christmas vacation, she imagined. She wondered briefly if he had grown much, but she so seldom saw him that it felt like wondering about a stranger. Kay would be there, probably dressed in pink, perhaps eyeing one of the young sons of Mummy or Daddy's friends, her hopes up. Amy hadn't heard from her at all since leaving. Like her parents, Kay had never written to her, but then girls of fourteen had empty heads. Hers had been empty at that age. She forgave her, but it hurt.

On the Boxing Day the younger set would go off, maybe to see car racing, parties of young people all bundled into motorcars, giggling and making a din. Later they'd go to see a pantomime, cram into the boxes to lean over the parapet and aim cocktail biscuits at the audience below, shrinking back out of sight and spilling champagne all over the seats they lolled in as offended people glanced up. They would poke fun at the theatre staff and ridicule the working classes in the 'gods' with their children howling back in response

171

to the quips and goading of the entertainers, and they would join in the singing as noisily as those they ridiculed, full of champagne and *joie de vivre*.

She missed it all so terribly. For several hours at a time, oh, how she missed it. So much that her heart ached and her stomach felt sick and her limbs felt weak. But there was no chance to share that special aching loneliness with anyone. Vi and Rosy wouldn't understand, at this time of year rushing off up West to ape the rich and to dance in cheap dance halls with boys despite their father trying to stop them. Tom wouldn't understand, he with his pub mates and girls on his mind. Willie was of no consequence, interested only in what halfway decent present would appear in his Christmas stocking. Mrs Jordan wouldn't understand, busy with her cooking ready for Christmas dinner when every relative she had came to sit down at her table. This year it was her turn, next year it would be at some other relative's table. As for Alice, she no longer considered Alice as a confidant, for Alice was too preoccupied with Dicky.

With a deep sigh, Amy turned away from the upstairs window where she had been gazing out but hardly seeing the narrow street below, the houses opposite, their flat faces identical to this, hardly aware of the cold feeble December sunshine that struggled over the rooftops, to peer eerily through a curtain of chimney smoke that one could smell even with the window closed and which yellowed the curtains a week after washing and left a permanent black line around where each window was supposed to open whether it did or not. And with her sigh, she went downstairs to see if there was anything she could do to help Mrs Jordan with her preparations for Christmas.

Christmas Day saw the Jordan house full of relatives as expected. The festivities would spill over into Boxing Day, so Amy gathered, some leaving to sleep at their own homes just a walk away before returning the next day. Many more, too drunk to find the immediate street door let alone their own, would spend what was left of the night finding sleep as best they could, menfolk kipping down on armchairs, two on the sofa, one who couldn't have cared less where he

172

was on the floor with a pillow and blanket, the rest, women and kids, in the main bedroom upstairs.

Those who'd gone home came back for the Boxing Day meal of leftover cold pork and to pick over the cold chicken carcass, with mashed spuds and pickles, followed by the lesser part of the Christmas pudding Mrs Jordan had made weeks before, eaten cold with custard; at teatime consuming as they had the day before bread and butter, shrimps and winkles and the remains of the Christmas cake, washed down by tea and later what was left of the beer and a little sherry.

Most of the fare had come by courtesy of the docks where Tom and his father worked – over the year clever sleight of hand conveyed out the odd tin of this, the odd packet of that, a bottle of something here and there, all for consuming over these two days and on New Year's Eve. The first day back to work after New Year would start the process all over again, carefully, stealthily, not too much, not too blatantly, never get careless, mustn't get caught, as that would mean instant dismissal and no likelihood of ever being taken on again.

Mrs Jordan told Amy she would die several deaths a year for thinking of what would happen if her men did get caught. 'There's some what do,' she said, 'but they're the stupid greedy ones – they ask fer it. There ain't nothing stupid about my Tom and my Arthur. They're good providers and Gawd knows we need a little providing for. They're good workers. Trusted.'

So Christmas Day saw the Jordans and all their relatives – Amy couldn't tell one from another, whose sister, brother, old aunt or uncle, cousin, niece or nephew was who – living like lords, the house near to bursting with them, eating, drinking, singing, laughing uproariously at every seamy joke, taking turns to entertain each other. There was no worry about disturbing the neighbours, who came in to share the fun if they hadn't a party of their own going. These two days of their working lives were reserved for themselves, the next being the Easter, Whitsun and summer bank holidays when a trip to Southend was sometimes on the books

173

although it hadn't been this year. Perhaps because of her presence.

Throughout the Christmas party Amy had sat at the end of one of the hard scaffold boards that had been ranged around two walls of the back room, supported on beer crates, the same in the front room where the bed had been curtained off for the children to sleep as they grew tired, all the softer chairs reserved for the older members of this, she'd discovered, vast family.

She had sat near the door of the back room for air in the fast growing airless confinement of cheap cigarette, cigar, pipe smoke and bodily fumes pressing back down on everyone from where it had all wafted up to the ceiling like a party all of its own and just as congested as the bodies beneath. Now and again she had wended her way through the busy crowded kitchen where Mrs Jordan and those of her relatives who wished to help made sandwiches while men came out to pour beer, and wandered into the concrete back yard with its dustbin and ramshackle wooden outside wc and its tiny strip of sooty soil meant to hold plants. It seldom did because cats came gleefully over the fence to piddle and shit in it. The soil stank. The back yard smelled of it, but even so it was to some extent better than the fug indoors.

Boxing Day evening found her repeating her exercise, glad to stand in the back yard with a slight chill breeze moving the tainted air away from her to adjoining yards. Alone for a while, she listened to the sounds of the East End celebrating Christmas: muffled by doors and windows closed against the night chill, singing coming from houses a few doors away; someone some way off ringing a bicycle bell, another erratically blowing a discordant trumpet; a dog or two barking – no sound from the cats who would withhold their celebrations for when people had gone to bed, whenever that would be.

Behind her the raucous bellowing of the Jordans' party made her small space out here seem silent, another planet. Amy folded her arms across her breast and gazed up into the shrouded night sky. But a sound came from just behind her right shoulder. She turned to see Tom had come to

174

join her. They hadn't spoken much these last few days with all the things she'd been doing to help his mother prepare for Christmas. Not that they ever spoke to each other all that much.

Now he said, 'You should be wearing a coat or something out 'ere. It's a bit on the chilly side.'

'I'm warm enough,' she told him, gazing up again at the sky which should have been full of stars if smoke from every chimney in London had not obliterated them.

She felt a light touch on her left shoulder, and realised Tom's arm had stolen across to rest on it. For an instant she wanted to let herself lean against him, but continued to hold herself stiff. Was he taunting her? She'd make a fool of herself by relaxing against him, her guard lowered.

She began to ease away, very slightly. 'It is a bit chilly. I'd best go in.'

The hand on her left shoulder tightened. 'Not yet. I've 'ad enough of in there fer a while. Let's just stand 'ere, quiet, enjoy a bit of fresh air.'

'Fresh air!' she laughed suddenly.

He didn't join in. She felt him looking down at her and turned her head to look up at him, seeing his face lit one side by the glow from the uncurtained kitchen window. His eyes were dark, his lips tight, his nose a strong line.

'I know we ain't much 'ere. Not ter you. We 'ave ter live among 'undreds of 'ouses with back yards what stink of cats and dustbins. We never 'ad the privileges your sort 'ave, but we do 'ave our own sort of pride. We 'elp each other and we don't let down our gels what get themselves inter trouble . . .'

Amy gasped. 'How dare you! How bloody dare you!'

The grip on her shoulder became even stronger as she made to escape. 'I'm trying to tell you something . . .'

'I've no intention of listening.'

'That's why we never turned you away,' he grated on, his words clipped and hurried. 'No more'n we'd turn our own away. We've taken you in, put up with you fer nearly a year, and if you need, we'll 'ave yer fer as long as yer need a roof over yer silly stuck-up 'ead. But me, I've 'ad enough. I ain't prepared to stand your bloody standoffish attitude a moment longer. It's driving me crazy. So . . . come 'ere!'

She felt herself pulled towards him with such force that it drove the breath out of her. His arms came around her, drawing her in even tighter. She took a great breath to cry out, but his lips were on hers, a crushing weight on her mouth. There was no fear, only outrage, her brain screaming again and again: how dare you ... how dare you! But her voice was paralysed. And even as she struggled instinctively against the embrace, so her arms began to feel weak and all she could do was to lift them up for support on his wide shoulders, to wrap them around his strong neck, and her knees all but failing her, she let herself be kissed.

He must have sensed her altered movements for the embrace lessened and she heard him murmur, 'I love you, Amy. Love you ...'

Something inside her said, 'I love you too.' And then she realised her lips had actually formed the words, her voice conveying it to him before he crushed her to him again in a second long, long kiss, she clinging to him with all her strength quite suddenly renewed and fierce with all the need for love of any sort that had been building up inside her these long lonely months.

Chapter Thirteen

There was no controlling Alice's exuberance as she displayed her ring again and again to any of her family unfortunate enough to come within range.

It was the first Saturday in January, Richard deeming it appropriate to make the new year of 1927 significant for Alice and her future with him. She had gone along wholeheartedly, agreeing to wait those long few weeks since his parents' eventual, to her almost surprising, blessing on his choice of a future mate.

'Just look at it, Mum. Look how it flashes.' Taking herself yet again to the back room window where the feeble January afternoon sunlight could just about catch it, she fluttered the ring gracing her engagement finger so that the band of five huge diamonds could flash and glint its rainbow of colours back into her mother's eye and her own. She felt herself continually mesmerised by each and every expensively blinding pinpoint of light. 'I never dreamed I'd ever own such a beautiful thing.'

Dutifully, Grace looked yet again, smiling indulgently and a little wistfully. She had never even had an engagement ring. Money had been more needed to set up home in two rented rooms all those years ago, and her wedding band had been good enough for her. It now lived on her finger embedded into it like a piece of her own flesh, immovable, unremovable, dark and rubbed by work.

'Very nice, luv,' she said sweetly and carried on with her afternoon dusting, which needed doing every hour let alone every day because of the London air thick with soot, until it was time to start on Arthur and Tom's supper.

They would be in well after dark. By then the fog would have settled down again as it had for several days, thinning just enough at midday to allow an hour of weak sunshine to filter through before closing down as the sun became lost behind the houses opposite.

The fog which settled in at night muffled the sounds of the river yet made them all the more noticeable, if ghostly: the long and solemn deep mooing of an ocean-going liner inching up to a berth if the tide was flowing; the lonely banshee wail of smaller freighters, the high disembodied hoot of tugs feeling their way through the peasouper that rose like a spirit from the water to spread itself slowly throughout London. November was the worst month for fogs, but January could come a close second. Grace's two wage earners would be late home for their supper and Alice would have to wait to inflict her ring on them.

Meanwhile Alice buttonholed her two immediately envious sisters and her younger brother when he came home after a day of racing through the streets getting rid of his papers and going back time after time to pick up more from the dropping-off point. Saturday was always a full, busy day for him, he was tired and his mind more taken up with the hope that this evening Dad would be home in time to take him to see a boxing match at the Stepney Social Club, than to stand gazing at some ring, cheap or expensive.

And of course she buttonholed Amy too.

'What do you really think of it?' she urged, once again acting as though she herself was still uncertain of its beauty when Amy quietly smiled her approval, having already twice expressed good wishes for her future. 'It really is too divine, but you don't think it just a teeny bit too ostentatious?'

Amy felt her mouth sour at these silly expressions Alice persisted in using as though needing everlasting practice for her new life ahead. This new brashness did not suit her.

'It's just right for you,' Amy said with more connotations behind it than she intended, only just managing to avoid adding, 'The way you've changed lately,' saying instead, 'It's a beautiful ring.'

'It is, isn't it? It cost Richard the earth. That's how much he thinks of me.'

'I expect it did, and I expect he does.' It was hard to keep the malice she still bore him out of her remark. She actually heard it creeping in, but Alice hadn't even noticed.

'But he's got pots of money anyway. And his family are so nice. His father is a bit grumpy, but his mother ... she has asked me to call her Margaret rather than Mother. They're giving us an engagement party this evening and Margaret has it all arranged, outside caterers, a four-piece band, she has been sending out invitations all over the place this week, and I shall be meeting all sorts of rich and important people. She's been schooling me on how to present and conduct myself and all the social niceties. She's been wonderful these last few weeks. I wouldn't have believed someone could be so nice. And as an engagement present and because Richard is twenty-one now, she has persuaded his father to give him the deeds of their house in Surrey. It's in a darling little village, only a stone's throw from London. I shall be lady of the manor.'

'You're very lucky.'

'Oh, I am! Margaret has really taken me under her wing. She will personally be presenting me to everyone who matters. It has to be done just right, she says. She has even concocted a past life for me. Isn't it a scream? Our little secret, she says – a bit of a joke, and she wants me to play along with it, because it will make everything so much easier for me to enter into society. Which I know I have to as Richard's future wife. I don't mind going along with it, of course. I'm supposed to have been brought up in India and educated in England, but my parents in India are dead ...'

'Alice!' Horror shot a stinging arrow through Amy's breast. 'Your parents are *here*. You can't do that! It's like tempting fate.'

'It's only a joke. People will forget once we're married.'

'It's not a joke. It's cruel. It's not nice at all. How do you think they would feel if they knew what you're playing at?'

'I'm not telling them. I shall still come to see them. I'm not deserting them. They are my parents. The ones in India are just fictitious. It's just for the time being, Amy.'

179

'And then you'll let it be known who you are?'

'Who I am?' Alice's face fell. Her voice wavered. Tears began to fill her eyes, the wonderful ring forgotten. 'I'm me. I hope I'll always be me.'

'A girl from Stepney.'

'No . . . I mean . . .' Her voice caught in a sob, tears almost splashed from them. 'You're being horrible! You're jealous because you don't have what I shall have, and you could have had it if you hadn't been so stupid!'

Amy stood very still upon Alice's headlong rush from the room to seek a quiet place to cry. Alice couldn't guess how near to the truth she had come with those last words, and the truth was now becoming an agonised pounding in Amy's chest, bringing tears to her own eyes but slowly, so slowly, unlike Alice's flowing torrent. She could never go back. She could never, never go back.

'We ain't ter be invited then?' Arthur remarked after being shown the ring, his daughter running upstairs again to get ready for the celebrations in Chelsea to be given in her and Richard's honour.

Richard was calling at eight o'clock and apparently she wanted to be ready so as to run straight out with him the moment his knock came at the door. It all pointed strongly to an embarrassment on her part that he might be expected to come in to receive her parents' clumsy and unrefined congratulations, to see them in all their impoverished glory.

Nor was Arthur blind to that point as he sat by the warm fire listening to the sounds of hurried preparations overhead while he waited for his and Tom's supper to be put on the table.

'Ain't good enough to be invited, that's wot.'

'I don't suppose there was time,' Grace said, a steaming plate held by both hands protected by a gravy-stained tea-cloth. The plate had a ring of dried gravy where it had been steaming for the last hour or two over simmering saucepans of water. Now the house smelt of the food kept warm for the men on their return home.

'Anyway, what do the likes of us want ter go traipsin' over

to there for at short notice?' She plonked the hot plate down on the tablecloth and made her way into the kitchen for Tom's plate, her voice going up a pitch or two, lowering again as she returned. 'We ain't got the togs fer one thing, an' fer another we ain't got the money ter waste on dressin' up – not fer them sort, not ter make ourselves a laughin' stock. Us an' them don't mix, and I'm more content not worrying about it.'

'She seems to manage it all right.' Arthur jerked a thumb ceilingward where Alice could be heard chattering to Amy, her earlier pique forgotten.

'Well, that's as it may be,' Grace said briskly. 'Come ter the table, you two, before it gets cold again. Twice warmed'll make it 'orrible. Once is enough.'

While Tom put away with a brisk rustle the *Evening News* he'd been reading, Arthur knocked out his pipe in the grate, put it to one side and spat into the fire above which the home-made chain of Christmas decorations, soon to be taken down, hung too heavy with the soot of three weeks to move in the rising heat. The two of them dragged up chairs and fell on their food like starving men, hungry as they were after a hard day's loading in the docks.

'I just 'ope,' Arthur said with his mouth full, 'she knows what she's doin'.'

It was April, and hardly credible to Amy that she had been with the Jordans for more than a year. This time last year she had been well out in front, unable any longer to wear the slim-fitting dresses that were in fashion. Incredible that she still wore the same ones that had grown too tight for her at the time, realising she would never be asked home again and no longer daring to spend what money she had on more high fashion. Now she made do with what she had, just as everyone around here did.

The time seemed to have flown, yet it seemed a lifetime away, those days when she'd return after some wild party somewhere or other to a large sedate well-kept home in Bayswater to be waited on by staff.

Where had her intentions gone, borne on the back of what she, a gently brought up girl of an upper-class culture, had first encountered in this most dismal poverty-stricken part of London? She really had thought it only a matter of time before she'd return to her rightful place or go off seeking her own life, perhaps become a businesswoman, though how, she had never thought to contemplate.

Such thoughts did return from time to time. There often seemed to be two of her – the one wanting to escape, be again what she had been, and the one who found herself totally incapable of taking the step, preferring to remain in what had become familiar surroundings, much as say a life prisoner might find the spartan cell he'd once hated becoming his world, rather than to voluntarily cast herself adrift into the unknown.

If she had been told to pack up and leave, she would have. Perhaps that was what she had needed, that large push from behind. But it had never happened, and so she stayed on and on, February becoming March, and March April. It had all become so static.

After that kiss in the back yard at Christmas, she and Tom had never been alone together again. She had quite expected him to ask her out, but he hadn't. What she might have done to drive him off, she couldn't think. Nor could she approach him with it. A somewhat shaky connection had been made between them at Christmas, no more than that, and it seemed he was content with that.

Tonight, a quiet drizzly night after several days of rain-bearing wind, Amy sat alone in the house but for Willie, long since tucked up warm in bed in the front room with a night-light and a comic, and no doubt asleep over it by now. His parents had gone off down to the Stepney Working Man's Club, a Saturday night ritual they rarely missed. Vi and Rosy were out, Rosy with a couple of girls from where she worked. Vi had a boyfriend now, had been going out with him for a few months and looked as if she might settle. He was a fair gangling youth, his face given to erupting every so often, but underneath that he was quite good-looking, except, his hats always looked too large for his head and his collar never tight enough. But Vi was in love with him, so Vi never noticed the ill-fitting headgear or the wobbly collar. He worked in a bakery, learning the trade while delivering bread and cake on his bike and in between sweeping and cleaning up after the master baker.

Alice was spending the weekend with Richard's parents. She spent the best part of her weeks there too, hardly ever here. She'd given up her job in Lipton's dairy, apparently being modestly helped financially by her fiancé's mother. The date of the wedding was set for the second Saturday in August. Invitations did not seem to have been sent out as yet, at least the Jordans hadn't received any and nor had Amy.

Where Tom was this evening, she had no idea. He never announced where he was going. Out with the boys no doubt. Or some girl. Again came that pang of jealousy she was wont to feel on visualising him with whoever she might be. She quickly got up from the sofa where she had been browsing through a copy of *Woman's Own*, no longer daring to afford, nor wanting the poignant nostalgia, of magazines like *Vogue*, and turned the cracked knob on the little square wireless on the shelf by Mr Jordan's armchair. The result was a squeak and a crackle with some tinny dance music behind it, hardly discernible. The thing had been on its last legs for months, Mr Jordan's tinkering with it in the evenings doing it more harm than good. Turning it off, she went back to the sofa, but then heard the sound of someone's key in the lock.

The clock on the mantelshelf over the fireplace showed nine fifteen, too early for the girls to come back, and Mr and Mrs Jordan never left his working man's social club until the last member had gone, he talking work with other men, and she gossiping with their wives on the latest price of cabbages and whose kid had gone down sick.

Still standing in the centre of the room, Amy waited, frowning, listening. The door opened, closed; someone was taking off their coat and hat in the passage, shaking it free of April drizzle, hanging it up on one of the crowded hooks by the door.

She knew it was Tom even before his muscular frame came to fill the doorway of the back room. Even so, she said, 'Oh, it's you,' as though surprised by his appearance. She stooped and retrieved the *Woman's Own* from the place she'd left it, the place he usually sat by habit. 'I didn't expect you home so early.'

He ran a hand over his dark hair, still a little flattened by the trilby he'd been wearing. The damp night air and an earlier lick of brilliantine had also helped stick it together and his action in lifting the natural wave it possessed when not slicked down had an unexpectedly self-conscious aspect to it.

'Didn't go out yerself, then?' he said, quite unnecessarily.

She gave a faintly bitter laugh. 'Where is there to go? I'm content enough here.'

He hadn't come to sit down. He still stood a foot from the doorway. He seemed on edge, unnatural, for a moment a stranger in his own home, uneasy. 'You should try to make some friends.' Even his words were stilted, jerky.

'I'm happy as I am, truly.'

Still he hadn't moved. 'It's not good for yer.'

Amy moved a little in an attempt to break the tension. She put the magazine she had picked up onto another chair, not looking at him. 'So what brought you home so early? Did your date stand you up?' Immediately she had said it she wished she hadn't, it sounded so acrid.

'I stood 'er up. I got there, the picture palace, and I saw 'er standing there waitin' and I just couldn't go over to 'er.'

'Had you been out with her before?'

'No. It was just someone I met a week ago, just made a date wiv, something ter do. She wasn't bad.'

'But you stood her up.'

'Yes.'

'Why?'

'I don't know. I just couldn't go over there. I kept thinkin' of . . . I kept wonderin' about you, 'ere, at 'ome, not goin' out anywhere, not seein' anyone, not 'avin' any friends.'

'I told you, I'm quite all right.'

'No you ain't. You're nowhere near all right. You don't ever smile or laugh or chatter on like most girls do. You're stiff and formal even when you try not to be. You're like a cardboard doll.'

She stared at him now, unable to reply, but words were flowing from him in a torrent. 'I've watched yer an' watched

184

yer, an' I've wanted ter tell yer to unbend, be natural. Christmas when I kissed yer, I thought then that yer might turn inter somethink real at last, but yer didn't. Yer never said another word ter me after that.'

'You didn't say another word to *me*,' she burst out, suddenly angry with him. 'How can I *unbend* as you call it, when you're totally unapproachable?'

'Not me!' His voice a little raised, he moved towards her for the first time, just a fraction. 'You. It's you what's unapproachable. 'Ow d'yer think I can approach *you* when yer still be'ave like the stuck-up, upper-class miss yer were when yer came ter stay wiv us? Fer Gawd sake, Amy! I ain't made of wood. That night in the yard, you said you loved me. I know you said it. I 'eard yer. But you made no move ter show it afterwards, and I was left wonderin' if yer'd really said it or not, and I'd just imagined it. So I said to meself, right, sod 'er! If she wants ter be the toffee-nosed little madam, then sod 'er. But . . .' there was a muscle twitching on the left side of his face, just above the corner of his mouth, and he faltered to a stop.

Amy felt tears sting her eyes although they remained unshed. She stood facing him. 'I can't help what I am, Tom. I can't fling myself into someone's arms, just like that. I did say what you heard out in the yard. And I meant it. And I still . . .'

It was her turn to trail off. How could she be the first to do the approaching? A girl didn't throw herself at a man and not look cheap. And what if he backed off again, if she made a mess of it? Instinct told her to remain where she was, that a false move now would kill any chance of their ever coming together, and suddenly she wanted so much for them to come together, to be one.

She stood very still, her eyes imploring him to make that first move. If time could be said to stand still, it appeared to do so now. The clock ticked on, a sharp ticking far too fast for its bulk, but it didn't seem to be registering time. In the fireplace a coal collapsed with a faint hiss of sparks, yet there seemed to be no movement at all in the room. Faintly in the distance a church clock chimed the half hour, a pale shadow of Big Ben. Perhaps it was that faint chiming which made him move. For a moment he seemed to lean towards her, and she wasn't sure if she should respond. She didn't. He straightened up abruptly.

'Christ!'

He was turning away towards the door, and Amy realised that she had ruined the crucial moment by not taking his cue and making some movement of her own. She was galvanised into action.

'Tom! I love you! Don't go!'

Her voice sounded like a wail, not at all like hers. She wasn't aware of him turning back to her but found herself in his arms, being crushed by them. She was sobbing, and he lifted her head to kiss her mouth, wet with her own tears she hadn't known she was shedding. They were down on the sofa, lying together on it in a fierce embrace she could hardly ever have thought possible between them, she crushed against the back and he lying over her. Thoughts flew through her head that here he would make her his and she wanted that. But instead, the embrace slackened after a while, and he sat up, bringing her up with him to cuddle her against his broad chest. She let him hold her so, lying weakly against him as though they had really completed the act of love. But it didn't matter that they hadn't. Being held to his chest was enough. They had become one in other ways.

For a long while they sat together, she cuddled in his arms, her head on his chest, both of them gazing into the fire. Then he eased her gently from him.

'Cuppa tea?' he asked.

Amy almost laughed, her lips curling at the edges of their own accord. Like a married couple, came the fleeting thought. Here would be no mad romance, but a gentle coming together, an acceptance of each other, and a life that would go on and on in the simplest way with a knowledge of love for each other. Behind her lay a life she never wished to have again. Yes, she would have liked to have money, marry into money, suffer none of the financial worries common sense told her would be her lot for the rest of her life, what was it they said – better be rich and unhappy than poor and unhappy? But suddenly all she wanted was to be with Tom, for better or worse and so on. With him beside her, she knew she could face whatever trouble would come their way and share with him whatever good times they'd have.

She smiled up at him. 'I couldn't think of anything better right now than a cup of tea.'

She let him get up, staying where she was as though still leaning against him. Her mind was a soft woollen blanket, her body warm within it. From the kitchen came the sound of the kettle being filled, the gas stove rattling as the kettle was placed on it, the light click of cups being put onto saucers, the tinkle of a teaspoon being laid beside them. The kettle began to boil quickly. She heard it die as the water was poured into a teapot. Then suddenly Tom was popping his dark handsome head around the corner of the doorway.

''Ow much sugar do you 'ave? I've forgotten.'

'Just one,' she answered, almost politely.

He stood there, looking at her, a teaspoon poised in his hand, the spoon looking tiny against the lean muscular fingers.

'What?' she queried, her eyebrows raised. 'What's the matter?'

'I just wondered . . . Like to come ter Southend with me, next Sunday?'

Amy's laugh must have made the next-door neighbours beyond the thin party wall jump out of their skins.

'I'd love to. Oh, Tom, I'd love to.'

No need for expensive five-diamond rings, fancy engagement parties, she was his girl and he was her beau, and she felt she had been proposed to, was even now engaged to Tom Jordan, the best man any girl could wish for.

It was wonderful sitting in a deckchair on the deep yellow, almost brown sand stained by the rich mud the Thames brought down to its estuary to distribute over the North Sea bed. Her nostrils filled with the ozone, as Tom called it, redolent of Thames mud and seaweed as well as vinegar from the cockle stalls and frying from the fish and chip shops. It was a smell she had never experienced before. She had never visited Southend before, had not known how else the ordinary people enjoyed their Sundays apart from littering the London parks and the Serpentine with their families and their rubbish. Now she was part of them, and Southend was an experience she found herself enjoying for all the hubbub going on around her.

Tom had said next Sunday, but he had meant the next day, today. And the day had dawned with as pure a blue-washed sky as any June morning. Warm too, growing warmer by the minute, the two weeks of wet April weather dismissed entirely from every mind, Southend's beaches crowded with day-trippers, families, some with their backs to the sea wall for that extra bit of sunshine, some behind breakwaters for that extra bit of shade.

People were paddling at the very edge of the water where it had become sufficiently warm to be tempting enough to bare toes; fathers with shoes and socks off and trousers rolled up as far as they would go just below the knees, mothers with their unfashionably long skirts held modestly up, stockings off. There were young girls with no need to hold theirs up, splashing young men who laughed and cringed and wondered if they should safely splash them back.

There were children in bathing costumes, squealing and screaming at the water's edge or, just out of reach of the tiny lapping wavelets, bent over silently intent on building sandcastles, spades as busy as those of navvies, or running down to the water for bucketfuls of sea for their moat, frustrated when the water in it disappeared into the sand and all the time keeping wary eyes on aggressive or exuberant contesters lest they come stamping on their laboriously built collection of sand pies that constituted their castle. There were young people in bathing hats and costumes, tentatively wading out, daring the piercing cold of water nowhere near yet warmed by summer heat, their arms well up, their breath driven from their bodies by the chill, the young males gritting their teeth as they showed how unaffected they were by the cold, while the young females gasped and called out to be helped and not to go too far out for all this resort was the safest for swimming that anyone could wish for. Further out a few round blobs among the gently rocking rowing boats tied to buoys denoted the swimming-capped heads of the hardy who would break ice to swim if they desired.

Amy sat drawing the sun to her face and watched it all. When they had arrived, the tide had been well out but already on its way in. A strange silence had hung in the air as she'd wandered down to the mud-line, the strong smell of the mud over which seagulls were quietly picking wafting up to make her wrinkle her nose and deign to touch it with her toe, since Tom had persuaded her to take off her shoes and stockings as everyone else did. Apart from the low babble of conversation from those already arrived on the beach she could faintly hear the mud plopping, a strange sound which Tom said was cockleshells closing and blood worms pushing the mud up through their gut. She'd hastily ceased any attempt to feel the mud with her toe.

Now the sea was in and the world had come alive in appreciation of it. Tom had taken her on the twopenny bus ride further up the prom well north of the pier that jutted out a mile into the estuary, the longest pier in the world, and where the *London Belle* had put them down with all the other trippers, past the gasworks and the funfair, to where the beaches were just a little more sedate. Even so they were crowded, the prom above full of humanity strolling up and down, licking ice cream and eating chips and half-melting chocolate bars, men in shirtsleeves and braces, women in light dresses brought out quickly for this one sudden hot Sunday, taking full advantage of it.

It was all a far cry from the boat train to Dover to take the cross-Channel steamer, then on to Provence and friends Daddy knew there. For a second the memory brought back a poignancy which she hastily shrugged off. Those days were behind her. They belonged to someone else. To combat the lingering after-feeling, she thought again of the little *London Belle* crowded to the rails with ordinary Londoners making the most of this one day of sunshine before going back to work the next morning.

Amy wondered if Tom had been able to afford the two pleasure steamer tickets, but hadn't dared offer to give him part of it and destroy his pride. She was finding herself weighing up all she did with him lest she inadvertently made

189

herself seem to be better than he – the very thing that had kept them apart all this time. It was hard work. But to destroy it now with a carelessly spoken word . . .

It was however Tom who broached it first, surprising and alarming her as she sat in her deckchair and he sat on the sand, either preferring it or finding it beyond his pocket to hire a second deckchair, she didn't dare enquire.

He had already paid out for a glass of lemonade for her, a packet of fruit jellies and an ice cream for them both. They'd had a pot of tea on the beach, he bringing it down on a tray after spending half an hour in a queue for it. They had eaten the cheese and pickle sandwiches, a banana and a piece of cake each and drank the flask of strong tea made up by his mother who had been absolutely overjoyed by their decision. She obviously fully approved of it, judging by her broad smiling face as she had waved them off that morning.

Quite out of the blue he turned his head to look up at her to startle her by saying, 'I expect all this is a bit different to what yer used ter do.'

It was as though he had been reading her thoughts as he sat there on the sand beside her, his back against the frame of her chair, his knees drawn up, his arms wrapped about them, his feet bare, his eyes, the colour of the sky, staring across to the Kent shoreline in the distance. Now and again he had pointed out the different seagoing ships that passed almost seeming not to move until one looked at them a moment later to see that they had. Then suddenly came this remark. She was taken off-guard.

'Yes, very different,' was all she could find to say on the spur of that moment, almost terrified that this might be the wrong reply.

He nodded solemnly. 'I wish I could afford ter take yer some place more expensive, grand, give yer a slap-up meal in a posh restaurant.'

'I don't want a slap-up meal in a posh restaurant.' She was aware of her refined accent, wished for a moment that she could ape the flat Cockney vowels he used, the dropped aitches and t's. But she couldn't. She felt almost ashamed

190

of sounding them. She was making him feel small, inadequate, and she didn't want to do that.

'I'm enjoying every minute of today,' she said hurriedly. 'I wouldn't want it any other way.'

'A bit of a novelty for yer.'

'No ... well, yes. And I have loved it, being with you. Please Tom, don't let any differences come between us. All that, my old life, it's behind me. I don't yearn for it any more. I just want to be here, with you. I don't want to go backward.'

He nodded and said no more, but she knew with a sense of relief that he was content, that she had put him at his ease, though how, with the few words she had said, she wasn't sure.

The sun had begun to sink behind a rising veil of cloud over London, rapidly losing heat. A faint mist rose over houses behind the beach and the marshes beyond. The thin clouds had a yellow look to them. Tomorrow it would probably rain, but today had been compensation enough for a week of rain. People were packing up. Soon they too must go, to catch the boat back. Tom had already risen and begun packing up. Together they picked up bags and wrapping paper, closed the deckchair and hauled it up the beach to where a man stood beside a growing pile in front of a line of beach huts. Together they mounted the steps up to the promenade, joined those all walking in the same direction, homeward. They'd not said much to each other the whole day beyond odd comments, happy merely to soak up the sunshine and sea air, and of course the matter of her feelings on her life.

Amy had put her hat back on, a light beige straw cloche she'd bought when she had first come to live with the Jordans. She wore one of her summer dresses brought with her at the time, one of four she had packed, this one cream with pink flowers, a little out of date now compared with the standard she used to set herself but today she felt really smart in it. They stood at the bus stop waiting for the one to take them back to the pier and the *London Belle*.

Suddenly Tom said, bending towards her: 'What yer said

this afternoon. Did yer mean it, that yer wouldn't want ter go back to what yer once 'ad?'

'Yes, I meant it,' she whispered fervently. Around her people were milling, jabbering, occupied by their own business. 'I meant every word.'

'Then, would yer marry me?'

Her breath all but knocked from her body by the surprise, she heard her own voice replying. It said, 'Yes.'

Chapter Fourteen

There were other outings with Tom that summer, Sundays going off back to Southend or rowing on the Serpentine in London or picnics at one or other of the East End's favourite bits of countryside – Epping Forest or Victoria Park which was like an enclosed bit of countryside in itself wherever the full-leaved trees hid the houses surrounding it. An evening or two a week going to the local pictures – he couldn't afford West End picture palaces or its theatres unless they stood in the queue taking a chance for the cheapest seats. But that always brought back memories of arriving at those same theatres to pile out in giggling noisy groups from taxis or a friend's car. Where were those friends now? It was as though they had never been. Such memories always carried an unexpected sting she'd rather not endure so she mostly declined any offer of going. Why torment herself when she had all she wanted in Tom?

It had taken her a while for the reply she had given him on that first visit to Southend to sink in. For a long time afterwards she wondered how she could have been so carried away as to commit herself so easily without giving proper thought to its implications. Instinct had told her almost immediately to retract that breathless 'yes', but even then it had been too late, and had grown later with every indecisive moment of delay. It had been one thing to enter into a life with the Jordan family knowing, no matter how vaguely, that she could leave and find another life of her own if it got too much for her; quite another to commit herself out of hand to becoming Tom's wife, cutting off every avenue of escape.

There was no going back. How could she put him down by retracting now? And she did want to marry him. For that she must sacrifice thoughts of choice. Her heart still cried out 'yes', she would share his life with him, and she staunchly ignored the brain that repeated and repeated, 'You're being foolish. It's not for you.'

Of course there would be a long wait before they could be married. Tom had to save. They would need a place to live, a modest couple of rooms, rented, with a down payment to find, money needed to furnish it, not to speak of the cost of the wedding, that too essentially modest when it came. At least a year of saving was necessary.

'Perhaps next April,' he suggested hopefully, and becoming romantic, 'the month I proposed to yer and you accepted,' and kissed her, his muscular frame smothering her slim one until her whole being cried out to be taken by him. But he never carried it further, as though holding her body in reverence to walk to the altar when the time came, untouched by what he obviously saw as mere lust.

'Yer too precious ter me to be treated like that,' he'd say when she pressed him to kiss her more fervently, to really make love to her and relieve the aching need of love.

At such times it was hard to wait for him to save up for their marriage. To perhaps bring the date forward, she had suggested using the money she had in the bank, now dwindled to around a hundred and eighty pounds, a fortune to some, rather alarming to her if she dwelled on it too much. And to think she had once looked upon such a sum as hardly enough to keep her for a fortnight, always assured of more if she needed it. She was indeed now nearly as poor as any of them around here, unless she one day swallowed her pride and went back to her parents cap in hand. But she would never do that. Not now. So what little was left of it must be conserved, yet for Tom she offered it readily. But he wouldn't hear of it.

'It would be like a sort of wedding dowry,' she explained. 'I want to play my part too.'

But he had frowned and waved it away. 'The day I take

194

money off me own fiancée will be the day I'll 'ang me 'ead in shame.' And he wasn't a man to allow himself ever to be shamed, she knew that and loved him for it. Not like that little worm Dicky Pritchard who'd let her give herself trustingly to him, and then, scared out of his wits, had shirked his responsibilities. Alice was welcome to him. She had become quite high and mighty, the Jordans seeing very little of her these days as though she were embarrassed by them.

An invitation to her wedding did finally arrive. Very late, almost as though an afterthought, it included only the immediate family, her parents and her brothers and sisters, and Amy of course.

It meant a hurried chase around for Mrs Jordan to get herself an outfit as cheaply as possible, Mr Jordan only needing to get his best suit – by the look of it at least twelve years old – 'out of moffballs' as he said.

Vi and Rosy were excited, though Vi complained long and loud about her Fred, the gangling youth whom she now seemed set to marry eventually, not being invited. The two girls bought bright dress material and cut and stitched frantically, at the same time bemoaning the lack of invitation to be one of their now posh sister's bridesmaids.

Willie shrugged and expressed a wish that he could crawl off into the earth rather than have to mix with a load of rotten stuck-up blokes he didn't know or care about all dressed in Eton suits and damned silly top'ats, and hoped he wouldn't be expected to dress up like a bloody dog's dinner, and was sharply told off by his mother for swearing.

Mrs Jordan herself went very quiet about it all, the lack of her normal loquaciousness very marked, and got on with her preparations, such as they were, in readiness to attend her eldest daughter's wedding.

'Yer can't blame the girl fer wantin' everythink nice and orderly an' well done,' was the only remark she'd stretch to. 'I'm pleased fer 'er, doin' so well fer 'erself.'

Tom had different ideas on it, refusing the invitation outright.

'I've thought about it and I shan't be going,' he said, startling Amy with his decision as they walked home on the Saturday evening before the great day from the tiny picture palace in the Mile End Road, their nearest. 'She don't want me there. She don't really want none of us. I ain't about to embarrass her by going.'

Her arm threaded through his, Amy glanced up at him. 'But you must go.' A week before the wedding was a bit late for him to get all hoity-toity about it. 'She's your sister. You won't embarrass her. You will if you don't go. Tom, you're as good as any guest who'll be there.'

Lately he had been making great efforts to improve himself, mostly his way of speaking. It was her influence, Amy knew. Ironic really, for while she did her best to modify her own upper-class accents which sometimes she now caught herself becoming aware of as if through the ears of others, so he was doing his best to hang on to his aitches and not drop his t's in the middle of a word – butter instead of bu''er and like words, even taking trouble to stress the 'ing' at the end of those words that needed it.

He would correct himself mid-word, which in an odd unexpected way, one which Amy hated when she considered it, seemed to lessen him as a man, a proud man, and make of him instead a shuffling illiterate fool, and Tom was no fool. She wanted to shout from the housetops that he was no fool. She wanted to feel proud of him. Instead she found herself cringing every time he made a correction. Would attending this wedding make him study his speech even more, laying more rather than less emphasis on his common upbringing, making him look a fool, embarrass him impossibly, and herself too? She could see the thinking behind his decision; knew his thoughts were for her as well as himself and had nothing to do with bitterness towards his sister who had done so well marrying into money.

The knowledge restored her briefly-shredded pride in him. Not many men would own up to a failing, if it could be called such. Even so she wanted him beside her at this wedding. She didn't fancy having to face some of her old friends who would undoubtedly be there, finding herself making up some story to explain her long absence from the scene. With Tom beside her she could face them squarely, announce him as her fiancé, and to hell with what they thought. Alone, she would be lost.

'I need you with me, Tom.'

He looked down at her, his hand gave hers a little squeeze. 'Yer don't 'ave ... have to go either.'

He was right, she didn't have to go. Why put herself through all that pain which would surely arise if she did – pain of what? Misgivings. She hoped not. But there was that risk, she felt it now – something of the old life drawing her to go, to test herself, see if she could survive being thrown back into that old life or not.

'I have to,' she told him. 'I need to.'

She wanted to add, 'Alice is my friend. She was there when I needed her.'

But she didn't, because he had already picked up the cry of the heart that had echoed behind her words even though she had hardly dared to admit it even to herself. He nodded sombrely and said, 'Yes, you do need to, Amy.'

She knew then that he was presenting her with an opportunity to get her previous life out of her system once and for all; was willing to face the fact that she would either do so or succumb to the temptation of going back to the settled and comfortable one she had once known and not return. She knew now that this was a test she had not been conscious of before, but of which he was. He knew her better than she knew herself, and all at once she felt everything begin to crumble about her. She felt suddenly terrified. Terrified that she could lose him.

'I don't want to go!'

Tom stopped walking, nearly thrown off-balance as she flung her arms about his neck, wanting the safety of his embrace to shield her from the world around them. Regaining his balance, he held her, gently rubbing her back.

'You must, Amy. I want yer to.'

'I don't want to lose you, Tom! I love you so much.'

He said nothing for a while, then his voice, low with a faraway sound to it, came quietly. 'I wish I could give you all what yer need, Amy. I wish I 'ad enough money to do that. Sometimes I dream. I dream of being me own boss, having me own business. Not being rich, but 'aving ... having enough.'

Hearing him correct himself, even now as he pipe-dreamed, revealed his secret heart to her. She wanted to cry out, no, be true to yourself. Speak the way you've always been used to speaking. I love you as you are. But she remained silent and listened as he mused on. She needed to hear him lay these longings of his at her feet. It made her far more part of him than anything else could. No one else knew of his secret heart but her. She let him continue.

'I'd like to 'ave a little business that would take me far out into the open air where I could be free ter breathe in the smell of water and be able ter look across at the far banks of the Thames instead of always being stuck down there in the 'old of some ship, loadin', unloadin', breakin' me back fer someone else and comin' up at the end of a day so tired out and fit fer nothing, I can 'ardly think. I'd like to 'ave me own craft, it don't matter how small. I'd even be a werryman, rowing all day taking other men across to their work. I could look about me and not see just walls and curtains of some stinking ship's hold, me filthy the 'ole day, me arms aching and me throat dry, and holding me 'and out fer me pittance at the end of it – when they've got work for me. But it's only a dream. I'll never make it.'

'You could.' She suddenly leaned away from him, gazing up into his faraway eyes. 'Everything is possible.'

'What on?' He was himself again, gazing down at her and grinning. 'Shirt buttons? Come on.' He put her from him but kept his arm about her shoulders, the two of them continuing walking. 'I was only dreaming, being silly.'

But she had seen that faraway look on him before. On the *London Belle* taking them to Southend that first time. He had leaned on the rails and his pleasure of the open water had shone in his eyes, utterly boyish, so different to the man she had at the time considered so sombre. It had fallen away from him like a shroud as he stood looking about, his chest filling with the salty air. She had sensed then, for the very first time, that the Thames was his life, his blood.

'This is what I'd like to do,' was all he'd said, his gaze cast wide, but she had been so completely happy just being there with him, she had given no deep thought to what raged within him; had been raging within him all his working life, and she did not know. But she knew now, only too well.

Walking on, in silence now, each wrapped in their own thoughts, ideas on how to help him achieve his dream harried her, all of them wild. Her own savings would go nowhere towards it. She could go to her parents, finally try to break the ice that had slowly thickened month by month, maybe so thick now as to be unbreakable. And what if they did relent? How could she reunite herself with them with the words: 'I want you to help my fiancé set up in his own business?' She almost laughed out loud at such a preposterous idea. And if she and Tom did have money enough, what did he know about business? What did she, sheltered most of her life, know about it? Tom didn't even know what sort of business he wanted except that it would rescue him from his present abysmal daily work. Best to forget it, let it remain a dream only.

It was eight o'clock on the Monday evening when the knock came at the door. Tom and his father were eating supper, his mother in the kitchen washing up a few bits and pieces. Amy, Vi and Rosy were sitting reading by the open sash window the easier to get some air on this warm August evening. Willie was outside in the yard with one of his mates messing about making a kite out of cardboard, paper and string.

It was Grace who answered the knock, drying her hands on a tea towel as she went along the dim narrow passage. Opening the door, her mouth dropped when she saw her eldest daughter standing there, face all puckered even though she tried to smile.

Grace found her voice. 'Good Lawd, luv, yer don't 'ave ter knock. Yer still live 'ere, yer know. Where's yer key?' But the look on her daughter's face was already giving concern. 'What's wrong, luv? Come in. Whatever's the matter?'

'Oh, Mum,' was all Alice said, quaveringly, as her mother drew her into the house to usher her along the passage and into the back room.

Tom and his father looked up from their eating. The girls

199

lowered their girls' magazines, Amy her book, to stare at the distraught Alice. No one said anything as Grace eased the girl down on the sofa.

'Now, tell us what's 'appened,' Grace enquired briskly. 'It ain't nothink awful, is it? You and yer Richard ain't 'ad a disagreement? Ain't called orf the wedding, 'ave yer?'

'No.' Alice found her voice at last. 'The wedding is still on.'

'But you and 'im 'ave 'ad an argument.'

'No.'

'Then what?'

Alice was biting her lips. 'It is about the wedding. Oh, Mum, I don't know how to tell you.'

'Tell us what?'

There came a deep shuddering breath. Alice straightened her back with an effort and she stared desperately from one parent to the other. 'The thing is . . . would you mind very much if I asked you not to accept the wedding invitations I sent you? You see . . .'

There came a shocked squeak from her sisters, seeing their lovely, lovingly made dresses for the occasion going unworn. But Arthur Jordan had already cut short his daughter's words.

'Not accept? What d'yer mean, not accept? What yer bloody talkin' about?'

'I don't know how to explain, Dad. It's just that I didn't think at the time. I didn't really consider the implications.'

'What's she talkin' about?' His knife and fork gripped in his work-gnarled hands, he shot his gaze at his wife as though she possessed some divine insight into her silly daughter's thinking. Grace complied meekly, her tone confused.

'Yes, luv, what're yer talkin' about? What didn't yer think?'

Alice took another deep fortifying breath. 'I didn't think it would go this far. And now I can't . . . I don't know how to remedy it.'

Mrs Jordan frowned with irritation at yet another pause. 'Fer Gawd's sake, luv!' she burst out. 'I don't understand what yer tryin' ter say. You mean you don't want us ter see yer married. Why?'

'Because she's ashamed to show us to her posh friends.' Tom's voice came suddenly deep and powerful. Alice looked at him in mute appeal. Her two sisters were on the point of producing some indignant weeping between themselves, little staccato noises of protest coming from them. Amy sat very quiet. What had Dicky Pritchard cooked up for this wedding that his own bride's parents had to be asked not to attend?

Alice had found her voice again, quiver though it did. 'It's complicated . . .'

'So yer said,' interrupted her father. 'It ain't complicated ter see yer don't want us there. Yer ashamed of us.'

'No, Dad! I'm not ashamed of you. Dad, Mum, I've something to confess. Something I did, and I didn't realise how serious it would become. I've been wanting to tell you for weeks and now with the wedding only a week to go, I don't know how to tell you what I've done.'

'Yer got yerself pregnant. Well, that's as near as damn it not ter matter.' Her father relaxed in his chair but immediately shot upright again. 'But that don't give no call fer you ter ask us not ter go to yer own weddin'.'

'It's not that, Dad. I'm not pregnant. Richard hasn't touched me.' She broke off, aware that she was getting away from the real purpose of her coming. 'It's something much worse. It began when I first met his mother. She accepted me with such good grace, no reservations whatsoever. She treated me as if I had been born into high-class wealth. She was really sweet and kind.'

'Yeah, yeah.' Arthur Jordan was becoming impatient on top of the shock he had been delivered, which still seemed unbelievable. 'Get on with it.'

Alice struggled on manfully, speeding up her story. 'But she, his mother, did have one reservation. She was concerned as to what other people might think of me. It's usual that everyone wants to know who the bride is, her background, that sort of thing, and she suggested that for the sake of appearances – and it would only be temporary, until Richard and I settle down and people forget about us – I pretend to have been of a good-class family myself.'

She paused and looked at them all, but no one moved or

spoke. It was as though they had been mesmerised by a cobra, she the cobra that would inevitably strike them all between the eyes before long. It felt exactly like that as she pushed on.

'His mother said that after the wedding people would stop probing into our lives and we could settle down and things gradually revert to normal with no one asking questions. It seemed so harmless that I went along with it.'

'Gawd almighty!' Arthur burst in. 'Fer Christ's sake, what're yer tryin' ter tell us?'

'It's that his mother suggested I let people think I have lived in India all my life and that my father had been a diplomat there, you know, part of the Raj? And when they both died in an accident I finally came to England where I met Richard.'

As her voice faded away, her mother's came softly, weakened, almost stupid: 'But we ain't dead, luv.'

'I know, Mum.' Alice's cry was beseeching. 'It was to make me look . . .' Out of her depth, unable to explain Lady Pritchard's reasoning, her words trailed off.

'But yer tellin' everyone we're dead.'

'Not you. *Them*. The people his mother made up, for the look of it.'

'But it ain't nice. Like yer was *wishin'* we was dead. It's horrible!'

'I'm not wishing, Mum! Please understand. It's only to impress . . .'

'You bloody ungrateful little bitch!' Arthur Jordan shot up from the table, Tom reaching out just in time to catch the toppling chair and steady it. 'If that's what yer think of us, then we wouldn't stoop ter see yer married – none of us. Yer can bugger orf an' go an' live yer posh life. An' we'll accommodate yer. We'll be dead to yer – all of us. Yer don't need ter come 'ere ever again. We won't want yer.'

'No, Dad, please.'

Alice was sobbing, but her mother didn't come forward to comfort her as she would normally have done. She just stood watching her huddled wretchedly into herself on the sofa, her eyes cold with pained disbelief. The eyes of all of them seemed to stare at her from all points of the room as though from a distance, not one soul making any move towards her.

Her father's voice filled her ears. 'You ashamed of us! I'm ashamed of *you*. If this is what your posh future in-laws 'ave done ter yer, then yer bloody welcome to 'em. Yer can go an' be the lady o' the manor if yer want, but don't come near 'ere again. Yer've decided ter make yer own bloody bed. Now yer can bloody well lie in it. Ter tell everyone we're dead . . . I just . . . Just sod orf! Go orn, sod off. We don't want nuffink more ter do wiv yer! Never!'

His face working, he swung away from the table, his back to her, to them all, facing the empty fire grate so that they would not see the unmanly tears as he blew his nose on the muffler from his neck and wiped his moustache in a coarse and clumsy gesture.

Grace Jordan hadn't moved. 'What sort of woman is she?' she asked now, her voice slow with shock. 'Doin' what she's doin'. Playin' with people. What sort of people can they be?'

'And what sort of silly cow are you, Alice?' Tom added, his voice toneless. 'Lettin' someone manipulate yer like that wivout a care fer the parents what's brought yer up ter live decent.'

'Don't talk to 'er! None of yer.' Arthur Jordan swung round, his face livid and contorted. 'What she wants is a bloody good 'iding – that's what she wants. I turn me back on 'er.'

Throwing down his kerchief, he stomped from the room. They heard him grab his coat from the hall stand so angrily that the stand rattled. The front door opened and crashed shut behind him leaving a trembling silence. He would come back hours later, drunk but not legless. A man who could hold his drink well, he'd not stagger around effing and blinding and causing a row. The most would be to grin ever wider the drunker he got and crack silly jokes. But he'd have no jokes on his return; instead would fall into bed and sleep, his misery obliterated for the time being.

'Yer could call the weddin' orf.'

'I can't, Mum. I love Richard.'

'In that case, of course yer can't.'

'I'll come and see you, Mum, afterwards.'

203

'No, luv, best yer don't.'

'But I want to see you. I will come.'

'I don't fink so.'

'Don't you want to see me?'

'It's like yer father said. Yer've made yer own bed. Best yer lie in it. We'll be all right.'

Rosy had been fidgeting for some time. 'What about our new dresses?' she began, but a look from her mother closed her mouth. Grace Jordan turned back to her eldest daughter.

'I'll see yer out, Alice. I wish yer all the good fortune yer wish yerself, and 'ope yer new 'usband will take care of yer.'

There was nothing else that Alice could do but follow her mother meekly, her head down, tears falling onto her handbag. On an impulse Amy got up too and hurried after them. Alice had been silly, wrong – it didn't change her pain. She had to give her a kind word to help ease it.

Mrs Jordan was closing the door. Amy was sure she hadn't even dropped a kiss on her daughter's tear-soaked cheek. Seeing Alice, she left the door half open and stood back against the wall to let her pass, her sad pudding-face averted.

At the door, Amy leaned out. 'Alice!'

The girl turned, her eyes wide with renewed hope, but seeing only her there, they dulled as she retraced her steps, pausing a couple of feet from her.

'I know how you feel,' Amy began as she came to a stop. 'I just want to say, if you ever need me, as a friend, I'm here.'

'Thanks.' The word sounded humbled, flat. Then she stared into Amy's eyes, her voice growing a fraction stronger. 'Thank you.'

'You were a good friend to me when I was in trouble. Don't forget, Alice, if you ever need help.'

The girl nodded. 'You're coming to my wedding though, aren't you?'

For a moment Amy stared at her. She was seeing something she had never considered before, having been too close, a part of it, but which the poor could see as clearly as looking through crystal – that the rich lived lives of constant pretence, sham, ever in fear of being discovered to be as human as the poor they despised, theirs a cardboard world compared to the hard, hearty, violent one of the less privileged, or so it all seemed to her. Perhaps neither world was honest, but she knew now which one she preferred.

'I don't think so, Alice,' she replied quietly, 'but I wish you all the luck and happiness you can find. And as I say, if ever you need someone to talk to, I'll be here.'

Yes, she knew now – no need to go to some society wedding to see which world she wanted to follow. This, with its poverty, its struggles, its unemployment, its day to day grinding down of many, was the world she found herself choosing. And with it there came a gleam of hope deep inside her chest. It was possible to climb out of a sewer. She and Tom together would climb out. It would be a long climb, and she didn't need her father's aid to do it. She felt suddenly elated. And all because of Tom. Just as Alice was doing what she was doing for the man she loved. It was just how things were.

'I wish you would come,' Alice was pleading, needing an ally.

'I can't,' she replied, hating the hurt in those imploring eyes. 'I hope you understand.'

But she could see by her look that she didn't understand at all.

205

Chapter Fifteen

Money was causing Amy some worry. If she and Tom were to be married next spring, now only five months off with time seemingly just whizzing by, it was crucial they must save more than she could see coming in.

'I must find myself some work,' she finally revealed to Tom as they felt their way back home from the London Shoreditch Theatre through a November peasouper that seemed to shut out all sounds except their own muffled voices and made them imagine themselves as the only two creatures alive in the whole world.

The buses had all but stopped and with what transport there was creeping along, it was quicker to walk, even from Shoreditch. It had saved paying the fare, added a little more to their pot. They shouldn't really have gone out at all, but staying in week after week tended to lower the spirits so that even the prospects of marriage dulled. At least the cheapest theatre seats at the humble little London Shoreditch were cheap indeed, even if its orchestra was very often out of tune and its turns mere try-outs for first-time hopefuls. Some could be really good, destined to go far, and it was the place to see them and say later of a growing name, 'I saw him when he was just starting,' or, 'I watched her long before she was well known.' Others were quite awful, but it was almost as good entertainment to listen to the audience's cat-calls and uproariously coarse remarks as watching the acts themselves. Amy was convinced the audience got as much enjoyment out of that as anything and came for the sole purpose of expressing their opinions as freely as they wished.

The question was though, she and Tom couldn't go on spending even this small amount of money with only his wages. She'd have to think of some sort of employment to help out. But what? She had no training for anything, apart from what her eighteen months at a finishing school had taught – to be a debutante, a successful wife in society and a good hostess. Before that, private school had taught a little maths, some composition, but mostly history, geography, music, painting, poetry – stuff suitable for a young lady expected to be successfully married by twenty or twenty-one. She had good French, passable German, but nothing at all that one could classify as food for the normal career of an ordinary working girl – no office skill, no clue how to serve in a shop, and as for factory work, she might as well be no brighter than the most uneducated factory hand, and also the thought of factory work made her cringe. Yet in a sense, with her impractical schooling, it was all she was good for.

Holding her close as they felt their way through the layers of fog, Tom's arm tightened on hers, the almost solid air deadening his voice. 'What's the point you going ter work now? You'll be giving it up again as soon as we're married.'

'The way we're going,' she said firmly, 'we'll not have half enough money to get married – not in a few months. We *need* another source of income.'

'A few months of you being in a job won't make that much difference. And I'm not 'aving my wife thinkin' she can go on working after we're married.'

This was how it was. Married women, unless they were in dire poverty, were not expected to work. Such a thing degraded both the woman and her husband and showed him up as being incapable of looking after his own wife. She wanted to say, 'What if you fell out of work?' but dared not – a superstitious shiver running through her that it could make her fear come true.

He had said that there was plenty of work at the moment, but she had come to know that nothing in his work could ever be predictable, and they needed money just in case.

Walking beside him, holding onto his arm relying on him to feel his way accurately through the peasouper, she remained silent, though her mind went on speaking to her. She would say nothing to him, but as soon as convenient would scan the newspaper ads for office staff vacancies if only as an exercise, for not for one moment did she imagine there to be anything suitable for someone who could not type, had never learned shorthand, had no idea of filing or the setting out of a letter apart from an ability to answer invitations with the customary socially accepted abbreviations or the usual convivial note to a friend.

There proved surprisingly little in the way of office staff wanted. Plenty of vacancies for domestic staff – her mother had always complained of the lack of good staff since young women had found other work more rewarding since the War and their emancipation. There were factory jobs, and again she cringed from that idea, but on the whole few shop or office staff cared to change jobs with Christmas just around the corner, preferring to hold fire until after the festive season and make a new start for 1928.

Christmas brought her a letter from Alice and a Christmas card for Alice's parents. Amy read the letter, three pages crammed with news of her marvellously wonderful life with Dicky and her still disbelieving view of her changed state with servants to wait on her – 'remember when I was one of them?' – and doing all the things that she'd never in all her wildest imaginings ever dreamed of doing. 'We're spending Christmas in Switzerland, with one of Richard's cousins, and we had a marvellous honeymoon in the South of France, and next spring we'll be going to Paris – Richard is such an avid traveller, we're hardly ever at home – that's Lyttehill Manor in Surrey which belonged to his father and which he gave us as a wedding present. It's old and so beautiful . . .'

Amy read the letter with a smile, glad to see her friend happy, glad that her horrid little plan of long ago had misfired. She'd have been consumed by guilt had Alice's life turned out unhappy. All her hatred of Dicky – he would always be Dicky to her – had dissolved completely. She had Tom now. She found herself not at all regretting Alice's acquired wealth and she wished them both every happiness as she folded the letter after reading.

Alice's card to her parents wasn't read, wasn't even opened. Recognising her daughter's spidery handwriting and the post mark, her mother left it for her father to open when he came home from work. This was usual. Everything addressed to them both, whether bills or personal, remained unopened for him to read first. As the man of the house, she would say, it was his right. Anyway nothing ever came for her personally, for she and he were one. Amy thought of her mother sifting through every post of which there were four, sometimes five, deliveries a day, the letters brought to her on a salver by, as it used to be, Alice. And she would take them to her little escritoire and there sit and slit open each envelope with the silver paperknife she used, placing bills in one pile, personal letters of which she had many in another, invitations in another, only her husband's own personal mail put aside.

Mrs Jordan's actions spelled out how behind the times the working classes still were, still clinging to the Victorian male-dominated attitude that the woman took second place to her husband, even though many a married couple might fight openly like cat and dog. Amy had seen it, often out in the open street. There would come a sudden screaming, a bellowing, doors would be opened and curtains pulled aside to see what was going on. Sometimes it would be two women, neighbours, a quarrel flaring up with physical results, but more often a husband and wife, he aiming punches at her, she screaming abuse and fighting back with whatever had come to hand from the kitchen. When a woman did not retaliate to her man beating her, the quarrel usually stayed behind locked doors only later manifested by her blacked eye or swollen lip. It was at such times that Amy wished she could go far away from this passionate, violent place, back to the sedate life she had known where most often quarrels were settled with words and silences, even if these could be more wounding. She was heartily glad there was never such behaviour in the Jordans' home. Arguments, yes, but Mrs Jordan's jovial nature often made her see the other side of things and even burst into laughter, and since Mr Jordan was a man who respected a woman, arguments were curbed before they went too far. Amy just knew that Tom would automatically follow their example, she and he settling differences of opinion in much the same manner as they.

There was, however, no laughter from Mrs Jordan that night as she handed the Christmas card to her husband to open.

For a moment he turned it over in his still work-dirtied hands, then without a word threw it on the fire, wiping his hands on his trousers as though his work wasn't the only thing that had dirtied them.

Mrs Jordan leapt forward but stopped before retrieving it from the flames. 'Arthur! What did yer do that for? She might've put a letter in with it for us.'

'Wouldn't be no letter,' he said as he turned away from the blackening envelope. 'No point writin' ter dead people, is there?'

She knew what he meant, but her ruddy face visibly paled. 'Don't say things like that, Arthur. I don't like it.'

'Well, we are dead to 'er, ain't we?' he said. 'She told us we was.'

Mrs Jordan's face had grown tight. 'Don't be silly, luv. You can't go on an' on 'olding a grudge. We'll 'ave ter learn ter forgive 'er some day.'

'Tell me 'ow do a dead man fergive?'

'Don't keep sayin' that, luv,' she said. 'It's creepy. It's like yer could make it come true. We've got ter forget what she said. It was just a silly idea got out of hand, that's all. It was just silliness.'

He turned on her, the look in his eyes as much that of a dead man as could ever be. 'It ain't up ter me to fergive or ferget. I'm dead, ole gel, remember?'

Had she been Catholic, Amy imagined Mrs Jordan would have crossed herself. Being merely Church of England, she held her hands as if in prayer and laid them against her lips before hurrying off to get her husband's supper.

Witness to it all, Amy was left wondering for the rest of that evening if her father had done the same to her one and only letter? She could more imagine him placing it solemnly aside to be conveniently forgotten somewhere at the back of one of his bureau drawers, that being all she was to him, something to be tucked out of sight and left to moulder away in some dark recess of his brain. Mr Jordan throwing his daughter's letter onto a fire might be more violent, more expressive, even more honest, but the same purpose lay behind it. It left her miserable for the whole evening. Even Tom couldn't get her out of it, asking what was the matter. She felt unable to tell him because she and his sister, for all their roles had been reversed, were in reality one and the same and it was all too close to home.

Christmas came. It being Mr and Mrs Jordan's turn to celebrate it at her sister's house just down the road where all the family would gather, Amy and Tom cried off, preferring to spend it quietly together at home.

Mr Jordan was definitely reluctant to leave the couple to their own pursuits but Mrs Jordan waved away his concern, proud and pleased that Tom had found himself a girl, if not with money, at least one from a background they hadn't any hope of aspiring to, and who could say there might not come a day when she'd come into money again, perhaps left to her by a father sorry for his attitude towards her. Blood was always thicker than water and Mrs Jordan still harboured a faith that one day her husband too might forgive his daughter the virtually unforgivable.

'Leave 'em be, bless 'em,' she said. 'Won't be long before they're man an' wife tergether. They're adult enough not ter do anything silly an' we're only just down the road, ain't we?'

She was incorrect there. Only down the road or not, the second they were alone, all Tom's carefully controlled ardour broke the bonds he'd clamped around it, and Christmas afternoon found them in his bed in each other's arms, he contentedly dozing off his first-ever knowledge of her. Their lovemaking had taken place with an ear trained for the sound of a door key turning in case one or other of his parents popped back from the end of the street.

It was this fear too that in fact stopped them sharing his bed that night, and just as well, as the whole family came trooping back around midnight for a more comfortable night's sleep in their own home than the crowded one of Mrs Jordan's sister. But love didn't need a night spent together. Boxing Day afternoon served just as well for a repeat performance of Christmas afternoon, both occasions afterwards leaving them as shy and awkward with each other as their lovemaking had been stimulating and unrestrained.

And what did it matter, Amy asked herself, when in a few months they'd be married. If she fell pregnant, they'd be married sooner. Tom would not let her down as Dicky Pritchard had. May was five months off. May, how she looked forward to it, to being Tom's wife.

But here again Mrs Jordan's prediction, indeed all their predictions of the marriage being only five months away, proved wrong. The enforced Christmas holiday had been no help to Tom's savings, because his work, as with all dock work, was based on the ruling of no work, no pay. Even two days without pay meant less saved. And with the passing of the Christmas season, work dropped off a little, leaving Tom and his father back on the stones at the dock gates waiting with the rest to be called on, his father's once-sharp wits dulled lately by thoughts of his daughter's attitude towards him.

'I wish he'd pull 'imself out of it,' Tom said to Amy, still having some trouble with his aitches for all he worked on them constantly. 'He's not the man 'e was.'

But Amy wasn't really listening. Their wedding looked like being put back to a later date, still she hoped before the autumn. Her resolve to find work and earn a little extra to help bring it forward again had become more urgent.

The new year well and truly over, she re-scanned the vacancies columns, which this time displayed more opportunities for office staff. She read the first of three likely local ones: *Well-spoken single young lady*, it announced, *wanted for busy telephone switchboard in small firm of solicitors.* She knew nothing of handling switchboards, but she was well-spoken and surely telephone work couldn't be all that difficult. She was at ease on the telephone where none were around here. It was worth a try.

The second: *Young lady for postal department of*

importers/exporters – high school leaver considered. Offices never considered anyone without high school or college education, they were fit only for factory or shop work. She wasn't exactly a high school leaver, but she'd had a college education.

With her background she'd be snapped up, she was certain, as she studied the third of her chosen advertisements: *Office clerk, young woman starter with some typing skills and willing to study shorthand at night school. Prospects of good promotion and reviewed pay as skill is acquired.* Well, that promised poor pay for some considerable time to come, and did she want to start learning shorthand at her age?

Carrying on down the page, a fourth held her gaze: *Small shipping office requires well-spoken young woman with knowledge of French and German to answer telephone and transcribe foreign mail. Some reception work so must be presentable.*

It looked perfect. She was well-spoken. She was presentable. She did have French and German. A shipping office caught her imagination too. Situated near to West India Docks, something which appealed to her because of Tom's work on the river, it sounded all too good to be true, but this one she would definitely answer. She'd try the other three as well of course though with less concern.

Amy lifted her eyes from the letter which had arrived a moment ago with the midday post. 'I've got it! I've got the job – the one I wanted.'

There was a new respect in the eyes of Mrs Jordan, envy in those of Rosy and Vi, just come in for their dinner break. No one they knew had an office job. Grace Jordan hurried forward and gave Amy a big kiss on her cheek. She had come to regard her as much a daughter as her own, her awe of the well-spoken girl from a wealthy background long since faded and her ear these days hardly noticing the refined diction that still lingered.

'Oh, luv, I'm so glad for yer. It's really commendable, you goin' out ter look fer work like yer've done. A real sacrifice, 'specially you not bein' used to it an' all that. Thank 'eaven

213

it'll only be till you and Tom are married. Pity that 'ad ter be put back again another few months. But you wait, luv, Tom'll get 'imself some lastin' work soon, you see if 'e don't. An' then yer can both bring the wedding forward again.'

'I do hope so,' Amy said, looking towards Tom standing silently to one side.

'Tom should be real proud of yer,' Mrs Jordan said, also glancing at him. 'Yer proud of 'er, ain't yer, Tom?'

But Tom was looking dark. Although he nodded, Amy knew what was going through his head: guilt at his own inability to provide for her without her help – a guilt too sharp to voice. To a strong, proud man it went against the grain, and already she wished she hadn't been quite so successful or boastful about landing a job on her very first try. Had she flunked it, he'd be stepping foward now, com-miseration on his lips, a sympathetic arm laid lovingly about her, offering protection against the disappointment she'd be feeling, telling her with confidence that it didn't matter. As it was, she had belittled him and that was the last thing she had wanted to do. Her excitement at her accomplishment melted away.

Mrs Jordan was still prattling on, not noticing anything untoward. 'When 'im an' my Arthur gets back on an even keel, an' with what you earn comin' in too – Lawd, you two'll 'ave a weddin' the 'ole street won't stop talking about fer months after. An' the time'll fly by, you just wait'n' see.'

'Be a bloody good day when work do come in more plentiful,' growled Arthur. He was seated in his armchair, which sagged even more than when Amy had first seen it and was likely to sag still more before they could ever afford to acquire better. He began to fill his pipe, tamping down the tobacco and lighting it from the fire. His body too sagged.

'Bloody 'ate this time of year,' he mumbled, staring into the fire. 'Ain't not one bit of cargo ter speak of comin' in or goin' out, us 'avin' ter fight fer every bit of work that do come in. Like a cattle market down there this mornin'. Me wiv a full gang of men, an' other gangs getting called on before us. I 'ate that ducking an' diving lark wiv everyone, even gangers, trying to get noticed by the foremen. Me and Tom showed out well before seven this mornin' but I just

214

can't seem ter put meself abart like I used ter. Must be gettin' soddin' old. Gettin' past it. Eivver that or it's just the start of another bloody bad year.'

Tom stopped in the act of rolling himself a cigarette and looked across at his father. 'It's just a bloody bad start to the year, Dad,' he said. 'You ain't lost yer touch an' yer never will.' But there was a flatness in his tone that he couldn't hide.

It was Tuesday, January almost gone, and both had returned home utterly despondent. Amy knew they would be back on the stones again at twelve forty-five sharp for the second and last call of the day in the hope of something turning up. If there was anything around, it would most likely give only half a day's work. If they were fortunate it might go on through the night and bring some much-needed extra pay. And who knows, the job might go on for several days. They could only hope. On the other hand there could be nothing more, good gangs of men left roasting on the stones as Tom had described to her the frustration of not being called on for work. All were continually at the mercy of the vagaries of other countries' affairs which could bring feast or famine to the dock workers. But there had never been anything permanent about dock work. And they knew that. It was part of the job they did, though it never made the lean times any easier to bear.

Seeing both men, who should rightfully have been working, idle and useless, Amy judged this wasn't the time to be rubbing salt into the wound by picking up again on her exciting success. Instead she followed Mrs Jordan out to the kitchen to help dish up their own dinners, the men and Willie, who had gone out to play for the remaining hour until afternoon school, having already eaten theirs.

'At least,' Mrs Jordan said out of the men's hearing, 'I can still put an 'alfway decent meal on the table for a while yet.'

There was a certain desperation in her voice for all she smothered it with a short laugh. Amy wanted to say to her, 'Never mind, after next week,' which was when she was to start with Bellows Shipping Company, 'I'll be earning enough to bring in a bit more of my share of my keep.' But she thought it better not to mention that at this moment in time.

Monday found her standing in the tiny dingy reception area of Bellows while the girl behind the desk went in search of Mr Curby, the office manager. Her stomach felt full of fluttering moths, her attire disastrously out of date. She hoped she was looking suitably smart in the fresh white blouse and carefully pressed dark skirt, her best camel-coloured outdoor coat now over her arm, none of them new, and she was grateful that 1928 had not altered the fashion for the short hemline. Hats too were still cloche-shaped, thank goodness, as hers was two years old.

She watched the small, middle-aged, balding man come towards her from the dim recess of a corridor, and for some unexplained reason found herself deducing from his pale freckled complexion that his hair, what there was of it, must have once been ginger, just when she should have been preparing herself for his formal greeting.

He gave her a large friendly smile, which showed his too-white dentures. He held out his fleshy hand for her to grasp. 'Welcome to our Company, Miss Harrington. I am sure you're going to be happy with us. If you'd like to follow me, I will show you where your desk will be. Then Miss Burt here will show you where you may hang your coat and hat. We have lockers, you know. Your own key. You can put your handbag safely in there. Handbags aren't allowed at the desks. Safety, you know.'

Following the direction of his crooked finger as he turned to lead the way, Amy finally entered a large open office with eight desks ranged in two rows down the centre. There were dingy looking windows at one end, two glass-paned doors in each of the other two walls, the offices of the senior male staff she assumed, and the door through which she had entered. The walls were littered with charts, maps of parts of the world, calendars, timetables, two framed, rather stained pictures of ships, one standing in dock, the other of a vessel ploughing through storm-tossed waves, dark and dingy, a peg board with notes and other bits of paper stuck on it with drawing pins, and a large bold-faced clock that ticked solemnly above the rattle of typewriters.

Mr Curby clapped his hands and the clatter ceased. Every girl looked up. 'This is Miss Harrington. She has come to join us. I know you will all help her with whatever questions she has, though I hope they'll not be too many. You may introduce yourselves to Miss Harrington later at lunch.'

Introductions over, he turned back to Amy. 'We have a small canteen, you know. Tea and coffee can be made, and you bring your own sandwiches.'

Amy nodded. She had already been told this and had come prepared. She followed him to an empty desk by the window that thankfully held no typewriter.

'This is your desk, Miss Harrington. Settle yourself in for a few minutes and I'll shortly bring out some work and explain what is wanted. There are some bills of lading, invoices, but mostly correspondence that needs to be translated, you know. I believe you have a smattering of Spanish? We do have a man who does that full-time, but if he becomes inundated, we may need you to help out with the simpler letters.'

Amy sat down, dumbfounded. She had no Spanish, not even a smattering, but it was best at this stage to say nothing.

'Well, I'll leave you to settle in for a while,' Mr Curby said, innocent of this oversight, and scurried off to the door at the far end on her side.

Left to herself, Amy scanned the empty top of the desk, opened its three drawers one after the other noting pencils, India rubbers, paper clips, elastic bands in the top one, a stack of paper in the second one, nothing in the third; she smiled briefly at the eight typists as now and again they glanced at her; looked around the cluttered walls once more and turned slightly to stretch her neck to peep out of the window. The window wasn't conveniently positioned and it did mean a lot of very obvious neck-stretching to do so, proving to all that the gazer was not conscientiously applying herself to her work. But at this moment she was at liberty to gaze.

To her delight, a long stretch of the Thames greeted her, its wharves and warehouses lying under a soft liquid light from a cold January sun not long risen. It was going to be a fine dry day and she breathed a prayer for the blessing of that, though why when she'd be in this office for the next eight and a half hours, she wasn't sure.

The thought brought a small sense of panic. What was she doing here? How had she, the pampered daughter of a comfortable upper-middle-class family, come to this – sitting in some office like a common working girl awaiting orders to be told what to do? It took some effort to control her jangling nerves, the fear that had assailed her stronger even than when she had set foot in the firm's reception area a few minutes earlier. She stretched her neck further for the comfort of the open water. This was what Tom meant when he yearned to be free of ships' holds to roam the open river. His job was a prison. He was like a prisoner. She felt like a prisoner too. There was no escape. Amy concentrated her desperate gaze on the open river flowing by with its ships and barges moving up and down almost at a snail's pace from her vantage point.

Further downstream where the Thames passed the West India and Millwall Docks, Tom was again working. His first call-on since Thursday, it might last a day or two and then he'd be back on the stones looking for another, or it might lead to a longer-term contract. No one could say.

He had been very quiet with her over the weekend. He was brooding, and had made no reference whatsoever to her new job and she in turn hadn't felt it right to mention it. It was as if it hadn't happened, with her still the stay-at-home girl she'd been ever since arriving at the Jordans'.

What had happened to the wonderful ease they'd had with each other since Christmas? She thought now of Christmas, when she and Tom had made love for the first time, and the overwhelming surprise with which it had happened – one minute content merely to be sitting just by themselves cuddling in the comfort of his home with no one else around to embarrass them with smirks and looks. They had never truly been alone together in the house since they'd fallen in love with each other, as either Willie was in bed if his parents were out, or one or other of the girls was hovering around. So conditioned to it were they, they hadn't anticipated what had happened.

Without warning, from a playful kiss they were clinging to each other, the kiss growing desperate and unforgiving, he breaking off sharply and, without a word, leading the way to his bed, his hand strong in hers and she following with her heart beating so fast and heavily, aware of what they were about, that she felt almost sick from it. Moments later she had lain beneath him receiving his kisses, his caresses, receiving him into herself, her arms tight about his neck, her lower limbs twined about his body, hers raised to meet him, feeling him deep inside her, hearing his gasps matching her own . . .

'Ah, now, Miss Harrington.'

Amy jumped at the voice, close to her shoulder. The littered office, the map-strewn walls, the double line of desks leapt back into view, the sound of typewriters being industriously pounded came loud in her ears. She was sure as she looked up at Mr Curby that her face must bear a look of guilt as though he had divined what she'd been thinking. But he was smiling benignly at her, entirely innocent of the scene that had been in her head.

He held a clip of correspondence which he placed on the desk, bending over to sort them out for her. 'Now, this is what you have to do, Miss Harrington. It's quite simple, you know. Most of the letters are in French. We'll start with the easy stuff first.'

Chapter Sixteen

Alice sipped her White Lady, her bored gaze taking in the slowly accumulating assembly of dinner guests over the flared top of her cocktail glass.

It was her birthday. The twenty-first of June. Richard was celebrating it for her in style. He celebrated everything, did everything, in style, to the limit, loved impressing her, impressing others, mostly others. To watch him, one would imagine he'd only just come into money with all the need of the *nouveau riche* to flaunt it rather than having been born into it. He, not she, had made all the arrangements, even to the choosing of the food with the help of his mother who knew exactly the sort of fare her sort of people preferred, overriding the suggestions of hired caterers.

Alice had seen the menu, which was quite brilliant, and had immediately wondered how good old fish and chips would have gone down with them had she suggested it. The idea would have been funny had it not made her feel so oddly depressed.

She still felt depressed despite the beautiful dress Richard had bought her for the occasion, a serpentine-slim black velvet Chanel gown with narrow diamanté straps, tiered from the hip to knee and dropping in a cascade at the back to the ankle, and the gorgeous emerald bracelet, her birthday present from him. She felt depressed despite the glittering gathering, everyone of note having driven down to Lyttehill Manor for this occasion; despite the breathtaking menu and the marvellous party that would go on after it into the small hours.

There were so many parties. Never ending, never any moments of peace to be by herself, to be herself, as Richard was ready to throw one for the smallest excuse. There were those given by others which she was obliged to attend with him. And then there was the business of calling on people and having people call on her, invitations from *friends*, acquired solely through Richard – her own friends long since put aside – to meet in London, for shopping, for coffee, she and Richard going to the theatre with parties of them. And then there were the holidays, endless holidays and trips abroad. Richard loved travelling, discovering pastures new. At first she had revelled in such unaccustomed excitement. Now it was becoming just tiresome, rather like eating too much caviar until feeling that one more tiny black fish egg would make her sick, preferring lowly . . . lowly what? Fish and chips from the local fish shop – the one in Commercial Road – well-salted, the oil and vinegar seeping from the corner of a bit of greaseproof into the newspaper around it, the whole hot mass burning the hands on a cold winter's night. She could almost taste the crisp batter coating on a succulent wedge of cod, chips crunchy on the outside and soft on the inside.

Alice took another sip of her White Lady. 'Do we have to be here?' she whispered as the couple who had been talking with her and Richard drifted away to another group while another two of Richard's friends came to take their place. 'Can't we disappear upstairs for a few minutes and be on our own?'

For a wild moment she wanted to let go of her glass, have it drop there on the carpet, the sound making everyone turn, and to run out through the open french windows and into the flower garden beyond to wander alone beneath the cool June stars. Or perhaps hurry off across the vestibule with its dated old paintings and its antique furniture and its parlour palms, and on through the wide entrance door and the imposing portico Richard had had built and which didn't go at all with the rest of the Regency-style house, and on towards the huge gravel drive where cars were still arriving. She would ignore the surprised expression of Hamlin their butler busy welcoming their guests as she rushed past him.

And where would she go from there? She knew where she would like to go. To that shabby little two-up two-down house in Stepney, that's where. Oh, how she yearned for Stepney at this minute as she stood, glass in hand, smiling at the approaching couple.

She had never heard from her parents since leaving her home even though she had put her address on the card she'd sent them last Christmas. One couldn't blame them for feeling bitter. She felt bitter too – at herself. Her treatment of them came back time after time to haunt her. But it was all too late to start trying to go back now. She'd come too far, and felt too much a coward to test their reception of her if she did.

'Don't be bloody crazy,' Richard hissed from the corner of his mouth, at the same time smiling at the approaching couple. 'Margie! Herbert! Wonderful to see you,' he greeted them.

'Dicky, darling!' And to herself, slightly more formally: 'And Alice. Thanks so much, darlings, for the invitation. Too kind.'

'Not in the least, Margie! You were the first people we thought of. Too long since we last saw you. How are things with you? How's the new house coming along? I heard you were moving to the South Coast. Hampshire, isn't it?'

The small talk drifted over Alice's head as she smiled and tried to make herself appear interested in what everyone had been doing since the last time they met. Richard was full of energetic conversation, his earlier impatient hiss at her as though it had never been. But she knew it would be there again as he censured her silly suggestion later.

Richard had changed. Mostly since Christmas when they'd had that blinding row during which she had screeched at him: 'I hate you! I hate this life. I hate the way you allow your mother to plan this for us and that for us all the time. You take more notice of her than you ever do of me.'

'How can you be so ungrateful?' he'd yelled back at her, his voice high with indignation. 'She's done so much for us, she and Father, this house. And what about all *I've* done for you? Now all you can say is you're bored! How can you be bored? You've fine clothes, money, this place, a car which, incidentally, you haven't yet bothered to learn to drive. I give you the sort of holidays those girls you used to know could never even dream about, let alone have.'

More and more he was throwing her origin in her face, and in most cases she ended it by fleeing from him in tears. He never now told her how fascinating her ways were to him as he had once done, and how he loved the enchanting way she spoke. Now he merely criticised, censured her for being ungrateful, entirely missing the fact that she was being swamped by his desire to be here and there and everywhere. It was all intended for her sake, she knew that, yet to ask for respite from it, just occasionally, made her appear ungrateful in his eyes.

Only recently she had said, 'All I want is a few weeks, months, here, to do absolutely nothing. I don't want to be on show all the time. It's as though I'm being put in a glass case to be shown off by you. I just want a little peace. I want us just to be together. I want to start a family, Richard. We've been married nearly a year and I'm tired of all this never-ending social life we lead. It can't be normal. When are we going to settle down and start a family?'

He had looked at her as though she had asked him to jump over a cliff. 'God!' he spat. 'You're not going to begin wanting to breed all over the place?'

'Why do you have to make it sound so crude? I don't want to begin breeding all over the place! I want to have a child, Richard. I want us to be a proper family. I want something of my own.'

'And I'm not good enough.'

'I didn't mean that. Something of yours too. Mine and yours.'

'It's not what you seem to be implying. You have all I can give you, a fine home, security, all you ever dreamed of, and now I'm supposed to take a back seat, is that it?'

'Of course not.'

'While you're here breast-feeding like some little Cockney housewife, what happens to me? What about our social life while you're doing all that?'

She'd hated his reference to Cockney housewives, voiced as if a form of insult. Her own mother, a respectable East

End woman, had successfully brought up a self-respecting family even if they didn't have much money, her mother as good as his any day except that she didn't have a title. At least she was honest, not like the socialite Lady Pritchard who in her forties dressed like a flapper, playing the social field and dolling up her face until it looked as false as her smile.

Alice had begun to dislike her intensely and blamed her entirely for the rift between herself and her parents. How could she have been so stupid and near-sighted to have gone along with that terrible lie but that she had been so in love with Richard that she had been totally blind to the consequences? She wanted to tell him all this, but she refused to be drawn into his argument.

'You won't be tied down, Richard,' she said haughtily. 'We can afford a nurse and later on a nanny. Having children shouldn't restrict *your* enjoyments.'

'You know damned well it will. I can just hear you moaning about being too long and too often away from *the children* – because I know you won't want to stop at one. Before long, it'll take a team of horses to drag you away from them. And I shall be expected to stay at home to keep you company. I married you, Alice, because I wanted you, not a horde of kids. I wanted you because I was in love with you and . . .'

'*Was* in love with me?' She caught at the words viciously, feeling the tears fill her eyes. 'You're not in love with me now.' She saw him wave his hands in exasperation at her.

'Bloody hell! Must you pick up on everything I say? I am still in love with you. But I wanted you for my wife and my companion too, not the mother of my children when we've hardly been married a year. Oh, for God's sake, Alice!'

The tears had spilled over as he had stamped from the room, leaving her crushed and bewildered. And it hadn't been the last time they had rowed over her inability, as he called it, to be grateful for all he'd done and was doing for her, for it was always her fault, wasn't it?

Recalling each argument, always the same argument, Alice felt the same crushed sensation as she had that first time they'd argued about it. But it must not show, not at this birthday party Richard had given for her. Clutching her cocktail glass to her, the fingers of one hand curled around its stem, those of the other curled around her wrist, the action forming a shield across her breast, she turned on a smile for Richard's friends, her voice light and cheerful as she joined in their conversation and her smile as beautifully false as Lady Margaret Pritchard's. She was learning fast. Richard could be proud of her.

Amy sat nervously on the chair provided, eyeing the General Manager of Bellows Shipping Company across his large desk and wondering why she had been so unexpectedly summoned by him. Mr Goodburn was gaunt, well over six feet tall, thin unsmiling lips, eyes of granite-grey and seemingly as brittle as that very stone, his presence in any department struck awe and discomfort into every young woman who worked there, even Amy for all she combated the reaction with the knowledge that her family would top his any day.

But she was to his eyes just another of his underlings, and as such sat facing him with nerves on edge trying to think what it was she could have done to be thus sent for. Was she to be given the sack? If so, why?

She watched him lean forward on the desk, forearms flat upon it, fingers clasped, every knuckle as proud as a miniature Mount Everest.

'How long have you been with us, Miss Harrington?'

Amy lifted her chin, her hazel eyes meeting his steely ones. If he was dispensing with her services, she would not take it submissively. 'Eight and a half months,' she replied firmly, refraining from addressing him as sir, or even uttering his name.

'Yes. And you have been doing the same job all that time?'

'I have.'

His mouth never twitched one fraction from its thin straight line. 'Do you not think it time you had a change?'

'If you think that in order.' She was not going to ask him what fault she was being accused of.

'I do think it,' he said quietly. 'I hear that you have been

225

applying yourself to other tasks of late besides the one for which you were taken on, that you have applied yourself to these tasks without mention of them to anyone, nor have you complained about the extra work asked of you, and I am of a mind to consider it time you had some recognition of your diligence in the form of promotion. But before I grant any form of promotion, I would ask you, have you any intention of marrying in the foreseeable future?'

For a moment Amy was dumbfounded. She had expected a reprimand, and was instead receiving commendation, promotion, praise. 'I . . .' she began. To tell him of her hopes to marry Tom as soon as they had saved enough would scotch all chance of getting on. Just in time she stopped herself.

'Not as far as I can see,' she told him. And that was the truth.

She and Tom had again been compelled to put back the date of the wedding. He'd had a run of poor employment this summer, not because jobs were scarce but because his father seemed to have lost much of his zest as a ganger, as though his heart had died within him for all he kept going.

Time and again Arthur Jordan had lost plum jobs to other gangs, letting down his own men, becoming aggressive when they had complained. He was losing his regulars, who were picking up other jobs that often made them unavailable when he required them, virtually cocking a snook at him when he attempted to give them a drilling for it. Without them he'd had to rely on floaters, men who did not belong to any gang but who drifted about with an eye only for work convenient to them. Arthur Jordan often refused them, knowing them unreliable, but the result often was that he and his regular men would be left hung up with an incomplete gang trying to entice the less dedicated to join it. The outcome of that was that he lost the best jobs and even Tom was expressing his dissatisfaction. But he could hardly leave his father in the lurch, so he had been stuck with poor paying jobs and the prospect of no wedding this year either. So Amy felt she wasn't lying to her questioner when she admitted to no marriage prospects in the foreseeable future.

* * *

'It'll mean at least two shillings and sixpence a week rise,' she announced as she fought desperately to push the point home to Tom. He hadn't displayed the least excitement about her news, though Mrs Jordan had flung her plump arms about Amy as soon as she had told her, congratulating her and hugging her close. 'It can all go towards the wedding. We could be married much sooner. You do want that, don't you, Tom?'

He nodded wordlessly and continued eating his supper. She knew how he must feel, striving to keep in work while she was getting a rise at the mere flick of a finger.

But she had worked for it. She deserved promotion. And she deserved much better from Tom. Not praise, but at least recognition that she was trying to help towards their marriage.

She would get him on his own later and have it out with him. But he'd say nothing to her complaints, she knew that beforehand, keeping his thoughts to himself. Of course it belittled him for all they badly needed the money. It was a bone of contention between them. But Amy wasn't prepared to give up her job just because her success made him feel that much less of a man. Men could be so short-sighted.

Angry and deflated, she got on with her own supper and neither spoke to the other for the rest of the evening.

In the early half light of the December morning the body of stevedores, now fully mustered, followed closely behind the foremen shipworkers onto the stones, the foremen themselves walking on one side of the road, the rest on the other. They would eventually form up opposite to where contractors stood waiting to take their pick of men for the day or the week depending on the length of their contract.

Each contractor had his own stretch of the stones, Arthur Jordan coming to a halt before one of them, having been approached earlier by the man's agent – not quite legal of course, but Arthur was putting himself about again with his old zeal.

Tom felt elated as he stood alongside his father, who, for the first time in months, had got himself a decent gang gathered around him, his old flair returning at last, for the first time since Alice had left home. He was beginning not to refer so much to himself as being dead, a remark once made with so much bitterness against her. It was a terrible thing she had done and watching the haunted set to his father's face day after day, Tom felt his own bitterness against his sister.

But that, it seemed, was all in the past. He had needed one good contract with a reliable firm for the old gang, seeing their opportunity, to muster to his side. Twice this month he had swung it, and now they clamoured to have him as their ganger. This morning was no exception as they were instantly called.

Today it was bagged phosphate to be unloaded into barges, a dirty dusty job, but in times of work famine they were happy enough to have it, especially as there was talk of being taken over onto other jobs by the same firm for some time to come plus the promise of plenty of overtime. Arthur Jordan was the hero of the day as the twelve climbed down into Hold Two ready for work.

'Overtime, that's what I want,' Tom said as he and his father manhandled heavy bulky bags into a set ready for the crane to haul up. He glanced up at the hatchwayman above him doing a balancing act on the combing around the square of the hatch, he who made sure each set remained clear of all obstructions as it was lifted and swung out and down to the waiting lighters.

Here in the hold the grey December light hardly penetrated and the portable lighting was already on, glowing yellow and ghostly. Midday, the hold emptying fast.

'With what Amy's making now and any overtime I get, we should be able to get married this spring.' It was the first time he had ever mentioned Amy's earnings and he made a face and then grinned in surprise at himself.

'Yer should be grateful to 'er,' his father said between heavy breaths from his exertions. 'Clever, that one. Sort of gel yer need to 'ave be'ind yer.'

But the smile had left Tom's face. Even his father didn't think he could be any good without Amy's help. 'I think I'm the best judge of that,' he growled and straightened up from the set they had completed. Taut-lipped, he glanced up, tugging hard on the rope sling to hoist away.

Up it went, slowly, swinging slightly. The hatchwayman would give it a twitch to send it clear of the overhanging wings. But the hatchwayman wasn't there, or couldn't be seen. The sling seemed to be swinging a bit too wildly.

The hatchwayman had been standing waiting for the ready when someone called to him. 'Got a match on yer, Alf? Bloody wind – can't get me fag ter light. Me bleedin' matches is all damp.'

Alf fished in his pocket, tossed the box of Swan Vestas to the other man. He watched him catch them deftly as the set rose to just below the deck level. Too late he turned to reach forward to be sure it cleared the deck's obstruction. The edge of the set touched underneath the protruding wing, caught, tilting the stack of nine weighty bauxite bags. As though in slow motion they slid, broke free, and toppled with increasing speed back down into the hold.

Tom saw them coming, the dim light of the hatch blocked out, each bag seeming three times its size as it fell towards him, felt the rasping fear of every man who knew the weight of these bags falling a hundred feet at an ever-increasing speed with himself directly beneath them.

'Dad!' The cry ripped itself from him. He made to push his father out of the path of the crushing power, and at the same time threw himself sideways.

Nine bags coming at all angles, how could anyone escape? Tom felt his legs plucked from under him as though by a giant hand. Thrown flat on his face, he lay gasping, both legs trapped by a tremendous weight unable to move as others crashed down all around him. For a moment there came a hanging silence. His legs felt as though they had been bent down at the knees into a hollow where the cargo lay uneven. He tried to ease them and experienced an excruciating pain that made him cry out.

The silence was ruptured by men's shouts, the hold already busy with rescuers. Twisting his head Tom found himself staring into a horrified face, the mouth hanging open to reveal stained teeth, the eyes fixed on him like the eyes of a doll.

'You orright?' came the inane enquiry.

Of course he wasn't all right. A bloody great bag of phosphate on top of his legs, his knees bent at some strange angle – he knew they were without seeing them. And when the man tried to move the weight, a shock of pain shot up to his brain, forcing a scream from him.

There were people walking all over the cargo, calling orders to each other, bending over him, going away again. That he was badly injured there was no question. There was a totally divorced thought in his mind. Dock workers never received sick pay, not even for being injured and off work, nor did any insurance company touch them. All one could hope for, for weeks of being out of work, was some kind soul sending up a kite for your mates to kick in with a few shillings for the injured party. How would his mother get on without his wages coming in for God knows how long? There'd only be Dad's wages . . .

The second thought struck him as he lay there waiting for someone to do something and help lift the crushing weight from his legs.

'Me dad,' he demanded of the nearest face, an older face, like his father's. 'Is he all right?'

'Which is yer dad?' came the question.

'Arthur Jordan – me dad.'

'Oh, Gawd.'

The words sent an ominous thrill of fear through him. 'Is 'e 'urt?'

'Oh, Gawd,' the man said again, then leaned closer. 'Son . . . yer dad's copped it. 'E's dead, yer dad. Neck's broke. Lad, I'm sorry. Another bloke's got 'is as well. An' there's anuvver wiv a broken arm. It's a mess down 'ere. I'm sorry about yer dad . . .'

But Tom couldn't hear him. The blood was pounding in his ears. He found himself struggling to free himself, crying out with the pain it caused, begging people to get him free so he could be with his dad, until slowly the pounding died away and his body went limp, but he didn't know that.

230

Chapter Seventeen

Silence lay over the house, silence that came from a lack of movement, a lack of will even to think, the woman stricken by the news that had come only seconds ago.

The three men, mates of Arthur, men of his gang, had stood in a sad uncomfortable group as Grace Jordan, her sleeves rolled up, her forearms damp, opened the door to their knock, her face smoothly unsuspecting slowly creasing in consternation then apprehension as the three men stood fidgeting, at first unable to reply to her question. 'What's wrong?' she had asked, then, even more fearful of what she would hear, knowing she must, 'Oh, Gawd! Tell me, what's wrong.'

Falteringly, as gently as they could, they told her the bare bones of it, and then, struck dumb by the sudden blow of grief so sudden that it hadn't yet truly registered, she had beckoned them into the house where she had been alone a moment before, happily and contentedly getting on with her daily chores. It was Monday and the copper in the kitchen could be heard bubbling gently, filling the house with the warm smell of soapsuds and hot water and half-boiled linen.

In the back room where she led the messengers, she sat down on a hard chair by the table, her eyes fixed on the middle distance, seeing nothing of the room around her, only the familiar face of her husband – grinning at her as he often did, his bristly moustache giving a little twitch, his slightly watery eyes amused by some secret joke that he'd tell her later – so that she felt she need only reach out and touch him and he would speak to her. Yet she knew that if she did reach out, she'd touch nothing; that his face would never again break into that crooked grin, nor would those eyes dance to some secret joke.

She could hear his voice ... 'Tell yer abart it later, ole gel ...' His deep voice, all too real for what these men were telling her to be true even though she knew what they were saying.

She heard her own voice speaking but distant as though some one else was speaking for her. 'We'll 'ave ter tell the gels. And Willie – 'e's in school. An' Amy ...'

'We'll tell 'em,' one of the men said as her words faltered and died. 'Where do we get in touch wiv 'em?'

Somehow she managed to give the information necessary, heard herself thanking them for coming, shook her head when one of them offered to stay with her. She saw them out and then came back into the room to sit down again on the hard chair by the table wondering why her head seemed so empty of thoughts, dark and empty, like there was only a hole there. Gradually she became aware of the gentle plopping sound of boiling washing in the copper. She ought to go and push the rising linen down with the copper stick before it boiled over the lid. That was what she had been doing, she remembered now, when those men, those mates of Arthur's, had come to her door.

Grace's eyes wandered around the quiet room. The furniture looked so still, so dead. Did it always look like this when nobody was here? With the family around her, it always seemed to have life. But she'd been alone many a time and it hadn't seemed like this before. If Arthur was to come in now, it would come alive again.

But he wouldn't come in, would he? She looked at the quiet room, wanting only for him to be here. Already he had gone to wherever he must go, and the room lay quite still, quite dead, only the quiet bubbling of the washing breaking the silence around her where she sat alone. She should go and see to it or soon there would be suds all over the floor, but she didn't get up. She merely sat on, staring blankly ahead trying to conjure up the man she'd never again see or touch or feel touching her, and all the while the chores she should be doing marched in slow procession through her head as she wondered at her lack of feeling. She ought to be crying but she wasn't, even though it felt as if her heart had been torn out of her.

Amy's legs felt as though they were made of jelly as, holding one of Mrs Jordan's arms with Vi holding the other helping to support her mother while Rosy and Willie followed behind, they entered the long casualty ward of the London Hospital in Whitechapel to where a set of off-white screens formed an awkward concertina construction around one of the beds.

It was afternoon. No one had eaten anything. They'd sat in the hospital for hours while the operation had been in progress, a nurse coming by at intervals offering cups of tea and words of comfort that she would let them know the moment the operation ended, and not to worry – Mr Jordan was strong and young which was in his favour. They learned, that the lower legs had both been smashed, the knees damaged but the main cause for concern was a fractured rib that had nicked the lung. However the surgeon Mr Sinclair was very good at his job.

His mother had sat staring ahead the whole time, nodding understanding of what the nurse was saying, and in all that time she had not cried, though the two girls and their brother had broken down at the sudden news of their father's death and were still tearful. A teacher had brought Willie home from school and a colleague had come home with the girls. Amy had come home alone, wanting no one with her to witness her stark fear for Tom. All she'd known was he'd been taken to hospital but as far as the docker knew, was not in danger. As far as he knew! What did the man know? Amy had come home, her body shaking, imagining the worst, thoughts of Tom slowly succumbing to his injuries and dying before she ever got to the hospital. Her first instinct had been to go straight to the hospital, but how could she leave Tom's mother in her sudden bereavement? She'd gone home first to be with her and her children to give her support as best she could. No one had notified Alice yet, but neither had there been time to tell the rest of the family.

233

The operation over, Mrs Jordan was informed, to Amy's intense relief, that her son had come through it very well and that they'd be able to see him in a short while but for only a very brief visit. They now followed the nurse down the long antiseptic-smelling ward with its highly polished brown linoleum floor and its dreary walls painted cream and green, the family allowed to come in a group, courtesy of the ward sister. She knew of the patient's mother's bereavement only a few hours ago and that Mrs Jordan was still in shock and need of support, so the customary rule of only two at a bed at any one time was waived.

'Is this the one?' Amy asked, fighting to maintain a steady voice as the nurse conducting them came to a halt at the wobbly steel-framed contraption.

The woman nodded, held up a finger. 'The doctor is just taking another look at Mr Jordan. He won't be long with him now.'

'How is Tom . . . Mr Jordan?' Amy asked on his mother's behalf, she still too stricken by the death of her husband to ask for herself. She looked ill, her cheeks mottled unevenly with pale patches amid the normal florid colouring

'He is comfortable,' the nurse answered.

Her reassurance was broken by a small groan of pain from behind the screens that made them all wince, but her smile didn't lessen one iota as she eased herself between the screens, bidding the family wait. Moments later she reappeared, pushing aside the screens to reveal the doctor who had been examining his patient whose eyes were closed, his face the colour of ash and still none too clean. The doctor, straightening up, dourly regarded the eldest of the group.

'You are the mother?'

Mrs Jordan gave a small nod, tears not far away as she found her voice. ''Ow is 'e, doctor? Will 'e be orright?'

The man didn't reply directly. 'I am Dr Ellmers, Mr Sinclair's registrar. Your son's sleeping now, but you can have five minutes with him, and then I shall need to have a word with you, if I may, before you leave. I shall be in the ward sister's office at the end of the ward as you go out.'

Mrs Jordan nodded, seeming to only half hear as Amy

and Violet helped her sit down on the chair placed next to the bed. Amy found a chair on the other side and sat; the others stood, looking lost, Violet hovering behind her mother to give aid if it was necessary. Rosy, sobbing quietly, and Willie stood together a little removed. Other patients alert enough to notice this intrusion of people where only two to a bed was normally permissible, came to their own conclusions about this bending of the rules. But none of the family was in any condition to care what they thought, as their eyes were only for the figure in bed, the cover tented up over his legs.

'Tom?' Mrs Jordan's voice sounded small. She had hardly spoken since her children had been brought home to share her grief. A shake or nod of the head, a negative gesture, an almost inaudible yes or no, that was all. But now she seemed to gain strength from that single positive word.

'Tom. Tom, luv.' He stirred, his face turning a little towards the sound, the eyelids, heavy from the anaesthetic, opening a fraction, the blue slit of the eyes displaying recognition. A shuddering breath convulsed him.

'Dad . . .' The voice was weak.

'I know, son. I've bin told.'

There was another sigh and the eyes closed, the body too full of anaesthetic to bear up any longer. The nurse came forward from where she had been hovering.

'We had best leave him. He'll sleep for quite some time.'

Violet helped her mother up as Amy came round to give any assistance needed, but there appeared to be a strength in the woman's carriage now. Hardly needing her daughter's help, she followed the nurse, and with the others being told to wait outside except for Violet, went in after the nurse to the sister's office where Dr Ellmers sat waiting, one arm lying loosely on the desk.

Through the small window shielded by a piece of net curtain, Amy could just make out the doctor talking to Tom's mother, she nodding, her expression fixed, like a child learning its lesson. Beside her, Violet was holding her hand while the doctor went on talking.

Outside, Amy's arm was being held by Rosy, tightly, as if the younger girl might fall down without her to hold onto.

235

Neither of them spoke, and it was Willie who broke the silence, his voice dull.

"Ow we gonna manage wivout Dad?"

Willie would be thirteen in May, growing tall and seeming to get thinner with each acquired inch for all he ate like a young horse. He reminded Amy of how plasticine gets thinner as it is rolled longer. He could broaden out like Tom as he got older, but mostly he took after his father. Usually he was so full of energy, seldom still, yet today he had moved with the family like an automaton. Amy felt the grief in the boy's voice and touched his shoulder gently.

'Let's not think about that now, Willie. We've got to think about your mother, how she will cope. And Tom too. He is going to need a lot of nursing when he comes home.'

Willie's tone didn't change. 'Tom won't be goin' ter work, not fer a long time, and now we ain't got Dad. We're gonna be tight fer money.'

'Don't worry about it,' Amy said. 'There's Vi and Rosy's income, and mine.'

'Dad's funeral's gonna cost Mum a lot,' Willie said, as though he hadn't heard. 'There ain't much insurance. Mum couldn't afford much.'

'Your father's colleagues will probably have a collection. They usually do, you know. Some sort of distress fund. That will help.' For a boy his age, he was far too obsessed by money problems. Probably most children of the East End came to that early in life. 'What you must think about is being a comfort to your mother.'

'Soon as I'm thirteen, I'm gonna get meself a proper job,' Willie went on.

'I'd advise you to keep at school until you're fourteen and then go on to night school and try to learn a trade. That would be far better for you.'

'An' what d'we use ter pay fer night school then? Shirt buttons?'

Amy ignored his rudeness, but Willie still had something to say and his tone sounded too bitter to be coming from the mouth of a twelve-year-old. 'You got money, ain't yer? Yer've lived wiv us long enough ter pool what yer got. Mum could do wiv a few extra 'alfpence now.'

She wanted to silence him with a reprimand but she couldn't. What he was saying was the truth for all it sounded impudent as all truths do when spoken by the young. She wanted to protest that what money she had was to help pay for her and Tom to get married, but any thought of marriage at this moment must fade into insignificance against the poverty that loomed ahead of the whole family with its main breadwinner gone and its second one looking to be laid up for weeks if not months to come. Of course she had no option but to offer all she had to help them, and that meant the most part of what she was earning too. Willie still had more to say, this time not directed at her, thankfully.

'Me mum ought ter get in touch wiv Alice too. She ain't let 'er know yet.'

Amy and Rosy looked at each other, the same thought in both their heads. Two thoughts in fact. First that there was a way out. Alice, married into money, would surely help her mother. Second, the more sobering thought, her mother hadn't even mentioned her, as if she did not exist, although she had been too shocked by grief and only a few hours had passed since the terrible news. There hadn't been time yet to notify Alice of her father's death. Amy resolved to contact her as soon as they got home. She would talk to Mrs Jordan about it first, if she was up to it, to make sure she approved.

Mrs Jordan and Vi were getting up, the doctor putting a kindly hand on the older woman's arm. Her face looked white, and Vi was sniffling into a handkerchief as he led them to the door and opened it for them, his voice becoming audible. 'I'm sorry to have to give you more bad tidings, Mrs Jordan, on top of what you have already suffered. And as I said, you have my very sincere condolences. Will you be all right?'

'I've got me family with me,' she said simply.

'What is it, Mum? What's wrong?' Rosy burst out, her voice echoing along the ward.

Mrs Jordan, her coat clutched about her, her handbag held tight under her arm giving the impression that she would fall to pieces if she did not hold herself together, gave a small flap of her free hand in a gesture of protest. 'I can't

237

talk about it 'ere. We'll 'ave ter go 'ome. I need ter get 'ome.'

'Don't worry, Mum,' Vi was saying. 'We'll get you 'ome and get you a nice cuppa tea, and you can tell us there what the doctor said to you.'

Amy said nothing. Whatever bad tidings he'd mentioned could only concern Tom. Her heart ached desperately to know what it was, but Mrs Jordan looked about to collapse. They had to get her home as soon as they could.

There was no money for taxis. In virtual silence they walked through the side turnings from Whitechapel, no eyes for the market that thrived noisily outside. It was a good twenty-five minute walk, but to people used to walking rather than paying out for transport when a good pair of legs cost nothing, it was no hardship and could be quicker than the two changes of buses needed. At least, although the December day was dull and slightly breezy, it wasn't raining, nor was it all that chilly.

All the way home, Mrs Jordan hung on to her daughter Vi's arm, her head slightly directed towards the pavement, her eyes apparently seeing only her feet. Violet was the only one to do any talking, short spurts of observations that needed no reply: she'd inform the family as soon as they got home; do all the arrangements necessary; Mum to rest as much as she could; and they would go back to the hospital tonight or tomorrow morning to see how Tom was.

'And do you want me to get word to Alice?' she asked at one point but when her mother made no reply apart from a faint movement of her head that could as easily have been a no as a yes, Vi didn't press the question.

And so they came home, Mrs Jordan automatically fishing into her handbag for her street door key and reaching out to the keyhole.

'No, Mum, don't bother. I'll let us in,' Violet said, taking the key from her fingers.

'It's no bother.'

But Violet already had the key, briskly opening the door as though she hadn't noticed the lack of life to her mother's voice.

They hastily made tea, then they listened in dread about Tom's condition as explained by the doctor, their tea untouched and turning cold.

Mrs Jordan's voice gained unexpected strength as she told them that Tom's injured legs were going to take a long time to heal – longer than any of them had imagined – that they might never heal completely. He would walk again, but not without a limp and most probably he'd have to use a stick. He would no longer be employable at the docks.

'But what's he to do?' Rosy cried. 'He don't know anythink else.'

'He'll find somethink,' her mother said firmly, firmer than she had been all day. This was something she could hold on to, to escape the empty place where her heart seemed it should be; seeing her son back on his feet no matter how long it took. She tried not to think of how they'd make ends meet. It had occurred to her that she could ask Alice for money. Alice had money and in the name of heaven she owed them all for what she had done to them. Grace remembered how she had predicted her father being dead and shuddered inwardly. That thoughtless bit of tomfoolery to make Alice appear to be what she wasn't just to please her betters had with hindsight been merely hurtful and unforgivable at the time. Now it had taken on the aspect of an omen. Or a curse. No, she would not go begging to her, cap in hand. She'd rather starve, see her family starve before she did that.

Vi and Rosy left her in the hands of Amy while they took on the burden of relaying the dreadful news to those of the family within walking distance, leaving them to contact further-flung relatives by telegrams, the cost with luck shared between them all, to save money. But they did send one to Alice, taking matters firmly out of their mother's hands. How ever she had hurt her parents, everyone really, this was a time to put the matter to one side. Her father was dead from an accident at work. She had to be told. From then on it was up to her what she did about it.

Arthur's body was brought home a few days later to lie in state in the front room for all to come and pay their respects.

Young Willie moved out to sleep on the sofa in the back room. Despite the next few December days growing steadily colder, the front door seemed to stand constantly open as family and neighbours and friends from the Working Men's Social Club and Arthur's colleagues at the docks – he had been a well-liked and respected man – filed in to stand awhile and look down at him lying in peace. The broken skull hidden under a white sheet neatly draped about his head like a monk's hood, his broken neck concealed, the bruised features professionally disguised by undertaker's paint and powder, he looked unnatural, but everyone left with the comment that he looked as though he was merely asleep.

After viewing, friends and neighbours came to murmur heartfelt sympathy to the widow, inadequate in their efforts to comfort, then went away sad but relieved to be continuing their lives. Family stayed longer, the female members breaking down in tears as they hugged her rigid body to them and hiccuped how dreadful it all was and that they couldn't find words to express how they felt for her, the men holding her close and blowing their noses as they released her, saying they'd be there for her for whatever she needed, help, support, little odd jobs, anything.

Grace nodded obediently, wordlessly. She still hadn't cried. That would come later when least expected, alone ironing, or peeling the spuds, or washing the floor, or going through Arthur's things – perhaps some trivial little thing, his shaving brush or a tie or a handkerchief falling out as she tidied a drawer. And she would hug the object to herself, bury her face in it trying to recapture the essence of him when he'd been there with her and which she'd taken for granted, so sure of their life together going on and on.

Such unexpected moments would go on for years, she knew. Someone had once said bereavement was a two-year disease and the pain would get less as time went on. She felt it would be more a lifetime's disease until she finally joined Arthur. But still she couldn't cry as she let herself be hugged and wept over, the loss more acute to them in being that fraction more removed from it for all their grief, where she, numbed in mind and body as though neither belonged to her at all, could feel nothing, as though she, this someone, floated in a great void.

Even sitting with Arthur, the blinds pulled down at the windows, the room in semi-darkness, gazing down at him lying so peaceful in his coffin – like they said, as though he was only asleep – she felt too numb to cry. She'd talk to him lying there, everyday things, what she was going to have to do alone now that he was gone.

'Went out yesterday, luv, and it rained. Fergot me umbrella and me black coat shrunk right up. I 'ad ter pull an' tug at it or it'll shown me bum in the end, I'm sure. Amy got the old treadle machine out an' she put on a piece of black from one of 'er skirts – she's got lots of skirts, luv – and made the bottom and the sleeves longer. So it fits again now. I must remember ter take me umbrella wiv me next time. Yer'd 'ave laughed, Arthur. Yer really would've.'

She would smooth his cold stone face with her hands, like marble to her touch, pretending it was warm again; she had even bent and kissed those rigid frozen lips, had with forlorn love for him caressed those hands, gnarled, the fingers curled from long use of a bag hook in his work, its wood handle gripped between the second and third fingers for long hours to get at cargo out of reach. His job had been a hard one, an unforgiving one, and in the end it had killed him.

Once, during this day that seemed to float, she had stared at herself in the oval bevelled-edged mirror over the fireplace and wondered at the woman staring back with what seemed to be the stare of someone quite different even though she had recognised her own reflection. Grace wondered abstractedly, as people came to hold her to them and murmur their deep shock at this terrible business, if she would ever be the Grace Jordan she had been before. From now on, without Arthur, it would be that woman in the mirror who would take her place.

The funeral took place the following Monday, Grace having spent most of that time in the front room sitting with Arthur. In a waiting silence the whole family, filling the little house, watched the undertakers arrive to carry the cheap coffin out to the hearse, and put on what flowers there were, a small wreath from a collection by neighbours, another from the Working Men's Club, one from Arthur's work gang, one from the company he had been working for when the accident had occurred – a flamboyant expensive thing and nice of them, but the Jordans would sooner have had the money to help tide them over, especially as the girls both lost a day's pay to be absent for their father's funeral.

Grace Jordan had gone to the expense of a small wreath of her own with a card: 'To My Dear Beloved Husband'. From his children there was a sheaf with the words: 'Our Dear Dad'. Amy had gone in with them on this, not knowing what message she should use and not wanting to look independent of them all.

She sat apart with Alice. Dicky hadn't thought it important enough for him to accompany his wife, and her own family making it obvious they were not including her in their collective grief, she looked so lost and not all that well that Amy felt she had to be with her, both of them as it were on the edge of the family.

Alice had arrived the evening of her father's death, leaving her home the moment the telegram had arrived. When Amy opened the door to her, she had been so distraught that she all but fell into the house, running in floods of tears to her mother, but whether Mrs Jordan was still in too much a state of shock or had no interest in Alice's grief, she was seen to almost push her away, saying tersely, 'I'm all right.'

How Alice felt about the welcome she hadn't said, but from then on she had kept her tears down, crying only to herself, her sisters not knowing whether to comfort her and upset their mother or to stay away from her. Amy, with no such dilemma, had taken her off by herself to weep unseen by the others until with nowhere for her to sleep here, Alice had left later, saying she'd be back for the funeral.

Returned from the cemetery, Mrs Jordan seemed a bit perkier, her family and friends about her, and even smiled at their chat as they ate the sandwiches and cake set out for them and drank tea and a little sherry, the men a glass of beer. But Alice remained apart, whether by choice or not,

Amy couldn't say, but she came and sat with her. After all, Alice had done her no wrong.

'How are you keeping then?' she opened, casually sipping her small glass of sherry. Alice smiled, eyeing the glass.

'Do you know, Mum hasn't four that match in this house. I wonder if I should buy her a set of wine glasses for Christmas. Crystal.'

'I don't think that's a good idea, Alice. Your mother won't have much use for crystal, or wine glasses of any sort for that matter – except to take to the pawnbrokers with hardly any money coming into the house now.'

Alice's lips turned downward. 'I didn't think about that.'

There were a lot of things Alice hadn't thought about, but Amy kept that opinion to herself. 'It's not going to be much of a Christmas for your mother, for any of us, Tom being in hospital too.' She'd told Amy how Tom was on the night of her father's death and what his future looked to be. 'But with your father's death so near to it, I don't think any Christmas will be what it was for her ever again.'

Alice bent her head and didn't reply, and Amy went back to her original question. 'So, how *are* you keeping, you and Dicky . . . I mean Richard?'

Alice didn't look up, intent on staring into her own sherry glass, her hands curled around it so tightly that the knuckles of the small slim hand had turned white. She had changed a lot since marrying Dicky, her hair still short about her ears but beautifully and fashionably styled and curled, her face expertly made up. The black she wore was today ostentatiously expensive, and she looked even thinner than when Amy had last seen her. Her hands fluttered more and her voice had become brittle. Amy could imagine her being quite self-assured although there was nothing of that at this very moment, something more like shame before this gathering. Even so, there was a brittleness about her that hadn't been there a couple of years back. Amy wasn't sure it was a change for the better – the kinder, softer Alice gone for good.

She had to repeat her question yet again before Alice finally gave a reply, and then she knew why she had been

243

side-stepping it all this time as the brown eyes began to swim.

'We're all right . . . Well, no, we're not. Oh, Amy, things have gone so terribly wrong. I don't think Richard loves me any more and I don't know what to do.'

'Of course he loves you,' Amy tried to console her but her heart felt as though it had turned over. 'You've been married only eighteen months, and he was head-over-heels in love with you. You're both probably just going through a sticky patch, that's all. Things will be all right again soon.'

'No, it's more than that. There's no one I can tell but you. I can't talk to his parents about it. He's their shining light that wouldn't go out if you threw a bucket of water over him. If I try to say anything detrimental about him, his mother looks down her nose at me as if to say, what can one expect but complaints from a common little slut who thought she was lining her pockets? It's awful. And I can't go running to Mum with it. Not now. I couldn't before. I can't now.'

'With what? What's the matter between you and Richard?'

'Well, you'll say it's nothing really. But he treats me so abominably. Ever since I said I wanted us to start a family, he's been so absolutely nasty to me. He blames me for being ungrateful for all he's done for me.'

'But he has done a lot for you, hasn't he?'

'Yes, of course he has. But he never stops doing it. We've been to so many places. Scotland, Paris, Venice, Rome, Vienna, South of France. All over. We've even sailed down the Nile in October with a party of his . . . our friends. As you say, Amy, we've been married only eighteen months, but he doesn't stand still for a moment. It seems to me he can't, doesn't want to, and I don't know why. There's not a day goes by when we're not invited out for the evening or invite people to us, or go with them to the theatre or garden parties. I still can't believe how we fit it all in, and it's wearing me down. I'd give anything for a week to myself, or us alone together. But he has to have all these people. He says this is the done thing.'

Amy didn't know what to say as she listened. Of course

those with money did the rounds quite frequently, went abroad, met friends. It could be exciting. But what Alice was describing did strike her as a little excessive. Alice, however, was still talking, almost as though to herself.

'Three weeks ago, I refused to go with him to a dinner party. I just couldn't. I had such a ghastly tense headache I could hardly see out of my eyes, and I begged him to cancel out. Instead, he flew into a rage. He pushed me and I fell down into a chair. He didn't even bother to help me up or apologise. Just shouted at me that I could stay there on my own but that he was going. And not long after that, when I didn't feel well again, he didn't even bother to row with me. He just said, "Stay at home then," and went without me again. And last week, he went with some friends to see Ivor Novello's new play *The Truth Game* at the Globe Theatre, and he didn't even ask me. Just . . . went. They all went on to a party afterwards, and now he keeps talking about someone called Annette Collier as though she is the top branch of the tree in his eyes. And when I demanded to know who she was, he said, "You're not jealous, are you?" and things like what right have I, who only married him for his money and to escape the sort of life I'd had, to tell him what he should and should not do, and who he could be friends with and who he couldn't.'

She finally stopped talking, her head bent, her fingers playing with the glass, its contents untouched. Now she lifted it to her lips and in one swift movement threw back the liquid into her mouth. Her voice when she spoke again was like the splintering of glass. 'I've bored you enough with my idiotic imaginings. Anyway, I think it's about time I left, don't you?'

She stood up sharply, the smile she directed at Amy like a razor edge. 'Do give my excuses to my mother. She won't want to see me off. I'll keep in touch with you, Amy, if that's all right. And do take no notice of my little outburst. I'm probably just low at the moment. My time of the month . . .' she gave a bright laugh. 'Things do get so amplified when one is a little under the weather. It's losing Dad like that as well, I expect.'

Amy stood up too, at a loss to know what to say. Some-

245

thing was definitely not going well with that marriage, despite Alice's change of attitude, full of smiles now as though she had merely been going through a silly moment. If she was upset by her father's death, it wasn't evident any more. He might have been anyone. Amy couldn't believe this girl could switch so quickly from grief to casual breeziness in the space of seconds.

'If you must go,' she said.

'Yes I must,' Alice said unnecessarily.

There was pain behind it, Amy was sure. They went to the door together, moving through the knots of family chattering brightly now that the ordeal of burial was over. Amy had an impulse to signal to Alice's mother that she was leaving, but thought better of it.

At the door, she said, 'Do keep in touch, Alice.'

'Oh, I will, of course,' Alice said.

'And if you do need my help at any time, don't hesitate to let me know.'

'Oh, I shall be all right,' Alice said brashly. She bent forward and planted a kiss on Amy's cheek, then without warning, clutched her to her.

'I want to thank you for listening,' she said. The hard tone had disappeared, giving way to the one Amy knew. 'I wish I had come here when my father was ... I should have come and tried to heal the wound I gave him, despite what he would have thought. It's too late now.'

She pulled away and though there were tears in her eyes, she smiled. 'Write to me, Amy, and tell me how Tom is. I'd like to know how things are. And if you do talk to Mum, try to persuade her that I didn't mean what I said when Richard and I were getting married. I don't know what I must have been thinking of. But it's done now. And Amy ... don't make the same mistake as me. Don't let too many years go by before you contact your own family again. Think of me, and my dad, and my mum.'

She was gone, hurrying down the dirty little street to the main road where she would hail a taxi to take her to Waterloo Station and then a train to her fine house in Surrey, leaving Amy to ponder her parting words.

Chapter Eighteen

There was really precious little chance to mull over what Alice had allowed to slip through. Whether things were going right in Alice's marriage or not, and why, Amy had her own problems.

After work she would hurry to the hospital and sit beside Tom until her twenty minutes with him was up, the rest of the family needing to see him in the hour allowed for visiting.

Tom was morose, quiet. He had been told the facts about his future then advised to think himself lucky compared to others in this hospital who had lost legs or were paralysed, wheelchair-bound or never to rise up off their back again, so on and so forth. In his present frame of mind it wasn't much comfort to a man whose life had been totally physical, who'd not so much been proud of his strength and bounding energy as taken it for granted, to be told he must think himself lucky to be destined to walk with a stick; as he saw it, he might as well have been paralysed, not realising or wanting to realise just what that meant.

'All I want to do is get out of here,' he growled to everyone who visited.

Amy held her temper, nursed her sympathy, sat holding his hand when he let her. There was never much to talk about. She avoided making him more fretful by talking about her work when it was obvious he'd never work in the docks again, not being educated enough for office work even if there was any going; perhaps good enough for sorting jobs, cleaning jobs, menial tasks, bringing his pride down lower than it already was. By the same token she could not mention how his mother was beginning to struggle, adding to his awareness that he was no longer bringing in money. His sister Alice was taboo. Bits of news about his other two sisters and his younger brother who could still help the family coffers no matter how meagrely, all of them fit and able to contribute while he lay here in hospital effete and useless, were best skirted around. The least mention of money, even to say that so far they were managing well enough, brought a tightening of his lips and a hardening of his expression as he visualised the time coming when the lack of money would inevitably become an issue. Attempts to comfort him only annoyed him and sent him into a fit of brooding. It was an almost impossible task talking to him and, feel for him though she did, love him though she did, Amy often came away as exhausted as if she had been doing a job of manual work.

So far things at home hadn't been too worrying if one didn't contemplate the future too much. Mrs Jordan was managing to cling to her placid expression, her tone one of unshakable Cockney bluff if a neighbour asked how she was doing.

'Oh, I'm orright. We get by, don't we? No matter what.'

If she cried for her husband, no one saw her. Only the eyes told the truth, sometimes noticed by the discerning as they gazed into the middle distance with the memories and the loss lurking there. In bed at night, Amy found herself listening over Vi and Rosy's gentle snoring for sounds of Mrs Jordan crying. But if she did, it must have been well-stifled by her pillow, for no sound of it ever penetrated the thin walls that hadn't been constructed to allow for privacy, snoring, chuckling, murmured conversation, lovemaking (though the Jordans had apparently thought themselves too old and too far into their marriage to bother any more about that).

Guilty though she was in listening out for any sound of weeping, Amy pressed her lips together, putting herself in the woman's shoes, knowing how she herself would have been had Tom been killed. As it was, she still shed her share

248

of tears for his present predicament in the secrecy of her own pillow.

Arthur Jordan's old mates were being extremely supportive. Apart from the money they'd collected, much of which had gone on the funeral, the least expensive that could be found, they brought goods to her door, none of it costing them but still a sacrifice when they could have kept such goods for themselves. They needed it as much as anyone. Every man working in the docks was something of a tea leaf. It came naturally to everyone in bad straits – nothing large, the pilferer careful not to flout dock security in being carried away by greed or financial gain – just the odd little something to make life a touch easier in a harsh world, a bit of baccy here, a handful of sugar there, a tin of fruit, a few nails; after all, the odd bit of tortoiseshell bric-a-brac which no man of slender means would dream of going out to buy adorned many a docks office worker's mantelpiece or lay hidden in some drawer. Each man felt justified in 'finding' the odd overlooked bit of fare to take home for his family.

Generously, a bit of extra came the way of their mate's widow – for a while – no sense overdoing it into the next century of course! A knock would come at her door. A man would be standing there with something wrapped in newspaper. A brief word wishing her well, a polite refusal to come in for a moment for a quick cuppa, and the item would be handed to her with a muttered, 'Look after yerself, luv. See yer.'

'They're good ter me, my Arthur's mates are,' she'd say to Amy and would turn away so that her expression couldn't be seen, and with a purposeful intake of breath would talk about some ordinary little chore she must get on with. Amy knew better than to comment on the remark.

Christmas was spent quietly. Grace's family came to see if she wanted to spend her Christmas with them, but she declined. The same with Arthur's people.

'I don't want ter be a burden on other people,' she said to Vi and Rosy. 'I ain't all that good company fer anyone at the moment.'

'It'd get you out of yourself, Mum,' said Rosy, visualising two days of sheer boredom. She missed her father terribly of course, but the prospect of sitting with nothing to do those two days alarmed her. 'And at least you wouldn't 'ave to pay out for food – Dad's family would provide that.'

It was a thought, but Grace Jordan couldn't see herself partaking of other people's food just to save herself money, or their company when she'd only be a wet blanket on any festivities they tried to make.

'I'd sooner spend it quietly,' she said. 'But you girls can go out.'

Vi knew she could spend Christmas with her Fred's people if she wanted, as she and Fred were unofficially engaged. They hadn't been able to afford a ring as yet, but he had a job now and eventually he might be able to afford something modest. She was, however, torn between wanting to be with her fiancé and knowing she should be keeping her mother company at this sad time. But from now on, Christmas would always be a sad time for her mother, and would she be expected to cushion the blow each year for ever?

'I'll stay 'ere with you,' she said bravely and was relieved to see her mother shake her head.

'No, luv, you 'ave yer own life ter lead. You go and spend the day with Fred Clark's people. It'll do yer good ter get out of the 'ouse fer a while.'

'But what about you?'

'I'll be fine 'ere. I've got Rosy and Willie and Amy. An' we can go an' see Tom in 'ospital. I'll be orright.'

Rosy wasn't the happiest of girls to hear her mother's words. She was going out with a boy now – a Cliff Carter – no talk of engagement or anything like that yet, but she was hoping. She was terribly in love with him but he hadn't yet said if he was terribly in love with her and she couldn't really ask him if he was, could she, not without frightening him off. He hadn't even mentioned taking her to meet his parents yet. So she could hardly go off out with him when he'd be spending it at home. She resigned herself to a very dull Christmas.

Willie didn't feel quite so resigned. 'Why do we 'ave ter

stay at 'ome? I miss Dad as well, Mum, but stayin' at 'ome'll only make us feel worse. That don't make no sense.'

'You can go on round to yer Uncle Tom's if you like,' she said. 'I don't mind yer goin'. I know there ain't nothink 'ere for yer, luv. A boy like you needs ter get out of this misery-'ole, but they won't be livin' it up much either, I don't suppose. Not this year.'

Willie shrugged, defeated. 'I might as well stay 'ere then.'

With Amy, of course, there was no question of going else-where. Where would she go? She would probably spend most of it anyway in the hospital sitting with Tom during visiting hours, the whole family taking their turn, their funereal black tainting the festive decorations the nurses had put up in the ward.

Tom was very down when she went in on Christmas Eve. 'They say I've got to 'ave another operation,' he told her during her turn with him, the rest of his family letting them enjoy their few moments entirely alone. 'It's me knee-joints. They're doing it after Christmas.'

'What have they got to do?' she asked.

'They ain't set right or something. They say I might not be able to walk properly – not for a long time. They hope the next operation might work.'

'At least your legs seem to be mending well. That's one consolation.'

'Consolation!' The bitterness came down like a sledge-hammer. 'Is that what you call it? I could be crippled for the rest of me life, and you sit there talking about consolations.'

'I'm sorry, Tom. I didn't mean it to sound like that.'

'What else did yer think it sounds like? Pat the dog on the head, give it a biscuit. It might shut up!'

'I really didn't mean it to sound like that. I'm sorry,' she repeated and saw his shoulders heave, his eyes trained morosely on the mound of blankets made by the cradle over his plastered limbs.

'I'm sorry too. Sorry to be a bloody nuisance to everyone. Sorry I'm being a bloody burden. You might as well go 'ome, Amy. I'm not very good company at the moment.'

'You're not being a nuisance,' she told him, anger at him

slipping through in her reassurance. 'You'll never be a burden to me, darling.'

'I will be. I'll never work in the docks again, not like this. They want men that are fit. I don't suppose I'll be fit again, ever.'

'Of course you will.'

'Oh, for Christ's sake!' He turned his head and shoulders away from her. 'Go home and let me be!'

She hadn't intended to get up, but she found herself on her feet, annoyance with him blazing out of her eyes. 'All right, if that's what you want. I shall go home and let you carry on with your moaning and groaning all through Christmas on your own. I shan't bother to come back until afterwards.'

But she did. Full of remorse, no longer seeing her attitude as justified, she was back that very evening. The others had gone in without her after their small Christmas dinner, a little bit of pork and the Christmas pudding Mrs Jordan had already made before her husband's death. As Rosy said, no use leaving it to go to waste, so she had determinedly got it out of the larder and had herself heated it up with custard because her mother couldn't bring herself to do it.

The four of them sat down to the meal. With Vi at her fiancé's people, Tom stuck in hospital and his father's place lying empty, it had been a silent meal, Mrs Jordan hardly eating a thing, saying she didn't feel all that hungry. She began getting herself ready to go off to the hospital as soon as the dinner had been cleared away for her by Amy and Rosy. Willie remained very quiet and subdued, sitting in his dad's old chair staring into the low fire, his few tiny presents from the family, put in his stocking for him, lying neglected after having been looked at, even the small bag of sweets untouched.

Mrs Jordan's haste to leave for the hospital was understandable. It gave her something to do other than have to sit dwelling on those past Christmases she and her husband had shared and taken so for granted. Amy, still smouldering from Tom's criticism of her, did not go with her and Rosy, saying she would stay behind and keep an eye on Willie. She hated acknowledging Mrs Jordan's grateful thanks with false reassurance that she didn't mind in the least. But by the time evening visiting came round, much of her chagrin against Tom had dissipated and she went alone to see him.

There was a warm comforting air about the ward when she arrived. The lights were switched off, the place glowed with candlelight and those dim lights where critically ill patients lay. The light of the candles twinkled off little Christmas bells fashioned by dedicated nurses from silver paper from cigarette packets and chocolate wrappings; handmade paper chains swung gently in the heat that rose from the central boiler, and the tiny sprigs of holly and mistletoe above each bed still retained their fresh green look, the berries bright crimson and translucent white.

Tom smiled at her as she came in, his teeth startlingly white in the dim flickering light. He seemed far more disposed to like his surroundings than when she had left. Perhaps losing her temper had done some good. Amy sat down, took his hand. It felt warm, perhaps too warm?

She began to speak, to tell him that he looked a lot better this evening, but he held up his free hand. 'Listen.'

Distantly she could hear the faint singing of women's voices. 'What is it?'

'Christmas carols. Chap over there told me he was in two Christmases ago and they always come round the wards singing. Usually it's Christmas Eve, but sometimes they do it again on Christmas night – those that 'aven't gone home and are on that shift.'

The singing grew nearer but no louder in volume. It sounded so sweet, so full of comfort and hope. Holding Tom's hand tightly, Amy watched as the light at the far end of the long ward grew stronger and the procession of half a dozen nurses appeared, coming slowly along the aisle, each girl holding a candle. The pale blueness of their uniforms and capes, the crisp whiteness of their aprons and caps, the scrubbed glow of their faces brought tears to Amy's eyes as she watched and listened to the soft female voices, the sweet tones of the women who dedicated their lives to people like Tom.

'Oh, Tom, it's so lovely,' she whispered through the tightening of her throat as the procession passed on to the ward beyond leaving only the echo of their voices filtering back.

She felt his fingers tighten around hers. 'No need to cry,' she heard him murmur in the dimness the departure of the procession had left. His fingers around hers became strong and she felt him draw her hand towards him, pulling the rest of her until, complying, she bent and let him kiss her. His lips felt hot, hotter than they ought to be.

'You are my girl, Amy?' she heard him whisper. 'You won't leave me, will you?'

Shocked, she pulled back, put her other hand gently against his cheek. That too felt unnaturally warm. 'Oh, Tom, how can you think that?'

'I'm not a lot of use to you at the moment. Looks like I won't be for I don't know how long. Maybe for ever. I wouldn't blame you fer crying off it all.'

'Don't say that, love,' she hissed urgently, her heart grown cold that he should even imagine such things. 'I want to marry you, Tom, more than anything else in the world. So don't ever again say things like that. And you are going to get better. Keep thinking you will. Just keep thinking it.'

He didn't reply and she bent and gave him another kiss just as the bell sounded for the end of the visiting hour. 'I'll come again tomorrow,' she said, straightening up.

He nodded, giving her a smile. 'You'd better,' he said and she dared to think that the little quip had substance to it, that his spirits were rallying at last. Amy vowed as she gave him a little wave from the end of the ward and saw his answering wave that with every last bit of strength she possessed, she would help them rally.

Two days later it was a different Tom she sat beside. An infection from the right knee, the family was told, had spread through his body. Everything was being done to combat it. No one could say what the outcome would be, but they were keeping a close watch on the infected knee.

It sounded dire and he now lay in a side ward, his breathing rapid, jerky, his eyes closed, his mother sitting by him, her gaze not once leaving her son's face.

'I can't lose both my men,' she whispered on one occasion,

and Amy felt she wanted to throw herself into the woman's lap to comfort and to be comforted, a solacer yet a child.

She had never felt so helpless, so frightened, Mrs Jordan's words bringing home the reality that she too could soon be sharing the loss and terrible desolation this woman had already suffered. God couldn't be so cruel as to take away both of this woman's men. He couldn't be so cruel as to take away the man Amy was only now coming to realise how desperately she loved now that she was in danger of losing him. Amy felt herself prematurely hating that God while at the same time praying with all her heart to the same God to spare the man she loved.

Even as she prayed, silently, Amy heard her own words come steady. 'Tom is not going to die, Mrs Jordan. He's going to recover. I know he will.'

But how could she be sure? Visiting hours no longer applied to this family – a special concession, they could be here at the patient's bedside whenever they needed to, day or night. A constant stream of family floated in, whispering together, talking softly to the recumbent comatose figure now in an oxygen tent, sometimes hovering fearfully outside a ring of screens while medical people examined him.

Amy and his mother hardly left the hospital, drank the tea and nibbled at the sandwiches nurses brought for them, dozed in shabby armchairs in a waiting room, said very little to each other although each knew the other's thoughts. Sometimes one of Mrs Jordan's relatives came to offer words of comfort, words such as, 'He'll get better, you see.'

Mrs Jordan would nod wordlessly without looking up at the comforter who patted her shoulder. Perhaps she believed them. But Amy no longer believed them. Tom appeared to be sinking ever-deeper into his comatose state for all the efforts of the doctors and nurses. She received very little information from any of them except that he was 'holding his own for the present' and, 'We'll let you know immediately there is any change.' It did little to encourage anyone to think positively.

The weekend dragged slowly by. Monday, and Amy took herself to work that morning. She begged Mr Curby for time off, without pay of course, now forced to confide in

255

him about having become attached to a young man, knowing that Mr Curby would keep her confidence for as long as it was possible to. She told him she needed to be with her young man as he was so near – she was certain now – to death's door. She felt dead herself, wondered why she was even bothering to go through the observed formality of asking Mr Curby for time off, yet doing so for all that.

She had told him of the accident to the husband of the woman in whose home she lived, and of his son. Working in a shipping company so near the docks of London such accidents and loss of life were not new to Mr Curby. Dock workers' lives were full of risks, more than a few of them fatal, even more than for coalminers. He knew that the son was Miss Harrington's young man who was in the hospital recovering from injuries, but her new distress as she asked for time off naturally made him ask the reason.

All she could say was, 'My young man is very very ill. They think he might . . .' She couldn't finish the sentence and Mr Curby's slightly bulbous eyes took on a look of profound sympathy.

'You trot along. Take whatever time you need.'

'I don't know how long . . .'

'Whatever. I'm sorry about the rules that you cannot get paid for unofficial time off. Company ruling, you know. If it was up to myself . . .'

'I do understand, Mr Curby.'

'If there is anything I can do.'

'Thank you. I shall manage.'

'And your job will be kept open. At least a week or two. I shall make sure of that, you know. Good luck. Hope things go well, Miss Harrington. Keep me posted.'

She promised, already seeing her job going, for all his assurances, but what did it matter? Tom was the only important thing in her life.

She returned immediately to the hospital to take up her vigil. The waiting room seemed full of people: two of Mrs Jordan's sisters and one of their husbands, Vi and Rosy – Willie made to go to school that day despite everything – and Mrs Jordan herself. She was in tears, the first time Amy had seen her so, openly, and Amy's heart plummeted.

'What's happened? What's wrong?' What if the worst had happened in her absence? 'What is it?'

One of Mrs Jordan's sisters came towards her, her eyes behind her glasses seeming to swim like pale brown fish. 'They told Grace first thing this morning . . .'

'No!' Amy voice was a shriek. 'Oh, Tom, no!'

'I know,' the voice floated through the drumming in her head. 'The poor boy, how's 'e ter survive? 'Im such a vital lad too. Fer such a thing to 'appen.'

It dawned on Amy that the woman was speaking of him still in the present tense. She took her hands from her face to stare as the woman went on sadly, 'As soon as Grace 'eard, she sent young Rosy running all the way ter tell us. She was 'ere all by 'erself but fer the two gels. We really 'ad ter come. She needed someone 'ere ter support 'er, 'earin news like that, poor thing.'

It sounded like an accusation aimed at Amy, but she ignored it.

'What news?'

'Tom. They might 'ave ter take 'is leg orf.'

'Oh, God!'

'They're still lookin' at 'im. They're worried about gangrene. When they got 'im in 'ere the night of the accident, when his poor dad . . . all dirty 'e was from what they'd bin unloadin' and 'e got an infection in that knee. It was all torn up from what I 'eard.'

All this Amy already knew, but Betty Drake, as garrulous as her sister in better times, went gabbling on. 'That's the trouble wiv the sort of stuff they 'ave ter unload. My Ken comes 'ome really filthy sometimes. It looks like it got really badly infected. If it goes green they're goin' ter 'ave ter take the leg orf above the knee. It's terrible. Young man like that, wiv only one leg. It's criminal.'

The worst news Amy had imagined put behind her, this now took its place. She understood his mother's tears – held back for so long in public over the death of her husband, flowing at last over what some might say was far the lesser shock of the two, much as a tiny matter like dropping and breaking a dish following hard upon that death so stoically weathered might have finally broken her down. Amy too

257

found herself breaking down in tears. Betty Drake's arm came around her shoulders and she murmured, 'There, there, luv. I know. It's awful, it really is.'

The words were heart felt but so trite. Amy drew in a deep breath and lifted her head, easing herself away from the comforting arm that seemed to her out of place. With the backs of her hands she angrily brushed away the tears.

'I'm all right now.' After all, Tom might have been killed alongside his father. As it was, he might merely lose a leg. A little thing to cry about. A leg lost against a life lost. How dare she behave this way!

Her thoughts began to resolve themselves. There was a lot to do. Tom would need a lot of looking after, nursing, a lot of understanding, a lot of patience. He'd not be the same man he was, unemployable except in some humble capacity. It would pull him down immeasurably. Thoughts went through her mind of those men, veterans of the Great War, mostly lacking a limb or part of a limb, who even after a decade still wandered along the kerbs of the big cities, solitary or in groups of twos and threes, playing trumpets and saxophones, a raucous wailing that passed for music, the banging of a drum, the uneven notes of a worn piano accordion; or would stand, rain or shine, with a tray of matches or shoelaces strapped to the chest by a string around the neck; or would merely sit, limbless, with a placard displaying their disability and their inability to look after the family they had.

Not for one minute would Tom be like them, but there'd be times when he would feel like them. She'd prepare herself for those times, be his support when he lost courage, his strength when he lost heart, his guide when he lost hope. They would make a life together and she would fight for him and never desert him. All these resolutions drove away her tears as she went to comfort his mother.

Chapter Nineteen

Tom was home. He had been home two weeks. The front room, hurriedly prepared for him, might well be called a bedroom now, the old bed he and Willie had shared still in its corner, another single bed bought cheaply off a neighbour by the window where he could gaze out at the blustery but bright early March weather. Which so far seemed to be all he ever did.

The old Victorian dining table and four chairs, inherited from his mother's parents and once used for family do's, had been put against a wall, leaving what space was left to her treasured if well-worn brocade three-piece suite bought second-hand when she and his father had moved into this house on their marriage. It would now be for Tom to use whenever he wanted.

Tom hadn't yet got around to using it; he was still cautious about getting out of bed except with the help of Amy or his mother. He'd laugh self-consciously at his efforts, making light of it, but Amy sometimes felt so useless seeing him, and she knew his mother felt exactly the same. If only they could steel themselves against running to cater to his every need, especially his mother, it might make him more confident about getting back on his own two feet. Yes, he had two feet, two legs, and Amy had lost count of the times she had offered up prayers of thanks to the God Who had listened to her pleading.

It had been like a miracle, the operation to remove the leg delayed because the surgeon couldn't be sure it had truly become gangrenous. Wait one more day, he had said. The following morning, Tom's fever subsided. The angry colour, they were all told, had moderated, giving hope of saving the leg. Tom's bounding good health had prevailed. But the knee would remain locked rigid for the rest of his life, the other also suffering permanent damage, so that he would be condemned to walk any distance only with the aid of a stick, maybe two.

As Amy saw it, it was a small price to pay compared to what could have been. Even so, she could see him never walking at all if she and his mother continued the way they were going. Where Mrs Jordan was concerned, she could understand the reason: doing something for her bedridden son helped to assuage much of the emptiness of the loss of her husband; as much a panacea for her as for Tom. As for herself, she had to hold back, bite her lip all the time dying to help him. It was courting disaster otherwise, but she couldn't seem to make Mrs Jordan see it.

'We mustn't make an invalid of him,' she warned after a week had gone by, Tom still not appearing to be getting on as fast as she had hoped.

Mrs Jordan regarded her with something like panic, pausing in the midst of getting Tom's breakfast to take in to him on a tray. 'He really does need ev'ry bit of 'elp we can give 'im. Mums know by instinct what's best for their kids.' Her smile was anxious, begging understanding.

Amy stood her ground with difficulty. She did know how the woman felt. 'There's a danger we could be doing him more harm than good.'

'Do you think so?' Worry creased the anxious face even more.

'We've got to allow him to do things for himself a bit more. We can't go on helping him for ever, or he'll begin to rely on you – us – everyone, to help him.'

'But he's crippled. He needs help 'Ow could I leave 'im ter get on as best 'e can in that state? I couldn't be so cruel.'

'Sometimes one has to be cruel to be kind. Being too kind could turn him into an invalid for life.'

'Not my Tom.' Mrs Jordan eyed the tray she held, her expression filling with pride. 'I know 'e's me son, Amy luv, but I've always bin proud of 'im fer bein' so determined.

Like that even as a kid. Never let anythink get 'im down. And 'e won't now, I know 'e won't.'

Seeing her face so set, so sure, Amy nodded and let the matter drop while Mrs Jordan continued on into the front room to feed her son his breakfast.

'Just one step, Tom. We'll give your mother a lovely surprise when she gets back.'

Mrs Jordan was out shopping for a pair of boots for Willie. It would be his thirteenth birthday in early May, and there was a stall in Petticoat Lane that sold hardly-used footwear.

The boots weren't merely a birthday present – they were very much needed. Willie had gone through his only pair until they were just sole and heels with the uppers barely holding onto them. She'd had them mended so many times by Mr Biggs, the snobber, as shoemakers were called. He lived opposite and mended shoes privately and did a good job, cheaper than proper cobbler shops.

Willie's dad had always mended the family's footwear, sitting in the kitchen cutting and shaping the shoe leather he bought down the Lane, thick for the men, thin and fine for the girls, the shoe hooked over the last that had been his own father's, a mouthful of nails withdrawn one by one to be hammered into the pliable leather. Came up as good as new, they had. But there was no man to do that now and Mrs Jordan was compelled to pay out the one and six to get them done by Mr Biggs.

The last time she had taken Willie's boots over to him, he'd shaken his head, noisily drawing his breath in through his teeth. 'Fink they've gorn too far this time, luv. Nuffink ter 'old 'em on wiv, see? Uppers is more like rag if yer arst me. Do wot I can though, but they won't last yer more'n a fortnight before them toes of Willie's poke fru, an' yer'll be payin' out all over again.'

So, one final mend to take Willie almost to his birthday, and off up the Lane with him for boots that must suffice as a birthday present. He took it in his stride, old enough to know that every halfpenny had to count now. He was still doing his papers, often skipping school and the school board man to get extra cash. His mother, hating the lies, covered

261

for him. Desperate times called for desperate measures and for biting the tongue when it came to lying.

Amy had taken advantage of Willie and his mother being out for at least a couple of hours this April Saturday afternoon to try and coax Tom into doing more than the single step he had so far been able to attempt. The stiff joint had locked but the other knee was terribly weak. There were times Amy wondered if it would ever hold his weight without giving way. What if he had to have callipers in the end? The thought was hardly to be endured.

'Look, I'll support you.' She had been chatting to him for about a quarter of an hour. A bit of a one-sided chat, with him just listening, saying little, mostly looking through the window at the lowering clouds threatening another shower. She knew the same thought was on his mind, but he would never mention it. Smile, try to look bright, his inner thoughts working away at him like a tiny parasitic bug.

'I 'ope Mum's taken her brolly,' he'd said, as if she hadn't made any point of his trying to get up.

'Did you hear what I was saying?' she persisted. 'Wriggle yourself to the edge of the bed and stand up, the way you always do. Come on, before your mum gets home. Let's show her what you can do.'

He had done this before, to the extent of getting his feet on the floor, his left knee bent, his right one stiff, taking his weight, while his mother put basin, soap, flannel, shaving brush, shaving mug and towel on a chair beside him together with the little mirror that usually hung on the kitchen wall and which his father used to use. She'd hook it over the tall back of the chair, ask him if there was anything else he needed, lay out clean if faded pyjamas, and then, instead of leaving him to it, would hover ready to help the moment he appeared to hesitate; would certainly be there to help slip the right pyjama-trouser leg over his stiffened knee, telling him he couldn't reach on his own.

'He'd have to reach if he *were* on his own,' Amy told her, but reaping one of Mrs Jordan's newly acquired dedicated looks, said no more.

Mrs Jordan was even there to help him with his toilet arrangement, herself emptying the chamber pot that sat beneath his bed, no question of his getting as far as the outside toilet. No question, with her being ever-protective, of his even getting to the nearest armchair to sit down instead of the edge of his bed.

'P'raps we could get 'im some sort of wheelchair,' she'd suggested only last week and Amy had flared up at her. 'Yes, make a real invalid of him,' instantly to regret the outburst as Mrs Jordan had caught her lip between her teeth but hadn't retaliated. The moment had been significant of the tension they were both under and she vowed angrily not to be so sharp again. The woman was only trying.

But it was crucial Tom begin to do things for himself. Amy watched as he offered her a wry smile and obediently edged over to the side of the bed until his feet touched the lino. She had already kicked away the little rag rug that saved bare soles from the cold floor but which beneath unsteady feet would slip.

'That's it, darling,' she encouraged. 'Now, stand up.'

His will seemed so much stronger when they were alone together. She prayed his mother wouldn't come back before she could get him to progress away from the protective edge of the bed. She had everything well-prepared, had already placed a dining chair within arm's reach should he falter and wobble unsteadily and she not have enough strength to support him alone.

'Come on, Tom, stand up.'

She held his arm as he lifted himself up from the bed, the springs creaking at the release of the extra weight on them. Slowly, he seemed to unwind, towering above her. She had forgotten how tall he was. Tall, broad and good-looking – all she'd ever wanted in a man, and now a cripple. But no invalid – she would see to that. She raised her eyes to his.

'That's perfect, Tom. There's the back of the chair. Put your hand on that and your other on my shoulder. OK?' She felt his weight come on her, tensed herself to take it. 'Gosh! You must have put on a few pounds lying there.'

She heard him chuckle, deep-throated, no bitterness, and her heart leapt for joy. For a moment he was his old self. Together they would triumph, and what was a walking stick between two people whose love for each other would give them heart to face the world?

His large hand sought the tall back of the sturdy dining chair. She saw his knuckles whiten as they took the rest of his weight. 'That's it. Lovely. Now, darling, get your right foot forward. That's it. Marvellous!' He was doing splendidly. 'Get your weight on it.'

His body shifted forward, but she and the chair were taking much of his weight, making it easier. Realising it, his voice sounded worried now. 'I don't think the left's strong enough to take me.'

'Yes it is.' But she too was not at all sure. 'Just bring it up to your right one. I've got you.'

But did she have him? Had she the strength to hold him if he toppled? Fear began to seep through her bones. God, what if he fell? What if they both fell, the chair unable to take his weight? How would she pick him up again? His confidence gone, as it inevitably would, how could she face it knowing it was all her fault? Questions tumbled through her brain like a torrent of water over rocks. Amy fought to throw a dam across the flood.

'I've got you,' she repeated firmly. Ignore her trembling muscles.

'I don't think I can, Amy!' There was panic in his tone.

'You can! Of course you can. One step, Tom. Just one step. Please!'

His body seemed a dead weight. She wouldn't hold it. Together they began to wobble, her body trembling under him. She felt so small, delicate, a tiny leaf being crushed beneath a giant's foot. She heard Tom take a deep breath to help him strengthen himself, his willpower; heard the drag of his bare toes on the lino as the weaker leg was brought on with an effort of will and muscle.

Her head bent, she saw the foot slowly come alongside the first one. His body seemed to sag to the left as the weakened left knee attempted to take his weight, knew at that moment that it would not only be his right knee that would make him limp through the rest of his life, but the bent left knee would cause his whole body to lean in that direction. Devastation gripped her with a vision of a man, not limping but shuffling – a figure of comedy. Oh, God, Tom! Tom! My lovely Tom. His mother had been right all along. To combat the sting of ridicule, he would wheel his way through life, helpless in the sight of others.

Desperation made her tyrannical. 'For God's sake, Tom! Take your weight on it. Push up! Come on, you can! You're almost there.'

The bent knee trembled as it held him. She could see it trembling, feel the effort he was making to put his weight on it. She could hear his breath rasping. It must hurt. She had gone too far. Who did she think she was, taking such a thing on herself with no knowledge whatsoever of medical matters?

Oh, Tom, I'm sorry! The words reached her lips but remained unsaid. The knee was holding. She heard his painful gasp change to one of triumph.

'Amy! Look! I'm doing it!' And yes, the knee seemed to lock. His weight on her shoulder lessened for a fraction of a second. He was definitely lower one side than the other. But he had achieved a goal beyond the endurance of any long-distance runner as far as she was concerned.

'Yes,' she said evenly. He would never know the indecision and fear that had consumed her in that moment. 'But I think enough is enough for one day.'

'Perhaps you're right, love.'

Getting back would be easier, just lift the bent left leg, and even if he fell backwards, it would be onto the bed and no harm done. Carefully they began to negotiate the manoeuvre, his body rising to the stiffened right leg.

The bedroom door opened. 'Dear Lord! Tom – Amy, What're yer doin?'

Amy almost leapt out of her skin. Her hold on Tom slackened. She felt him go, heard the bed springs shriek as his body landed on them, heard the smack of his head connecting with the windowsill and his cry of 'Ouch!' – She swung round but heard his painful laugh, saw him lying on his back, his head away from the sill as he rubbed vigorously at it, his broad handsome features creased in mock agony.

'That made a dent in the windersill,' he chuckled. But his

mother, her face twisted by fear for him, rushed forward in a hopeless attempt to lift him.

'Oh dear. What did yer think yer was both doin'?'

'It's all right. Really.' Amy tried to soothe his mother while Tom lay on his back across the bed, his stiff leg stuck out over the bed edge, free of the ground. She still felt excited. 'He took a step – a whole step. He *will* be able to walk.'

Mrs Jordan wasn't listening, but by the bedroom door, Willie was. 'That's good news, Mum, ain' it?'

'It ain't if he's done 'imself some 'arm,' she shot at him, her reply sharp with anxiety, then diverting her attention to Tom, it moderated. 'Come on, Amy, we'll 'ave ter 'elp to get 'im back inter bed between us, luv. Yer shouldn't 'ave let 'im try this with just you 'ere. He ain't ready yet.'

'But didn't you hear, Mum?' he cut in. 'I walked. One step, but I . . .'

'One swaller don't make a summer and one step don't make a man fit ter be expected ter walk 'alf a mile. Now let's get yer back inter bed.'

'Mrs Jordan . . .'

'Please, luv,' Mrs Jordan swung on her. 'Just come and 'elp me. I'd rather you and 'im didn't try this again. Not till 'e's fit and well enough.'

'But if we don't let him try to walk, he'll never be fit and well,' Amy argued as together they got him straightened out, though he seemed capable enough of doing it himself. 'I want him to get strong. One day we'll be married and I want us to walk down the aisle together.'

''E can't never get married in 'is present state. What good's 'e ever goin' ter be ter yer, like 'e is?'

Amy threw a look at Tom, saw his expression. She felt she wanted to fall on the woman and shake her, but she stood, mouth agape, knowing they had been discussing him as though he wasn't here; as though with his physical state impaired, his mind was too. And she could find nothing to say to repair the damage she and Mrs Jordan had done. Without intending to, she turned and stalked to the door. There she stopped and looked back, Mrs Jordan, still unaware of the impact of her words, busily replacing the bedcovers over her son as though he were a baby.

'I *am* going to marry him,' she announced from the doorway, but no one heard her, apart from Willie, next to her, his thin face agog.

Whatever his mother might think, Tom had taken his weight on both legs, had taken a proper step. It was a start.

If only she could have more time with him. But with no money coming in but the poor pay of both girls and Willie's few pathetic pennies, Tom still to be fed, there was nothing for it but for her to keep working. Mr Curby had kept her job open for her, bless him.

Five and a half days a week she must spend away from Tom, his mother free to mollycoddle him, her love for her son holding him back from any progress he might have made, that spark of hope she had seen in him draining away again for lack of incentive. He needed to get his enthusiasm back so that he could again feel useful, even if unemployable except for humiliating inferior tasks.

But first they would be married, and as soon as possible. Marriage would restore his self-respect, his self-confidence. There was still nearly two hundred pounds in her bank, more than enough to get married on. The only problem had always been that he had stubbornly refused to bow to using her money. *Her money.* He, the man, must be the provider. It had angered her more times than she dared to count, even though she saw his principles as commendable, admirable. But things had changed. He could no longer be the provider.

She spoke to Vi for advice. Vi and her intended were struggling hard to get enough together for a halfway decent wedding, a rented roof over their heads and a little furniture – all that went to make up a married life together. Another thing was that early in March she was sure that Vi had been pregnant. (She had suddenly been under the weather last March. Her mother had attended her, taking her into her own double bed and closing the door on everyone. Vi could be heard crying out and sobbing and not long afterwards Mrs Jordan had come downstairs with a pail covered by a towel and had gone into next door, not saying a word to any of them. Vi had stayed in her mother's bed looking wan and tearful and had come down after two days to go back to work to tell her employers that she'd had a touch of 'flu.)

Vi, by virtue of those circumstances, would be someone to confide in. There had been times when Amy had confided in Alice, but those times were gone. Alice lived on a different plane now, would probably no longer understand or want to remember the problems of too little money and too great a pride. Amy still wrote to her occasionally, but Alice's replies were always full of her own woes – Richard not doing this, and Richard not doing that, how tired she was at being taken for granted – shallow letters, no longer from the thoughtful, sympathetic, philosophical girl Amy had once known. She turned to Vi.

'How can I make him see that there's nothing belittling in using whatever money is available, even if it is mine.'

Vi looked solemn. 'I thought yer knew Tom by now.'

'I do.'

'Not enough to see my brother's always bin a proud man and always will be. What's 'appened to 'im 'as taken away all 'is dignity and 'e's fighting to get it back. You flinging your money in 'is face won't 'elp 'im get it back, will it? We may be poor, Amy, poorer than we've ever bin, but we can still 'old up our 'eads.'

'So what do I do?' she asked, a bit put out by Vi's almost rude bluntness.

'I don't know. You two'll 'ave ter work out yer own salvation, like me an' my Fred are doin'. No one can give yer advice – not the advice you want.'

So that was that. Left seething over Vi's off-handedness, she had to bow to the truth in what she said – she couldn't use her money and insult what dignity Tom had left. Yet it seemed so silly. No doubt it would sit there doing nothing for the rest of their lives, more than likely to be used to bury one or the other of them.

It would be hard. She'd have to keep working, hope to achieve promotion and a somewhat higher wage. There were two other ways: without letting on to Tom of course, she could go cap in hand to her parents and throw herself on their mercy, but up came the old problem – she'd been too long away from them, too silent; how could she spring her request on them now? So many times she thought about Alice's words to her: 'Don't let too much time go by before you contact your parents.' But she'd left it too late to heed them.

The second would be to approach Alice herself. She might provide a little something from the allowance Dicky Pritchard must obviously give her. No need to ask for too much – just enough for her and Tom to get married and rent a place near his mother. It would be a loan, to be paid back little by little out of her wages. But again there was a problem, this time her own pride. Alice had been her maid. How could she, of upper-class breeding, go begging to a girl who'd once been her maid, a girl who'd virtually taken her place in the world?

The only choice was to work hard and efficiently, try to get promotion, and hope to save enough for the pair of them to share a life together. Some hope of that. Obliged to give Mrs Jordan the lion's share of her wages so as to keep the family going, there was little left to save. Nothing for clothes, yet she must continue to look decent for work.

That was another thing. As spring progressed, fashion had taken a great new leap. Hemlines had begun to creep down and according to magazines like *Vogue* which Amy, unable to afford, covertly thumbed through in paper shops, they threatened to reach calf-length by summer, the classic look as it was being called with long slim lines and waists back in their proper place. The cloche was at last going out, giving way to hats with wider brims, more hair shown, styled longer to curl below the ears. Amy found herself tugging constantly at her skirt to get it below the knees and praying for her shingled hair to grow as quickly as possible. But there was nothing she could do about hats and she breathed a sigh of relief every time she saw another person still wearing the cloche. By now she'd learned to look after her clothes – gone the days when she'd fling a dress aside after only three or four wearings – and they still looked in pretty good shape when seen alongside those of the girls with whom she worked.

* * *

269

Amy sat in Mr Goodburn's spartan office – say that much for the man, if he afforded his staff small comfort in their surroundings and conditions, he afforded himself just as little.

All that earlier talk of promotion hadn't come to much except a lot more work, typing mostly, with its compensation of two and sixpence a week rise. She had become very proficient as a typist but *promotion* had merely meant that she was in reality doing the job of two for a rise hardly acceptable as an office cleaner's wages. Seven months on and this appeared to be all she was worth.

Bidden to sit down she watched Mr Goodburn close the frosted glass door between his and the outer office after giving the area a leisurely inspection to reassure himself that the staff were working as hard as they could, which of course they would with his pale grey eyes upon them.

She watched him return with slow measured strides to his side of the desk, wondered what he could want of her, and at the same time thought of Tom, though why, she didn't know, except perhaps to make comparisons. This man, now in the act of sitting down in his scuffed leather wing chair, every action done with deliberation, was the antithesis of Tom who seemed to be failing by the day.

Tom had progressed little beyond taking a few steps with the aid of two sticks, which he hated, as far as one of the armchairs and back. A commode in the room erased any need to venture beyond to the outside loo, his mother willing to take charge of the emptying. It made Amy mad to see, but she was up against mother and son with Tom in danger of becoming quite apathetic. He hated being seen on his feet. She knew why. It had to be awful for him, knowing that people who had once seen a strong and virile man would now see a wreck hobbling on a pair of sticks. Yet Amy felt that if he were to pull himself upright, learn to balance properly without the need to lean on those sticks so, he'd master a much better gait. He would always limp of course. But even that could be done with dignity. His stiff knee thrown forward and his weak left knee growing in strength, he with his broad chest and his fine height could still command a place of note in this world.

Sometimes she daydreamed of him, owner of a thriving shipping company, moving with an arresting limp through an office full of young women typists as they bowed to every word he spoke in that full deep voice of his, much as they did to the tall, gaunt Mr Goodburn himself. She could imagine Mr Goodburn not having a friend in the world and wondered if he was married, and if he was how he had ever come to court a woman enough to marry her. She could visualise him proposing marriage as though announcing the commencement of a board meeting. And did he have children? Virtually impossible to imagine the man engaged in the most basic performance of copulation, gasping, sighing, at his most vulnerable. Mr Goodburn vulnerable? More she could almost hear his clipped instructions: 'Right, my dear, ready when you are – one, two, three, four . . .' Amy felt her lips beginning to curl.

'And how are you coping these days, Miss Harrington?' It was a command rather than an enquiry, pulling back her wandering thoughts, obviously alluding to her work rather than her social life.

'I think . . .' She paused. Be positive. 'I am coping very well, Mr Goodburn.'

'You enjoy it here?'

'Yes, very much.'

'And we in turn are pleased with your progress.' He used the collective pronoun more to encompass the company than in the royal sense. 'Indeed, we are very pleased.'

Lacing his thin bony fingers together, his forearms resting on the scratched desk, he leaned towards her in a confidential manner. 'So saying, there is an offer of promotion for you, Miss Harrington, should you care to take it.'

Not another promotion! More work, another shilling or two? Amy kept her smile rigid on her lips, hoping it looked obliging or at least reached her eyes.

'We are planning to offer you a position as my personal assistant.'

Amy's gulp almost choked her. 'But . . . I don't have any shorthand.' It had the element of a protest, but startled, for it was all she could think of to justify herself not being up to such esteem.

Mr Goodburn almost allowed himself a smile. 'That shouldn't matter. You're very bright for a young lady, Miss Harrington, and I have known many shorthand typists who have virtually nothing between their ears. There are quite a few such young ladies there in my outer office.' His long thin lips quirked into what Amy would definitely describe now as a smile. The next moment they had straightened. 'Are you willing to take the position?'

He hadn't yet said what rise would accompany this glittering advancement but the courage to ask had failed her. He was watching her closely, grey speckled eyebrows raised as if asking a question. She had to say something.

'What does the position entail?' she asked weakly.

Mr Goodburn's eyes held hers so that she momentarily felt like a small animal held transfixed by the cold unblinking stare of a cobra as his voice filtered through to her brain, explaining the duties of a personal assistant. It held out great promise, but at the same time sounded daunting. She would be at his side and under his eye constantly, never able to escape, imprisoned by his imperious authority which she must respect yet not quail from and do his bidding even before he requested it. In other words, she must take over from him whenever and wherever necessary, take command of any situation in his absence, do what he would do but at a lower level and be answerable to him on his return, and at all times be at his beck and call and remain humble enough to take any criticism he might deal out without answering back.

He never said as much, but as he explained her duties, this she gleaned. Her first instinct was to quake in her shoes and refuse this awesome post immediately. In fact a little knot of rebellion had begun to rise up inside her as she listened until as he finally came to the end, finishing with the words, 'Have you anything you wish to ask me?' the words leapt into her mouth, from where Amy didn't know.

'Yes, Mr Goodburn. What will my salary be? I assume it'll be substantial.'

His great guffaw, so unexpected, made her jump. She'd never before heard him laugh all the time she had been here,

272

thought him incapable of it. In that moment, he seemed no longer the god he allowed his toadying staff to think him.

'That was what I was waiting for, Miss Harrington. Had you not asked I'd have advised you not to take the post at all. I am looking for a young lady who can conduct herself with some authority in any given situation and discuss her findings and opinions with me on even terms. Such posts are usually filled by men, but I am of the opinion that most male personal assistants merely seek to fill their peers' shoes. A woman by her very nature is in no danger of doing that. And I also like to think of myself as a radical. It would be quite off-putting to the people I deal with to see an efficient and attractive young lady as my aide-de-camp as it were.'

Amy was gaining confidence. The man was so arrogant. 'What will my salary be?' she reminded him, unsmiling. She saw him frown. Well, if she had blotted her copybook, she might have escaped a fate worse than death anyway. She felt suddenly resigned to the inevitable.

'What are you earning now, Miss Harrington?'

'Twenty-two shillings and sixpence a week.'

'Then what do you say to another twenty-two shillings and sixpence?'

Amy looked at him. Two pounds five shillings! It was a fortune. A man's wage – or nearly. Wordlessly, she nodded.

'Good!' He got up and came round the desk to her, helping her to her feet. 'Well, Miss Harrington, from Monday you will be working with me. In there.' He indicated a small glass door leading from his office, an inner sanctum, a cell from which there would be no escape. 'That will be your office. I am sure you will like it. You have made the right decision, my dear, and I look forward to our association.'

Moments later, Amy stood outside in the general office, wondering just what she had got herself into. But the money. Oh, the money. In no time there would be enough for her and Tom to get married, live in comfort, so long as he didn't get on his high horse and get uppity about her being the wage earner. But he would, she knew he would. The next few weeks, perhaps longer, were going to be fraught.

Chapter Twenty

Adversity, as it often did, closed the Jordans' ranks ever more tightly against the outside world, growing suspicious of its motives in offering help if offered too frequently. It could be overdone, could be seen as excessive pity, a revelling in another's downfall. Some understood that and let the family get on with its own life. Others hounded, reluctant to let go: 'How are yer, luv? Must be 'orrible for yer wiv no man now. If there's anyfink I can do, yer only 'ave ter ask. I just thank God I've still got me own family round me.' They were given short shrift as Mrs Jordan lowered her portcullis against them.

Drawn in behind it, Amy felt the same way, fiercely protective, as if this was her true family. She seldom thought now of her own family, and if she did was struck by how false they'd been compared to this one standing shoulder to shoulder against all odds. Looking back, it struck her that hers had been fragmented from the start, her father taken up with his work and seldom out of his study when he was home, her mother taken up with her various charities, both of them following separate paths, hardly ever together. Her sister Kay had most likely gone off to a finishing school. She must be due home soon, coming out like young ladies still did, the idiotic dated parading of debutantes looking for an excellent marriage. Her brother Henry hadn't lived at home since his prep school days – boarded out at seven, he was fifteen now and preparing for university, never seeing his family, not bothered anyway, destined for greater things, not a word of thanks for the money they'd paid out for him.

She was no different to them in leaving home, which was probably half the reason why her parents had never striven to bring her back. People of their class, at least in her experience, took it for granted that their offspring must seek pastures new, unlike the poor who clung tighter to each other the poorer they became.

Thinking of her old life, it seemed so false now, so full of affectation and concern about image that she wondered if she hadn't been merely marking time until this life of struggle and honest reality had embraced her; that this was what she had been destined for all along, like a missionary perhaps.

She thought of Alice. Had she married a plain man she'd be living around the corner now, popping in maybe every other day for a chat with her mother, still as much part of the family. But marrying into money she had left, only now and again these days thinking to drop her mother a line. She had done so regularly after her father's death. Mrs Jordan would look sadly at the envelope as it arrived, would gaze into the low flames in the fire grate as though her husband were bidding her to do what he would have done, throw it unopened into the flames, but instead would put it on the mantelshelf. Later she'd succumb to temptation, open it, draw out the expensive-looking notepaper and read, her eyes brimming with tears, then fold it, tuck it away somewhere, keeping its contents to herself as though she'd committed some crime against her husband by the mere fact of reading it. But as Alice got over her father's death, so her letters to her mother diminished.

She still wrote to Amy occasionally – letters that spoke of unhappiness, making her in her turn feel her own small guilt in having introduced an innocent unsuspecting girl into a life she hadn't been prepared for. But that was the life she had accepted and Amy told herself that she had more to concern her than worrying over Alice's troubles – if she really had any.

Alice watched as the travelling bags were brought in. She was glad to be home. July in Vienna had been miserable, the way Richard had behaved towards her. And it wasn't her fault. She'd every right to feel jealous, neglected. That horrid woman, Enid Smythe, blonde, waif-like, disgustingly pretty, and so sickeningly childish, fluttering her painted eyes at him, pursing her scarlet lips, waving her hands about like a drunken butterfly, her golden bracelets rattling on her slim, suntanned bare arms as she twittered, 'Dicky darling . . . I haven't a drinky – oh, do get me one, darling, would you?' The way he'd fawned on her. Openly. Pandering to her every tiny whim.

Then had come nights when he came to bed late. He'd been with her, Alice was sure of it. If it was true, then she could demand a divorce. With alimony. She'd be a wealthy woman with her own money. Trouble was, she was so in love with Richard still that the mere thought of losing him tore her poor heart into pieces, especially as all the way home his mood had been dark and she knew he was missing the silly little Enid terribly.

Two days later she caught the maid who usually picked up Richard's mail on her way out to post it. Going through the envelopes, on the silliest of pretexts but the only one she could think of on the spur of the moment, that he thought he had put the same address on two envelopes, there was one addressed to Miss Enid Smythe. Of course, she couldn't open it before the maid's questioning stare, nor even take it away. And with what excuse? But she knew it contained words of adoration, love even, was even more sure Richard had slept with her while they'd been away. And he was being so short with her. He had to be in love with someone else – Enid of course.

It was confirmed when he invited her to Lyttehill Manor for the weekend. With a few other people of course, to make it look correct. But they'd go off horse-riding together, just the two of them while the others played tennis or sat drinking martinis on the terrace in the sunshine, unaware of the clandestine canters. She had never been able to master horses, and she imagined them laughing at her way out there hidden among the trees, Richard revealing her origins, a confidence one bestowed on a lover. She stood at the window, blind to her guests, in her mind's eye seeing two lovers sinking down in the bracken wrapped in a hot embrace.

Yesterday she had caught them in the old weather-beaten vinery which had been built against one wall of the kitchen garden generations ago by other owners.

Standing well apart but looking guilty as she burst in, they had been in each other's arms, she knew, the sun beating down on them through the stained cracked glass panes, adding to the heat of their stolen love.

And in the evening, Richard had wound up the gramophone and danced with Enid the whole time while she had to dance with other of their guests or sit out and look too obvious for words. And he had come to bed late, kissed her on the cheek but had shrugged off her attempt to snuggle closer, just as he always did these days. And there were still no babies.

All this Alice put in her latest letter to Amy, but Amy dismissed her complaints as Alice's spoilt imaginings, no proof to any of it, and trifling compared to what Alice's mother was going through. Amy had far more to concern her than worrying about Alice's frivolous life – probably half the girl's own fault anyway.

Her job was taking up all her time. She was at Ronald Goodburn's constant beck and call, and was often required to work late. It was bringing in much-needed money, almost a man's wage, but little ever seemed to go to swell the savings for her and Tom's marriage.

Despite his mother's coddling, Tom was beginning to get back on his feet. His natural strength of character at last prevailing, he was coming to terms with his disability, accepting it, would conquer it. With Amy's help he had made it out of his room and into the back room, their progress unsteady, a stick to help his stiffened right leg propel him forward, his other hand on Amy's shoulder to take his weight off his still-weak left knee.

Amy felt proud of him on that score. But he hadn't accepted her success at work as easily. It could even have been that which had forced him back on his feet – determined not to be put down by a woman. If it was, then it was a good thing even if not comfortable for her as she prudently refrained from talking to him about work. He'd have done better still had it not been for his mother hanging about him, worrying about him, using his disability to fill her loss. Nine months after his dad's death, she still wore deep black.

'You could be forgiven for wearing a brighter blouse or at least a scarf with a little colour in it after all this time,' Amy told her, but she tightened her lips and shook her head.

'I intend ter stay faithful to me poor Arthur's memory.'

'But it's such warm weather and the girls are back in summer dresses. And Vi will soon be in white come next month, and Rosy will be her bridesmaid.'

Vi, getting married in September, thought herself quite at liberty to wear white for her wedding, since no one was aware of her earlier condition or even her present one. She was pregnant again – four months she thought. It must have happened in May when Fred had got careless again, recovering from their first fright before she had lost it. But now who cared? Next month, she would be getting married. She wasn't showing, and as far as anyone knew, she would walk down the aisle in white with impunity.

'What they put on,' Mrs Jordan said to Amy's urging, 'is their business. And what I put on is me own. Anyway, black don't need ter be washed so often like coloureds do an' that saves on clothes, don't it?'

This was her first and last aim nowadays, how to make the money go round. Needing everyone, except Tom obviously, to pull their weight, even she was trying to do her bit, taking in little bits of sewing – she had always been a neat if not gifted needlewoman – turning old sheets for neighbours for a couple of pence, mending curtains, lengthening dress hems or altering them, even making simple new ones for a shilling or two from a bit of material they'd bought up the Lane. It wasn't regular by any means but the few shilling were welcome. She treadled her old portable machine bought twenty-odd years ago, the lino around her feet littered with cotton ends and offcuts to be swept up later. The machine had become a permanent fixture, standing in the corner of the back room like a patient sentinel, blocking part of the window onto the back yard.

Grace Jordan's greatest dread was to be forced to pay the pawnbroker a visit. Her greatest boast had always been that she had never had to do such a thing in her whole life and had always looked upon those who did as worthy of her pity. But if she had to starve, if they all had to starve, she told everyone, she could never bring herself to go through that door with its three brass balls hanging over her head ready to drop on her 'like the sword of Dominic' she stated roundly. So they must put up with cotton ends clinging to everything and bits of material littering the floor and meals delayed while she finished off some garment or sheet on time to be collected. 'I put me 'ands together whenever someone knocks on me door with a little job fer me, no matter what it is. I ain't too proud ter turn nothink away what promises an extra penny fer bread or a bit of marg.'

They hadn't yet come down to starvation level, but come September she'd be losing Vi's money; Vi and Fred were to live in his parents' spare back room until they could afford the rent of the two-up-two-down next door that Fred's father with his ear to the ground had been told could become vacant in about a month or two. The tenants were having trouble paying their rent and beginning to fall badly behind.

That could equally happen to this house, Amy thought, were it not for the money she herself was bringing in. Without Vi's money there'd only be hers and Rosy's, and Rosy too was courting now. Which left only Willie. And what he got from selling newspapers could hardly be counted as supportive, even though he worked long hours these days, the summer holiday having closed school for six weeks.

An agile runner, loud of voice, his call, '*Star, Standard*, all news!' echoing from one end of a street to the other, he'd race back and forth from first light to well after dusk, papers under his arm, first, second, midday editions, afternoon, extra, late extra, never letting up, his thin face running with rivulets of sweat from beneath his old cloth cap, his tall thin body weary by the time he came home to fall into bed.

'That poor kid's gonna kill 'imself,' wailed his guilt-ridden mother, accepting the pennies he gave her. But he was young, he had the indefatigability of the young, and by next morning would be off again as fresh as a daisy.

''Xactly 'ow old are yer, lad?'

Willie gazed at one of the *Daily Chronicle's* van drivers as he dropped the tied bundles of the early morning edition for the group of lads to cut, grab and be off with. He resented the delay the enquiry would cause: the others would be off before he could be away.

'Ain't got time now, mister.'

''Old on, sonny. I'm astin' yer a question. Could be in yer favour ter listen.'

'Why?'

''Cos if yer old enough, could be a job fer yer down at one of the *Chronicle's* sub-offices wot I've just 'eard abart. Messenger boy. They need a school leaver. I've watched yer, fella-me-lad, an' I think yer might be well advised ter get along an' 'ave a shufty at it. Kid there bin given the push this mornin'. Lazy little sod from what I 'eard, an' gave the manager some lip. But yer'll 'ave ter be quick before word gits out. So what's yer age?'

Willie put down his bundle of papers. 'I'm in me fourteenf year.'

It wasn't exactly a lie. He'd turned thirteen in May. It was now August and he'd heard somewhere that the Chinese took a person's age from the day of him being conceived – that was when a man got a woman pregnant like, so his mum had been got pregnant with him nine months before he'd been born. So by Chinese reckoning he *was* fourteen. But he said fourteenth year just to be on the safe side. Anyway he only had two terms to go at school before they chucked him out into the world. He could have passed for fourteen at any time, and indeed the man looked appraisingly at him, but at the same time grinned knowingly.

'I'd've taken yer fer older than that, lad, ter look at yer. I expect yer still at school really. Well, I'm goin' back ter pick up me next delivery. I can take yer back wiv me if yer like. Tell 'em yer've already left school and they won't be too bovvered. If they find out you are, they can only sack yer. They can't kill yer.'

'Why pick on me?' Willie asked as he clambered in beside the driver. 'Why not one of the uvver kids?'

Again the man smiled. 'I live in the next street ter yer mum. She did a bit of sewin' fer me wife. She knows abart yer dad bein' killed in the docks. Your street sent round a collection for 'er for yer dad's funeral, and me wife's sister lives there. I just felt yer might take well to a job, if only temp'rary like. But if yer get it, you make sure yer don't let me down, see, 'cos I'll be vouchin' fer yer.'

Willie came home at seven that evening, earlier than he usually did, alarming his mother, the expression on her face as she looked up from mending a hole in a pair of old curtains a neighbour had brought in one of immediate concern.

'You ill, luv? Yer've bin overdoin' it. Yer look all flushed.'

'That's 'cos I bin 'urryin' back from Fenchurch Street.'

She dropped her repairs over the machine and got up, coming towards him. 'All that way? What was yer sent all that way for? Yer a local lad. Yer shouldn't be doin' any London rounds. I've a mind ter . . .'

'I got meself a job, Mum.' His narrow face was grinning from ear to ear.

Quickly he told her what had happened, how he'd been taken on there and then by a *News Chronicle*'s sub-office as a messenger boy, eight till six, seven days a week at five and sixpence a week.

'Five'n'six!' she echoed descending on him and inflicting a huge bear hug on him. Then she drew back from him, her face creased with concern. 'But you ain't left school yet, luv. What they gonna say when they know yer still at school?'

'I told 'em I'd left. If I 'ave ter go back after summer, they'll 'ave ter get rid of me, or I can tell me school I've got a job and don't need ter go back. There's lots of us don't go back after we've turned thirteen. They don't care. Not much else they can teach us, and if we've got a job, what's it matter ter them?'

'They could cut up rough.'

'Let 'em,' Willie said lightly. 'What's fer tea?'

She gave him another warm cuddle then went back to her work. 'Steak, chips and caviar!'

'No . . . really.'

'We'll 'ave sausages.' That in itself was a feast when usually there was only something on toast midweek. 'I'll go out up the pork butchers this minute an' get some. It'll be open until eight. We was goin' ter 'ave sausages fer Sunday, but we'll 'ave some tonight. This can wait!'

Tossing the curtain back onto the machine, she got up and took off her apron, ready to put her now well-worn black cloche hat to go out in. No need for a coat in this warm weather with the sun still shining.

Thus clad, she stood in the doorway looking back at him, pride in her youngest spread all over her blunt features. 'To think – my Willie, grown up and gettin' 'imself a job. Just like that. An yer can keep two bob out of yer wages each week fer yourself, if that's all right.'

'That suits me, Mum,' he answered, as proud of himself as she was of him. Two bob was a fortune.

'Seems like everyone's keeping this family afloat except me.'

'Don't be silly, darling.' Amy had trouble disguising the irritation in her tone. Everything that was said, everything that was done, was to Tom's mind a reflection on him.

He looked up at her from the back room sofa, where he had come to rest, puffing from his efforts to get there. Amy felt that if he did it a little more frequently, he wouldn't be so out of practice, but his mother was always venting her sympathy on him: 'Let 'im stay where 'e is if 'e don't want ter. It's a lot ter ask of 'im.' She seemed unaware of the damage she did him.

His blue eyes as he looked up at Amy were hard with the unaccustomed effort and what was going through his brain since his younger brother's news. 'I'm no use to anyone, am I? I just take up room, eat everyone out of 'ouse and 'ome. No bloody use to anyone. Now silly on top of it.'

'I didn't mean it that way, Tom.'

He relented a little. 'I know you didn't. But you must know how I feel stuck 'ere. I try to get on me feet. I do try, Amy.'

'I know you do.'

'But I can go on trying and it won't ever get me a job, except for selling matches ...'

'Don't talk like that!' The sight of those crippled veterens, still to be seen eleven years after the War's end, plagued her, frightened her. Aware of Tom's own unemployability, it was too close to home.

'Well, what do you suggest?'

'You wouldn't talk like that if your mother was here,' she scolded, ignoring the question.

They were alone for the moment, Mrs Jordan gone off to buy her celebratory sausages, leaving Willie to convey his wonderful news to Amy before going off out to tell all his mates. The two girls were upstairs getting ready to go out to see their respective beaux and already complaining at the lateness of dinner, having peeled and cooked the potatoes ready for mash as soon as the sausages appeared back home.

Amy had taken the opportunity to coax Tom out of his armchair in the front room, almost needing to get angry with him before he'd move, his mother lovingly indulging him while Amy was at work and not there to goad him on. It was a bone of contention between her and Mrs Jordan, the woman sure she was in the right as his mother and Amy feeling something of an interloper for all she and Tom had declared they would be married one day.

'I suggest,' she said to him, refusing to bend to his point. 'I suggest you stop thinking about getting work and concentrate on getting better. You've got to keep at this day after day, for as many hours as you can. Slowly you'll get stronger and stronger, and perhaps you might be able to do something else, perhaps work for yourself.'

'Doing what?'

'There's lots of things. Look, your mother's taken in machining. Perhaps you could ... I don't know ... do woodwork, make things to sell. Oh, Tom ...' she dropped on to her knees before him, looking up into his face. 'Tom. I love you so much. I want to see you be strong again. There's nothing I wouldn't do to see you strong, darling. I want us to get married and have a life of our own ...'

283

His face had begun to crease up as though all she was saying had become unpalatable to him. 'What sort of life d'you think I can give you?' he demanded, his tone gone suddenly harsh and unforgiving. 'Don't you know you'll be spending the rest of your life looking after me. Doing ... that?' He indicated with a stab of his finger the way they had travelled into the room, weaving, she struggling under his tall weight. 'No, Amy, I want to spare you that. You don't need me. Yer've got yerself a bloody good job now. Yer can go off an' make yer own life.'

The carefully studied diction he used when she was with him fell away in his hatred of what the future held for him as he saw it. 'Yer came 'ere 'cos yer was in a mess. But you was what you was. You'd get yerself on yer feet no matter what. You've got that sort of breeding. I ain't. I ain't got nothink to ...'

'That's not true, Tom!' She was near to tears. 'You've got me. You'll always have me, no matter what you say. I love you. I'm not going away, leaving you. I'll never do that, no matter what you say to me, or try to hurt me because you've been hurt. If we have to eat the dirt off the street, I shall stay with you. And don't throw my upbringing in my face. You've got the pride of those people I've come to know since I've been here. You've got that, my dear. And one day, one day we'll come up in this world – if it's the last thing I do, I shall see you raised. I don't know how, but I shall.'

She stopped, breathless from her outburst. He was looking down at her and there were tears in his eyes. 'I know. So long as I've got you, Amy, I know it'll all be right in the end. And I promise you, Amy, you won't be disappointed in me.'

Seconds later he had leaned down, caught her arms and lifted her up to him. His lips were on hers, she was crying and kissing him and crying and kissing. He held her firmly, a man in charge of a situation, if only for a few minutes; a man she felt in that few minutes who would fight his disability and come through it. She suddenly had trust in that, and she knew that one day they would be married and that nothing would stop them.

284

They didn't hear his mother come in through the front door until they were aware of her standing there in the room. Then they broke apart, both of them smiling through the tears they'd shed. Their smiles fell slowly away from their faces as Amy got up, seeing the blank look on Mrs Jordan's face.

'Anything wrong?' Amy enquired. The woman's expression, as though she had intruded upon something very secret, made her feel oddly uncomfortable.

'Nuffink as I know of,' came the stiff reply, so unlike her usual warmth.

'Are you all right, Mum?' It was Tom who spoke, but she didn't look at him, her gaze seeming unfocused.

'I'm orright, luv. I just came in ter tell yer I'm doin' sausages fer dinner.'

She left the room without another word, but Amy had already interpreted the trepidation in those eyes. It spoke of a woman already seeing her eldest son leaving her to cope alone with the emptiness his dead father had left. It spoke of a woman who, despite her loving nature, would feel the need to strive to keep him so as to escape that terrible black void she could see stretching out in front of her.

Amy had a terrible feeling that in the long run she could lose to this meek and loving woman, merely because she *was* so loving. Should Tom yield to those fears of loneliness, she'd lose. Should he break free and marry, she'd live with the knowledge of having taken away this woman's only anchor. Either way she knew, as she went out to help his mother prepare their meal, that she couldn't win.

Chapter Twenty-One

It was a revelation viewing Ronald Goodburn from the other side. A man who had only to walk into his general office to cause every young typist's head to bow over her machine as though she hadn't looked up from it for days, who set office boys running at top speed and brought a stammer to every male employee's reply should he ask him a question, even made Mr Curby's elderly hands come together as if in supplication even if he didn't bow his head or stammer, sometimes seemed to Amy now she was working alongside him a man inexplicably unsure of himself. He kept it well-hidden but there were times when she saw the cracks of wistfulness appear, a weakness in such a man making him appear startlingly more human than was expected of him.

'I'd give a lot to have my life over again,' he once said to her quite out of the blue, as he handed her his diary of the day's appointments to copy into hers.

'Would you, Mr Goodburn?' she answered dutifully.

It was always difficult to hold a conversation with him in the normal sense of the word. He spoke, she replied. He never mentioned his private life, nor she hers. All they had in common was work, and her work she knew she did to his entire satisfaction. She suspected he felt more at ease with her than with most people, even his clients to whom he would chat along stilted lines. She had never seen any of them give him a jovial slap on the back, and when they shook his hand it was formal with no warmth to it, a deal clinched, nothing more; and if a joke was shared all would laugh uproariously except Mr Goodburn who would allow the joke one of his restrained smiles.

With her, his smile was relaxed as far as he could relax and she would feel trusted by a man who feared to trust anyone. It was probably why she had been given this position and had kept it. The rare personal snippet had made her feel even more trusted, if a little surprised.

'Yes,' he answered, his eyes on his diary, opened at the day's date. He said no more than that and Amy felt compelled and daring enough to delve a little further.

'In what way?'

'In that I would have done something more worthwhile with it.'

Startled by the statement, Amy pushed no further, applying herself to jotting his appointments into her desk diary in silence, receiving his curt thank you as he stalked from her office into his own, leaving the glass door between them a little ajar as he always did.

Through the fluted glass, she saw his distorted figure seat itself behind the large desk, the riffling shape of an arm reach out to the telephone, heard his voice requesting a number.

His muffled voice talking into the mouthpiece of the telephone filtered through the half-open door. She looked away, back down at her diary, took second note of where he would be this day and with whom, a normal day. But Amy's mind wasn't on her work. Why had he said that – he would have done something more worthwhile with his life if he had it over again? What could be more enviable than the position of command he held, unless he had secret longings to be knighted or own this company entirely or be a Member of Parliament, or the King himself?

Amy smiled as she got on with her work. It didn't matter what Mr Goodburn wished from life, what mattered was that he had expressed a wish, something he had never referred to before.

It was to be the start of many confidences that drew them together, not physically – he never so much as laid a finger on her arm – but because he had a need to unburden those thoughts and feelings he had locked away long ago. It seemed he had lost his wife early in marriage. A fall from a chair on which she had been standing to hang a picture had broken her neck – this before they'd had time to consider having children (Amy felt guilt rise up in her that she could have once ridiculed the man by imaging him having sexual relations with his wife). He hadn't remarried, had sunk his grief into his work and now thought it too late and too inconvenient to relinquish his widowed state. He lived alone and had a housekeeper, an ugly woman with a heart of gold who mollycoddled him. Again it was difficult for Amy to imagine Mr Goodburn allowing himself to be mollycoddled, yet it made him unexpectedly human. Why was it always unexpected, a shock to see him as human, even now?

He seemed not to want to hear anything about her life, using her as a sounding board for his own inner longings. This was fine with her. After all, it was her job to be his listener, his aide, his adviser. She was his personal assistant. She listened, nodded, gave her opinion when needed, and began to know the man.

'What I've always wanted,' he said one morning in early September as he sat in her office drinking the cup of coffee a trembling junior had brought in for them, 'would have been to have my own boat – not a yacht – not that sort of thing – but a boat capable of taking people up and down the river. One of those pleasure steamers I often see going to Margate or Southend.'

It always amazed her that such a taciturn man outside this sanctuary could have so much to say in it.

'That's what I always dreamed of before I married. Not specifically that, but something like it. As a boy I used to stand gazing at that little winding river – the Thames – I lived in a place called Lechlade, on the borders of four counties – the river was quite wide even there – and I used to wonder how wide it must be at its mouth. And when I moved to London when I married, I was still besotted by it. After my loss, I would stand on the Embankment to look at it. I longed to be on it. Such wide horizons even in the centre of England's capital city that not even those noisy docks with all their cranes could take away. They were, and still are, horizons to dream by. Do you know, Miss

Harrington, I have never been to Southend or Margate on one of those boats I once dreamed of owning. I am not a lover of people in crowds. I imagine I wouldn't have enjoyed it after all. I've never been anywhere, Miss Harrington, on that river. Too busy. Still I regret that I never took the opportunity.'

'You still could,' Amy said. 'On a Sunday.' But he shook his head.

'I usually take work home with me. I am a man of work, Miss Harrington, and nothing can change the habit of a lifetime. But I still regret not throwing over the traces, when I was younger and first came into this firm, of taking a gamble and investing in a pleasure boat of my own. A big gamble, Miss Harrington – not one for a man who fears to gamble. That has been my trouble: fearing to close my eyes and jump.' The small stiff smile touched his lips and was gone again.

'I know all about such a business though, Miss Harrington. I have studied it. I could run such a business with one arm tied behind my back, but I have never had the courage to physically do it. I am a man who is naturally set in his ways and my dreams are not worth a fig, Miss Harrington.' Again the small smile. 'I don't know why I am telling you all this.'

'Because if you don't tell someone eventually, you'll burst,' she said simply.

He nodded wistfully. 'Had I had a son, I would have seen him go into such a venture before he had time to set himself into a pudding of a job as I did.'

Draining his cup suddenly as though he knew he had revealed too much of his true self, thus subtracting from his own authority, he got up. 'Ah, well, back to work, Miss Harrington – back to work.'

He never spoke of his birthplace again, nor of his lost ludicrous dream of being captain of a pleasure boat, but he did speak of the business itself as though it were part of the one in which he had submerged himself. Amy gathered together these small tidbits of information like a gleaner following a harvest, her mind beginning to weave all that she picked up into definite form as listening quietly prompted more and more snippets of his secret mind from him with growing trust in her complete trustworthiness.

She knew that, like him, hers was only a dream; she'd never have a quarter enough money to mould it into reality. But had she the money, that would be the sort of business she and Tom would set themselves up in, Tom who also had a secret longing to be out on that wide artery of London whose horizons were not mere places where earth and sky met as an escape from claustrophobic existence.

Even as she continued to learn about the business in which she worked and that of which Mr Goodburn dreamed, collecting it all in her head and on bits of paper stored away as a miser stores coins, at intervals to be brought out and studied, common sense told her that it could only ever be wishful thinking. But if nothing else it was escapism, a panacea against the drabness of life, much as Mr Goodburn's personal idea of Utopia was. Had it not struck her as so sad, she would have laughed, not at him, but at herself.

Vi's wedding was a frantic affair. Frantic in the sense that the tiny two-up two-down tenement was forced to spill its guests out onto the street for the want of room.

'We didn't invite all these people,' Vi gasped, looking glorious in her short wedding gown made by her mother and her long veil once worn by her new husband's mother, which being both lent and old fulfilled (including the dress) three of the requisites of a bride, the fourth being a blue brooch her Fred had bought her for one and six off a stall for her last birthday. 'Good job they've brought their own grub.'

Indeed, Fred a popular chap and something of a dedicated athlete, had all his friends from the swimming baths and the training centres he frequented as well as those from where he now worked at the brewery who incidentally had supplied some of the beer that was flowing. While all Vi's friends from Lipton's Dairies came, supplying bits of butter, cheese, bottles of milk, cream to go with bananas and strawberries, and offcuts of ham and pressed tongue, everyone in Fred's short street (the reception was taking place at his parents' home, the bride's mum as a widow was unable to cope with it) had joined in once the gathering had spilled out onto the pavement. Their in their turn brought a bit of grub, a bottle of beer, bread and marg; helped to cut sandwiches for the ham and pressed tongue and cheese. The family proper had brought wedding presents as well, mostly home-made: bedsheets, pillowcases, cushion covers with material bought off stalls; doilies and tray cloths painstakingly crocheted in the months leading up to the important day; an unwanted flat iron polished up with black lead and with a bit of coloured ribbon tied to its handle to make it look new; a knife tray made by a relative fancying himself as a carpenter, likewise a towel rack, a set of coat hooks, a small stool – all of them accepted, with good grace and gushing thank-you's, from guests who had little by the newlyweds who had even less.

Vi, all smiles, clung to her husband's arm to be congratulated over and over again while the seldom-played piano from his parents' house, brought out into the street because it couldn't be heard from the front room even with the window open, was having all the popular dance tunes banged out on it, every note out of key and ringing like a bell.

'Fancy me, Mrs Clark, don' it sound nice?'

'You an' me's goin' ter 'ave an 'appy life tergevver, Mrs Clark,' he proudly yelled to her over a raucous singalong, and drew her to him before they paraded off to greet all those they hadn't yet greeted. September dust raised by stamping feet slowly settled on the new bride's bleached wedding veil and home-made posy of a couple of roses, a dozen white Ezra Reed daisies and a few fronds of asparagus fern lovingly plucked from her father-in-law's cherished back yard.

In simple pink as one of Vi's bridesmaids, Rosy being the other, Amy stood thinking about Tom. He'd had to be left at home, as there was no way to get him here with him unable to walk any distance. He had insisted long before the day that he preferred to stay at home, and anyway wasn't interested in being a peep-show at his sister's wedding.

'I'll be in the way and spoil it for her. I'll be there in spirit, but I'm not ready to go anywhere yet. Not until I can walk better than this.'

He still hobbled spectacularly and he knew it, and there was no kidding him that he didn't. Amy, being completely honest, agreed that if he preferred staying at home, then that was his right.

'And I'll stay with you,' she said.

But Vi had specifically asked her to be her bridesmaid. 'Alice would 'ave been,' she said. 'I always planned she'd be, but I can't ask 'er now, way things are.' And she had pleaded with Amy who had felt obliged to accept, officiating for Alice as it were.

Alice had been invited. Mrs Jordan saw to that, had forgiven her up to a point and insisted it was proper she should be asked to her sister's wedding, but whether she came or not was up to her.

Alice was at the church and kissed Vi good luck as she came out, but made her excuses not to attend the reception; as Rosy said, 'Too good fer us now.' She hurried back to Surrey after a word or two with Amy who, asking how she was, had received a shrug and a piqued expression and a promise to write and tell her all about it later on.

Tom understood the importance of the bridesmaid bit. 'Go along and do Vi proud. I'll be fine 'ere – honest.'

So she had gone, but all through the church ceremony she ached to get back to him, as she was aching now, wondering how he was. These sort of frolics weren't her cup of tea – without Tom there she felt alienated. It might have been Alice's brief presence reminding her of better days with people who conducted themselves with more decorum than this gathering. Leopards don't change their spots, she thought, eyeing the jigging and jumping to the ringing out-of-tune piano joined now by a mouth organ and a couple of upturned saucepans and wooden spoons to give the tunes, many of them out of the ark, music-hall stuff, a bit of a beat. No matter how hard you try to scrape its coat. She knew. Her mother once owned a leopard coat and on cutting away a bit of the fur as a child when it had been tossed away, Amy found that the skin underneath also matched to some extent the fur that grew from it. Like the leopard of that maxim her upbringing was still ingrained beneath the veneer of this life she had built around herself. She felt disconcertingly above all this and it alarmed her. If only Tom was here.

Suddenly she needed his protection, needed to feel his arm around her, hear him say, It's all right, darling . . . But he never called her darling, did he? It was 'love' he called her. Loneliness in the midst of this revelling Cockney crowd began to assail her. All she wanted to do was to run home to him. But how could she go, leaving his mother behind?

She looked across to where his mother sat with three or four of her own people, a fraction removed from their chatter in that she seemed to be gazing into the middle distance, her eyes glazed and unfocused, perhaps seeing times past, the small glass of beer in her hand untouched. Amy watched her, glad of someone to watch, glad to have something else to think about.

She had expected Mrs Jordan to continue as stoic as she had been when she had first lost Mr Jordan. But as time moved on she seemed more and more to lose hold of that stoicism, until she behaved quite helplessly at times. She would have been in black even today had she had her way. As it was she sat in a dark grey cotton skirt and a light grey blouse, that in itself a sacrifice.

'It's me weddin' day, Mum,' Vi had protested a few weeks before. 'Yer can't wear black on me weddin' day. 'Ow d'yer think I feel? Yer can't spoil it fer me.'

She had relented by choosing grey that to Amy looked even more sombre than the black she'd have preferred as she sat apart from the chatter going on around her. She'd not really spoken to anyone at length, and had certainly not said much to Amy herself. These days she hardly said much to her at all, in stark contrast to the chatterer Amy had first known her to be.

'Alice gorn, and now Vi,' she'd mused in Amy's hearing on the way to the church. 'Soon it'll be Rosy. Then Tom, I s'pose. Everyone going. Soon Willie will be all I'll 'ave left.'

'You'll still have everyone,' Amy told her. 'Living nearby.' Except Alice of course.

'Not quite the same. But I don't want ter talk about it. It 'urts.'

Then why raise it, Amy thought with a small unexpected

stab of annoyance, to feel instantly sorry. It stemmed from her own sense of guilt wanting to marry Tom, but even so she was determined not to let it ruin her vow to marry him as soon as he felt able to name the day.

Never had she felt so heavy of heart. Swamped by feelings of total isolation for all the crowded carriage of the four forty taking her back to Surrey, Alice stared with unfocused gaze through the grimy panes as they left London behind.

Sooty London. The swaying train, puffing out more smoke for the City to breathe in, had drawn slowly out from Waterloo Station, passing Vauxhall Bridge, catching a glimpse of the Thames. High tide. Winding in a clean sweep away from her, it had been like a friend going its own way, leaving her to go hers, cocking a snook at her as it went off through the rest of London snaking off to the west. She was travelling west too. She'd not see the river again, though they would cross a tributary near Byfleet. A tranquil waterway a few dozen feet wide over which her train would trundle, it slipped between trees and fields; tideless, well-mannered, softly reflecting the pink and blissful September sky as the sun sank. Plied by small elegant craft that only the elegant rich could afford, it would tell her that she would be back to her own life which the quiet water divided from the one she had left behind. Yet did she want that kind of life she had just left behind? Nostalgia, that was all it was, fine enough when she'd known no other. Not that this life she now had was anything to talk about either. She was in limbo; hated her life, yet could never go back now, not after the way she seemed to have been treated.

Alice seethed with anger against them, her family, who had hardly noticed her at the church. Hullo, how was she – how was everything? Then they would edge away, distracted by someone or something: going to take a snap on a battered Brownie of the happy couple; need to talk to that chap, that woman, that family over there – not seen her, him, them for ages. They hadn't seen *her* for ages! Was it her money, her apparent grand circumstances that embarrassed them, made it hard for them to talk with her? Was it jealousy? Taking the form of lack of interest, always the easier option.

Little wonder she had come away early.

Mum had embraced her as though guilty in doing so, releasing her too soon, her face concerned, age-discoloured teeth worrying her lips. 'Are you 'appy, luv?'

She in reply said yes, she was. A lie, her mother's face still looking slightly concerned yet relieved that she wouldn't be called upon to offer sympathy to a girl who had everything but perhaps not happiness. 'That's good, luv.'

Vi had been too ecstatic in white to talk to her, giggling, had offered her cheek for Alice's kiss and murmured good wishes. Rosy had been openly disapproving, a lingering legacy from her father. Willie, not interested, and Tom ... Tom hadn't been there. What would his reaction have been? She hadn't had the courage to go on to Albert Street to find out. Better not to know than to be sitting here with his unforgiving anger ringing in her ears. Then again he might have been kindness and understanding itself. She'd never know now.

And Amy – she'd had a long conversation with Amy. Felt an affinity with her, both of them in the same boat. She had at least made an effort to see her parents. Amy never had. Strange, but knowing how the upper class was, perhaps not so strange.

Alice felt the hatred of her life rise up in her. The magazine lying open and unread on her lap, she gazed with unfocused eyes while tracks, fences and the back gardens of suburbia slid by. Her eyes did not see the scenery changing to fields and hedges and distant villages. They saw only fragmented snatches of their own scenes within her head.

Richard was becoming a bastard and there was no one to turn to for help or advice. His mother had been the pinnacle of support at first, nurturing, teaching how she should conduct herself, what current little sayings she should use that wouldn't make her look what she really was, a product of a lower society – she had prickled at that, but knew Margaret Pritchard was right – *Lady* Margaret Pritchard! Under her guidance she'd become what she now was, or at least what Margaret's world thought she was, but there was no erasing those ingrained memories that rattled around in her brain, the inborn instinct that struggled to rise to the surface every now and again, so that while her voice said one thing her thoughts said another. 'Darling, how too ridiculous,' she said out loud, and in her head, 'Bugger off, you silly cow!'

Nor had Margaret's tutelage prepared her for Richard's behaviour this past year, and the way her sort of people viewed it – no raised eyebrows except towards her when she made a scene. To them it was a scream that he was up to something, an occasion for a little bit of gossip over coffee, not quite the magnitude of a scandal unless something special about it hit the headlines. No one bothered to wonder or care how she felt. Slowly coming to realise it, she had thrown tantrums, had run to her husband's mother rather than her own which instinct told her would have made her look the failure she was becoming. But Lady Margaret, already tired of her protégée, washed her hands of her, told her in no uncertain terms that she had married Richard with her eyes wide open and should get on with it.

The magazine on her lap as the train pulled slowly into Woking was still open at the same page as when the train had left Waterloo, not one word read. Closing it, she dropped it on the seat and with her clutch bag tucked tightly under her arm, the wide brim of her summer hat low over her eyes against the strength of the sinking sun, she got out, briefly thanking the person who opened the carriage door for her. All that remained was for a taxi to take her on to Lyttehill Manor.

She knew full well the reception she'd get. A quick peck on the cheek from Richard if he were around, he hardly pausing to ask how things were with her, she left to her own devices, not seeing him again until tomorrow morning.

They slept in separate rooms now, had done these last three weeks since she had flown into a rage about his cancelling the theatre that Saturday saying he was too tired to go to the theatre and needed some peace. He'd gone to London to his club for the evening to unwind but she discovered later that he'd 'bumped into' that Smythe woman and they'd gone to a nightclub. He'd not come home until next morning, saying he'd stayed the night at his club. But she had already telephoned his club as the hour had grown late to be told he'd left hours ago, and she knew where he'd spent his night.

Confronted by her screeching fury the next morning he'd thrown it in her face, the first time he'd ever openly admitted to it.

'You must have guessed,' he'd taunted as though she were a complete idiot. And when she'd asked in tears, why, he'd said, 'Because I'm sick of you and your everlasting carping about wanting to stay home, never wanting to go anywhere, always going on about starting a family. Yes, I want a family, but not yet. I want to have some fun first. Enid Smythe *is* fun, she makes two of you. And she doesn't go on at me all the time.'

His reasoning had been that if Alice would only alter her ways, return to being the person she'd once been, enjoy being with him wherever he went, their marriage would brighten up, they'd be as they were when they first married.

'You're ravishingly pretty,' he'd bawled at her. 'But you've become a wet blanket. You could be an absolutely smashing hostess if you'd only try, but you never stop moaning about people coming here. I want people here. I want to have fun! And when I've tried to make love to you and do things, you end in tears saying that the sort of love I want us to enjoy is crude and dirty. Good God!'

'Well, it *is* crude,' she'd shot at him in tears. 'I don't want to watch us in a mirror. I don't want you doing . . . the things you do. The way you do.'

'That's how love is,' he'd railed. 'The missionary position? That's not loving. That's about as good as shaking hands. You need to experiment, enjoy it. If you'd just have let yourself go, I wouldn't have needed Enid Smythe. She knows how to make love. Can't you see that, Alice? It's you that's driving me away.'

'But I love you, Richard,' she'd wailed, but he had sneered at her.

'Richard! Everyone but you calls me Dicky. Why can't *you* call me that? It's the embodiment of what you are, Alice. Deadly dull.'

'If I'm so bloody deadly dull,' she'd exploded, 'if that's how you feel about me, why don't you go into another room to sleep? Anyway, I don't want you in my room after you've been with *her!*'

He'd given her a long slow look. 'That's fine by me,' he'd said, and had moved out.

Now she was left with no sense of this being home, if she had ever thought it was. She longed to be back in dirty old Stepney, sitting with her own mother, telling her all her troubles. But, as she had once advised Amy, the longer a gulf is allowed to widen the harder it becomes to bridge it. She recalled advising Amy to write to her parents and heal her rift. Now she had formed one of her own and she too had let it widen too far to leap back.

What hurt most as she with Vi's wedding still vivid in her mind, alighted from the taxi, leaving Hamlin to pay the driver was that Violet would never know any rift between her and her family. Like all good East End girls, she had married a nice steady boy of her own type, would live with him a couple of streets away from Mum and would live a happy contented life visiting her several times a week. Alice felt the acid sting of jealousy grip her stomach like a real pain as she passed through the portals and the wide open door into her gorgeous, lonely mansion, ignoring the maid who curtseyed to her as she entered.

Vi and her new husband had settled into his parents' back room. Only two streets away from her mother, Vi visited her every afternoon. She had given up work of course. No married woman expected to go on working with a husband to support her, her role now to look after the home and children when they came. Her mother, with everyone at work, her son mostly keeping to himself in the front room, and no Arthur coming home at the end of the day, welcomed this new filling of her life and she and Vi would chat for hours.

It didn't take much for Vi to look after her one room. She'd made it into a little haven for herself and Fred in the same sense as a little girl might look after a doll's house. It *was* her doll's house, everything to hand, set out nice if cramped, second-hand double bed in one corner, her mother-in-law's not-too-badly-worn fireside chairs each side of the fireplace, a rag rug – a wedding present from an uncle and aunt – in front of it covering the existing lino; small second-hand dining table in the centre and two dining chairs for now; a print or two on the wall, a pair of vases given by her mum and a small clock given by Amy. It felt like heaven.

The kitchen, naturally, had to be shared and she must wait her turn to use it after her mother-in-law had done, or she'd cook for the four of them one day and Mrs Clark senior the next, the two women participating in the general washing up. But Vi's room was hers, hers and Fred's, a heavenly retreat.

Two weeks later the house next door fell vacant. Mr Clark senior had had a word with the landlord whom he knew in passing. As a painter for a firm of outside decorators having recently painted the windows of the man's privately owned residence, he had already come to an arrangement with him over key money. A matter of five pounds, Mr Clark senior's wedding present to his son, his one and only child. Even so, five pounds was a sacrifice, collected by hocking a few items of good silver cutlery, a wedding present to him and his wife twenty-four years before, selling a couple of dining chairs to a neighbour, the rest borrowed with a promise to pay back at tuppence per week interest. Of course he didn't tell any of this to the grateful couple, who went gaily off to their new home next door.

From a cosy little back room the newlyweds found themselves rattling about in a whole house echoing emptily with nothing to fill it. But Vi was over the moon. Her own home. Fred was in work to pay the rent without fuss. Furniture and furnishing could wait so long as there were curtains at their front room and bedroom windows for privacy for the time being.

Chatting away the afternoons with her mother, Vi would plan how to fill the house when she got enough money. It would have been nice to have the sort of money Alice had and buy whatever she wanted at the flick of a finger, and every so often Vi would feel a small pang of jealousy and resentment that it wouldn't have hurt Alice to put her hand in her purse now and again to help. But then she would think of her and Fred's life together and shrug. Sod Alice and her fine life. But it wouldn't have hurt her sometimes.

Chapter Twenty-Two

Summer almost over, Tom sat with the family now. It was good to see him getting from one room to the other, leaning on her and his mother. But Amy missed those precious moments together in his room, he in bed, she sitting on its edge, longing to slip in beside him and make love. He had often tempted her to, but they never dared. Willie was liable to come barging in at any moment to get a comic from his curtained-off side of the room, or his mother would pop her head round the door, asking if they were all right.

Those snatched moments, low conversation melting away to little kisses, lips barely touching, playing gently, they'd never been allowed to lead to anything more – just as that tingling need began, would come a tap at the door, Mrs Jordan enquiring: 'Orright, Tom? Anythink yer want, luv?' She never seemed to realise she was intruding on their privacy.

To turn her away would look suspicious. In a scramble, Amy would leap off the bed, adjust her dress or blouse where Tom had been fondling her, and hurry to sit in an armchair. Tom, throwing her a look of resignation, would sit upright in bed, endeavouring to look innocent, a look that would have made her laugh on any other occasion, and would call, 'Come in, Mum.'

In she'd come, bright smile naïve, face benign. Surely the embarrassment on their faces should have told her what they'd been up to as she sat on the bed Amy had just vacated, relating some inane little thing she'd forgotten to say earlier. It was as though she had stored it up for this very reason. Finally, giving up on any further chance of lovemaking, mild and cautious though it had been, Amy would leave with her, leaving Tom alone. And now, even those moments were gone, with Tom mostly going to bed only at night, so she was hardly able to creep in without it being noticed by all. She ached for the day when they could marry and finally be alone together.

Now, the only time she spent in his room was with Mrs Jordan, helping her to get him to walk unaided. He could, but it was a terrible shambling walk. Amy had devised a way to make that gait not quite so shambling, so he wouldn't see himself as ridiculous. She had tried to drill it into him, but it was such an artificial way of walking that time after time he gave up.

'It ain't natural to me,' he protested. 'I lose my balance every time. I need more practice.'

'You're trying too hard,' Amy told him. They were on their own, his mother out shopping. An ideal opportunity to make love, but his walking properly was more important at this moment. 'Try to relax a little.'

'And fall over,' he chuckled.

'Not if you concentrate. Look, give me your hand.' She was beginning to sound like his mother, in danger of coddling him just as she did. His efforts to be again what he'd once been pulled her heart to pieces and she was coming to know the pain his mother must feel, loving him, seeing him so helpless, at a loss to know how better she could help, tempted to help, her resolve not to breaking down.

She must have looked stern, for his chuckle died on his lips. 'What's the matter?' he asked sharply. 'Can't I laugh now?'

What came over her, she didn't know. Tension maybe. 'Laugh if you want. But this isn't funny, Tom. I'm trying hard to get you back on your feet.'

'Then p'raps yer shouldn't be tryin' so 'ard.' He always resorted to rough speech when he thought she was being critical of him, to annoy her it seemed.

'Perhaps I shouldn't,' she shot at him, and leaving him to get back into bed his own way, swept out of the room.

* * *

In brooding silence, he watched her go. It was only after the door closed that he spoke again. 'I can't be what you want me to be, Amy. I wish I could.'

If only he could say that to her face. She fostered such high hopes of him, expected such impossible standards he couldn't yet acquire. Some day perhaps, but not as miraculously as she wanted.

He watched the door. In a while it would open and she'd come back in, tears in her eyes, to throw herself at him, apologising for her behaviour when he should be apologising for his own outburst. But he wouldn't need to apologise. He'd take his two sticks in one hand, put his free arm around her waist and draw her to him to kiss away her tears, their love all the stronger for the little tiff they'd had.

While he waited he'd practice on his own. He took a deep breath, the dining chair within reach to support him should he need it. He could walk. September, nine months since his accident. It was the *way* he walked that troubled him, this rickety gait: stiffened leg thrown forward, the weak, slightly bent leg brought past it, the tendency of the body to lean over to the weaker side, the result a profound and spectacular limp that made a bloody fool of him.

Time after time Amy had told him to lean towards his stronger stiff leg as he put his weight on to his weaker one. The result were infinitely better, giving him something of a swagger. Trouble was, he still couldn't keep his balance, with the result that he staggered about as she held on for dear life, finally collapsing into laughter. Sometimes he laughed too. There were other times when he didn't, when self-respect was at stake and he could find nothing funny in it all. Or he'd laugh and she couldn't. Today had been one of those times. But it would all come right. When Amy came back into the room, he intended to be standing in the centre to greet her.

Concentrating hard, he managed six steps in the way she would be proud of. He was standing in the centre of the room feeling pleased with himself, his only support one still very necessary stick, as the door opened. But it wasn't Amy who stood there.

'Oh, luv, no!' His mother's voice was filled with panic. 'Not on yer own. You could fall and do yerself an injury.'

She was in front on him, trying to support him, easing him back to the bed. In the doorway he could see Amy, her slim body rigid, her hazel eyes bleak.

'Please, let him do it for himself. He can.'

The conviction in her voice for all her bleak expression, filled him with a sudden determination to prove himself. He'd show them, show the pair of them, hovering like mother hens about him.

'Leave me alone, Mum,' he commanded. 'Just stand back a bit.'

'Yes.' Standing at the door, Amy's voice was a whisper of encouragement. Her expression was no longer bleak but vital, full of hope, full of trust in his ability. 'Let him be, Mum. He can do it. Come on, Tom.'

It was the first time she had ever called her Mum, but none of them noticed as he put his mother's helping hands gently away from him, fixing his eyes on his tutor. One hand on his single stick for support, the chair comfortingly nearby in case his efforts failed, he went through the drill, first in his head, then transferring it to his body. Stiff leg first, weak leg forward and past it, lean towards the stiffened leg while doing so, take the weight on the bent one, moving the stiff leg forward, and so on. It felt unnatural, yet the result was far better to look on. He gritted his teeth as he continued past the chair. No aid now but one stick, and Amy, just a foot or two away should he fall into her arms at the end of it, his self-esteem still intact.

He could see her eyes shining with his own achievement, beckoning him on, giving him strength. Behind him his mother was giving out little noises of fear for him, but he ignored them. Amy was his goal, no one else.

How he had got to her he wasn't sure as they fell simultaneously into each other's embrace.

'I did it, Amy! I did it!'

Neither of them saw his mother's lips begin to tremble, then grow tight. If they had, they would have read her thoughts. She had been excluded from this little scene of triumph, would be excluded for always, the two young people too in love to notice. Minutes later, she had pushed the knowledge aside, though it would always be there to raise its head at unguarded moments, and came towards the two to add her own words of pleasure at her son's achievement.

For some days after she said very little while Amy exuded unbounded joy of the remarkable feat they had witnessed, but if Amy noticed she didn't probe into her failure to share in it. All Amy knew or cared about was that from now on Tom would be a different man, leaving his room unaided by either of them, and as he gained confidence his posture would slowly straighten, the new walk he was fast adjusting to becoming a faint swagger. Grace could no longer hold back the tide that sooner or later would flood past her to the very feet of her son – in her heart the embodiment of his dead father – who stood ready for it as he took Amy's hand in his, young people in love with all their lives before them and no thought to spare for those they left behind.

But, came the thought for all she tried to ignore the reasoning behind it, Tom still had to take his first steps beyond this house and out into the world itself. When that day came would he be as confident? She hoped so, for his sake, angrily closing her ears to the devil whispering into them that if he didn't, she could still have her son here with her.

Money. It always came down to money. The more Amy listened to Mr Goodburn's airy-fairy aspirations, the more she longed for them to come true for herself – that pointless enthusiasm drawing off pointless fervour. His confidant, Amy allowed herself to wonder if any of his colleagues were to know what she knew, their awe of him would melt in an instant. Mrs Jordan, who would have no awe of King George himself, had a saying: 'If yer bovvered by someone what thinks 'e's above yer, just imagine 'im sittin' on the lav – that brings 'em down ter bein' 'uman bein's again.' By the same token those who quaked in their shoes in Ronald Goodburn's presence would see him as a laughing stock were they to know his secret heart. Such a ludicrous secret – that a man who appeared to have no close friends, no family, held his colleagues at bay and frightened the life out of his staff could ever see himself with hordes of people aboard his imaginary pleasure craft. Such were dreams.

Her own stood far more chance. Tom had always been gregarious, or had been until his accident. He could be again. But of course, it was all illusion, not the remotest chance of ever having that sort of money, even if Tom would accept it from her. It all came down to money in the end.

Amy gave a light derisive chuckle, making Mr Goodburn glance at her, sobered quickly and continued making notes of what he required of her today. Correspondence, she dealt with most of it. No need for shorthand, copying down words parrot fashion, she had enough good working common sense to write letters on his behalf. This morning one to the PLA, another to an export company, reply needed to a letter from a Mr R. A. Gravesbrook of HM Customs and Excise – she would dictate them to one of the girls from the general office, call her in when Mr G had left for the appointment he had in half an hour. Hotel accommodation had to be arranged for someone coming over from Paris this afternoon, and there was that file to be sorted out, that marine insurance thing that had been going on for months, and . . . a dozen and one things that made her day fly by.

A trembling office boy tapped on the formidable Managing Director's glass door, hurrying in with the second post of the morning, jumping as the great man's deep voice rang out, 'In here!' to come and lay it with a few mid-morning edition newspapers on the equally formidable Miss Harrington's desk instead, before scurrying out.

Several early edition papers already sat on her desk waiting for Mr Goodburn to read when he had a moment. She allowed herself a passing glance at those the boy laid on top. 'Wall Street In Panic As Stocks Crash' said the black headline on the first one, but it didn't impress her with so much work in front of her today, and Mr G would be late for his ten-thirty appointment if he didn't hurry.

'I'll take good care of everything here until you get back, Mr Goodburn,' she told him confidently and hustled him from her office.

* * *

306

Mrs Jordan stared at the smartly uniformed boy. 'Telegram? For us?'

She couldn't remember ever receiving a telegram. Letters came swift enough. Local ones posted in the morning arrived around teatime. There was a fleeting moment of anxiety that it could only mean bad news, but from whom? The only person who'd be sending telegrams would be Alice, who could afford to be that extravagant.

'For Miss Harrington,' the boy said smartly. 'Sign for it please?' He held out a pencil which she took, signing the small form he held out. 'Any reply?'

Mrs Jordan wasn't sure what to do. 'The lady in question ain't at 'ome at the moment.' She couldn't read another person's telegram. The boy shrugged.

'Don't matter. She can send a reply from a Post Office.' He was hovering, his face expectant, his hand held at an unnatural angle from his side.

Mrs Jordan fell in. She'd heard about this. 'I'll get yer a tip. Just wait a tick,' she said.

Amy stood holding the telegram Mrs Jordan had pressed into her hand the moment she arrived home from her office.

'Came this mornin',' Mrs Jordan said as Amy quickly slit open the yellow envelope. 'Didn't open it. Ain't any bad news, is it?'

Amy's face had already begun to blench as she read the few words. She looked up at Mrs Jordan, her expression tight, angry, frightened. 'Why didn't you get this to me earlier?'

''Ow? You was at work.'

'You should have telephoned me.'

'I can't use telephones. Never 'ad ter.'

'I needed to know!'

'But I couldn't open your letters.'

'This isn't a letter. This is . . . You should have opened it. It was urgent. Oh, my God . . .'

The words flashed up at her again from the yellow form: YOUR FATHER SERIOUSLY ILL STOP HEART ATTACK STOP PLEASE COME STOP MOTHER. She crumpled the piece of paper in her hand. 'I've got to go.'

'Where?'

'Home. My father's ill.'

'Oh, luv. Anything I can do?'

'No, nothing.'

From the back room came Tom's voice. 'What's going on?'

'Amy,' his mother called back, her eyes on the girl's face. 'She's 'ad bad news. 'Er dad's ill. She's goin' home.'

There came the sound of sticks clicking, uneven laboured steps on the lino. Tom was at the door, but Amy had already picked up her handbag from the kitchen table where she had put it to take the telegram from Mrs Jordan. She gave him a look.

'I've got to go home. This very minute. It's urgent. My father is very ill.'

'You're coming back?' There was fear in the cry. The sound wrenched her heart, but her errand was stronger.

'I don't know yet.'

'Amy?' Again the sound of fear.

Her love for him temporarily overrode the urgency of her mission, but its very urgency made her tone sharp. 'Yes, darling, of course I'll come back. But I don't know when. I just know I must go now.'

'Yes,' he said simply. He sounded like a man who had just heard himself sentenced to death and again she felt that wrench in her heart. Tom really believed she would never come back.

Quickly she went to him, reached up and kissed his cheek. 'I'll come back, Tom, don't worry. But at the moment . . .'

'Yes. You go.' Putting his two sticks into one hand, he reached round her, pulled her to him and kissed her, hard. 'I love you, Amy. And I need you,' he whispered in her ear before letting her go. It was only later, when she had time to think, that she recalled never before having heard those words from him – I need you. And it struck her how much she needed him. But at this moment she hardly heard them as she broke away from him and let herself out of the house.

Lawson Harrington died of a second massive heart attack an hour before his eldest daughter, whom he'd not seen since she walked out of his house four years before, got to St Bartholomew's Hospital where he had been taken.

Staring uselessly down at the still figure, numbed by remorse at having arrived too late, Amy felt she would never forgive Mrs Jordan for not relaying the contents of the telegram sooner. A woman too stupid to know how to use a phone had done nothing. They were all stupid people, those denizens of the East End – not a pennyworth of brains between them, and Mrs Jordan had to be the worst. It didn't strike her as an unfair judgement at that moment.

At the moment, gazing at her father's heavy features with regret more than grief that she would never see those grey eyes look at her again, a shadow stole over her that it was she who had erred, not Mrs Jordan, letting time go by, allowing the years to stretch out, the pain of separation to dull with the passing of that time. Her father's deep voice wafted into her head. The years had gradually obliterated that part of him while he'd lived and now he was gone she could hear him speaking, as clear as anything, like an accusing echo. She should have gone to him, made it up with him, or at least tried to keep in touch. All those years of pride and anger, refusing to be the first to break the deadlock – what a waste it had all been.

Behind her in a close little group stood Kay and Henry and her mother. Her mother was quietly sobbing. A nurse came and touched her arm, then Amy's, the touch feather-light and discreet.

'When you're ready,' she whispered, 'there is some tea for you all in the sister's office. We'll leave you alone in there. No need to hurry.'

Amy slowly half-turned, hating the fact that she remained dry-eyed. 'Do you want to go now, Mummy?'

She saw her mother nod, a handkerchief held against her nose. 'There's nothing more we can do. You go on, I'll follow.'

As they made their way, slowly, grievingly away, respect, in some strange ritualistic way, of the dead dictated that it must be done in silence, no words said. Amy saw her mother bend over the still form of her husband, his face pointing ceilingwards, and lay a kiss on his stiffening lips; heard her whisper, 'Safe journey, my dear,' the words caught in a sob. Straightening, she came and joined her family and together they went to drink the tea in the sister's office where they would not be disturbed in their grief.

Chapter Twenty-Three

In her mother's spacious lounge Amy sat with the others, informal. A meagre gathering of relatives, they numbered nine in all, plus the servants who had also been mentioned.

The funeral two days ago had been well attended, church and graveside spilling over with his and Mummy's friends and acquaintances, her charity ladies and their husbands, his business colleagues and their wives, the church rafters vibrating to the words and music of 'Abide With Me'. But Lawson Harrington's family wasn't large by any means. There was Mummy, of course, and her, Kay and Henry, her father's brother Edgar, his wife Anne, and two cousins, and his childless widowed sister Maud, whose husband had been killed on the Somme. Amy hadn't seen any of them for years, since she was a child, and then only seldom. The Harringtons had never been a close-knit family.

For her, sitting here didn't feel right. That she had been summoned could be merely as a formality, because she was his eldest child. His will would have been altered in the four years since she'd left. He could only want her here to show his displeasure to her, even from the grave. As if those years hadn't been painful enough.

She glanced towards the solicitor, Mr Gregory, smoothing out the stiff parchment with dramatic deliberation as though about to enact some ritual sacrifice. She hastily looked away.

Across the room from her and Henry, Mummy sat on a sofa with Kay at her side. She was holding the girl's hand with a grip that looked vice-like. It declared Kay as her sole companion, Amy not having been there to share that privilege. Kay hadn't a young man as yet for all she had grown beautiful. Her hazel eyes, wide and arresting, should have attracted the glances of dozens of the opposite sex by now. But that grip had the semblance of a steel cage, Kay ensnared by her mother's need of a daughter. Amy felt a surge of relief that she had left when she had. Escaped might be the better word. She too might have become Mummy's prop, especially with Dicky Pritchard jilting her and running for his life. And Kay might have been free to seek a husband. She felt suddenly deeply sorry for Kay.

She felt sorry for Mummy as well. Her face looked white and strained, though she held herself well in check, her back ramrod straight, a woman of good breeding, or that was what she conveyed. Amy wondered if she had cried yet. She hadn't seen her cry all the ten days she had been here. At the funeral her white angular face behind its black veil had floated seemingly disembodied and no one could tell if she shed tears or not. During the buffet later when people had conveyed condolences to her, her replies had remained quite steady, her lips composed, her eyes still hidden by the partially lifted veil betraying nothing. Her only concession to grief was that she hardly ate, was still hardly eating. What little light food was brought to her at mealtimes by a silent maid – a thin piece of bread and butter, an egg custard in a tiny earthenware pot, a small bowl of clear vegetable soup – was hardly nibbled, anything heavier waved away making the rest of them feel guilty just by eating. Mummy carried her grief magnificently.

If she hadn't cried, neither had Amy. During the funeral there had arisen in her a resentment against her father. He must have known he had a heart condition, that his days were numbered, yet he hadn't sent for her, knowing she'd inevitably return at the news of his death suffering all the remorse of not seeing him again in life. It wasn't unreasonable resentment, she told herself, looking across the table at her mother while beside her Henry fidgeted chin on fist and sighing with all the short patience of the sixteen-year-old. He seemed not unduly upset by his father's death either. Why should he when he'd spent nearly all his young life away from home? She'd known them more than he, and had once been close to Daddy. Now she felt she'd hardly known him. Why then should she cry?

Kay on the other hand looked deeply distraught. Her beautiful hazel eyes red-trimmed and slightly puffy, she held a small embroidered handkerchief at the ready in her free hand. She had cried openly throughout the funeral, obliging her mother to talk to her in sharp whispers every now and again. She had always been the apple of Daddy's eye, and despite her present thoughts about her father, Amy experienced a small surge of jealousy even as she felt her anger rise against him for what he'd done.

'How long had he had heart problems?' she'd asked her mother when she'd dared to broach it.

It was probably the only time her mother seemed to droop. 'Some two years. Dr Lombard said he might have been having a problem before that. But you know your father, disdained the need to go seeking medical advice if he could.'

'But what could have brought it on?'

'It could have been that terrible Wall Street thing. Oh, he came out of it well enough, financially. I don't know the rights of his dealings, but he apparently sold a good deal of stock that very morning ready to make transfers or something. I don't understand such things. Quite beyond me. I had my work, my good causes, your father had his. It seemed America being so many hours behind us, he happened to do just right in what he did. He merely happened to be lucky . . .'

She'd stumbled then over those words, but recovered herself, took Amy's hand with a warmth Amy wouldn't have thought she warranted after four years without contact, apart from her one unanswered letter. At that moment it had seemed she'd never been away as her mother gripped her fingers.

'I think it was the terrible repercussions Wall Street caused to the stock markets in general. His escaping so miraculously, yet seeing his associates going down around him. It affected him terribly. I'm sure it was that which brought on his heart.'

She had let go Amy's hand, grown cold again towards

her. 'It had to be that,' she'd said and went to open the dozens of telegrams that had come, each containing their sad messages of sympathy, her final words to Amy completely disconnected from what she had been talking about. 'I expect I shall have to wire replies to all these.'

'There's no need, Mummy. They won't expect it,' Amy said from the distance her mother had again put between them, but her mother hadn't answered.

Mr Gregory's voice reached her, reading out the will. Amy listened without much interest. It was her duty as one of her mother's children to be here but of course she expected nothing, or at most a little token. He wouldn't leave her out entirely. She was still his daughter. But slowly her mouth dropped open.

Her mother told her after the reading that her father hadn't changed his will after she'd left home. He had never been able to bring himself to answer her one and only letter, had requested she too stay her hand until he could bring himself to reply, but when no other letter came he'd been hurt, terribly hurt, refused to write that crucial one that might have brought her back home. Listening, all Amy's resentment fell away, as snow on a summit might vanish leaving the cold granite bared to the sky. Who had been in the wrong? Her father? Herself? A chain of misunderstandings. Forgiveness and the need to be forgiven were now lost.

Tears flooding her eyes at last, Amy heard how he had refused to change his will, maintaining that it was the last vestige of the love he'd always had for her, despite all. Knowing now what she should have known all along, she let her mother hold her as four years of pent-up emotion she hadn't even imagined she harboured flowed out of her. She couldn't recall her mother crying even then, but the hand that gently patted her back as she clung to her was all that was needed. Mother and daughter again, they stood, arms around each other, but how pitiful that it had taken her father's death to bring them together.

'Yer've got ter stop it, Tom, luv,' he heard his mother saying through the clogging apathy into which he had sunk these last couple of weeks, or was it more? Weeks that seemed to him a lifetime. 'Yer've got ter pull yerself tergevver. If she don't come back, there ain't anythink yer can do about it. 'Er's is a different world to ours. She was bound ter go back to it sooner or later.'

Cold comfort. Amy had written him two letters, one to say she was dealing with things there, a bit about the funeral arrangements, and that she'd be back as soon as she possibly could. The other told him of the reading of the will, her reconciliation with her mother – she sounded elated, relieved, a different person in that second letter – and the money she had been left. Money people like him couldn't even imagine let alone dream about. A different world. She had re-entered it. Not one word in her second letter spoke about coming back. Inheriting money, it had made all the difference. He knew now, she wouldn't be coming back. What would she want with this hole? Her with all that money, her lovely home – it must be – all friends again with her mother, her family, what could she want with him?

He didn't reply to his mother's efforts to make him face up to the inevitable, merely gathered up his sticks and not bothering to concentrate on the way Amy had told him he must walk, took the easier one and shambled back to his corner in the front room.

His mother was right, he had to put the past behind him. He and Amy came from different worlds and he should have foreseen its conclusion. He'd been a fool to have thought otherwise.

But he couldn't put the past behind him. Memories of that Christmas flooded back, he and Amy locked in each other's arms in the back yard, oblivious to the cold night air. And that other time, that evening with her in his bed, his hand still remembered how her breasts had felt, small and firm under his palm, his body still remembered how her hips had arched to him, that hot preciousness as he joined himself to her.

He remembered too the times after that when they had wanted desperately to repeat it, but never dared, knowing his mother was just the other side of the door. Lost and wasted times. And where did he, crippled, useless, no man at all, go from here? He knew where Amy was going. He not included on that route, unable to reach out and touch her across the chasm her money had created.

No, he didn't reply to the truth of his mother's common sense. His heart was too full of his loss and the tears that pained his throat to reply to her.

Amy had taken herself up to bed early, leaving the others downstairs. These days she couldn't wait to come up here. It was heavenly lying in her room, snuggling in her soft cosy bed. She had forgotten how soft and cosy it was, the eiderdown puffed up all around her chin, its pink pattern the same as the curtains, the frills around her dressing table and upholstery on the stool. The wall lights and her bedside lamp were pink too, and the fluffy rugs into which her feet could disappear entirely. Everything remained as it had always been, as though she'd been away just one night instead of four years.

Hard to imagine how she could have accepted the cramped poorly-decorated poorly-lit little bedroom she had shared with Alice, Vi and Rosy. She thought of that tiny folding bed she had bought, unable to bring herself to sleep in the same bed with another person. After Alice, then Vi left to get married, the room had become less cramped. But it hadn't altered the meanness of the room. How often she had thought longingly of this one. Expecting never to see it again, she'd forced her thoughts of it to seep away, firmly prepared to look at a future she in her wildest nightmares would have never dreamed would be hers. But now she was back, how could she ever have imagined she could become inured to what seemed now to be squalor?

Snuggling under the eiderdown, soft pillows puffing around her ears, the lights still on because she felt reluctant to get out of bed to turn them off, Amy sighed with deep contentment and closed her eyes, the room silently, protectively stealing in around her, its solid walls permitting no word of the conversation going on below her to enter.

'It's not fair!' Henry was in a sulky mood, had been ever since the reading of his father's will four days ago now.

He'd said little in his mother's hearing. She would have

316

rebuked him. But she had gone up to bed soon after Amy, and he could hold it in no longer. 'If I were older, I'd have a good mind to contest the damned thing. It's totally unfair.'

He was with Kay, the two of them listening to the radio gramophone, the volume knob turned down in case they disturbed Mummy and so they could talk, occasionally going to lift the cabinet lid to change the record. The instrument needed no winding up as the record kept going to its end, the black bitumen disc only needing to be turned over to the other side.

Henry came back from selecting yet another record, and to the strains of the gentle but cheery little tune 'Why Do I Love You', came back to lounge on the sofa opposite to where Kay sat trying to read the page on the new styles in clever make-up in the magazine she'd bought that morning. She did so want to be the height of fashion and attract the young men, but Mummy would keep saying she looked far more presentable with just a moderate brushing of powder and the barest touch of lipstick, and as for her eyes, why spoil such pretty ones with lots of black pencil? She wanted to absorb as much of the new fashions as she could before going to bed, but Henry would keep interrupting.

'I'm sure Mother ought to do something about it. It *is* unfair, you know. Utterly unfair.'

Kay put down her magazine. Hopeless trying to read. 'I expect Daddy thought he was being fair at the time.' Tears misted her vision at the mention of him, her brother seeming to swim for a second or two before her gaze, but she blinked them away. She felt cross with Henry, not only for disturbing her, but for being so mercenary and causing her tears to come. She didn't want them to come. They made her throat hurt and she wanted to be free of that for a while.

'Then he should have made sure he altered it after what she did. I wouldn't have let the grass grow under my feet.'

'Perhaps he didn't want to.'

'After what she did? I think she must have sent him a bit funny in the head. He couldn't have been in his right mind after being treated like that by someone he loved. You could contest the will on that point alone.'

'*I* could?'

317

'Well, Mother could. And I expect Uncle Edgar could. Look at the paltry little bit he got. I bet he'd be all for it.'

Kay looked at him. 'You mean you'd like to see Amy cut out of Daddy's will entirely?'

'And why not? He owed her nothing, behaving the way she did, not even writing a single word to him or Mother. She cocked a snook at them.'

'I don't know enough about it,' Kay shrugged and looked longingly down at her magazine. 'I was never told anything, and I didn't ask. I wished she'd written to me, though, at least. I'd done nothing to her.'

'Exactly. She didn't care a fig for any of us.'

'It couldn't have been nice for her. I think she was living hand to mouth.'

'She had what Father gave her. A blasted couple of hundred quid.'

For the baby, Kay thought, but she didn't say so to Henry. He was too young for talk of illegitimacy, and she'd have felt embarrassed discussing it with him. She wondered vaguely if Daddy had ever thought about the baby, his grandchild, would ever have liked to have seen it. Neither he nor Mummy ever spoke about it. It might be dead for all they seemed to concern themselves. She'd often wondered, though, whether Amy had had it adopted – no one even knew the sex – or whether it still lived with those people she apparently went to live with, the family of a maid of theirs, Alice, who Daddy had let go. There had been an address.

'She did write to Mummy and Daddy once,' she said.

Henry shrugged. 'First I've known about it. But it doesn't alter the issue, does it, that after the way she behaved, he could still leave her in his will. He couldn't have been of sound mind, that's for sure, and on that alone we could ...'

'Contest the will, yes I know, Henry, and I'm sick of hearing it.'

'But that way, you and I would have got a damned sight more. Half each of the remaining half, instead of a bloody third each.'

'Henry! If you're going to start swearing, I'm going to bed.' She closed the magazine. She'd be able to read it in peace in her room. And perhaps practice the way they told how to put make-up on, using her limited supply to its full potential.

Henry's lips curled into a little sneer. 'All the chaps I hang around with at college swear and curse. If I didn't do the same they'd call me a pansy.'

'I suppose you've had lots of girls too,' she shot at him, angry. 'Just to prove you're not.'

He grinned, a slow wise grin. 'More than you've ever "had" boys.'

The quiet emphasis on the one word and the grin conveyed that he implied something more than she'd meant, and she blushed deeply, feeling her face start to burn.

'I didn't mean that kind of . . . You're disgusting!'

He burst out laughing and got up to change the record, its needle now scraping round and round in the groove with a regular rhythmic sough and click.

He chose a new tune, 'Tiptoe Thro' The Tulips With Me', one that suited his altered mood. As the cheerful dance band began, he came back to sit forward on the edge of the sofa to gaze into his sister's sullen eyes, his own alight with avaricious possibilities.

'Just think, Kay, half of fifteen grand would be seven and a half each. Plus all that interest when we're twenty-one. If Father hadn't been out of his mind.'

'What about solicitors' fees for fighting it in court?' she parried. She felt suddenly much wiser than he. 'Amy wouldn't let it go without a fight, and I don't blame her. Solicitors know how to charge and string it out for years. They're the only ones who come out well off from contesting wills in courts of law. Even if Mummy did agree with you, we'd see even less than we have now with it split the three ways. Anyway it's in trust for us. Five thousand will make plenty of interest.'

'Bloody nonsense!' Henry scoffed, forgetting himself.

'I said don't swear, Henry. You can say whatever you like with your chaps, but not in front of me. Nor do I want to fall out with Amy again. I don't suppose Mummy would either. I think she's overjoyed at having her back, even though she tries not to show it. It's perked her up immensely and taken off some of the grief of losing Daddy. Though nothing can make that grief...' She stopped, swallowed hard against the renewed threat of tears. 'I'm going to bed.'

'And I'm going to speak to Mother in the morning, tell her how I feel.'

'Yes, Henry, you do that,' she told him from the door. 'But I'm happy with what I'll have. I'm not greedy – like some.'

'You needn't be,' he told her, going to lift the gramophone needle and scratching the record in the process. 'One day you'll marry money. Me, *I'll* have to do the providing. I'll need that cash.'

'By the time you marry,' she told him, 'you'd have spent the lot. Anyway it'll be five years before you ever see any of it, if you do persuade Mummy to fight it. And it means that Mummy's money will be frozen while she is doing that. Have you thought of that? No one could touch Daddy's estate until the whole thing is settled. How do you think Mummy will live during that time? Can you provide for her? She's been used to a decent standard of living. Amy will understand that. She's been poor and knows what it's like. And Mummy couldn't continue to pay your college fees, could she?' That would deter him.

From where the radio gramophone stood, Henry's young gaze grew crafty. 'Then it could be settled quicker than you think, dear clever Kay. Our dear sister wouldn't want to see *Mummy* impoverished. I reckon she'd give up her share not to see that happen, so long as *Mummy* looked after her. Mother could give her all she needed, and one day, like you, she'd marry someone with money, so what's she got to cry about?'

'Oh!' Kay had had enough of him. 'You've turned into a horrible person. I think you're just beastly.'

'Only looking after my inheritance,' he murmured at her retreating figure.

Upstairs Amy, oblivious to the argument concerning her going on beneath her room, dreamed on, not quite asleep, still blissfully aware of luxuriating in her new-found surroundings. It had been a shock, but a marvellous shock, hearing of the money she had inherited. These last four days she'd been a little benumbed by it, by her mother's change of heart towards her, by the joy of being home again, even through the trauma and sadness of her father's death. She had meant to write to Tom this evening; realised she hadn't included anything about seeing him soon in her last letter, so excited had she felt about the result of the will. But he'd understand, know automatically that he'd see her, although when, she still wasn't sure. There was still so much to do here, and Mummy was being so loving towards her she needed her for a while longer.

The blissful meanderings had become more purposeful at the thought of Tom. Amy opened her eyes, the room's comfort leaping into focus about her. Tom. A small prick of remorse made itself felt. She hadn't thought of him as much as she might have these last four days. Now she did. And now all her love and all the things her money might do for them both began to replace these last two weeks.

There'd be a lot to do. Five thousand pounds. To Tom and his family it was a veritable fortune. But to sink it all into a business which she and Tom knew so little about was taking a fearful chance. It could all be lost in one throw. Such gambles actually happened in casinos in the South of France, and this wish to see Tom in his own business, on the river, wasn't that just as risky? She knew as much about the pleasure boat business as he did, and that was virtually nil despite all her avid listening to Mr Goodburn's fairy tales. It needed a lot of serious thinking before venturing into such a scheme. It began to consume her, brushing away sleep to leave her wide awake, her mind whirling like a windmill. By the small hours she knew that in the face of everything, this was what she wanted to do.

But first, she had no intention of living with the Jordans in their horrid little dwelling. A small house in the suburbs was the solution. Rosy could easily get a job in a local shop. Amy was resolved that Rosy and Willie would continue to work. No one must imagine they could live off her money. Willie would have to commute by train to London, if he still had his job. His school was making moves to claim him back until he was fourteen.

She thought of the price of a modest suburban home. In

the type of magazines her father used to read, houses and desirable bungalows were priced between six and nine hundred pounds. Nothing that grand would be needed, just a little terraced house for say two to three hundred, a token of thanks for all the Jordans had done for her. She and Tom would be married, and as the business got going (she was sure now as the hours grew that it would be successful) she and Tom would buy themselves a finer house. In time they might even have one as good as Mummy and Daddy's. Oh no, it was Mummy's now . . .

Happy visions of fleets of pleasure steamers and fine living burst with a gentle pop as Amy steeled herself against the lump that came unbidden into her throat at the realisation that she could still think of her father as being here. That he was no longer here felt so frighteningly unreal. Even though she hadn't seen him these four years, knowing that he was in this world hadn't made the rift so hard to bear as now, knowing that he wasn't. The final severing. Amy bit at her bottom lip and took control of herself, forced her thoughts to back to their original purpose, but they no longer had the golden aspect they'd had before thoughts of her father had invaded them, even though she knew with certainty that they would be made into more than just dreams. She had the money to make them so.

Constance Harrington glared at her son. 'Certainly not. I think Amelia has paid quite enough for her mistakes, Henry.'

Henry stood his ground. 'Why should she get the same as me and Kay? We've both done everything you and Father asked of us. We haven't thrown your love for us in your face. We never walked out. Yet we're to get the same as her. She comes back, large as life, and she's welcomed with open arms and . . .'

He wanted to say out comes the fatted calf, but that sounded much too grandiloquent. He was thinking of the prodigal son, but he didn't think quoting the Bible at his mother would be quite appropriate. He ended with, 'given exactly the same as us. After the way she's behaved. There's no justice in this world.'

That sounded petty, not half as grandiose as fatted calf,

and now he wished he'd said it, as it wouldn't have made him sound so much like a mere sixteen-year-old boy and would have carried far more weight.

His mother continued to glare. 'You don't know the half of it, so be very careful what you are saying, my dear.'

'So I don't know the half of it.' He felt brave enough for this. 'No wonder I feel unjustly treated. Perhaps if I did know, then I might not feel that way.'

'You are too young for such things.' His mother's lips had stiffened with a sort of embarrassed expression, but he ploughed on.

'If it affects my feelings of unfairness, I think I should be told.'

'Then stop all this blazing and sit down, there.' She indicated an upright wing chair in the morning room where he had found her sifting through several recently arrived letters of sympathy. She went and sat herself on a similar chair quite some way removed from him, as though distance might lessen the sense of awkwardness she was obviously experiencing.

'To start with, your sister did not so much walk out as was ordered to leave by her father. I would not have done that, for all I agreed with him in his anger at your sister's condition, but he was master of this house and father of his daughter and I felt obliged to support him.'

'Condition?' Henry picked up on the word, his young, well-informed mind already racing ahead. But he still asked. 'What condition? Was Amy . . . you know?'

His mother's head on its thin neck inclined, the faintest of movements, but enough to rescue her from further awkward explanation.

Henry sat back with a soft whistle that made his mother's eyes widen in a warning that this was not a matter for amusement. He straightened his expression accordingly as his mother continued.

'I did not truly realise the anguish your sister was going through or else I would have gone against your father. But I didn't know. And I have suffered the guilt of that for four years. I ached to write to your sister, but your father would not bend and I could not find it in me to go against him. He was so terribly hurt.'

He watched in silence as she rose and began to pace the room, her clasped hands twisting. 'I know the young man who did this to her, and I consider him utterly despicable in refusing to stand by her. He had proposed marriage to her and she honestly believed him. Your sister was a victim.'

Henry tried to control his grin. Fancy Amy doing things like that. He'd only got as far as a fumble with girls in the town, a slobber of kissing, a stolen handful of breast, but he got a swift slap and a 'Get your hand off!' when his hand attempted to steal up their skirts. It invariably led to the girl stalking off. A chap had to learn to be crafty. He hadn't quite got the hang of it, yet, but hoped to before long. And now his young mind visualised his sister going the whole hog. He was in danger of showing himself up, but he kept his face impassive.

His mother had stopped pacing, stood looking down at the Turkish carpet on which she had come to stand, though he suspected she wasn't seeing it. The look on her face swept almost all lascivious thoughts from his mind.

'Your sister was rejected by us. She went to live in squalor. A gently brought up young lady, forced to fend for herself in some horrid slum in the East End of London, among total strangers. That's what your father and I did to her. And when she tried to write to us, we ignored it. We refused to forgive. We didn't stop to see how frail virtue can become when a girl is in love. We didn't stop to recognise our own frailties. Standing on our principles, guarding our pride behind our battlements of good behaviour, we did your sister a great wrong. She lost the baby, you know.'

Henry sat quite still. It was as though his mother was speaking to someone other than he. Herself perhaps? His father?

'She told me all about it just after the funeral. She told me without a tear, but her face was dreadful. I shall never forget that look, or the wrong I did her. It will remain with me for as long as I live. I should have been there with her when that stillborn little baby was taken away from her. But

324

it was a stranger, a grubby woman of the East End, who held her and comforted her.'

Any remaining luscious thoughts that had been in Henry's head of his sister rolling in the hay with a man, seeing the 'act' as though he were actually watching, his young manhood squirming – all that dissipated as he saw tears slide unheeded down his mother's gaunt face. In that moment all he could visualise was a young mother's agony, losing her child. In that moment Henry Harrington grew up.

'So you see . . .' his mother began again after a pause, but he didn't want to hear, a cold sweat broken out on his brow.

He got up from the chair. 'I'd better go, Mother. Sorry I bothered you.'

It was a crass way of excusing himself, but he wasn't yet old enough to excuse himself with decorum, not under these circumstances. It had been in his mind for a while those moments before he became suddenly older to taunt Amy with innuendos that he knew something she didn't know he knew. Now he knew he would not, could not, face her, ever.

He longed to be back at college, be with his chums again. They were real, they were fun, uncomplicated, uncluttered by profundity, chaps who had no reason to bother about life's pangs.

And anyway, by the time he came of age and was able to do what he wanted with his five thousand, the interest it would have accrued would more or less have come up to the hoped-for amount.

Chapter Twenty-Four

It was hard, this leaving home a second time, hard leaving her mother; Mummy in black and grieving without tears. She would be coming to see her often enough, now her mother's house was once more open to her, but it was still not easy to leave her.

As Amy prepared to leave, she and her mother stood in the hall, Amy in hat and a new winter coat she had bought against the fogs of November, her small case ready to be picked up and carried out by the maid hovering by the door waiting to open it on a signal. Outside a taxi was ticking over in the kerb.

'You will be all right, Mummy?'

'I have Kay.' The words touched a jealous chord, but Amy smiled.

'Of course you have. I shall see you very soon, Mummy.'

She had been here a month. A month without Tom. She had written several times, but he had written only once, reminding her that not only had she never before had occasion to note his angular rather uneven hand, but how stilted the letter itself was. More a friendly one than a love letter, it contained no mention about missing her, loving her. But she put that down to the limitations of the written word. After all, she too had been cautious at putting feelings of love down on paper, which could read so sloppily and sentimental. When they saw each other again, his true feelings would pour out, and so would hers.

From now on they would have a new life together. She was sorry to leave her mother, yet eager to be on her way.

It was the actual going that was so hard. Once away her thoughts, unfettered by this momentary loyalty, could fly ahead of her to the future that lay waiting for her and Tom.

'I'll come and see you as often as I can, Mummy.'

'Whenever you wish, dear.' Mummy, preparing herself to be distant again, was not expecting too much of her. 'I shall be well looked after here.'

Yes, by Kay, poor domesticated Kay, designed to exist within the bounds of her mother's love. Amy felt sorry for her, yet still jealous of her role. Mummy didn't need her eldest daughter any more. Every word she spoke indicated that she had stayed away too long to take up her old place in this house. Of course she could come and visit, but her mother didn't consider it obligatory.

'Will you wish me well, Mummy?'

She had told her about Tom, how they hoped one day to marry. Her mother had listened without comment, that itself a disapproval ... no, more a silent washing of hands in that Amy was old enough to know what she was doing and was anyway not her responsibility any more. She had made one mistake in her life and if that hadn't made her wise, then nothing that could be said would be of any benefit.

'I do hope it works out for you, Amelia.'

So that was it, no warmth in this guarded response even though her mother came forward to put a hand lightly on each of her shoulders and draw her close enough to peck each cheek in turn, her pursed lips giving forth a small smacking sound – the way she might greet or say farewell to one of her charity friends. Amy knew then that this was all the blessing she could hope for. There was a distinct feeling that she had overstayed her welcome, that a wound is never truly healed, its scar noticed again and again, reawakening memories no matter how dim.

She was almost grateful to climb into the taxi and be on her way, the quiet little maid following out after her through the descending afternoon fog to put her case in the vehicle for her.

She gave a wave to her mother from the taxi window as a form of a promise to come back soon, but already the front door was being closed as the taxi drew away. Mummy had her own life, she had hers. She had been too long away.

Having answered the knock, Mrs Jordan stood there, her eyes lifting from Amy to follow the course of the departing taxi as though establishing how she'd come here, then moving back to her again.

'Oh, it's you. We wasn't expectin' yer.'

The guarded tone threw Amy off balance for a second, found her apologising. 'I'm sorry. I should have let you know I was coming.'

'No, that's all right.' Mrs Jordan seemed to collect herself, an appropriate smile touching her lips. 'You'd best come in then.'

She was making an effort to speak nicely, the way Amy remembered when Alice had first brought her here. A studied caution. It made her feel a stranger all over again as Mrs Jordan stood back to let her in.

Not having set foot in here for a month, the place struck her with a new force of unfamiliarity: the narrowness of the dim passage, the ancient wallpaper, the old second-hand hat and coat stand, the lingering taint of earlier cooking, of floor polish and washing day, just as the smell of the area had hit her full in the face as she got out of the taxi, a pervasive odour of drains and the nearby brewery hanging on the thickening November fog.

Tom was sitting at the table, engrossed in a newspaper crossword, as Mrs Jordan conducted her into the living room, his cigarette burning away in a black chipped ashtray with the words Worthington's Ales embedded into the glass. He looked up and immediately struggled to his feet, his eyes lighting up. She'd forgotten just how wonderfully blue they were.

'Amy! For the love of God, what a surprise! What're you doin' 'ere?'

As she came forward he took her hand but surprisingly merely laid a kiss on her cheek, something seeming to forbid his kissing her lips. He seemed almost wary.

She stood back from him, laying her clutch bag on the table beside his crossword. She had already dropped her

328

case in the hall, unsure if she was truly welcome here or not, whether she would be expected to stay here at all, so strange had Mrs Jordan's welcome been.

'There was no more for me to do at . . . at my mother's.' It didn't seem right to say home, any more than this place seemed home now. It struck her, with a catch in her throat, that really she belonged nowhere.

"Ow is she, yer mum?' Mrs Jordan offered with slightly more warmth.

'Not too bad,' Amy obliged formally. 'She's a very stoic person.'

'And the rest of yer family? Yer poor father goin' like that.'

'They're taking it well.' How could she go into any detailed preamble about people of whom Mrs Jordan had no conception? The room fell quiet. It was Mrs Jordan who bridged the threatening hiatus.

'I expect yer'd like a cuppa tea, wouldn't'cher, luv?' Her earlier efforts to speak correctly had been short-lived but in a way helped ease the atmosphere.

Amy smiled. 'I'd like that! I really would.'

'Good. Well, sit yerself down then, luv.'

More at ease now the first surprise was over, she bustled out. With the sound of the kettle going on the gas, teacups industriously clinking onto saucers, Amy and Tom looked at each other, a shy sort of smile passing between them.

'I'm glad you came back,' he said quietly, then more significantly, 'came back home.'

A lump had begun to form in her throat. It was an effort to speak through it. 'I'm glad too,' she managed. This place, for all its poor state, *was* home. *She* was home. And Tom's arms were about her and he bent and pressed his lips to hers in a long slow kiss that spoke as much for his relief in having her back as her own to be back.

Amy had hoped coming back would be easy, but realised almost immediately that it might not be. She had money now and already she could feel a premonition of it proving a barrier which might keep coming down at odd, unexpected times.

329

It began almost immediately in the presents she'd bought for the Jordans – an afterthought as her taxi took her through Bishopsgate. Nothing too ostentatious to embarrass Mrs Jordan, who must have been reduced to struggling on next to nothing all these weeks she had been away without her share coming in. (Whether she still had a job at Bellows, Amy hadn't bothered to find out with the trauma of these past four weeks; but she would contact them, for courtesy's sake).

For Mrs Jordan there was a peacock brooch with glass stones, white, blue and green. For Rosy a lipstick. For Willie a half-pound bar of Nestlé's chocolate whose red wrapper he immediately tore off with all the excitement of the schoolboy he'd again become now his school had claimed him back until nearer to his fourteenth birthday, good job or not as messenger boy on a newspaper. (The paper had at least promised to consider him again when he did leave school, good worker that he'd been.) But as the chocolate was pounced on with a rush of thanks, Amy saw Mrs Jordan's small frown at this unnecessary flourish of generosity, and bit at her lip.

For Tom, Amy had brought only her love. A gift would have somehow lessened the way she felt for him, her longing to see him mounting with each mile the taxi took until she'd hardly been able to bear it, cursing the fog that slowed the journey as the taxi negotiated weaving droves of bikes that helped save fares, trams and buses filled with those home-ward-bound workers who could afford them. Willing her taxi to move quicker, despite the growing fog, Tom's face had hovered in front of her, and she felt amazed that she could have kept away from him for so long.

Tom had understood the significance of receiving no present, giving her a secret smile that intimated he intended to claim his personal one later.

Over the supper scraped together for the extra unex-pected mouth, it was good to see Mrs Jordan's cautious reserve melt away as she related what had been going on during Amy's absence. It wasn't much, but Mrs Jordan had always been adept at stringing the briefest most mundane bit of information out into a long tale. Less so since the death of her husband. She still wore a good deal of black for him, old-fashioned to the limit: a year would have to pass before she'd consent to wear anything brighter. But her old loquaciousness was returning, so different, Amy mused gratifyingly, to the studied absence of chatter considered good behaviour by her own mother.

Finally exhausting herself, Mrs Jordan sighed and rose after the bedtime cup of Fry's cocoa, ushering Rosy ahead of her.

'Well, I need me beauty sleep and so do Rosy with work in the morning. You two can wash up the cups fer me. Don't stay up too late, the pair of yer.'

Amy watched her departure, speechless. Mrs Jordan had previously got the spare bed in Rosy's room ready in a flurry of energy which in its way indicated a welcome home, as did that departing request. Willie, already gone to bed, would leave Amy and Tom quite alone downstairs.

Left sitting at the table with the remains of her Fry's cocoa, hearing the two pair of footsteps going on up the stairs, Amy shook her head. Left alone together, and willingly? This was a different woman to the one of four weeks ago. Where was the fear she tried stoically to hide of Tom being taken away from her?

The place quiet at last, Tom drained the last of his cocoa and got up on his sticks – he still used the two when not practising – going to the sofa to sink down, the sticks being propped against its curved bulky arm. He was definitely getting around more easily. Still awkward, still an effort, but it had become much easier. In time he might even attempt going out of the house, though that, Amy contemplated, would be to him like contemplating the scaling of Mount Everest, in other words, almost impossible.

It crossed her mind he might need help getting to his room. Or should she leave him to it? He had enough coddling from his mother. But she should at least ask. His reply was a grin, his blue eyes roguish. He patted the place beside him on the sofa. 'Come here.'

The way it was said told her what he had in mind. 'Your mother might come in,' she whispered, her heart beginning to thud against her ribs.

'No she won't. I had a word with her while you've been away, Amy. Come and sit down.'

While she sat, his arm going about her shoulders, he told her his mother had voiced the likelihood that having returned home she wouldn't come back, that with all that comfort and nice living to go back to, what would she want with their sort of life? 'I told her we loved each other and that should be enough to bring you back to me,' he told Amy quietly, his arm motionless across her shoulders. 'But as the weeks went by, I began to believe she was right. I began to get frightened.'

The word 'frightened' made her start, turn, and in panic cover his cheeks with kisses of remorse for what her absence must have put him through, trying not to doubt her loyalty yet forced to believe his mother's fears.

'Oh, my darling, how could I ever leave you? How could you even believe I would? I don't care if we haven't one penny between us – if we have to beg a room from someone to live in, I couldn't stop loving you. I want to marry you. I want us to be together, no matter . . .'

The flow was cut short by his lips, his arm tightening around her, bringing her hard against him. He was in command and she, for once, the follower, the recipient, neither of them daring to make a sound as he brought her to her climax lest those upstairs, or the lad in the adjacent room, heard them. But it was the most wonderful moment of Amy's life, that overwhelming surge of love, until now her first time.

Still close in his arms, the time drifted. She slept, woke enough to think that she ought to be freshening herself up from their lovemaking, but it would have destroyed everything to go out into the kitchen to do so; might even awaken his mother. Lying very still, a haze of contentment settled back upon her as she asked quietly, 'Are you awake, Tom?'

'Huh,' came the dreamy response, and she went on talking in the same quiet tones.

'I'm glad I'm back. I'll never go away again.' She felt his chin against her head move slightly in a nod of agreement and she went on dreamily. 'We will get married, won't we, Tom? And we'll make it as soon as possible.'

Again he nodded. With this confirmation, she could embark on the other thing that had been forming in her mind for so long. 'We could start up in business now, darling. Now we . . .' She wouldn't say 'I'. 'Now we have a decent bit of money coming our way.' She hadn't yet told the family how much money she had been left, not eager to see them squirm uncomfortably at the sound of such a sum. Five thousand pounds! The eyes of some, she imagined, would light up with avarice, but these people, she knew instinctively, would be embarrassed and not know how to face her.

She waited, but Tom didn't correct her by saying it had come her way, not his. She was encouraged. 'You've always wanted to be on the river. You used to tell me how you felt so imprisoned working in ships' holds – how you loved being taken by barge to some other place to work. The way you'd describe how wide and clean the river felt from where you stood, and the way the water smelled, all fresh, and the sound when it churned under the bows of the barges. You made me feel some of the magic you felt, the freedom you felt, and I would think how lovely it would be to have enough money for your own boat and take paying passengers up and down the river. I don't mean those big pleasure steamers that go from Tower Bridge to Southend or to Margate like the one we went on, remember, darling, to Southend? I mean a small one. At least to start with. We could probably afford something like an ex-ferryboat, work it on a regular tripping service up to some place like Richmond.'

Mr Goodburn had often mentioned it. 'It's a very popular place,' she went on, being carried away, lovemaking and its comforting aftermath all forgotten. 'It could be absolutely wonderful. Your own business. Your own freedom. I can see you, darling, on your own boat . . .'

He stirred sharply. 'Huh?'

'But you could be,' she persisted, unaware she was entering dangerous waters, the captain with eyes only for the beautiful sunset failing to see the rocks below the bows of the dreamy ship she guided. 'Oh, Tom, it can happen now. Now we have the means to do it.'

He sat up, startling her, leaving her half-lying in the place where he had been. 'And give 'em all a bloody good laugh, I suppose, them *paying passengers*. Why not chuck in the comedy show as well? Me.'

A small prickle of impatience rose up. 'Don't be silly, darling! Don't spoil it. I was being serious.'

'So am I. Serious and practical.' He swung his legs to the floor with that awkward movement he was forced to adopt, one leg struck out straight in front of him. 'What good would I be at that sort of thing?'

She too sat up, angry now. 'Yes, Tom, I know. Your legs. Always your bloody legs.'

He turned and looked at her, the minutes stringing themselves out. A row was beginning to brew, she knew, and she was powerless to stop it without having to back down, and she was determined not to do that. She had got this far. How could she let it all go for someone who was threatening to become pig-headed? All she hoped was she wouldn't lose the argument by stalking off in a huff. Or perhaps he would get up instead, in silence reaching for his sticks to hobble off to his bed leaving her sitting there with no more allowed to be said, nothing solved – yet again.

She was almost on the verge of crying out, 'Well, say something!' when he began to straighten up from his slumped position, stretch his back, seeming to grow in stature before her gaze.

'I wasn't thinking about me legs,' he said very slowly. 'I've decided they ain't goin' ter stop me any more. I'm sick of bein' looked on as a damned invalid. No, Amy, what I was thinking, or at least what I'm thinkin' now, is, I ain't got the faintest idea how to 'andle a pleasure boat. A rowin' boat'd be more my mark.'

For a moment she could only stare at him, then realised that he was in fact making a joke. A small hint of a grin had even begun to stretch one side of his lips a little. And there was something else. He was talking as though he had accepted the offer of her money. She couldn't believe he was. But then, of course, it could be looked upon as a windfall, nothing to do with her skills, no case of her providing for him by the sweat of her brow, making him less of a man with his inability to work. A windfall, it seemed, was permissible. Amy felt the tension melt away from her.

'Oh, Tom, you are a fool!' They were both fools, and she told him so.

The next minute they were both laughing, giggling more than laughing, both trying hard to keep it down and not wake up the whole house. But upstairs nothing stirred and Willie was sleeping the deep sleep of youth, not to be awakened by laughter or even a death scream for that matter.

Falling against the sofa back, they clutched each other, revelling in the joke he had made, she more than he, relieved that he could at last make light of, if not accept, his disability. Revelling in their closeness, in their love, they slowly sobered enough for lips to meet, passionate.

But lovemaking was too recent for him to repeat it for the moment. They broke apart, gazing into each other's eyes, hers even brighter than his, mutual agreement needing no words. Even so, Amy spoke, becoming serious, hoping that what was in her mind was in his also. 'It's *our* money, Tom. We can do what we like with it.'

He nodded, his blue eyes growing as solemn as her hazel ones as he posed a valid question. 'We wouldn't have half enough, would we, for such a thing?'

'I don't know,' she replied. 'It amounts to five thousand.' His incredulous whistle made her hurry on. 'I'm not sure if that would be enough. And for us to get married on as well. We'd have to have a house of our own. I'd like us to afford a nice house in the suburbs. There are lots being built now, bungalows, at around seven hundred pounds.'

She saw his eyes widen, and knew just how it must sound. Living in luxury this past month, grieving luxury it was true, had tended to make her a little blasé again. But she'd also had four years living in poverty and it struck her as incredible too that she could speak so easily of several hundred pounds, several thousand pounds.

'Tom, I want us to do this,' she said in earnest. What did it matter if she was again taking up the reins? Someone had to. 'It's our chance to get out of this ... this trap. I want to see you having a life of freedom, my love, able to make your own choices. It's going to be hard, of course. Being in business isn't all the strawberries and cream it seems to the man who works for others, but you'll be your own boss, free to make your own decisions. Your own mistakes as well. We'll probably have lots of those. But we can do it, Tom. I know we can. And we now have a chance . . . that's if you still want to,' she finished, for he'd sat up, away from her, was looking down at the floor. Was he looking at his legs, wondering if he had the go in him to do what she was asking of him? Was he wilting, having second thoughts?

She sat up too, trying to sound practical. 'We don't have to do it straight away, darling. There'll be a lot of planning to do first. I could see Mr Goodburn, my old boss. He'd advise us. He knows all about that sort of business. Anyway, I ought to go and apologise for leaving so suddenly . . .'

'Sod Mr Goodman! Or whatever his name is.' Tom came upright, took hold of her and bore her back with him against the sofa arm. 'All the business we need to do now is this business.'

That second time was as marvellous as ever the first had been. More so, perhaps. But she couldn't tell, really.

Chapter Twenty-Five

The visit to Mr Goodburn proved a waste of time. He'd been sympathetic to the loss of her father, but whatever friendship had arisen between boss and secretary was gone. He received her formally, and when she told him about her ideas he listed a half-hearted set of requirements: registration of the vessel; operating licence insurance; passenger liability insurance; a master to manage the boat, seeing that her husband had no knowledge of such things, one who could be trusted; an engineer. There'd be outlay for solicitors' and accountants' fees, advertising, docking fees, perhaps a broker's fee, and the cost of the boat itself, and dozens of other expenses.

'And remember it will be seasonal, your boat laid up during the winter but maintenance still eating money.'

If anything his advice merely served to pour cold water on the scheme. Not only that, but when she referred to his own dream of owning a pleasure boat, he'd turned on her with an astonished smile.

'Did you honestly think I'd give up a good and reliable senior position that affords me a comfortable existence to embark on such a ridiculous gamble?' To her shocked ears, he continued almost sadly, 'My dear, I am sorry if I misled you. All of us enjoy a little immersion in the happy wanderings of the mind. To be the master of a vessel full of happy, carefree people was mine, that was all. It may be because I've never had occasion to be among such people, but in reality I think I would find them most irritating.'

'I didn't know,' Amy said lamely, and after a few more minutes made her embarrassed exit.

She didn't tell Tom about the meeting. It had been so humiliating it was more comfortable not to. She did make a lot more enquiries, but these too she kept to herself. Underhanded perhaps, but it would be seen as managing, taking up the reins Tom should be handling. Not that she intended to rush headlong into anything just yet. Mr Goodburn had been right, there was a lot at stake. But she discovered he'd been wrong about one thing – some craft weren't as prohibitive as he'd suggested. Out of her five thousand she could have change of at least three, surely more than enough. She could afford to be generous with herself and Tom, and with his family. They'd done so much for her, they should share in her good fortune. Pushing aside the pang of sorrow at the manner in which that fortune had come about, she thought instead of Mrs Jordan who had unstintingly taken her in when she needed help. Some of what she had should go to making the woman's life a little more pleasant. The idea that formed was bound to thrill and amaze her.

Mrs Jordan didn't think so. Shocked, she looked up from her scrubbing board over which she had been energetically doing the Monday wash when Amy broke the news of her wonderful idea. 'Oh, luv, it's a nice thought. But I don't want an 'ouse in the country. You save yer money.'

'It'll be away from all this smoke and dirt,' Amy told her. 'I'd like to do this for you. It's the only way I can say thanks for all you've done for me.'

Mrs Jordan looked embarrassed. 'I don't want no thanks. luv.'

'But you've done so much for me.'

'Nice of yer ter say so, luv. I know yer mean well, But I don't want ter be uprooted from the people round 'ere. They're me friends. There's the Workin' Men's Club – they did well by me when I lost my poor Arthur, an' they still look after me. I couldn't walk away wiv me nose in the air from people like that. I'd never forgive meself. And who'd look after me like that if I moved away among a lot of strangers?'

'Tom and I would be near you,' Amy said. 'We'd buy a house nearby when we marry, and he can pop in every day to see you.'

For an answer, Mrs Jordan returned to her scrubbing board, if anything, with more energy than before. She was washing a well-worn pillowcase off Willie's bed – Willie who got his grubbier than anyone she knew. Amy watched the reddened hand rubbing the case up and down the board with its fluted metal strip, plunging the thin cotton into the sink full of suds to bring out and scrub again, plunge and scrub, the smell of hard green soap and dirty linen rising up around her.

'When d'yer mean ter get married then?'

From its previous warmth, even in its refusal of Amy's offer, the tone had grown a little tight, as though something had begun to restrict the woman's throat. There still remained a tender spot that she was losing her son to another. Amy felt she must tread carefully, not just for this mother's sake but for her own.

'We hope to . . . eventually. But Tom would never dream of living miles away from you. We could even buy a house right next door.'

'Won't yer be spending a bit rash? Two 'ouses.' Mrs Jordan straightened up, wringing suds from the pillowcase with a powerful twist of her wrists. 'Won't be much left by the time yer need it. I'm sorry ter say it, luv, but there may not be any more where that come from, once it's gorn.'

'If the rest is put into a business,' Amy began. She hadn't yet told Mrs Jordan of her business plans – not before they were properly formulated. 'We'll never have to worry about that.'

'Business? Is that what yer thinkin' of doin'?'

Cautiously lifting the lid of the steaming copper beside the sink, she let the wrung pillowcase fall in with the rest of the bubbling bed linen. Drying her hands on a scrap of cloth she turned to face Amy. 'And what if it don't work out, this business? Do Tom know about what yer plannin'?'

'We've talked about it. Not enough yet to make it official. It was an idea.'

Mrs Jordan gave her a searching look. 'You shouldn't start counting yer chickens before they're 'atched, yer know.'

Amy had no idea if she was referring to business and money or to Tom and marriage, or even to the still nagging likelihood of being expected to uproot herself, an order rather than a good deed. She decided it must be the latter and hastened to soothe any fears she had.

'How about a nicer place around here if you like?' Rented of course. No one would *buy* houses in this area. 'I'd provide whatever extra rent it cost.'

'Look, I don't want yer money, luv.' The tone was unexpectedly sharp. 'You keep it. Don't go silly with it on my be'alf. You'll probably need it yerself.'

'But I really want to do something for you, don't you see?'

Mrs Jordan's smile was wise and slightly sad, as though saying she rather suspected the giver of trying to ease her conscience, or so Amy interpreted it. Even the sigh that issued forth was full of appeasement. 'Well, if yer want ter 'elp, luv, the place could do with a bit of decoratin' and paintin' up. I wouldn't want all the worry of movin' somewhere else. This 'as bin my 'ome since me an' my Arthur was first married. I wouldn't ever want ter leave 'ere knowing that bits of 'is memory is in every corner of this 'ouse. I could never do that. It's still 'is 'ome, yer see.'

Amy felt her eyes grow moist at the simple words; strove to collect herself. 'I could buy a few things as well, a few pieces of furniture?' she offered, defeated.

Mrs Jordan smiled again, almost apologetically, gazing around the kitchen all steamed up from the copper. 'If yer want, luv.' She brought her eyes back to Amy. 'But I'm not askin'. An' if yer do, I would like ter keep my Arthur's old armchair, if that's all right with you.'

Her possessions, and she was pleading? Amy felt suddenly an intruder. This wasn't at all what she had intended. She almost wished she hadn't broached the subject at all.

Grace Jordan was genuinely worried. 'Tom, yer sure yer doin' the right thing?'

She had gleaned from him the nature of the business

venture he and Amy were talking of embarking upon – if ever it came about, which it wouldn't do until next spring with no one wanting to take boat trips in winter.

'Don't get me wrong, luv, but Amy can be a bit headstrong and managing-like. It's all very well for her. I know she means well, and she's got all your interest at 'eart, but she's got all 'er 'ealth and strength, and she comes from people used ter business. You don't know nothink about that sort of thing. None of us do. We're not business people. An' on top of it all, you ain't all that well ter start embarking on things like that.'

'I'm not ill, Mum,' he corrected sharply. 'It's only me legs. I don't need to work the boat. We'll employ a skipper to do that.'

'Employ? The means more money. It ain't a bottomless pit, luv. She won't 'ave any left time she's done spending it all like it grows on trees. One day she'll turn round an' it'll all be gone. Then where will yer be, the pair of yer?'

But she could see she was talking to a brick wall. His eyes were bright with excitement, following her about the room as she dusted; he manoeuvring out of her way on his two sticks, not quite as clumsily as he might once have.

They were alone. Rosy was at work, Willie at school, and both had gone off complaining about having to, huddled miserably against the late November drizzle which at least had kept any fog at bay. Amy, not working now, was upstairs making the beds. As far as Grace was concerned she'd have been better keeping her job. The money had gone to her head. Well it would. It would go to anyone's head. Grace had gasped at the size of the amount, hadn't quite known how to take it, in fact had felt alarmed by just the sound of it, and still did. But the way she seemed intent on throwing it about as if there was a bottomless barrel of it was even more alarming. At least she was still putting a decent sum into the house-keeping, often too much.

And she had set about having the place done up. Another worry at the rate all that money was disappearing, on trivias, tins of paint, rolls of wallpaper. A man, one of her neighbours along the road, was coming in to start the decorating next week. He was very grateful for the money, being out of work.

Not that she wasn't grateful. It was very generous of her. She pursed her lips, bringing her mind back to the subject in hand. 'You may *feel* well enough son, but what when it comes ter meeting people what's hale an' hearty with all their wits about 'em and know what they're talkin' about – an' you on two sticks?'

Tom's eyes gleamed with determination. 'I don't intend to be on these *two sticks* for ever, Mum. I've been practising. I intend going out soon.'

'Out? But you ain't never bin out of the 'ouse. What if yer fall out there for everyone ter see. Indoors, there's only us, but out there . . .' She paused, shaking her head in brief self-criticism. 'I suppose I'm just bein' a bit too over-protective.'

'You are, Mum,' he chided mildly and she shrugged.

'Well, it's how mothers are. Wives are 'arder, as yer'll find out when yer do get married. I suppose that'll 'ave to 'appen one day.'

Tom put his two sticks into one hand and laid his free arm affectionately around her shoulders. 'Don't worry about me, Mum. I'll be all right.'

She stood with his arm about her, but her mind would not be embraced. 'I do worry, Tom. Amy, with 'er business ideas, I can see 'er takin' over an' you in the background. Like them film stars you read of. What's that one? Norma Shearer – it's 'er film name and someone called 'er 'usband Mr Shearer. I think that's dreadful. I don't want that to 'appen ter you, Tom . . . No, don't laugh.' For he was chuckling at her. 'I know it sounds silly, but it can 'appen. I know she's done good for yer. But this boat thing worries me. It's 'er money, not yours. And what've you got to offer? You could find yerself left standin' in the background . . . 'er husband. If yer ever do decide ter get married, that is.'

'If?' Tom echoed, but his voice had dulled. 'Of course I will. It's what I want, Mum. To marry her.'

'Maybe,' she sighed. 'But do be careful about what yer gettin' yerself into, luv. Yer could be bitin' off more than yer can chew,' and leaving him frowning, she went on with her dusting.

Amy, talking about their plans, stopped as she noticed the expression on Tom's face – contemplative, as though he'd lost interest, or perhaps wasn't sure it was all as rosy as she made it sound.

'I'm not boring you, am I?' she asked sharply.

He brightened immediately. 'Of course you're not boring me. There's a lot to discuss. It's a big thing.'

His speech was so much better these days. He seemed to have so much more determination in everything. This last month he had achieved a lot, had even ventured outside into the street after hesitantly negotiating the one shallow step down to the pavement, Amy in front of him lest he fall, his mother behind him, both of them anxious for his safety. He had stood there leaning on the two sticks necessary for this major attempt. That achieved, he had stood surveying the wide expanse of naked openness before him and had decided he'd done enough for one day; that to go any further would be pushing things a bit too much.

'Just a few steps,' Amy had tried to persuade him, but he had shaken his head, master of his own decisions.

'Not today,' he'd said firmly. 'Perhaps tomorrow, eh?'

She'd been disappointed. 'No one's going to stare at you, Tom.'

'I know how he feels, Amy, luv.' Mother-like, Mrs Jordan had come to his aid. 'Everyone in the street watching. I'd feel the same.'

'If they're watching, it's because they're willing you on,' Amy had insisted, hating to go against his mother, but this was a crucial moment for Tom and she had no intention of his breaking down now. 'We've got good neighbours around here, Tom. Sympathetic people. They really want to see you do well.'

It occurred to her much later that she had actually said ' "we" have good neighbours', rather than 'you', as though she had always been part of this neighbourhood. At the time there had been more important things at stake to notice than what she had said, her heart swollen with pride and

Tom looking with triumph on this his small achievement. A December wind had begun getting up around them; he had shivered then and she knew this wasn't weather in which to attempt any more so they had returned to the comfort of the house. Tom had got up the step better than he'd got down it. By spring he would be walking the length of the street, unaided except for one stick, she proudly holding his other arm like any couple.

But it had been a flash in the pan. Winter, with winds howling and rain and snow and damp, penetrating pea-soupers, wasn't weather for anyone to go walking in, much less someone out for the first time leaning on sticks.

With little to do but sit around the house, now bright with paint and new wallpaper, a new three-piece suite in place of the old tatty things, though Mr Jordan's sagging armchair still reposed in one corner as Mrs Jordan – whom she now called Mum, knowing that by spring she and Tom would be married – had wanted, everything seemed to have come to a full stop.

Trying to keep the impetus going, Amy contacted an agent who said this was the time to buy. With boats laid up and money short, a snip or two could come on the market any time, especially with Christmas approaching. He would keep his eye out and tip her the wink.

It was six of one and half a dozen of the other when it came to buying. Laying out money before Christmas, paying the berth and maintenance until April when the tripping season started was wasteful; but waiting to after, say, February, prices would go up. She asked Tom what he thought.

He shrugged. 'You're doing all the business.'

She sat at the table busy stoning raisins for the Christmas pudding. Now she looked up sharply at his tone. 'What does that mean?'

'Nothing.'

Sitting in one of the armchairs, he was staring into the blazing fire. His mother sat in the other, on her lap a basin of hot water in which she was blanching almonds. Life was being kind to them. Amy's money had made all the difference, where some hardly had any fire, any food, except by courtesy of a pawnshop, the slump biting as Wall Street's crash in New York so far away began to make itself felt over the whole of England. Further afield it was worse – in Germany, the papers said, they were literally starving, and in America itself millions were being thrown out of work as businesses failed, the unemployed in their thousands queuing at soup kitchens.

Even Amy had begun to wonder if she were doing the right thing, ploughing money into business. Yet if she waited it would all get frittered away, which money had a habit of doing. Beginning to feel just a little desperate, she needed Tom's advice. 'What do you mean, Tom, nothing?'

Again he shrugged, his gaze on the fire. 'You seem to be coping all right. Why do you need to consult me? You don't usually.'

'I'm consulting you now,' she said, mystified.

'After you've already made all the decisions.'

'That's not fair, darling!'

He looked up at her. 'You've found an agent. You've talked everything over with him on what best boat to buy. You've asked him to go ahead and look for one. I wasn't there. Though I can't be, can I? Now you ask me what I think, now it's all done. What advice do you need?'

His mother remained sitting quietly opposite him, saying nothing. A thought sped through Amy's head, completely uncharitable: what had she said to make him so oddly hostile? It took but a few words to turn a person's mind to another's thoughts – or fears – if they were well-chosen. Instantly ashamed, Amy pushed the notion from her. His mother's fear was very real – the prospect of all one's children leaving home must be hard to bear. But that fear itself could prove an invisible barrier to her and Tom's marriage. Were he to find himself compelled to pamper his mother, how would she ever break it down? Even now she could see it forming. Blood was thicker than water.

'It isn't done, Tom,' she hurried on. 'I have to . . . We have to . . .'

He cut in, catching on to the mistake. His tone was gentle, almost sad. 'That's what I mean, Amy. *You* have to, not me, not we. It's your money in the first place. It's your business.'

'It's ours,' she corrected desperately. 'Tom, darling, it is *ours*.'

He smiled, nodded, but didn't reply, instead he looked up at the clock on the mantelshelf, scratched his head with both hands and yawned – all very normal and ordinary, as though no difference of opinion had ever taken place.

'Ah, well, time for bed for me.'

A trite phrase, an escape. She wanted to shake him, prolong the argument until he saw it her way. But that was the crux of it all, wanting him to see things *her* way. She made herself a vow as he got up, leaning on his stick, to drop a kiss on the top of her head, murmuring, 'Goodnight, darling,' and louder to his mother, 'Night, Mum,' that she would have to see things his way, *their* way from now on. For the sake of the business, their eventual marriage, their love.

Chapter Twenty-Six

Christmas was no longer a happy time for Grace with its memories of her previous one, her husband killed just a few weeks beforehand. Even so, she refused all invitations to spend it with either his or her family. The result was that they all came to her instead, with good intentions and arms laden with this that and the other to make her Christmas enjoyable, and if it necessitated a lot of preparation and catering for them all, at least it kept her mind off things.

The house bulged with relatives, except for Alice wintering with husband and friends in Tenerife in the Canaries. To enquiries as to how her rich daughter was, Grace said that by all accounts, and occasionally when she saw her, she seemed well and very happy.

Neither she nor those she told this to knew just how far from the truth that was, but so long as she believed it wholly, Alice's pride let her mother go on believing her life was tip-top. It was only to Amy that she was able to confess how truly miserable she was.

'Dicky is being just horrible,' her last letter read. 'He's still carrying on with that abominable Smythe woman. I'm so dreadfully miserable. Don't tell my mother, will you? We're off to the Canaries for Christmas and New Year, taking a passage to Santa Cruz and staying until the end of February. And that bitch is coming too. Dicky won't hear of her not coming, the wretch. Two friends of his, Beverly and Roland Hutchings, will be with us, and some effeminate young man the Smythe woman knows. I know why. To make it look good. But of course, it leaves her and Dicky free to go off on their own, and I'm stuck with the silly man. Bertram Sully I think his name is. He's a very nice person. I met him once. Very kind. But that doesn't make things better for me, knowing what Dicky and the Bitch are up to. Every time I face him with it, it ends in a screaming match. I can't face much more of it, Amy. I shall end up going mad, end up in an insane asylum, or filing for a divorce. But he'll deny everything. He always does. If only I could catch them at it. I don't know what to do . . .'

Amy wondered what her mother would say were she to know what was really going on. Perhaps it was best she didn't.

Dicky watched his wife throwing herself about their sumptuous apartment in their Santa Cruz hotel, his manner as calm as hers was wild.

Her voice had risen to a shriek, enough to wake up the whole of the stately old Victorian hotel. 'I don't believe you. You can feed me all the lies you want. But I've seen you two creeping off together. I've watched the way you both look at each other. I know, you see. I know! I know!'

Dicky smiled slowly. It was a taunting smile, tinged with irritation. Her tantrums could both amuse and annoy him. At the moment, however, it was six thirty in the morning, the dawn just beginning to grow strong in that rapid eager way it does nearer the tropics, one minute pitch dark, the next bright with the rising sun. So what if he had just come in, still in his evening clothes? It didn't warrant her waking up the whole hotel this time of the morning.

'What do you know, my sweet?' he asked, impassive. 'Have you any proof?'

'I mightn't have proof,' she screamed at him. 'But I know what's going on. You out all night. I know where you've been. In her bed.'

'You knew I was going on to a nightclub with some friends. We were playing the tables until half an hour ago.'

'Who?' she shot at him. 'Who are these friends? I don't believe you. It was a ruse, to be with her. All I know is you left me here, all night, on my own. Why didn't you ask me to go with you to this nightclub, Richard?'

'You dislike nightclubs, Alice, and staying up all night, or else we'd have been there together and I wouldn't be listening to all this rot.'

'The sort of clubs you go to? No thank you. My head spins enough without all those blaring and shrieking trumpets and trombones and crashing of drums and cymbals until all hours.'

Life with Richard was still hectic, even after all this time. If she didn't follow after him playing the society woman, he promptly left her behind without a thought for her.

It had been the same on the ship, the four-day journey out with a brief stop at Madeira, everyone gallivanting off and getting drunk on the island's wine. She had pleaded to be taken back to the ship, her head muzzy, not from wine, but from the heady, overpowering perfume of the island itself, ablaze with flowers.

The cruise here had driven her mad, everyone playing incessant deck games, lounging about on the first-class sun deck or in the sumptuous lounge from which third-class passengers were barred, sitting at the captain's table indulging in inane conversation about nothing, Richard sitting opposite Enid where they could exchange overtly . . . oh, yes, overtly meaningful glances, all of which she knew full well she wasn't meant to miss. Because she refused to associate with Enid Smythe, for obvious reasons keeping her loathing of the woman to herself, Enid and Bev went shopping together, talked together, partnered each other in the deck games, leaving her, the odd man, the third person, out of it entirely. What should have been a wonderful voyage was instead boring, long, and fraught with jealousy.

'All I want is peace and quiet,' she screamed at him. 'I'm sick of this life. All I want to do is go home, live a quiet life for once, and have a . . . have a . . .'

'And have a baby,' he finished as she stumbled over a plea that had become far too repetitive. 'That's all you talk about. Good God, Alice, I'm twenty-four. I'm not ready for that sort of thing yet. Life's just too exciting to miss out on.'

'Yes, don't I know. Oh, I know. Jumping into her bed every chance you get. Consorting with someone else behind your wife's back – far too exciting to settle down. Don't try denying it, Richard.'

'I'm not denying it,' he said quite suddenly, making Alice stop, mid-screech, to stare at him in disbeblief.

'What?'

'Nor am I confessing to it. You've no proof whatsoever.'

'But I know you sneaked into her bedroom last night.'

'Did you see me sneaking in?'

'No – but I know you did. Oh, I know you did.'

'You saw me go into the lift with Bev and Ro-ro.'

'They came up again later, to go to bed, and you weren't with them.'

'Of course I wasn't. I went on to a nightclub, as I said. I told them.'

'You might have told them that. But I know where you really went. Two doors down the hall.'

'Then why didn't you knock on Enid's door and find out?'

'Because I couldn't. How could I, in the middle of the night, and make a fool of myself? But when I do catch you. When I do . . .'

'You'll write another long letter to your friend Amy about it, won't you?' he finished for her as the words trailed off in a series of gulping hiccups, genuinely angry with her now. 'I know you write to her about me, accusing me of infidelity. She's the epitome of good behaviour, eh? Well, I'll tell you something. Did you know she had an illegitimate child?'

'Of course I knew,' Alice shot back, recovering. 'And the poor little thing died when she was six months pregnant. She was devastated, inconsolable, so my mother said.'

For a moment he sobered, looked as though he could see Amy in her devastation. 'I didn't know that.' Seconds later he'd collected himself. 'And did she ever tell you whose baby it was?'

'No, she didn't. It was her business, not mine.'

'Then let *me* tell you. I knew her well, before I met you. We became quite serious about getting married at one time. And of course . . . Well, you can guess. The silly little idiot got herself pregnant. Wouldn't wait for me to take precautions. Not her. Wanted me there and then. Well, she was extremely tipsy that first time. We did it a couple of times.

And there you are. Well, after that, I couldn't marry her, could I? What would everyone have said? Couldn't have held up my head in front of society in general and my people in particular.'

'You knew she was carrying your baby when you first met me?'

He shrugged. 'For all I knew at the time she might have got rid of it. You can blame her just as much as you blame me. As far as I was concerned it was over by the time I met you.'

'I don't blame her,' she railed. 'It's not a thing a girl boasts about. She must have felt so ashamed. No, Richard, I blame you.'

He made a mute mocking appeal to her, spreading his arms as if utterly innocent, but she wasn't going to be appeased.

'You pig! Knowing what you did, making a play for me. Treating her like dirt. Now you're treating me the same. Worse, because we're married. She trusted you and you abandoned her. You're the most hateful selfish person I know.'

'You married me,' he grinned at her. 'You didn't think that when there was the prospect of money and a cushy life.'

'Oh . . .' Unable to find words, Alice snatched an ashtray from a table and aimed it at him. He easily dodged it, the thing exploding against the wall. But his face had grown angry.

'Why don't you just take this mayhem you're creating out into the hallway for the entire hotel to listen to? One simply cannot have a discussion with you.'

'Discussion! You call this a discussion? You carrying on with that Enid Smythe right in front of me? Throwing your adultery in my face? Then calmly telling me you fornicated with my best and only friend and left her with a baby? Well, I've had about all I can take from you, Richard. I want a divorce.'

'On what grounds? Adultery?' He chuckled. 'Divorcing me, my sweet, will leave you without a bean. Mind you, it can take three years, and I shall pay you maintenance until then. But afterwards? Not a thing, and I'll be within my rights.'

The shattering crash of the ashtray against the wall, the mark it had left, its ruby glass scattered all over the expensive floor tiles, had both frightened and calmed her. If the wall had been his head, he would be lying dead at her feet now. Her voice trembled at the thought but had quietened. 'I don't care. You call me a gold-digger, but I don't want your damned money. I want you to give me a divorce.'

'And be cited as the respondent, my name in all the newspapers? Oh, no, my dear. I'd be more than happy to see the end of you, but if anyone does the divorcing it will be me. So you'd best see to it, hadn't you? Sort it out. What about being found in bed with young Bertram Sully? You'll be safe enough with him. And he wouldn't want it put around that he's queer. He'd be happy to oblige you. It's the only way out for you, I'm afraid, my love.'

'I could put a knife into you!' she hissed, but his expression was adopting a look of boredom.

'Isn't that just typical of someone brought up in the slums? I should never have married you. Look, my love, I'm tired of all this bickering. Either get yourself dressed or go back to bed. I'm going down to the bar.'

'How dare you refer to my upbringing!' she yelled insanely at him, but he'd already gone out of the room, the door closing behind him.

On the second of February, Vi had a baby boy. If anyone was counting, they'd have known that Vi had been three months pregnant on her wedding day but most had already forgotten when the wedding was except that it was last summer. She named him Michael Arthur in memory of her father who had been Arthur Michael, and her husband was quite in accord with those wishes.

Vi, pale after her ordeal but her eyes sparkling with achievement and pride, looked at the faces gathered around her and her tiny son. 'Ain't he lovely?'

'The loveliest baby anyone could wish for,' agreed her

352

mother, taking in every inch of her first grandchild. 'Absolutely perfect.'

And there were gentle kisses rained down on the tiny squashed face buried in the shawl she'd knitted with her own hands, and kisses for the mother, and hugs for the father. 'I just 'ope you 'ave many more, luv.'

To which Fred, tall and athletic and as proud as Punch, laughed, ''Old on, Mum! Let's git started bringin' up this one fer a year or so.'

Gazing down at the newborn squirming delightfully in its little crib, Amy felt a strange vague ache in the pit of her stomach, a longing perhaps, but more a hunger for the baby she lost. She had almost forgotten that, but the sight of this little scrap just one day old with its screwed up face and its tiny fists and it fine fluff of gingery hair that would wear off in a few weeks to make way for a more permanent colour, sent a knife through her heart for that child she never saw.

Yet, there was hope as there was fear. She'd not seen her period last month and niggling in the back of her mind had come the memory of those evenings she and Tom were left alone. Not often, it was true, but the times they had, they had not taken precautions. Tom was not able to get out to buy what was required, and she could hardly do so, and how could he ask anyone to procure for him what was needed? It had remained for them to 'be careful' but they had not always 'been careful' enough. And it hadn't seemed to matter.

Gazing down at Vi's baby, Amy was torn between a wish for herself to be pregnant and a fear of the pointing finger. If pregnant, then she and Tom would have to marry soon, no matter how his mother took it.

Mrs Jordan still alluded to 'her loneliness'. She'd continued with her bits of machining for neighbours for all the decent housekeeping Amy insisted she took. 'A bird in 'and's worth two in the bush,' she'd say when Amy hinted of the needlessness for her to work, nine times out of ten ending with the codicil, 'Anyway it keeps me mind occupied, which I expect it will have ter be when everyone's gone off and got married and I'm evencherly left on me own.'

Rosy and her intended, Clifford Carter, were planning to

marry soon, probably in May, a wedding to be done on the cheap with only immediate family and a few friends present. Cliff at twenty was still an electrician's mate. But Rosy had refused to wait until he became a fully-fledged electrician and better able to keep her. She had told Amy she was scared of getting pregnant before the day, just in case he jilted her, that she wanted what they were already doing made legal as soon as possible.

Where they would live they hadn't yet decided. With little money and Cliff being one of eight children all still at home, Rosy had asked her mother if they could live with her, but Mrs Jordan had said truthfully that there wasn't room.

Amy felt that was putting the cart before the horse because when she and Tom married they would obviously get a place of their own on some of the money she now had, leaving a room empty for Rosy and her husband. But it seemed to her that the woman actually looked forward to the prospect of being able to wallow in her loneliness.

It made Amy angry, but she felt it best to let the matter go. However, there was no getting away from the fact that Tom would have to marry her if she was pregnant. He would, of course. She decided to let another month go by to be sure before telling him. Meantime there was work to do.

Tom was walking much better, on one stick only, if with a pronounced limp.

'Gives me a bit of a swagger, don't yer think?' he'd joked, aping the upper crust. But Amy detected the tiniest undertone of pain in having been robbed of the youth more fortunate young men often took cruelly for granted. Even as she hurt for him, she felt the bursting of love for him, pride in him, knew she'd be there for the rest of his life to help him make something of himself, make him strong again.

He still couldn't walk far, hated neighbours seeing him, exacting their pity. At least with money in the bank they could use a taxi now and again. Mrs Jordan's lips would tighten at good money wasted. 'You should look after it,' she said again and again.

Time was rushing by. Soon it would be April, the start of the pleasure boat season. They still hadn't sorted out what they were going to do. They had held fire for long enough. But for Amy it was becoming urgent. She'd missed another period. She was pregnant. Soon they must get married.

On the first Tuesday in March came a letter for Tom from the man engaged to look out for a suitable boat. 'I think we ought to go and look at a few of these,' Amy said after she had read the letter. 'And there's something else I have to tell you, Tom. I'll tell you while we're out.' It was private. She didn't want his mother knowing just yet.

With the coming of the season, boats for sale were getting scarcer. Of the three they'd come to see, one was in a poor condition, another in very good shape but too large and expensive. The last was capable of holding just under a hundred fare-paying passengers with possibilities of using a small area for serving tea, coffee, soft drinks, sandwiches and cakes.

'Not too bad, eh?' queried the man in charge, a beefy middle-aged man in overalls and an oily sweater, with bowed legs, broad chest and a smile that split his weatherbeaten face almost in two each time he used it. 'Bin kept in pretty good shape. Well, these ferry people do, don't they?'

Amy said nothing, waited for Mr O'Brien, the man she'd engaged, to give his opinion. He would arrange surveys, insurance, everything. He toyed with his double chin as he spoke to Tom directly, who as the man would be the one to address in these matters, she merely a woman come along for the treat and of no importance. He had even given her a funny look when she had put her spoke in as it were, no doubt thought her interfering and his client long-suffering.

'Seems a good buy to me, so she does, Mr Jordan. I'd advise yer to think on that one very carefully, so I would, sir.'

'Y . . . es.' Tom responded slowly, a hand to his own firm chin as though in deep thought. But Amy knew he had as much idea about the thing as she had, except she'd done all the business side of it, using his name for the reason that was obvious at this moment. Few men would do serious business with a woman. Better to use Tom's name in everything. And it made him feel better about things. *Her* money, *her* idea – it still haunted her although he hadn't referred to it again.

At home they had already gone over what he would say and Tom's enquiries appeared to be his alone. 'She looks OK to me too. Needs a bit of looking over, but yes . . . I'm happy to take your word for it, Mr O'Brien.'

Two days later, surveys done, insurances arranged, having signed papers and gone through all the necessaries, they came away slightly glassy-eyed owners of a pleasure boat. Fingers crossed, once it was fitted out to the specifications Mr O'Brien was advising, they'd be up and running before April. Preparations were already half-completed for mooring it at Westminster to do trips to Richmond and back. Amy suggested that trips from somewhere like Westminster could bring in people better able to afford it than people around here. Hopefully money would come rolling in, more than enough to pay a skipper and engineer's wages, maintenance, insurance and other overheads. But above all, Tom would once more be his own man. He was already, she felt, as he held her to him, kissed her, made love to her, and he would be even more loving when finally she told him about the baby.

Chapter Twenty-Seven

In all the excitement of the purchasing of a boat, their boat, Amy said nothing after all about being pregnant. It could still be just a false alarm even with her missing those two months and she wanted to be a hundred per cent certain before saying anything and raising his, their, hopes.

They had spent the whole journey in the taxi home wrapped up in talk about all they hoped to do in their new business, having jitters about doing it. For both of them it was something so new, they were hardly able to believe they were doing it. The moment Tom got in the door he was excitedly relating their day to his mother who had listened in virtual silence, unlike her usual loquacious self, except for two remarks: that she was pleased for him, and that she hoped he knew what he was doing.

For Amy, harbouring her own news, it wasn't the time to announce the fact that she could be carrying Tom's child. She had found herself wondering if she did announce it, would her prospective mother-in-law come and hug her with delight, or hold back aware that it would bring their marriage further forward and also her own expectations of Tom going blithely off leaving her forsaken and alone. No amount of reassurance from Tom ever seemed to convince her that she wouldn't be so left.

There was plenty of time to tell them, Amy thought, shying from being the one to invoke Mrs Jordan's imagined prospects of loneliness just yet. Meanwhile there was much to do. Next month the boat would be in the water ready for their first paying passengers, a skipper at the helm. She and

Tom had someone in mind, recommended by the helpful Mr O'Brien who certainly knew his stuff. Then she and Tom would start on their wedding arrangements, this time definitely. They'd been talking about it, and about the business, almost non-stop, Tom eager for both to take place as quickly as possible.

So it made Amy blink two weeks later, when all the business was concluded, a small mortgage raised on the advice of Mr O'Brien, thus conserving some of the money for other things, the boat almost about to be taken from the boat yard where it had been done up and converted when Tom said, 'Do you think we're doing the right thing?'

The question came out of the blue. Amy glanced up from where she was sensitively twiddling the knob of the wireless, trying to lessen the crackle it produced nowadays. It was old, and she planned the next item on the agenda of replacements for the house to be a gleaming new radio set. Though with all the money being laid out at present, she ought not be too free with it.

'What do you mean, doing the right thing?' she asked.

'Just that I'm wondering if we're not getting ourselves into deep water a bit, going into business. It's a big step.'

Tom had been morose all day. Now Amy straightened, leaving the radio to crackle on uninterrupted, her heart beginning to thump a little unevenly at this culmination to it. 'We've been talking all this over for months. It's all settled. I thought it was all settled. We can't have a change of heart at this late stage.'

Willie looked up from the comic he was reading at the table, his narrow face screwed up with disappointment. 'You mean you ain't gonna buy a boat now?'

All Willie had talked about to his school chums was the boat, bragging, feeling ever so wealthy, enjoying their eyes popping out with wonder and envy.

'Yes, Willie, we are,' Amy told him. 'This is nothing to do with you. Go back to your comic.'

She hated discussing things in front of the family, there was no privacy. Fortunately Rosy was out with Clifford, and Mrs Jordan was in the kitchen cleaning round the stove after she and Amy had washed up, having asked Amy to go in and find something on the wireless to listen to for the evening.

Willie gave a grimace and she turned her attention back to Tom. He'd had a bad day, there was no denying that. After what had happened last night, it was understandable. She couldn't blame him. But this, this turn of events, to let one little setback destroy all they'd talked about, all they'd planned, could even put the lid on their hopes of marriage yet again. No, she wasn't having that.

They'd had such a lovely time yesterday evening. She'd persuaded him out to one of the big West End cinemas. A treat, a chance to get out of the house, and for once he'd been more than happy, fed up watching the March day drizzle to its close. Sacrificing a little bit more of her money, they had taken a taxi so that he wouldn't need to walk very far from the vehicle to the foyer and into the back stalls which were not only cheaper but convenient for him.

It had been wonderful. Eighteen months or more had passed since Amy had last set foot in any big cinema, for fear of using up too much of her then small bank balance. When she'd been working her anxiety to get home to Tom had prevented her making friends with anyone enough to go anywhere, and then had come his accident. Now the brilliant lighting and opulent decor of the cinema came fresh again. Tom had remarked on it too, he who had at one time gone as often as he could afford with his friends.

In the darkness of the back stalls she and Tom had sat close, like lovers, his arm about her shoulders, she snuggled against him, his head every now and again bending to kiss her upturned lips. All about them were like couples. She felt very much part of it all, not wanting it to end. She and Tom were alone, others too busy with each other to ogle or care.

An all-talkie programme had been a novel delight – Marlene Dietrich in *Morocco* followed by the second feature, the Marx Brothers in *The Cocoanuts*; even the Mickey Mouse cartoon was a talkie with weird, incomprehensible American gabble. And then the newsreel, the English newsreader's voice coming over just as unevenly, one moment soft and blurred, the next blaring and fuzzed.

But it didn't matter. It was a novelty and Tom was here to share it with her.

The only other talkie she had seen was Al Jolson's *The Singing Fool*, the rest of the programme silent, with live entertainment during the interval. No one here in this large imposing theatre was concerned by the loss of live entertainment. It was the audience that was now silent, forbidding anything to distract them from trying to catch the foreign American accent on the screen, and every now and again came a harsh 'Ssh!' if anyone dared speak aloud. Amy had in fact made a comment to Tom and had been shushed, and Tom's resulting chuckle had received another shush.

Recalling it on the way home – spending out on yet another taxi – laughing unrestrictedly at the marvellous change in cinema audiences, once so noisy through every silent film, now themselves silenced, her and Tom's merriment had come to an abrupt end seconds after they drew up outside home.

How it happened Amy had no idea, but his foot had caught on the edge of the running board of the taxi as he got out. Before she could steady him, his stick had gone flying and he'd ended up on his hands and knees. Fortunately it had been dark, and late, but it hadn't stopped him imagining a face at every window witnessing his fall, his humiliation. Mrs Jordan had been in a flurry of consternation for him even though he assured her he hadn't hurt himself.

'He shouldn't never 'ave gone out,' she kept saying as if anyone could have predicted this outcome, her insistence undermining his already ruined confidence.

Today he'd been thoughtful, growing more and more withdrawn as the day went on, and Amy could swear that while she had been out that morning doing a little shopping for Mrs Jordan, she'd been at him, warning him of endless pitfalls.

'Mum was right,' he said, totally ignoring Amy's previous words. 'She said I shouldn't've gone out last night like that. Trying to do too much. A lot of things I shouldn't be doing. Kidding myself. What if that had happened when we'd been going into the cinema, or coming out, or if I was in front of a crowd of day-trippers? Give 'em a bloody good belly laugh, that would.'

Amy fought to hold onto her patience. 'You don't have to be there, ever.'

But wasn't all this so that he *could* be on the river, could be with people? It occurred to her abruptly that this wasn't so much a business venture as a means to give him freedom from the confinements of four walls, allow him to have the full enjoyment of dignified work rather than the other alternative of begging for employment, probably forced to do some degrading job for the rest of his life, if he worked at all. This was supposed to be the fulfilment of a dream. She was being a fool, and even she was having reservations about what she was doing.

'Of course we're doing the right thing. We've done it now.'

'It can still be undone.'

After all that striving, coaxing, planning, loving. It felt as though the shattered glass of all the world's broken dreams had gathered there in her heart, slicing it to pieces, acute as any physical pain.

'Is that what you want, Tom?' Anger suddenly exploded out of her, filling the whole house.

Willie was looking startled, his comic forgotten. In the kitchen she heard Mrs Jordan put a pot down on the draining board with a crash. Any second she'd be in asking what on earth all the shouting was about.

Amy wanted to run out of the house, grab hat, coat and handbag, rush out into the wet March afternoon and never return. There was a roof for her at her mother's house. Forget all of this and go home, start again, one day marry a man of good income and property. What was she doing here anyway, tying herself to a man who saw himself only as an invalid, who had lost all his courage for all he tried to make light of it. Yet she knew that was untrue. He did have courage, he was strong, and she loved him. The very thought of leaving Tom or his leaving her made her feel sick. And she was carrying his child. She gazed up bleakly, already feeling Tom's indecision spreading to herself as Mrs Jordan came into the room.

The woman's expression was one of consternation but it

was also directed at her with such caring concern that Amy found herself immediately appealing to her.

'Mum, Tom wants to throw in the towel about the boat.' Panic had gripped her. 'I don't know what to do. Should we pack it all in? Should we?'

Mrs Jordan staring at her with a blank look. 'Pack in? But yer've done a lot of work towards it all! Yer can't let it all drop now.'

'It was that fall yesterday taken the wind from out of his sails.' Before she realised, Amy found herself sharing her problem with this woman who had before ever seemed to be trying her best to block every decision she made. 'He can't let one small tumble set him back like that. We've worked hard for this, and what else can I do with all the money if we don't go ahead?'

'I don't know, luv.' Mrs Jordan was out of her depth. 'It's up to you, really.'

'If it's up to me, I want to go ahead. But I want Tom to be with me.'

Mrs Jordan turned ineffectually towards her son. 'You should listen to 'er, luv. She knows what she's doin'. I don't know what ter say. But yer should listen to 'er. I'll just go and finish off in the kitchen, luv, and then we can settle down to a nice bit of wireless fer the evening. Won't be a tick.'

She disappeared back into the kitchen. Foolish asking a woman like that to play-arbitrator on such a question. Amy turned back to Tom ready to smile away their differences, a smile that faded immediately at his grim look, and she felt the hopelessness of all she had tried to do sweep over her again. If he was ready to fall so easily by the wayside on this venture, how would he take marriage and would they ever be married? She felt sick at the prospect of telling him about the baby.

Amy leaned with her head over the lavatory basin in the outside wc. How she had made it that far was a miracle. Hardly had she got out of bed than her stomach convulsed, sending her headlong down the stairs, past a startled Mrs Jordan and out into the chilly March morning, flinging open the outside lavatory door, glad no one was using it at that moment.

A hand each side of the wooden seat supporting her, she waited for the spasms to die away, then pulled the overhead chain, the rattle and gurgle of the flushed pan enough to signal the wc's occupation to neighbours three doors down on either side and those backing onto the yard from the next street as well.

Coming back indoors, feeling weak but better, Amy found herself confronted by Mrs Jordan's astute face.

'Is it what I'm thinking it is?' she asked. Amy nodded. Mrs Jordan nodded too. 'First time yer've 'ad ter do that, luv – run fer the lav. Yer about two – three months?'

'I haven't seen my periods for two months, and I think I've missed my third now.'

'Well then, luv. Tom's is it? No . . .' she corrected herself with a quick smile of apology. 'I put that all wrong, didn't I? Course it's Tom's.' Again Amy nodded, too abject to argue on points of nicety.

Mrs Jordan gave her a grin. 'I s'pose it 'ad ter 'appen, sooner or later. Trouble is, you won't be in no fit state in a few months' time ter go runnin' about tryin' ter work a business. Tom'll 'ave ter do that. Yer goin' ter 'ave ter leave a lot more in Tom's 'ands.'

'But he . . .' Amy began, only to be interrupted by her.

'That's bin yer trouble all along, luv. Too blessed managin'. Thinkin' you know all about everythink, and my Tom don't know nothink. He's had a rotten deal this past year or so. We've all 'ad a rotten deal, my poor Arthur goin' and Tom bein' injured like 'e was. It's nat'ral 'im acting like he did, like 'e still does. It'll take a long time fer 'im ter get 'imself back tergether again.'

Amy forced a word in edgeways in defence of herself. 'I've tried to help him all I can.'

'We all try to. P'raps a bit too much at times. We've all bin a bit guilty of that I suppose and it's time we all realised 'e 'as ter do things fer 'imself too. But that takes time. You're goin' ter 'ave ter 'ave a lot of patience with him, luv, if yer take 'im on.'

'Take him on? You mean marry.' She could hardly believe this was what was being intimated.

'Yer pregnant. Yer've got to now. No two ways about it, is there?'

'You wouldn't mind?' Amy questioned in surprise but the question was brushed over, deliberately she felt.

'Can't 'ave you with yer stomach swellin' up in front, and all the neighbours talkin' about you and my Tom. I won't deny it's goin' ter be strange fer me ter 'ave someone else lookin' after 'im instead of me. I only 'ope 'e appreciates what I tried ter do for him, and 'ow 'e took 'is father's place fer me.'

Giving Amy no time to assure her of Tom's appreciation for everything his mother had done, Mrs Jordan continued, well into her stride as she pottered about the kitchen. 'What with Rosy gettin' married in two months' time, I'll only 'ave Willie left. It's goin' ter be funny, all on me own 'ere with just 'im. But I s'pose that's the way of life. They all 'ave ter go off and leave yer one day. Willie will too, I expect. But not fer a long time yet. Thank God there ain't no more wars like the last one ter take 'im orf. I can feel good about that at least.'

She was wandering on, but all Amy could think about was that she had received a backhanded blessing for her and Tom to marry. She felt she wanted to kiss her in her joy, but the woman, back to the old talkative person she had once been, allowed hardly a breath between sentences, let alone an embrace.

'As fer this boat business, well, yer can't drop it all now, can yer? Not when it's got so far. But it's Tom yer goin' ter 'ave ter consider as well – 'is feelings about it. Yer goin' ter 'ave ter get 'im out of 'is doldrums some'ow. Let 'im make a few more decisions of 'is own, without you inter-fering an' takin' over as if 'e ain't got two pen'orth of brains between 'is ears. And yer goin' ter 'ave ter let 'im do all the work from now on. You won't be able to with a baby ter look after. An' p'raps that's just as well. A woman shouldn't be messin' about tryin' ter run a business. That's a man's job. It's a man's right.'

She was speaking as though all this had been Tom's idea,

his money, and that Amy had merely been interfering in it. Of course it was his money now as much as hers, but it was hard to stand here and listen to a monologue on how Tom had every right to the reins.

'And now 'e's hired a skipper for the boat, 'e don't ever need ter go on the river 'imself. He can just sit back.'

'But that's the whole reason for all this,' Amy managed to get in. 'So that he *can* go out onto the river. It's always been his dream. He used to talk to me about it when he was working as a stevedore, how he always wanted to get out on the river itself and enjoy the freedom of it.'

She thought suddenly of Mr Goodburn and the dream he would never realise, a dream he'd take with him to his grave, too busy working for others, and when he retired, too old.

She felt suddenly very sorry for him and turned her thoughts back to Tom who, through her, had all this ahead of him – made for him. Yet Mrs Jordan was right, it was he who had to take the reins, sink or swim, and she who must now take a back seat. It was going to be as hard for her, without whom Tom wouldn't have had any of this opportunity, to do that as it was for him to take over. She just couldn't see him taking over without her there to help him. He needed her. And she needed him to need her, just as Mrs Jordan had, and that she supposed was the irony of it all.

'He never used ter talk to me about them dreams,' Mrs Jordan said softly.

The words had a lonely ring to them, the cry of a woman being isolated from all she had been during her son's life, perhaps realising for the first time that she had never been to him what she'd thought she had been. Amy wanted to cuddle her, tell her she knew how she must be feeling, having another woman about to take over, how she felt exactly the same knowing she too must allow the man his head, that her help might no longer be needed.

But something in Mrs Jordan's bearing as she moved around the kitchen doing chores that had already been done once prevented a display of affection or understanding. Tom was to be given up to another and she was preparing herself to face it. Any attempt to cuddle her, thus turning her stoicism to water, would not be welcome. Amy moved off, leaving the kitchen to her and to the grief Mrs Jordan preferred not to share with anyone.

Tom stood staring at the boat, his boat, bobbing at its moorings, refitted, its new paint bright in the sunshine. Thirty-first of March. Nineteen thirty, a new decade ahead of him, a new sort of life. He wasn't sure if he wanted a new sort of life, which if he admitted to it, scared him, though he'd have rather died than let anyone see how much it scared him.

'She looks a picture, don't she, Mr Jordan?'

The man who was to be his skipper stood beside him, a tall, gangling, sinewy man, the skin of his sunken cheeks seamed and scored, like a map, tawny eyes narrowed from gazing into the sun and long horizons, an old sailor of wider waters than the Thames but now, near retirement, happy to navigate the narrower banks of the river above Chiswick.

Tom nodded. He was trying with all his might to look pleased, but his mind was split between what Amy had told him this morning and the prospect that from now on he was on his own. He was happy and worried both at the same time.

At this moment she stood behind him, not beside him. As though she had already relinquished her place, leaving him to do all the business. It not only felt strange but as though having come this far, she needed to come no further with him, her mind now on the baby she would have, the project for her brushed aside.

She had come to him this morning as he sat in the back room reading the newspaper. Her face had been pale and he'd asked her what was wrong.

'I've just been sick – again,' she told him.

'Again?' he queried, and then it was that she'd given him a significant look, said this was the third or fourth morning in a row that she'd been sick and that his mother had had a talk with her about what he and she should do about getting married as soon as possible. There had been no need to say more. Overwhelmed by what it all meant, he had got up and gathered her in his arms. Here was something he had

366

achieved, that made him wholly a man. They had clung together, him laughing, her crying – at least it was a mixture of crying and laughing so he knew she wasn't upset.

Finally letting go of their embrace, they had sat across the table from each other, each gazing at the other, their eyes sparkling. Well, hers were. He was not sure what his were doing for his head seemed to be spinning. He did remember saying, 'We must get married,' a silly statement but she had nodded, for once not trying to take the rudder from him, just sitting there waiting for him to name a date. He had felt like a tower of strength then, had set the date for four weeks' time, gratified to see her eyes shine in mute agreement.

It was only when standing gazing at the boat, his boat, all ready to go tomorrow, that it hit him what he was taking on. He was to be husband, father, breadwinner, Amy in the background, from now on needing to rely on him, their roles reversed.

Misgivings were already racing through his insides like a pack of ravening rats. Could he do it? How would he ever be able to face the people going on board this boat tomorrow, happy trippers to whom he'd have to smile and look efficient? For he had to be here, something he hadn't envisaged. Knowing little about the sailing part of it, he had John Mottram, his skipper, and Albert Shaw, his engineer, at the moment wiping oily hands on a bit of rag after inspecting the workings. But neither could be asked to collect fares and socialise. His job. Day-trippers would look down on just being left to a somewhat taciturn skipper. It was daunting.

All this time he had envisaged Amy doing the socialising part of it. She was so good at that sort of thing, meeting people, talking easily to them, self-assured, her poise and authority blending as she made sure everyone was safely aboard and comfortable; she who'd stand behind the little counter they'd had built, pouring teas and serving biscuits, crisps and sandwiches, smiling at them, efficiently ironing out any complaints they had. But at this moment she looked as if she would do none of this. She hadn't once opened her mouth to voice an opinion of the craft, leaving it all to him.

Panic was beginning to grip him, yet he mustn't show it, must grin affably and control the quaking in the pit of his stomach at the prospect of tomorrow. He almost wished none of this had been started. He had to be mad.

'All set then for tomorrow,' said Mottram. He had a Norfolk accent, slow and thoughtful. 'Seven in the morning then. Get some steam up, everything nice and shipshape. And you'll be along around eight, Mr Jordan.'

'Yes,' Tom said, more tersely than he had intended.

'Right then, see you tomorrow, Mr Jordan. Here's to good luck and fine weather.' To which Tom nodded silently as he shook hands with him.

Chapter Twenty-Eight

'I'm going to look a bloody freak.'

They had been discussing tomorrow's event in fits and starts over their lunch through most of which Tom had sat dejectedly picking at his toast and bacon and chips.

Amy frowned. Of course he'd have first-night nerves. They all had. She and his mother too. But his announcement that he'd rather let it all go overboard than show himself in that way in public had shaken her and his mother.

'You can't, Tom. We've advertised ourselves. We're ready to go. Mr O'Brien has to be paid. We've employed people. We bought the provisions, fuel, everything. You can't turn round the day before and say you want us to back out.'

He was obdurate. 'I've just not got the guts to go through with it.'

'Of course you have,' she said angrily while his mother looked on, her own food forgotten. 'It's last-minute nerves, that's all. Tomorrow's a big day.'

He seemed not to be listening. 'Me, stomping up the gangway like bloody Pegleg Pete. Everyone grinning.'

'Oh, for God's sake! Who's going to grin? All right, so you use a stick. I can't see what all the fuss is about.'

'What if it was you, Amy – if you were like me?'

She fell silent, unable to answer that. The truth of it hitting her, she stared at him through a film of mist. Her condition seemed to be causing a vague, inexplicable lack of confidence completely alien to her which she tried to tell herself was the natural instinct of a woman guarding her unborn child from harm. But it was more than that. In following his

369

mother's advice and letting Tom make his own decisions, a cliff had been cut from under her own feet, the solid ground of her natural dominance collapsing. She felt strangely weakened, given to tears, as now.

'Oh, Tom. You've got to be there, love. I can't do it. No one wants a woman standing there helping people on board. I shall look ridiculous.'

'Then you know how I feel.' He pushed his hardly touched food from him. 'The skipper can take over. Mottram. And the engineer, Shaw, will be there.'

'Don't be so silly, luv.' It was his mother suddenly putting in her word, her tone authoritative. 'Yer can't leave it to a couple of employees on the very first day. Yer've got responsibilities now. Sod what other people think. You ain't got ter see 'em again after termorrer. The next day it'll be a new lot of passengers. It's your boat. You've got a business. They ain't. So sod what they think. And Amy'll be there anyway, ter do teas and things. An' I'm comin' too and so's Vi with the baby. So's Willie. I'm lettin' 'im 'ave a day orf from school. And Rosy's takin' a day orf work ter be there too. We'll all be there with yer. Every one of us.'

Except Alice, Amy thought but said nothing as Mrs Jordan went on. 'Be like a real 'oliday. I've never bin up the river before. Bin down it once or twice, down ter Southend when Arthur was a bit flush with a few bob on a couple of occasions. I'd like ter see what the other end of the Thames is like – the posh end. I've bin told Chiswick and Richmond an' them places is full of rich people in boats and that. Be a luv'ly change. And yer'll 'ave us lot ter support yer.'

But Tom didn't smile as she had obviously expected him to; his lips set grim, like those of a man condemned to a stretch in prison. She gave a big sigh and said, a little defeatedly, 'Well, let's see what termorrer brings.' Then a little more positively, 'You're going ter 'ave ter buck your ideas up, Tom. Yer'll be a married man soon, and a father. Amy's goin' ter need ter rely on you.'

Amy saw his eyes liven a fraction as he looked at her and smiled. But it was more the smile of love than bravery. But he was brave. It was young days yet. He would see it through and she would be there to help him. Tomorrow would dawn with a better light, and he would become a different man to the one sitting here worrying.

The day passing, Amy fought to think up new ways to get Tom to snap out of his misgivings, and herself as well, for she was beginning to dread tomorrow.

'Let's spend an hour or so up West,' she suggested. 'We could go by taxi.'

She shouldn't be spending on taxis with the outlay of the past months. There was their wedding to think about, now with his mother's blessing. A simple wedding. Mummy and Kay would have to be invited and, she knew, would accept, though Henry (who now preferred to be called Hal) was away at school. She'd have to ask Alice, perhaps even Dicky, for the look of the thing. It would be up to them if they came. A simple affair she might hope for, but with people like that coming, a hall would need to be hired for the sake of making an impression. That cost money. Spending it on taxis when Tom ought to be getting on buses and tube-trains by now was being extravagant. But today circumstances called for sacrifice. She needed to get him out of this house and away from thoughts of tomorrow's ordeal, if only for a while.

To her intense relief he agreed to her suggestion – but it was a concurrence that spoke of a couldn't-care-less-what-he-did attitude. But beggars could not be choosers and she was grateful that he had even agreed to go out.

The taxi dropped them in New Oxford Street, Tom not wanting to go as far as the bright lights of Piccadilly or Oxford Circus. She had conceded to his wish, wondering what on earth he'd be like tomorrow in the bright light of day. In the cab he'd been so silent the driver must have thought they were going to a funeral. After they'd alighted, Tom had merely shrugged when asked what he fancied doing, had shrugged again at her suggestion of a drink in a pub just off Drury Lane, where they had found themselves without really thinking where they were going. He was now sitting at the table with an air of complete disinterest through the smoke haze of his cigarette.

Amy stared disconsolately out of the window, wondering

what next they could do. Strolling was out of the question, Tom hating to walk any distance on his stick. She could see them going home. What else was there? She didn't fancy a cinema. A theatre? She hadn't been to one for ages. From where she sat gazing through the pub window she could just see the New Theatre with a great queue outside. Over the bright entrance the title of the show was emblazoned in lights: *Symphony in Two Flats.* Ivor Novello's New Play.

She had read about it. Newspapers proclaimed it a raging success, a hit, Novello himself as the English Theatre's Most Promising Playwright, a Man With A Golden Touch, seats sold out ever since its start last October. From the beginning she had been dying to see it, but always something interfered. Could there be seats available after all this long run? The queue said there wouldn't be. But that was for the cheaper seats. They couldn't queue – Tom with his legs. How expensive would dearer seats be? Amy swore silently. Money again! But this was important. They must do something or they would just end up going home.

'Come on, Tom, let's go there.' She pointed out of the window and saw him shrug non-committally, but it was encouraging. 'I'd just love to see that. We can at least see if there are any seats going.'

'Hm,' he mumbled affably if unenthusiastically. 'Could do, I suppose.' He, as much as she, had had enough of doing little so far but sit in a pub.

There were seats – just four, rather pricey – because of a cancellation moments before. Amy did a hasty calculation of what she had with her. In seconds they'd be gone.

'How much have you got, darling?' she hissed and watched him bring out the wallet she had bought for his birthday in February.

'Enough. But,' he confided in a whisper as they were shown up to the grand circle, the other cancelled pair beside them filled almost immediately with another lucky couple, 'we can't buy sweets or ice creams or drinks during the interval.' And he gave a chuckle that cheered Amy's heart.

The theatre lay bright all around her. This was what had been needed. Tom's mind would be taken off the prospect of tomorrow for a few hours. They would go straight home after the show, have a mug of cocoa, and he would go off to bed. Whether he'd lie awake worrying, Amy would not know; at least she'd be plagued only by her own worries about tomorrow.

As seats filled up, the low murmur of their occupants drifted upwards to the rich decoration above them to be held there. From the orchestra pit came the quiet, almost self-conscious cacophony of musicians warming up. The fire curtain had been lifted to reveal the crimson and gold and blue of the drop curtain, itself soon to go up on the first act.

Amy felt her stomach churn in anticipation. In the warm brilliance of the chandeliers she took in the spectacle surrounding her before the lights dimmed, felt rich and privileged. Like the old days . . .

'Isn't it gorgeous, darling?'

'It's . . . fine.'

Amy glanced at him, saw he was having problems with his stick, laying it first across his legs, then on the floor, but in both cases it was too long to go anywhere.

'Put it between us,' she whispered urgently. 'It won't be in the way there.' Any moment the lights would fade, the orchestra strike up, the babble die away to expectant silence. 'Give it to me.'

She made to take it, but his fingers curled around it. 'Leave it!'

His tone was a harsh hiss, turning a few enquiring heads in their direction. Amy had a momentary vision of him getting up and stalking out to the disruption of everyone around them. She let go. In the swift wave of darkness that swept over them, she felt him lean it between them, exactly where she had suggested, but that, she realised now, was his decision and not hers.

A little dejected by such a small incident, she leaned back and away from him as the curtain rose slowly, majestically. But as the time passed, she forgot about the hurt she'd felt, lost in the story of the young composer, David, his sight taken from him and his wife too, almost, by the wealthy philanderer, Leo Chevasse.

She had known it for a serious play, different from Novello's previous one, *The Truth Game* (an outrageous comedy, so she had read in the papers), but she hadn't anticipated having her heart wrenched by Novello's overwhelmingly sensitive portrayal of a gifted man blinded, robbed of his most cherished vocation as well as finding himself powerless to prevent himself being robbed of his wife. By the interval her handkerchief was wet with tears; by the end, soaked.

In all this, Tom remained impassive. He had to be made of stone not to be moved by it, she thought as she dabbed self-consciously at her eyes with the lights coming up. Men were different, believing emotion was not something to be displayed in public, but at least he could have blown his nose now and then. They left the theatre in silence.

'Shall we get a taxi?' she asked frigidly. 'Or could you manage going home by bus?'

'Bus I think,' he answered, the decision taking her by surprise.

'It'll mean standing in a queue for God knows how long.'

'It's a nice enough night.'

'A bit chilly.'

'It'll blow the cobwebs away after the warmth in that theatre.'

Terse, formal, they might have been nothing to each other. Standing in the lengthy bus queue, the chill beginning to creep into her bones despite her warm coat, creeping into his bones too no doubt, what little conversation there had been grew even less as they sat on the bus when it arrived. The journey home seemed interminable, each lost in their own thoughts. In silence they got off, Tom holding his stick in his other hand to help her off. Together they went from Commercial Road through side turnings, Amy wondering how he'd take such a lengthy walk but whether he felt its effect or not, he remained silent until they were almost home. Then he stopped abruptly, pulling her to a halt with him.

'Sorry I've been quiet,' he began. 'I've been thinking. That play. I know it was only a play, but it did say something to me.'

Amy, still prickling from their earlier silence, had an urge to be caustic, say who'd have believed that? But what was the point in starting up an argument over something so silly?

It had been a good evening, or could have been, but for his moodiness.

'What did it say to you?' she asked instead.

He must have detected the faint sarcasm in her tone, and was struggling to ignore it, for his voice was low and tinged with embarrassment. 'It seems a bit silly, really, trying to say what went through my mind.'

'What went through your mind?' She wasn't being sarcastic now, rather she felt a need to help if she could, annoyed at allowing herself to become irritated.

He drew in a deep breath. 'You won't laugh?'

'Of course not, darling.' Thoroughly chastened, how could she?

'It was just that . . . well, all through the play . . . I kept thinking . . . that man's gone blind. What could be more terrible? I know it sounds bloody silly. It's only a play, out of someone's head. Not real at all. But it felt so real. I suppose it does end up being real in a way, because although it is only someone's imagination, it does have some truth, don't it? It's what playwrights and all them sort of people what write do, don't they? They look around and see what goes on in other people's lives, other people's minds, all the problems they have and can't always express. They put it all down on paper for other people, people like me, not clever enough to see what them sort of people can. I suppose that's what I felt while I was watching that play – it was real. I'm not crackers, am I?'

'No, darling.' She felt she wanted to cry for him. 'You're not crackers.'

'It was just that I *felt* it was real. I kept thinking to myself all through it, no wonder he behaved like he did. It was how I felt after my accident, and afterwards, knowing I'll never walk properly again, won't be able to do the things I used to, like play football like I did with the lads over the school playing fields, go cycling . . .'

'You could still cycle,' Amy cut in, and immediately cursed herself for sounding so trite, in danger of breaking his thoughts, destroying them.

He hadn't noticed. 'I kept thinking, you bloody moaner, what happened to you ain't half as bad as what happened to him. And then I thought of all the people out there blind, or stuck for the rest of their lives in a wheelchair. That hasn't happened to me, so what the hell am I moaning about? Amy . . .'

He turned to her suddenly, his grip on her arm so tight that it pained.

'Amy. I've come to a decision about tomorrow. I'm goin' down to that boat and I'm goin' to stand there and take the fares and speak to everyone.' In his surge of enthusiasm, his words slipped back into his old ways but he didn't notice, and neither did she. 'Then I'm goin' ter walk across that damned gangplank, me and me stick, and I'll show 'em who's the owner of that boat. An' another thing – next week we'll go and put up the banns for our weddin'. What d'yer say?'

She was taken aback. 'We can't make all the arrangements that quickly. What about the hall, and the invitations, and . . .'

'Bugger the hall! Bugger the invitations. We'll send 'em out as they come. And if we can't find an 'all in three weeks, then somehow we'll 'ave it in me mum's 'ouse. Well?' He was waiting for her answer.

'Yes.' Qualms melted away like thin frost before the rising sun. 'Oh, yes.'

'Right.'

He gathered her arm beneath his, his stick in his other hand, and walked her the last few yards to the door, his gait, that peculiar strut he had developed, jaunty and sure. Amy felt she could have wept with pride and pleasure.

It was a marvellous day. The *April Lady*, the name of the boat, making her maiden voyage, and April, the month, making hers. The sun shone for them both.

On the day trip to Richmond and back, the vessel, crammed with some sixty-odd people on their first day out of the year, seemed to lift its bows clear of the water in response to their joy at being on the river at four and six return, children two and six, enough to make the boat all but fly. The engine chugged, the tunnel spouted smoke that left a dark smudge trailing behind them. But in front everything was fresh and sparkling as far as the smoke of all the other craft making for the same destination allowed.

'I thought the Thames'd get much more narrower as we go,' Grace Jordan laughed as each bend in the river revealed gently wooded and meadowed banks, her earlier squeaks of fear in getting on board across the flimsy pontoon forgotten.

'It is narrower,' Tom told her, watching Willie hanging precariously over the rail vainly trying to touch the smoothly flowing water. 'It'd be wider back in London but it's been embanked on both sides. I suppose that's why it flows a lot stronger through all the bridges there. Below the Pool of London, that's when it really gets wide. I think it's all the open space around here that makes it seem less narrow.'

'Well, it's a wonder for all that,' sighed his mother, holding onto her new straw hat against the breeze their moving caused. Otherwise not a puff of wind disturbed the still air of an April morning.

The air might have been still, it wasn't quiet. Dozens of families yelled their conversations as though they sat or stood at least fifty feet apart and needed to be heard, children were squealing, laughing, bickering, and someone had started up a singsong at the front beneath the tiny wheelhouse. 'Margie-e . . . I'm always finking of yer, Margie-e . . .' A song at least ten years old but still very singable, followed by several others as old and even older – the songs every Cockney sang at every party they'd been to since the beginning of the century and probably even earlier. And from other, larger, boats came sounds of actual music.

Behind her little counter with Rosy to help, Vi being occupied with baby Michael while proud Granny Jordan waited to have her turn with him, Amy cut and handed out cake and sandwiches and filled thick china mugs and tough drinking glasses and took the money.

By the time they reached Richmond her back ached with bending over the counter.

'It's too low,' she told Tom, but he laughed.

'We'll make it higher as soon as we get a chance.'

This seemed an impossible promise because they had had to turn passengers away this morning. By the look of it,

April Lady would be continuously busy with people looking for midweek trips as well as weekends.

Richmond, like most Thames resorts along the way, was alive with people all seeking pleasure in the Sunday sunshine. Those wealthy enough to own their own private craft moved about their decks generally doing what rich people did, or sat disdainfully observing the poorer classes disembarking at the pier. Others were enjoying Sunday boating in skiffs and rowing boats, men and women all rowing leisurely about. The grass banks held picnickers, ice cream vendors, men with trays of linen sunhats strung from their necks, children paddling in the shallows. There was a brass band playing somewhere and a continuous babble of voices floated across the broad curving sweep of a smooth flowing Thames. Richmond Pier, even with its extension built four years earlier, seemed too small to accommodate all those getting off boats already tied up alongside it. *April Lady* had to wait ages for her turn to tie up.

Mr Mottram guided the boat to its designated place at the pier, their own passengers moving off across the pontoon to firm ground. It was still hard for Amy to believe that this was their very own boat, that they truly owned it. Whenever she had glanced at Tom he too had had that look of disbelief as he went among the passengers explaining this, explaining that, pointing out places of interest – mostly out of a guide book from which he had memorised as much as he could.

'We've taken our first fares,' she whispered to Tom as the boat emptied, and he nodded wordlessly, but pleased with himself, pleased with his day. A few hours and they'd be taking everyone back on board and turning the vessel away from the fresh airs of Richmond beneath a late afternoon sun and towards the grimy sooty airs of London.

A few hours though would suffice for them to relax, go and get something to eat, a proper meal, though they must not afford that luxury every time, at least not before they saw some profit from all that outlay. But this was their first time and something to celebrate.

With Mum, Vi and Rosy keeping a watch on Willie and the baby, Amy and Tom went off for a little while on their own, the boat in the good hands of Mr Shaw. In a secluded little spot among some trees, Tom spread his coat on a patch of last year's fallen leaves for her to sit on, levered himself down beside her, his stick propped against a tree and they sat watching the scenery, the river winding away below them. It was so quiet, made more noticeable by the confused hum of many people enjoying themselves reaching them only faintly, though every now and again came nearby voices growing louder and fading, the shout of some lad and the tramp of feet passing by the unseen couple.

While Amy, her arms around her drawn-up knees, gazed through the thin group of trees where they sat into the far distance and at the blue April sky with tiny puffy clouds floating on it, reflected in the river just below, Tom smoked a cigarette. Neither had much to say, and hardly needed to. It was too peaceful for words to break the magic of it. For Amy it was the most wonderful feeling of contentment she'd known since she could remember, it seemed, and when Tom finally finished his cigarette and took her gently in his arms and kissed her, she lay beneath him, savouring their love, although with caution in case someone walking by saw them, stumbled over them, or even trod on them.

The thought struck her as ridiculous and mentioning it between his kisses had him laughing. The spell broken, the hour to make way approaching fast, Amy got up, brushed her dress down and helped him to his feet, his stiff knee giving him purchase.

When they arrived back his mother gave them a funny look, but Amy didn't care. In little less than a month she and Tom would be married. That they had talked about, if briefly. They would talk about it in more detail that evening no doubt.

Going back behind the counter again, and even though it was not so busy now that people had already eaten and were growing tired, Amy felt all in, some of the disbelief she had felt during the day about owning this boat dropping steadily away from her as they neared more built-up areas. Would all this remain the pleasure she'd anticipated, or would it become just sheer hard work? Next time she wouldn't have Vi to help her, and Mum, as she was now starting to call Tom's mother, wouldn't want to come along every trip. Nor would it be long before she too would have to let go. Then it would be just Tom, his skipper and his enginer. Between them they would no doubt cope, but would Tom be happy? All this had been for him. What if after a while he wasn't happy? Amy pulled herself up sharply. Of course he would be.

The boat moored, John Mottram and Mr Shaw each went off in their own direction. She glanced at Tom as they made their way to the tube station and home, trying to ascertain his reaction to this his first day as an owner now that he too must be tired. His face was bright from the sun and open water. His face was bright from something else too. Bright with the satisfaction of something achieved.

'How was it?' she asked even so, falling in step with him, his erratic step, Vi and Willie going on in front, Mum and Rosy trailing behind.

'Good,' was all he said. His face, however, said so much more than that.

Chapter Twenty-Nine

Alice had turned up on her mother's doorstep just an hour ago. She now sat in the back living room with its new furniture and its new radio and its new curtains, none of which she appeared to have noticed, though the last time she'd set foot in the place had been 1927, nearly three years ago, and everything had been old and shabby.

For an hour her mother had sat through her tale of woe. Rosy was at work, Willie too, having finally left school on his fourteenth birthday and had returned to his job as a messenger boy at the *News Chronicle*'s offices. There was only Alice's mother, Amy and Tom here, as the boat was not operating on Tuesdays or Thursdays.

The *April Lady*, up and running this past month, had enjoyed nothing but success so far, the boat crowded with trippers every weekend and busy on all the other days that she ran. Amy could see only good times ahead. She and Tom were to be married the Saturday after next, the banns read, the dress made, accommodating the gradual thickening of her waist. Invitations had gone out, caterers had been hired, a nice flat above some shops in Cambridge Heath Road, not too far from his mother, stood all ready for them to move into. Grace would have liked them to have lived in the same street as her, but Cambridge Heath Road was an improvement on Albert Street. Amy's real dream was a house out in the suburbs in time. There promised to be enough money, and if their present success continued, they might even have a little car, the cheaper Vauxhalls selling at around five hundred pounds. If Tom and she learned to drive it they could visit his mother, take her out for rides to compensate for forsaking her, though she still had Willie. Lovely to dream when those dreams could come true. There was the baby to think of too – it should have all the opportunities their new lifestyle could offer it. If a girl, it would be Kay after her sister. If a boy, it would be Thomas, after his father.

Only half-listening to Alice, she thought of her baby, a lovely warm feeling spreading throughout her body. Poor Alice, her life was in such a mess while her own was improving by the minute.

For a long time she had felt at fault for Alice's plight. So much so that in the end she had confided in Tom. It hadn't made very nice telling and she had half expected him to grow disapproving of her cruelty all that time ago, in its way a penance for what she had done. But he hadn't condemned her at all.

'Alice didn't have to go and marry him, did she?' he pointed out. 'She was probably dazzled by his money. I suppose anyone would be. And he happened to see something in her that made him want to marry her. All you did was lead the horse to water, and the horse promptly drank it. So don't go blaming yourself, love, and feeling miserable about it for the rest of your life.' And he'd cuddled her to him so protectively that she knew it had really never been her fault at all. Nor must she think of it now. Alice had made her own bed.

She returned her attention to what Alice was saying. Her pretty face was a picture of grief and desperation. 'I can't stand it any more. I had to come home, Mum. I hate him. I really do.'

She sat there looking suntanned and · healthy, her hair lightened either by Canary Islands sunshine or a bottle of peroxide, immaculately styled and marcel-waved, yet she held herself as though she were the drabbest person going.

'I've made up my mind, Mum. I want a divorce from Richard.'

Sitting opposite her, her mother, who'd been gnawing at her lips throughout her daughter's tales of woe, released them in horror leaving the flesh bright red.

'Divorce? Yer can't do that, luv. Not divorce. Surely the two of yer can patch things up.' To her divorce was a dirty word. It was a woman's place to make a go of her marriage unless she was being knocked about, and even then it was a case of grin and bear it or find somewhere away from the violent husband. Certainly not divorce! 'An' look what yer'll be givin' up. All that nice life . . .'

'Nice life! Christ!'

'Oh, dear!' Grace Jordan didn't abide swearing, not from menfolk in her hearing which properly put her back up, and certainly not from women. 'What sort of language 'ave yer picked up, luv? Whatever yer've 'ad ter put up with, it don't warrant that sort of talk – an' not 'ere in my 'ouse, luv.'

'I'm sorry, Mum.' Alice, twisting her tearsoaked handkerchief round and round between her fingers, wasn't really sorry, except for herself, and the apology was sharply given. 'But I've been driven to it.'

'Well, not 'ere, luv, there's a good gel.'

'If I told you all the things Richard has been up to, it would make your hair curl.'

'I've no doubt it would, Alice. Yer've told us enough as it is. It must've bin 'orrible for yer an' you with no one ter talk to. I think 'is mother must be a strange sort of person, tellin' yer you was just making mountains out of mole'ills even after yer told 'er about yer 'usband's fancy woman. But then, them rich people are a bit odd in their ideas. But, well, I don't want ter back his mum up or anythink, but if yer do leave 'im, yer'll be turnin' yer back on all that money.'

Alice sniffed loudly. 'I've found out that money isn't everything.'

Amy, who had thought it best not to interfere in all this, now said quickly, 'But if you sue for divorce on grounds of adultery, he'll have to pay alimony to you, though I'm sure he'd be more generous than that.'

Whatever else Dicky was, from her experience of him he had always been a generous person and he had plenty of money not to miss a little of it to Alice. 'And you must have some money of your own by now. Jewellery and suchlike.'

Alice's eyes gazed at her through glistening tears. 'I expect he'd see me all right. But it's not that at all – Richard wants me to give him grounds to divorce *me*.'

'What?' After an hour telling them of all her various woes, this was the first time Amy had heard this one. Mrs Jordan looked blank, having no understanding of the ins and outs of divorce. Tom gave a strange kind of growl.

'That's the trouble,' Alice went on miserably. 'I can't stand being married to him any longer, but I can't see any other way out.'

'What is he suggesting?' Amy asked, already knowing the answer, and was not surprised when Alice, holding her hanky to her lips, told her.

'I could arrange some sort of hotel evidence,' she whispered, her voice muffled by the linen. 'You know – be found in a hotel bedroom with a man and be seen as the guilty party. He says it's the only way I can get what I want because I haven't as much to lose as he has.'

'Good God Almighty!' Tom burst out, risking his mother's wrath.

'His family being so well up in society,' Alice went on in a tiny voice, 'he says he can't have his name splashed all over the newspapers as the guilty party.'

'But yours can.'

'I'm nothing.'

'That's bloody disgusting!' Tom growled. 'You're not nothing. If I get near 'im I'll knock his bloody block off!'

Mrs Jordan held up a mediating hand. 'No, stop it. All of yer. I don't know nothink about these matters. All I know is Alice 'ad best come 'ome here ter live until whatever she wants ter do is sorted out. I've listened to it all till I'm fair worn out by it. Alice, you come upstairs with me, and we'll sort out somewhere ter sleep if you don't mind kippin' in with Rosy. Amy's got the other one, but 'er an' Tom's gettin' married in two weeks' time so yer'll have a bed all ter yerself then.'

'Married!' Alice looked at Amy with something like resentment, or was it despair?

Amy nodded but deemed it best not to enlarge on the subject. Alice looked shocked and unhappy enough without

384

rubbing her nose in it, her once considered successful marriage on the verge of breaking up.

'We've got to find a way of stopping this,' Amy said that evening when she and Tom were alone, everyone gone to bed, his mother not averse to it these days with the wedding only two weeks off, and Amy pregnant anyway.

She had ushered a still swollen-eyed Alice up to Vi's room early, but for the couple left downstairs there'd be no fondling and lovemaking tonight. They were too full of all Alice had told them.

'Obviously Richard will be giving this person whom Alice is to be found with some money for his trouble,' Amy mused as she lay on the sofa with Tom's arms around her. 'Why can't she offer him more to say that Richard had approached him with the idea and offered him money to do it?'

'He'll want a damned good sum, whoever he is, to cover what that swine's probably offering – could be a couple of thousand.'

Amy fell silent, thinking. 'What if she hasn't that much money?'

'We could ask her. The bracelet she was wearing when she arrived this morning must be worth a few bob. It can't be all she's got.'

'It might not be.' Amy felt her heart sink at what next entered her mind. 'If it isn't . . .' She couldn't finish the sentence, said instead, 'I can't stand by and see her name smirched like that. In a way I still feel a little responsible for what I did to her.'

She felt his arms tighten about her. 'I told you to forget all about that. It was a long time ago, love.'

But Amy wasn't listening. 'I think we might have to help her, Tom, if she doesn't have enough for what she needs.'

Now his arms loosened about her. He half rose from his recumbent position. 'You mean use your money?'

'Ours, darling.' But the correction made it seem all the worse as though she was suggesting commandeering *his* money for her own whim. His outburst seemed to bear it out and she hurried to correct it. 'She's your sister, Tom,

385

and my friend ... I'd like to think she was still my friend, for all I did to her.'

'I've told you,' he interrupted. 'All this is no fault of yours.'

'I know, but I want to help her, and you do too, Tom. Your sister. We can't stand by.'

'No.' He relaxed and lay down again. 'We'll talk to her in the morning about it. You know it could mean losing all we've got.'

Silently, Amy nodded. Deep inside she wanted to cry. All her hopes, the business promising to go so well, the little house in the suburbs, all of it could go. That night, lying in the bed next to Rosy and the sleeping Alice, she couldn't sleep for seeing all her hopes flying out of the window. Cruel justice, retribution – for all Tom had said, it boiled down to that.

Christ Church, in Dean Cross Street, Stepney, echoed with those sibilant whispers people adopt when conversing in church, and the organ was emitting quiet nondescript music as Amy entered the grubby church porch on the arm of her brother.

Hal, as the closest member of her family, had agreed and been allowed to come down from college to give her away, reluctantly, except that his mother who, now on her own, had swiftly learned how to bend most people to her will, had talked him into realising that he must do his duty by his sister, as his dear father was obviously unable to.

From where Amy stood she could see the half-filled church, the back pews empty, one side emptier than the other. She hadn't much family, few friends; one or two from where she had once worked had thought to come along. She had written to the office in general about it, not wanting to single anyone out in particular.

Old Mr Curby had come along, and three of the girls she had known, but not Ronald Goodburn. Amy felt at once relieved and disappointed, glad and sorry. At one time she had suspected Mr Goodburn of looking upon her as more than just a secretary, had been made vaguely uneasy by it in a different way to the discomfort he normally instilled in people. Had he been in church today, she would have felt distinctly ill at ease on a day that was exacting anyway. On the other hand she felt a certain amount of disappointment and sorrow in that she felt he still blamed her for leaving after his taking her into his confidence as he had. He need not have worried, his secret would remain intact because he was in the past, meant nothing. But she did feel sorry he had judged fit not to attend. If nothing else he would have helped to fill those four rows on her side.

Tom's side was full to the eighth row with family, and further back still with mates from his leisure and work days, neighbours, his mother's cronies from the Working Men's Club who still kept an eye on her as Working Men's Clubs did for all widows.

The organ swelled to the first resounding solemn chords of Wagner's Bridal March from *Lohengrin*, the alert-eyed organist catching sight of her standing there ready. To its stately sound Amy began on her long slow walk down the centre aisle; approaching the occupied pews, she caught the sighs of admiration from the women at her satin dress that reached to the floor in a figure-clinging shimmer, a long sleeveless satin jacket hiding from sight any thickening of her waist. Her veil sheer and long, at the moment covering her features, also helped, as did a bouquet of cream roses held appropriately. No gasp of detection came from any watching her, the sighs proclaiming only envious approval of the bride's calm and stately progress, though Amy alone knew that what felt like a swarm of butterflies was fluttering about inside her stomach.

Tom had moved out into the aisle, his best man, a friend from childhood whom Amy had met once or twice, standing beside him. Seeing Tom, she felt near to wanting to break into a run to reach him quicker. The butterflies would vanish once she was standing beside him. But she kept to her steady pace, to arrive at his side right on cue to the thunderous final chord of the Bridal March that had dictated her pace all the way.

It felt strange, to stand beside Tom, in half an hour to be his wife. This man who had once looked on her with scorn when Alice had first introduced her, a bewildered, lost soul, to the Jordans (she'd glimpsed Alice as she came down the

387

aisle, standing with her mother, the forgiven, sheltered Alice). This man to whom she had taken an instant dislike for his looks of contempt was the man she had come to love above all else, shielding her from a life she had never thought possible to endure. Now they would soon be husband and wife, and, she noticed as the butterflies fled, he didn't have his stick with him. Love and pride swelled inside her so that she hardly heard the opening words of the Reverend Thompson: 'Dearly beloved . . .'

In a daze she went through her wedding vows, feeling she would remember none of it when in the future she tried to, except that very precious moment when the ring was slipped onto her finger, at last proclaiming her a married woman.

The rest of the unbearably lengthy ceremony, the minister's endless prayers at the altar for the newly wedded couple once more became a blur, a wish to have it over and done with now the main, most important part to her had been concluded. It seemed to go on and on, blessings called down on their heads, the congregation's responses, the long drawn-out sermon; Amy felt herself grin secretly at the beseeching for the couple to be assisted in being fruitful. If this man were to know that she was already fruitful . . .

Even the walk to the vestry, the signing of the register, one of Tom's uncles taking photographs of them with a well-used Brownie camera, all this too Amy felt would become blurred in time so she would feel guilty in not remembering it. But she'd remember well the kiss Tom gave her as he put down the pen, a long and lingering kiss until his uncle chuckled, 'Enough of that, you two. There's a time an' a place, yer know, an' it'll come soon enough ternight,' and the minister smiling primly at the joke. For some reason or other Amy felt that smile would always stick in her memory. That and Tom's first kiss as her husband. The two would always go together, she was sure.

Coming back from the vestry into the church, the organist gave forth with an enormous rendering of Mendelssohn's triumphant Bridal March, shaking every rafter and managing to bungle a few notes in his enthusiasm. She was on Tom's arm, her heart and mind lifted now it was all over.

Amy caught sight of Alice again, and again felt a weight lift from her shoulders.

The morning after coming to that difficult decision to assist her with any money she might require to avoid darkening her name, they had told her of it. Alice's eyes had brightened, then entreated. 'I couldn't take anything from you,' she'd said, but shortly after she had gone off back home to 'sort things out', as she told her mother.

A week later she was back, her pretty face no longer gentle but set with the look of a woman who had found her feet and was totally in charge of herself. It was a look of fierce, almost cruel determination that Amy had found quite frightening. A woman no longer to be trifled with.

'It's all sorted out,' she said firmly. 'There is no need for you and Tom to use any of your money. I know now how much it would have set you back. It would have taken all your business with it. But I want to thank you both for what you were prepared to do for me.'

Amazement and some degree of fear quashed any relief Amy might have felt. 'What have you done?'

'I've confronted Richard, and he said he would give up that woman of his. He actually pleaded.' She gave the high, harsh laugh of someone enjoying revenge. 'But it was too late. I now have concrete evidence of his adultery, you see.'

Before their awed gaze, she had explained. Richard had sent a note to the person with whom it was planned she'd be discovered in a compromising situation in a sleazy little hotel bedroom, offering him money for the favour. When Alice had said she would better the offer if the man, Bertram, would testify to this deception in court, he had shown her the note. She had been stricken dumb by the amount offered which she, even with Tom and Amy's help, could not have hoped to match, much less better. In desperation she had begged, had seen herself forced to endure Richard and his woman, or women, for the rest of her life. It was only as she was leaving that she saw the note with its incriminating offer for the favour still lying on the coffee table where it had been dropped for her to see. Without Bertram noticing, she had swept it up into her handbag, hurriedly leaving in tears.

'So,' she said to Tom and Amy, 'I have all the proof I need to virtually hang him! I'll never forget what you both offered to do for me, but I no longer have any need to take anything from you. As for me, all I have to pay out for is my solicitor's fees. I showed it to him and he made a certified copy of it to send to darling Richard. So I, my dears, am divorcing *him*, and his name will be splashed all over the newspapers for his titled family and their friends to see. And all his abject pleadings to give up his woman have fallen on deaf ears.' The vicious glee in what had once been a gentle, forgiving, generous girl was painful to see but, Amy felt, justified. 'In three years I shall be rid of him. Pity it has to take that long. It's to give time for the parties to come to a reconciliation. But I shall never forgive him. As for reconciliation, once bit, twice shy, as they say.' And again she had laughed.

For all that, as Amy moved down the aisle on Tom's arm, she couldn't help thinking how Alice must be feeling watching her. Poor Alice, for all her tanned features speaking of a holiday most people here would have given their eye teeth to have had, a lonely figure among them. Turning hastily away, Amy concentrated on getting out of the church as soon as decently possible, and with Tom comfortingly beside her, moved into the early afternoon sunshine of a late April day, breathing a prayer of thanks and putting aside all thoughts of Alice.

At the porch door, Tom kissed her again for the few cheap box cameras to record. But what they could not record was what he said to her as he kissed her: 'I love you, Mrs Jordan. And tonight I'll show you how much I do love you,' sending a shiver of delight and anticipation through her.

Mrs Jordan. One day she and Tom would amount to something, owners of a fleet of pleasure cruisers, Jordan's Pleasure Boats. The vision floated before her. She and Tom would be going up in the world; but the vision clouded a little as Amy's glance fell again upon Alice.

Alice was standing on the perimeter of the knots of guests as though she had purposefully removed herself from them all. Perhaps to be alone, lament her own marriage that had started off so full of promise, only to fail. All she had for company as she stood there was some stranger, a man who had perhaps wandered there as a spectator with nothing better to do.

Poor Alice, who had thought herself fortunate beyond dreams, to become a divorced woman three years from now, compelled to return to the squalor of the East End. Again Amy turned her mind from that thought. This was her day. It must not be marred by concern for poor Alice's future.

But what Amy didn't know as yet, or any of them, as the bride clung to her new husband for photographs to be taken again and again, re-arranging her dress, posing and smiling and trying not to look at Alice standing quietly to one side, was that Alice was savouring thoughts of her own that were far from dismal – had been savouring them these past eight days or so. For Alice's eyes had fallen on a Mr Jeremy Forsett, a widower in his thirties and heir to a nice little emporium in Houndsditch, while she had been recently browsing in there. Better still, Mr Jeremy Forsett's eyes had fallen on Alice. And he was more than halfway handsome.

And her thoughts at this moment were: 'Don't worry about me, Amy dear. There's no need to look at me so pityingly. For I shall be fine from now on, you'll see.'

And she looked up into Mr Forsett's grey eyes and smiled.